Lethal Woman

by

Carrie Pierce

The Lethal Series

Lethal Woman

Cover Art by *Kim Mendoza*

The Wild Rose Press, Inc.
PO Box 708
Adams Basin, NY 14410-0708
Visit us at www.thewildrosepress.com

Publishing History
First Edition, 2022
Trade Paperback ISBN 978-1-5092-4507-9
Digital ISBN 978-1-5092-4508-6

The Lethal Series
Published in the United States of America

"I can't ever imagine you not being the Lethal Woman, Lindsey. Whether you like it or not, that is who you will always be." The look in my father's eyes breaks my heart. But I walk away anyway. I can't help him now. It's time that I live by my own morals and forget the words of my past. I turn my back on the man that stabbed my family in theirs years ago and walk toward my chance at a new future.

As I approach the open metal door, I grab onto Thomas, knowing that one way or another, this battle will end with us.

Dedication

To those who are still with me and to those who aren't,
this is for you.

Chapter 1

Meeting the Pavlovs

As soon as my feet hit the pavement below, I feel the biting cold as the storm roars from above. Pulling my coat tighter across my front, I lock my front door, and charge to where my parked car waits, abandoned, and empty. Shivering in the chill, my hair coils around in the wind.

With one foot in front of the other, I attempt to tame my nervousness. "You can do this," I encourage myself. Placing my hand on the side of the vehicle, I prop my door open and let it air out for a few minutes. I can battle the cold. I can endure the pellets of rain. It's worth it. I feel slightly as if I deserve the torture. For what I've allowed people to go through, I deserve this.

"No." My brother would sigh if he heard my trail of thought. "You don't. It was a mistake. An accident, Lindsey."

Wiping my nose, I shake my head as the water from above begins to seep from my hair into my eyes. He's wrong. I know he is. Jonathan is a great man, but he isn't always right. He is brilliant but doesn't always know the truth…it has to stay that way.

Flipping my wrist over, I shiver as I take in the time. Shoving my hands in my mass of hair, I use my reflection in the mirror to adjust my appearance. Late and a mess,

I curse myself as I boost my way into the car and start the ignition.

Overall, nothing is more embarrassing than being late for a meeting you planned. But my brother had a different idea, let's go have lunch, catch up, and complain the whole evening about a defensive girlfriend, or who he thought was his girlfriend. She cheated, and I got delayed.

I love my brother, Jonathan, but seriously he has to stop coming to me and complaining about his love life since I don't have one. I can't. Not with this job, this profession, it's not for the faint of heart or open-hearted. It kills and destroys all that grows.

My car's rumble lures me on, and as it sails through the late evening traffic, my heart rate begins to even out. Waving on the young woman in the opposite car in front of me, I catch a full look at my grubby appearance. My hair is still a blonde mess, so I can just claim that I had training that went into overtime—sounds like a great plan. Hopefully, the man that asked to meet with me will buy it. Lord knows that I need another contract. Someone with my reputation can't afford to stay down long.

The man that's willing to hire a twenty-three-year-old is none other than Anthony Pavlov. He's gotten into some deep stuff. New businesses are joining, contracts are expanding, and now he needs to think about his future and protection reinforcements. When he called, I was sure that he had the wrong number, but as I listened, I knew what he wanted. I accepted his offer of the job after reviewing the contract. The file was thick, but still, I knew that he was hiding something. Everyone always has something to hide. Small or large. Simple or chaotic. A secret always has a weight, whether or not it has an effect.

But simply after chatting for an hour, he agreed to meet me after I told him about a few of my other clients. He did a background check and even looked at my references. He wants the best, but not for himself.

I wasn't hired to protect him. That part, I nearly learned too late. It seems to be a theme of mine.

He wants the best security for his son, Thomas Pavlov. He works at the company in his free time but attends the local college, majoring in Business and English. Anthony doesn't trust his son to follow the rules and get protection on his own, so that's where I come into play.

He wants the lethal force that many in England know about, but what he doesn't know is that I'm not as fierce as many promised him.

Shifting in my seat at the red light, I try to keep myself calm. "I'm not lying," I tell no one. "I've just changed." I hum to myself. "Evolving is natural." Yeah, but my new boss may not be as happy as he sounded on the phone when he finally sees me. I floor the gas at the green light and roughly pull away from the line. Looking at the dash clock, I see that I'm roughly ten minutes and thirty seconds late. But as I said, the man can't fault me for training. He wants the best, so he will have to trust the idea that I am trying to be the finest version of myself for this mission.

Liar, liar, liar, my mind keeps taunting me. You are a *failure, failure, failure.*

Ignoring myself, I focus on the dark, slick road. Looking around me, I contemplate what I know about this man. He isn't a widely known public figure. He goes to work and then comes home to his son, his only family.

Lonely, I predict. Just like me.

As my black sedan sails through traffic, my heart is beating rapidly. I need this contract. I need to build up my credibility again. I've lost so much already, and I can't afford to lose this opportunity. Breathing out one, two, three, I tighten my hands on the wheel and swallow the lump in my throat.

Stick to the facts, my mother would say. Anthony Pavlov has been the only person in a long time that has taken an interest in my abilities. He has trust in me that I don't quite understand, but I can't prove him wrong yet. I have to make him understand that he made the right choice. We both need this deal to work, so I promise to do my best, even if it is overly complicated. "I can handle it." I say as my hands tighten on the wheel.

As I float through the congested intersection, everything around me becomes a blur. My thoughts, my breaths, my hammering heart. The worry is settling in, and as I glide into the private estate of the Pavlovs, I'm pulled back into reality, but the knot in my stomach trembles and comes undone. Like a shattering object, my breath comes out in complicated pants.

Demanding the best of myself, my brain becomes focused and alert like I've trained it to do. Taking in my surroundings, I notice there are three different cars in front of the estate. All different colors and models. Analyzing the spaces, I pick the closest parking space to the door.

As the car comes to a jolting stop, I take a few deep breaths. Closing my eyes, I mutter to myself about why I am here and that I need this chance. "You are your mother's daughter and your father's soldier. Prove the legacy right." I lock eyes with my pale reflection in the side mirror.

Knowing I'm stalling, I shut off the ignition slowly and pocket my keys and phone into my trouser pockets. Climbing from my seat and making my way up to the grand oak and glass door that is the size of a whole wall, I ball my hands into fists. Shit, I think as my feet streak the expensive mat below my feet. Gawking at the expense of the stone estate, I allow myself to think selfishly about the wage I might be receiving. "It would be nice for a change," I mutter with clenched teeth.

Just as I reach the knocker, a bitter fall breeze sends blistering chills down my spine, ruffling my hair. A few strands fly loose from my ponytail as I glance up at the darkening sky, and the drizzle falls in my eyes. A storm is gathering, and as I watch the heavy gray clouds come together the door creaks open.

A man of a different era opens the door and waves me inside. "You must be the new hire?" The man's voice creaks. With stiff and slow movements, he waves me into the warmth of the house.

"Yes," I say, keeping my voice even, and straightening my back. The old man's eyes show no dazzle, no recognition. "We have tea in the reading room," is all he says as he offers a dismissive expression.

Turning away from me, he shuffles toward the reading room. Keeping in step with him, I give the older man his space as his movements become a rhythm of wobbly then jerky.

In the doorway of the room, I'm left gawking. The reading room speaks so many different volumes about the inhabitants. Wandering around the room, my gaze travels to the heavy leather-bound books that fan from one wall to another. A thick wooden desk resides in the far corner, and two leather couches face the desk. Not wanting to sit, I choose to stride to the windows. The metal and glass artwork is wide and expensive.

Again, feeling uneasy, I shift and settle my eyes to focus on the aging man that led me to the room, who is now off to the side by the door. Smoothing out his blazer, the man just watches me from the sideline. Cocking my head to ask a question of the man, I'm interrupted by my watch as it buzzes to signal that a new hour has arrived.

Blasting through the entry, another man stands before me with a grand smile on his face. "Ya! Yes, Lindsey Vasiliev! So nice to finally see you in person. I've heard many great things about you." The tall but faded man takes my hand and shakes it aggressively. The tremulous voice matches the voice that spoke to me on the phone. He seems more composed and less feeble than I first imagined.

Remembering my manners, I speak. "Likewise, Mr. Pavlov. Sorry for my sudden appearance. Training ran a little later than normal. I hope that I'm not too late?"

Nodding, but still smiling, Anthony Pavlov keeps his eyes even with mine. "Shall we get down to business now?" My accent peeks through slightly, but Anthony doesn't say anything about it.

The man in front of me just waves off my words, and as he seems preoccupied, I watch him. He's not a day over sixty. His gray hair is slicked back, and a crisp gray suit is pulled tightly around his chest. Today is the day I prove that my parents taught me well. Both my mum and dad taught my brother and me a lesson on life, no one can save you or challenge you as much as yourself. That we all have the ability to defend ourselves, it just needs to be unlocked. And overall, we can only ever truly rely on ourselves.

From a young age, my brother and I had to know how to take care of ourselves and how to defend each other. That was what my parents wished and vowed since my brother and I were young; we had to be soldiers. We had to be dangerous because of our parents' past. My mother was a bodyguard, too, while my father was a military sniper who worked on classified missions until he vanished and my brother's and my lives were ripped apart.

Shaking out of the past, I know for a fact I carried on with the family's legacy, while my brother is a real estate agent. A damn good one too. But not many people know the full story about the Vasiliev family secret. No one knows how deep it truly runs in London's rich history. And not many can ever know. That is something Jonathan and I pledged to take to our graves.

Cutting me from the curtain of thought, Anthony Pavlov chants cheerfully, "My son is in the living room. I shall go get him, and we can get down to business." For an older man, he moves fluidly, almost childlike. There is humor in his voice, but experience is rooted in his eyes.

Left alone, I cross my arms around my chest and continue to take in the features of the room. But with distrust, my gaze continues to land on the butler. I can infer he too is waiting calmly for a command. He seems poised but also reluctant to leave me in the room alone. As my eyes stare into the hall, I hear voices and then footsteps as the two men make their way into the room. Silence forms around the rich wood-smelling room as we all look at one another. An awkward expression is shot my way by the son, a plea to his father that he doesn't need a babysitter at the age of twenty-four. Standing calmly, I wish to wipe the smirk off Thomas Pavlov's face.

"Who are you supposed to be?" Thomas Pavlov, the one that I'm supposed to protect with my life, asks pointedly. Something tells me that protecting him will be easier said than done. There is defiance in the way he stands. His brown eyes hold nothing special but a huge ego and something locked away deep within him. Not something I haven't seen before, but it is something that gets unnervingly old to face.

By the look he's giving me, I can tell that with me being his bodyguard, I'm going to bruise his constructed ego that is bigger than the front door that I had to walk through. "I'm the one that's going to keep you alive, Thomas." The truth always offers a calm sense of knowledge. The truth is what reminds people like me about how dangerous this job truly is. Truth is what sets people straight…always.

Forgetting the son for a second, I turn my attention to the man that picked me. "Sir, if you don't mind, can we talk about the contract now? It's getting late, and tomorrow's going to be an early day." I feel like I'm guiding these two to the point. Maybe that's why I'm here?

"Okay, Ms. Vasiliev, there are three important rules that you must follow." Anthony rams his shoulders back and squares up to me. The older Pavlov's voice is demanding, vibrant, and knowing.

"All right." I cross my arms and look anywhere but where his son is standing. "Shoot."

"You must follow them to the T, Vasiliev." Anthony's voice sings through the room, and he looks at both me and his son as he reviews the necessary points. He holds up one finger. "One, don't get involved with my son." Another finger goes up. "Two, protect him at all costs." With one final designated finger and pointed look at me, Anthony finishes his statement, "And three, blend in. Do you understand? You are here to protect my son from harm, keep him out of danger's sickly fingers, and from doing stupid shit. Remember what you told me? 'The moment you slip up is the second you accept a bullet.' I hope you can take your own advice, Ms. Vasiliev. Don't mess up."

With the older man recycling my words at me, I feel stunned. The audacity of this man sends a chill up my spine. Never has that happened to me before. But again, I accept the truth at all costs.

Knocking my head back, I see the look in the older man's red-rimmed eyes. Not feeble at all. Maybe it was a trick to trip me up, but either way, I agree with him. I'm here to do my job and nothing else.

The man standing in front of me shows respect, and he is silently waiting for what I'm about to say next. Anthony has power, but he isn't treating me like I am lower than him. I like the attitude. No one I have previously worked with showed respect for what I do before. No one has accepted or acknowledged the risks I'm forced to take. But knowing that I have analyzed the older man enough, I turn my attention to the son. He is the one I was hired to worry about after all. He's the one I need to know inside and out. He's the one with the actions I must be ready to correct.

Thomas is now standing in front of me as well. Dressed in blue jeans and a fancy sweater, his eyes even and cool. His hair is fluffed and mannered, but there is something in the way he is projecting himself that I can't yet buy. I understand his anger, but does he think looks of distrust bother me? It's like a bee sting compared to being shot.

But this is my life and my new job, and at times it means working with people you don't want to, or don't yet understand. It also demands that I take command and do my best to serve my clients. But these people better understand I'm not a servant. I'll help and protect, but the moment anyone crosses a line, they'll be the ones catching a bullet. I've learned my lesson the hard way, pretty faces tend to be the most dangerous. I have begun to learn that not everyone you put your faith in can be wholly trusted.

"I do understand, Mr. Pavlov, and I agree to the terms." I shoot a look at Thomas and finish my sentence, speaking low and fierce, "All of them, you can trust me, Mr. Pavlov."

With that, Anthony Pavlov smiles, and his dark eyes shine. "Then you're hired, Lethal Vasiliev." The chip on my shoulder shifts, and I frown at the calling card. That was before, and this is now. Without a comment, I have everything I need to complete this mission. Shoved in my hands are my contract, a licensed weapon that the father insisted I use, Thomas' college plan and classroom settings. I have a new work phone that Anthony said, depending on the situation, I may never have to use. I also receive a key to the house and a new black car.

Sighing at all the contents in my hands, I shudder at the sudden responsibility and understanding of what this man is asking of me. But lightening my expression, I nearly mutter to myself that it would be so nice to have money that I could throw around. But not everyone gets to live a dream like this. Not everyone gets the chance to have endless fortune and prosperity.

Staying silent, I just stand rod-like as everyone moves throughout the room. I can hear Thomas protesting to his father, but Anthony shuts him down with the knowledge I still can't live up to. "She is the best there is. The Vasiliev line is straight and professional. She's the only one that can help."

Swiveling back, Anthony stares down at me. "Report here tomorrow morning at seven sharp." Again, he takes my hand and shakes it with serious aggression. "Goodnight, Ms. Vasiliev. I'm glad to be in business with you, and if you need anything while you are with us, let me know." He smiles a toothy grin as we finish shaking hands. His rough hand shows age and a lot of wear and tear, another thing that I can keep stacked away about the man. Remembering his words of farewell, I choose to smile back. From the mirror behind me, I can see my white teeth shining in the darkness of the room. With a gentle tug of warning, I get Anthony to release my hand completely.

"Goodbye, sir," I say. The butler's far-off look tells me he is tired of his job. He doesn't come forward to show me out, so I just march my way to the door. I'm left with my thoughts as I follow the passages to the front door. The roaming walk seems endless, but the ancient figures on the wall along the grand staircase catch my eyes. Ancestors, I choose to conclude. My white-shod feet come to a squeaky halt as I take a closer look. Humming at the line of paintings, I bathe in the warmth for the last time before continuing my way out.

I open the heavy wooden door, and the smell of rain welcomes me. With a deep breath of delight, I leave the house. The rain begins to beat down on my battered skin as I approach my car. As my jacket flaps open behind me, my bruises and scars are in clear view. I don't have to take a look at myself to figure that out.

As I step into my car and turn on the radio, I look up to see Thomas watching me from the office window. Testing my eyes, I question if it is a smirk I see or a frown? Mechanically, I go through the motions of getting my car ready for the drive home.

He better pray to God he doesn't act like that tomorrow because if so, hell's gonna rain down on him. I'm not a pushover, and I'm done being walked all over. It's my job to protect him, not to play his boyish games.

"Lethal my ass." I feel no need to prove myself wrong. I just peel my wet coat off. In my T-shirt, I feel the cold, and I welcome it. "You're alive, you're breathing—that's the important part." Jonathan recited those words to me when I woke in the hospital, littered with tubes and machines humming and clicking around me. "You got out of there alive."

Remembering the feeling of the achy knowledge that I failed on my last mission, I shift to look over my shoulder. I back out of the parking spot. As I make my way down the driveway, I make a list. I met my new boss, my new detail, and now it's time to be the lethal shadow that no one will see coming. I just have to get back to that mindset. It can't be that difficult. I faked it until I became the best, so I will just have to do it again.

If there's one thing I know how to do, it's make hell rain down on someone if they threaten the client I'm working for. I've done it before, and I know I can do it again. I've had time to adjust and welcome the person I had to become. It's what my parents wanted, and it's who

I have become over the years. I've worked long and hard to build up my client list, and it's how I got the name that everyone recognizes.

Lindsey Vasiliev is the Lethal Woman of England's prized occupants. I just have to be able to honor that title and keep my crown.

But, tomorrow is a new day, and it's time to let the past go. It's time that I try to start over. I'm no longer the lethal shadow that makes people back down. I am no longer who I used to be. I have become more cautious, more tedious. No more mistakes. I can't afford to go through losing a client again. That is a mistake I refuse to repeat again.

This client isn't the same as the one before. I refuse to fail this time.

Failure isn't an option. I will do anything to win, no matter the cost. No matter how painful it will be for me, I can't slip up this time.

I know this mission will be different. There are two routes I can take with this one, be lethal, or let that version of myself die. Soon, I will have to choose: let those who see me cower or see me as a real person and not just a myth.

A woman on a mission is dangerous but put a gun in her hand, and then she becomes lethal. The choice is mine, and as time floods through, I know I will have my answer.

In due time, I will know who I need to become.

Chapter 2

First Day on the Job

The sound of my alarm makes me instantly jump out of bed. Knowing I have to leave soon motivates me to get going and leave the warmth and comfort of my bed. With a thumping heart, I shove my hair out of my face. A voice within me whispers not to go. But I have to. This is my job. Now and forever.

As I stand, I look over the schedule to see what today has in store for me, and I know instantly that this job won't be easy. Nothing ever is. What's on paper doesn't mean that is what you will have to face. Life is unpredictable and unrecognizable when you need trust and faith.

Sighing, I look down the hall and take in the stillness of the place I call home. My house is dark as I walk into the kitchen, preparing my coffee and meals for the day. Bending my neck from one side to the other, I go through the motions of my meal prepping. Keeping my feet light, I prop one over the other to avoid the chill from the wood.

Swiveling, I take two containers of shredded roasted chicken with two sides of a mixture of green beans and baked potato from the side pantry. Hitching my arm up, I reach into the fridge to gather the breakfast container of plain oatmeal. Having everything now ready to be packed in my travel bag, I turn on the coffee maker so it can begin its brew.

Knowing I should be getting a move on, I retrace my steps to my room but stop dead at the note on my calendar. My brother is supposed to stop by after work and get all the gossip from my day. Biting my lip and slightly rolling my eyes, I simply choose to let it go. But still, I'm worried. What if I fail? London's most ruthless just feels like a coward at the moment. Smacking my lips, I wrinkle my nose at the thought of being a leader to others.

Reluctant to start this new chance, I jog my way back to my bedroom and pick out my attire for the day.

Trying to soothe my subconscious, I list the things I have done. One step is marked off of my morning routine.

Now on to the second, I look to the left and once again mourn the picture of my parents smiling and carelessly happy. Blinking at their smooth faces, I gather my clothes. Quickly, I shuffle to the bathroom and turn on the shower. Hot water is a necessity to wake up my muscles in the morning. I am so close to finishing step three, I chant to myself as the doubt starts to web in again. "Almost there, Vasiliev." I can hear my mother's expelling voice as I rinse out my smooth hair.

Dragging the washcloth over the tight ridges and dips of my body, I shut my eyes and allow the steam to wake me up. Ever since day one as a bodyguard, I made a promise to always serve with an angry heart and strive for perfection. Nothing has changed, but this is one of the riskiest jobs I've ever taken. Never has a business put anyone in danger like this before. I don't know if the Pavlovs are hiding something or not, but either way, my guard is up, even more so than ever. Even worse, never have I worked with such a young client before.

I've never worked with a client so distrusting of me as Thomas is. Understanding that he may not want help or approve of the help, I get it, but all I've been asked to do is protect him. With or without his trust, I'll make sure he stays alive.

This will definitely be a different ball game than I'm used to.

Feeling warm and clean from all the soap, I pull my hair around my head. I shut off the water, draining some of the extra drips from it. Looking into the mirror, I see how pale and cold I have become. The woman looking back at me with the familiar blue eyes is a shell.

During my last mission, I lost control. I lost focus of the end product. I can't lose control ever again. If I do, there might be a chance that I won't come back again. That I can't regain what I lost. That I can't dig myself out of the trouble that plagues my mind and heart.

Drying off and patting at my damp hair, I let my brain drift. I let myself go into autopilot. Rubbing at my sore neck, I release a series of pops into the empty silence of my room.

Pulling on a tight black tee, I regain my composure and focus on the job at hand. I need to get my shit together. I need to be getting ready for work. Next, I tug into my black military pants that perfectly hide the weapon I carry.

I've learned many skills since taking on this profession, and one is blending in the best you can is the most effective way to protect your clients. But looking at my reflection one last time, I see the dark circles that have invaded my face, showing just how tired I feel.

There was once a day when nothing could get under my skin, but everything's changed. I'm not as strong as I claim to be. Is anyone ever truly as confident or strong as they claim? At times, we are all liars.

I know I am. I'm not the person whom great masses of people have come to respect. I'm a tired, faded, and retired version of the Lindsey Vasiliev that helped protect London from swarms of evil acts.

I'm pulled out of my self-conscious thoughts when the beeping of my alarm goes off. Feeling composed but breathless, I know I am right on time. It's now or never.

Jogging back to my room, I pull on an old pair of boots and an ordinary black jacket. Snaking my way back to the kitchen, I take the coffee pot and pour it into my travel mug. Once finished and with my bag tugged over my shoulder, I know it's time to face the day. Looking for my ceramic bowl that holds my keys, I quickly shuffle my keys into my pocket. Checking my phone for any final reminders and seeing none, that too, ends up in my pocket.

Taking my gun out of the drawer by the door, I place it in the holster against my hip. The weight is extraordinary and uplifting, but it also gives me a twisting feeling of guilt in my gut. I thought I would never again get to hold this weapon. Having a gun, it allows you to be a force that many back away from.

It gives me an edge. My weapon tends to be my saving grace.

Chuckling at the uneasiness in my trembling body, I remind myself to finish my hair. Tangling it on the other shoulder, I put my bag on the floor and weave my hair into a tight braid. My appearance doesn't determine how I do my job. So if being comfortable works for me, it should work for Thomas and his father. But oddly, I want to impress everyone around me. I want to earn the respect that I lost. I want to regain everything I've lost.

I have the skills that will keep Thomas alive, and I hope they can trust my word on that because recently I, too, have been having clear thoughts of doubt.

Peeking at my watch, I feel like hooting with delight. I'm about ten minutes ahead of schedule. I smile. Thomas has class at eight thirty, and that gives us thirty-four minutes to get to campus, get to class, and get this two- to three-hour-long class done with. I never went to college myself, but I can tell this is going to be the most boring part of the job. But, I understand now, sometimes boring is better than excitement in this line of work.

****

The drive to the Pavlov estate is made up of an abundance of stop signs and red lights. Grinning as I pull through the gate, I am greeted by the security post. I inform them of my name. Being approved, I stop my car by the shade of a tree and park it, knowing that during the times I have Thomas with me, I will have to use the car Anthony Pavlov has provided. Making sure everything is put away, I approach the front door and wait silently for someone to answer. A little bit of yelling, frantic footsteps, and the echo of a voice stream through the wooden door, and then the door is opened so fast a gust of wind almost knocks me off my feet.

"Oh, you're here? Come in, come in." Thomas half turns to me, his eyes dilated and his hands tight around the doorknob. "I still have to get ready. I'll be down soon."

Stuffing my left hand in my pants pocket, I silently enter and close the door as Thomas jogs back up the stairs. I decide to wait by the entrance until he's ready. Soon, with all the noise gone, the world seems empty. Getting bored, I quickly unlock my phone and look over the missed messages.

One from my brother and two from my dog's vet. I type out a reply and put my phone back on silent. Just as I'm sliding it into my pocket, the senior Pavlov is standing before me. He looks the same as last night, composed, elegant, and powerful. But scruffed at the collar, seeming to be watching me a little harder than necessary.

"Lin—" Stopping, he corrects himself, "Ms. Vasiliev, how lovely it is to see you. Do you want coffee? I'm sure I can find some. Tea? We have plenty of that. Anything I can get you?" His eyes are glassy, and his steps are uneven. "You have no idea how important it is and how glad I am to have you on our team."

Grinning, I simply look down at my feet, not sure how to handle the compliment. But, remembering my nature, I lock eyes with the poised man.

Team? That's all that rings through my head. It is not something I hear very often, but pride swells up inside me to know that someone is excited to have me on their side and have me working with them. Chewing on the side of my cheek, I pay attention.

Knowing that Anthony is waiting for a response, I remember to speak, but refuse his offer. "Thank you, Mr. Pavlov, but call me Lindsey. It's much easier. And no, I have coffee in the car. Will he be ready soon?" I inch my chin up, gesturing to where Thomas disappeared moments ago. I hear movement but refuse to shift from my post unless given the say-so. Searching the older man's face, I try to gauge his emotion.

A rough cough and a steady hand are resting on the stairwell railing where Thomas is leaning all his weight on the banister. Looking between his father and me, Thomas levels his shoulders as a frown forms on his face. Stepping slowly down the stairs, Thomas keeps a hand on the railing.

He locks eyes with me and gives a tight grin. "I'm ready. Do you need a few more minutes before we leave? If so—" I cut the younger Pavlov off before he can say anything else.

"No." My voice comes out clipped and meaner than intended. "Let's go. We have twenty-two minutes to get you to class." I want Thomas to know that I am the one that calls the shots, if I am responsible for him, then he better respect my words.

He can think whatever he wishes. I won't hold it against him. As long as he understands to respect me, our relationship will work more efficiently.

"I will be seeing you later then, Mr. Pavlov. Call me if you need anything." I turn and start to walk out the door. I don't turn back to see if Thomas is following me. To my surprise, when I reach the company car, I see him slowly heel tapping toward me. Signaling to the car we will be using, I tell Thomas, "You get in. I just have to get my bag."

Taking a second, I think about what else I may need. I need to get my coffee from my own car as well as my bag. Tapping my waist, my gun is still fastened and tight. Looking over my shoulder as I walk to my car and fish out my bag and travel mug, I continue to watch Thomas. He's in the passenger seat and doesn't seem very happy. Returning, I toss my bag into the back seat of the Pavlovs' car. Before I start the engine and begin our advance to his college campus, I take a needy swallow of my lukewarm coffee.

Five minutes into our drive, Thomas begins to click his fingers together. My eyes remain trained on the road while Thomas taps his foot.

"You don't talk much, do you? I mean, you always have this blank expression and, baby, you're going to get frown lines."

Rolling my eyes, I make a right turn.

"You seemed happier when we first met. Why aren't you talking to me?"

Pursing my lips, I decide not to reply. Let him suffer a little. What could it hurt? I mean he's used to instant attention. He has to learn quickly that, with the type of danger he's in, if he draws too much attention, he and I will both be dead.

Knowing my place but also being curious, I break my silence. "What type of trouble did your dad get both of you into? I mean to hire one of the best security services, you must be pretty desperate."

I don't hear him speak. All that comes from his direction is a long exaggerated sigh and the movement of his seat as he adjusts himself.

The directional signal clicks as I make the first turn to the college campus. The drive is about twelve minutes, so I feel no hurry, but Tom's silence makes me want the truth even more. As I look into the passenger side mirror, Tom finally speaks.

"My dear old dad had no idea this would happen. Trust me, no one did. No one at the company knew these people were bad news." Thomas looks down at his feet, avoiding my gaze.

"Now everything we have ever worked for is

crumbling at our feet, so, Princess, that's why I need you." Sneaking a foul look at him for the nickname, I let him continue. "You're the best at what you do. These people are the best at whatever the hell they do. I don't know much of the details. Dad doesn't trust me enough to tell me." Turning his head in my direction, he leans back. "So maybe one day, when he's in a great mood and has a few shots in him, you might get the answers that I can't get." His voice seems to echo in the cabin of the car.

This is deep shit, and no matter how skilled I am, I truly understand the risk with this job. Also, I understand why Anthony Pavlov offered to pay me so much. He wants his secret to stay dead. I also know why he wants his son to have the best protection; love is a force that never ends.

Coming out of my thoughts, I glance quickly to my right. Thomas has his sunglasses on, phone in hand, and slender fingers moving rapidly on the screen. I notice how he pulls his bottom lip inward and rests it between his teeth. As I turn the car into the college parking lot, he looks up and lets loose another sigh.

The drive was quicker than I imagined, and it startles me a bit when Thomas smiles at me and whispers in a low voice, "Ready for this, *Bodyguard Lindsey?*"

****

His first class took three hours to finish. Notes, a lecture, and a film were shown to represent and broadcast the different forms of literature written over the past three decades. My eyes hurt from looking so intently around him and me. I should have known there would be no threats in his freaking classroom.

As soon as the class is over, Thomas stops at the cart

to get more coffee, two scoops of sugar, and a pinch of milk. Fancy, but not overdone. He once again surprises me when he hands me a hot cup of coffee as well. Lifting the lid, I note the plain black liquid. How did he know that's how I like my coffee? The plain blackness of the liquid has a punch but just enough flavor to not be deadly bland.

As I prepare to ask how he knew about my drinking preferences, I'm cut off when Thomas beats me to the punch.

"I read online that service people like yourself tend to drink strong liquids, but guess what?" Thomas looks at me fully and takes a greedy gulp of his coffee. "They don't add flavoring, which is believed to hinder the effects of the drink, such as coffee."

And I just thought I enjoyed my coffee simple. "Do you really just randomly search these things?" Is he the type of person that has a million questions flowing through his brain and refuses to forget about them? Add that to my list of new details about Thomas Pavlov.

"Sometimes, when I'm bored, I do." His voice is laced with an expression I can't quite pinpoint. But ignoring the nagging questions, I try to get us back on track.

"Anyway, when's your next class?"

My head is pounding, and the strange amount of heat radiating off the pavement from the sun isn't helping. I have this dreadful need to go home and take a nap. I can skip eating and my workout for the evening. All I want right now is to crash on my bed, turn down the lights, and forget about the world. I rarely get these feelings, but since this is my first real job since the one that went sideways, I think I have to readjust to working again.

"I have only one class today." Thomas reels closer to me. "Did you not read the schedule my dad gave you?" Looking at me with heavy eyes, Thomas shrugs. "But anyway, I'm exhausted and have tons of homework. You'd think that after three years in college, I would already be used to the pressure and all, but I'm just not." Not understanding what he's saying, I offer him a blank look of defeat. "I think I'm ready to head on home. How 'bout you?" Thomas bellows loud enough I nearly wince. He seems so different from before. When not in the presence of his father, Thomas is more laid back and calm, less arrogant. That just proves to me I don't have a clear handle on my skills just yet since coming back.

I simply nod. Glancing to the side, I take in our formation. I don't stand behind or in front of Thomas. I stand beside him. Blend in—rule number three.

The walk to the car is long and silent. A much-needed rest is required for the both of us. I have never talked so much to someone I work for, but it's nice to have a relationship and build trust with someone other than my brother. Having Thomas beside me is a new but somewhat comforting feeling. It's a feeling that is starting to grow on me. Bringing the car to life and taking a sip from my coffee container, I feel a little more relaxed.

Maybe Thomas and I just need to get to know one another. Maybe after a few days we will be able to build a routine with each other.

Gently wheeling the car forward, I make sure nothing seems off. In public areas, I have to be on high alert all the time, face blank and serious. I thank God that the estate isn't far from his college. It seems odd to me that Thomas would be going to a low-key school when he could be going to a prestigious and secure one, but so far he has already proved to me that I don't have him figured out like I wish I did. Thomas is a multi-layered person that I will have to peel back bit by bit. Piece by piece, I will get to know the true Thomas. I want to get to know him not because of this job, but for a more unexplainable reason. His calmness cancels out my chaoticness.

Just as I make a right, my phone just starts to ring. As we pull through the front gate, I shift so I can reach my phone. Stopping and looking at the caller ID, I see that it's Pavlov senior. Sighing and taking a deep, calming breath, I prepare for what's to come.

"Hello, sir. What can I do for you? Is everything all right? Are you in danger?" I start to question, and my hand on the wheel tightens with pressure. Do the men that he's trying to protect his son from have him? Is he still at work and just checking up on us? Damn... maybe I shouldn't have come back to work yet. Maybe I'm not ready. I scold myself for worrying. Maybe I'm not as stable as I believed myself to be. Maybe, I shouldn't have come back at all...

A deep laugh sounds through the phone. "Calm down. No, I'm all right. I was wondering, since I'm working late and the security detail at my house is different than you, could you—" Mr. Pavlov stops short then resumes, "—look after Thomas until I get home with my detail?"

Without a second thought, I already have the answer. "Yes, I'll look after him. Talk to you soon. But seriously, contact me if anything changes." The older man chuckles before he hangs up the phone.

As soon as the call is over, I turn my phone to vibrate after texting my brother, saying I can't meet up with him tonight. Sighing, and giving one final look at the guard at the gate, I ask him to open it with a pleasant, "Lindsey and Thomas returning," pulling the car forward up the driveway and parking. I turn to Thomas. "Your father is working late so he wants me to stay until he returns home."

Thomas smiles, and with a beam of happiness, he jumps out of the car and bolts toward the house.

"Thomas!" I shout. Damn it, he's supposed to wait for me. I mutter under my breath along with a few added curses. As I put my phone and keys back in my pocket and then grab my coffee and bag, I make my way to the house. "That boy, I swear." Shaking my head, I add another thought. "He's gonna get me killed."

I enter the house, and a beautiful wave of homely heat welcomes me. Thomas stands in the doorway peeling off his thick jacket, but he keeps his hoodie on. I sigh. I finally have a job where I'm allowed to come into the house. It feels odd but acceptable.

Looking at me, Thomas asks, "Do you want tea? Let's eat some early lunch?"

Glancing down at my watch, I raise a brow at the time.

Thomas then looks down at his, a slow creeping red of embarrassment rises on his cheek. "It's earlier than I thought. Maybe some cookies? Care to join me?" He smiles down at me, my heart speeding just a little faster than normal.

Nodding, I follow him into a part of the house I haven't seen. As I watch the spot between Tom's shoulder blades bounce, I think to myself; I came back to work just at the right time. I may not be the dangerous person many once knew, but I will do the same things I always do. I will guard my client with everything I have. I will use my training to defend them.

This was my calling and now, I just have to honor it.

Seeing Thomas move in front of me, I know things will be different this time around. No more mistakes and no more missed signs.

Thomas Pavlov is my client and no matter what happens, I will honor that contract I signed.

This is the rebirth of the old me. The fatal version that my parents wanted me to be.

Chapter 3

They're Coming

As my eyes open, I instantly feel the pain in my neck and back. The stinging and vibrating of my spine makes a whisper of a hiss slip between my parted lips.

Seeing the light streaming in through the room, I gasp, knowing that I have once again forgotten about the time. Peeking a solid glance at the rays, I begin to rise.

Slowly rotating my position and hoping for the pain to subside, I notice my bodyguard asleep with a frown on her lips and blanket hugged tightly around her on the next couch over.

Affectionately, I wish to wake her. But wisely, I know I should be dashing to get my day started. But, as I rub at my sore neck, I find myself just watching her while there is time.

Her jaw is clenched and tight. I can see the muscles working still; she seems to always be on guard. Drinking in the human side of her, I can see her eyes rotating back and forth beneath the lids. Lindsey looks so potent but poised with her mannerisms. "Always seeing a threat," I whisper as my eyes adjust to the light streaming in from the curtains. "I wish you had the ability to relax, Lindsey."

Shifting slightly, I position my head on the arm of the couch and silently think about yesterday. Our talks, her silent laugh, her scolding, the way she does her job. Being a jerk wasn't much of my idea. I don't even know why I acted that way when Lindsey walked into the estate. But, as I gaze at her, I know now: it makes everything that my father has done real. She's the reminder, the one person that might be able to redeem and save us, but that isn't something I want her to do. In my mind, it should be the man that caused these issues that solves the problem. But my father has never been a truly clever man. He's never been able to fix anything he's broken.

As my mind reels through the thoughts, the house begins to settle and creak. At the top of the landing, a few boards groan in matching tremors. Hearing footsteps coming down the stairs, I already know it has to be my father. He rises with the sun and settles with it too. Sighing, and deeming that I am out of time, I simply shut my eyes, hoping that he will let me lie here in semi-comfort a few moments longer.

The chuckle that bounces through the house tells me he has seen Lindsey and me asleep on the couches. Knowing I have to get up before she does so she doesn't get alarmed, I begin to shift from my false slumber.

Frowning, I know that I need to get ready for today. Then like a demonic whisper, a careless thought bounces into my head. Can I just skip class? Shaking my head of the cobwebs, I let my body settle again. No, that's a bad idea. I need these degrees. I need to show that I don't live off my daddy's money. Proving myself is one of the reasons why I enrolled in these classes. I need to work just as hard or even harder if I want to pave my own road. I can't let anyone do my work for me. I need to earn what I get. I need to travel the hard road just like everyone else. I need to prove myself just like Lindsey does.

Forgetting where I am for a second, my father's voice startles me. "Son? Come on, it's time to wake up. You gotta get to class in two hours." Faking a groan and then swatting at his rough hand, I try to get him to take a step back, but he just shakes me harder and threatens to wake Lindsey. And at that remark, my eyes bolt open.

"No, don't!" I exclaim as his wide, dark eyes tear a hole through me. "I'm up. I'm up, see?" I stand from the couch and let the blanket that was wrapped around me flutter to the polished floor.

"Then I suppose you should get moving. I could always just—" as my father takes a semi-step toward Lindsey I raise my hands, showing him that I'm moving.

"I go up to my room, and you leave her alone?" I ask, with my eyes trained on my father's tailored suit.

"I'll give you a head start. After all, she's gotta get up too."

Taking small steps and with a heavy stride in my walk, I make a beeline for my room. The unextraordinary walk to my room is filled with flustered thoughts. My father seems different with Lindsey here, more careful, I assume. But his actions seem more calculated and measured. He's faking who he is.

He fears her, my forethought whispers as I crack the door to my room open.

Smiling a little, I let my mind loose as I gather what I need for the day. I've never felt so weird but oddly comfortable around one of my bodyguards before. My dad has assigned me only two in the past, both males, but distant, and very noticeable by the passing crowd. Lindsey is different, not just because she is a woman, but because she makes it her purpose to blend in with those around her. Lindsey is heavily trained but also so flawlessly human. You feel her strength radiate off her, but she always knows how to seem inviting. She refuses to intimidate. She seems to want people to be themselves around her. Maybe then if they are honest she can get more information? Sighing as my feet travel on, I can't help but keep thinking about her.

She speaks her mind, stays with me, and even tells me off when I'm not doing what I'm supposed to. Sighing and leaning my weight on the wall adjacent to the window, I look out. The birds chirp and play in the shallow breeze. They even toss some of the bird feed on the ground as they fly around. Opening the window to take in the softness of the morning, a breeze wanders in and rustles a few loose papers on my desk.

Sinking lower on my heels, continuing to listen to the early morning, I let the kissing wind hit my bare arms, making me shiver. Winter is dipping in, and it looks like it's going to be a beautiful one.

Focused and content, I steal a glance at my clock. Cursing and shoving off the wall, I know that I have to hurry if I want to get to campus early. Grabbing anything that resembles clothes, I shove them under my arm. Swinging to the bathroom, I set everything down on the counter—a plain dark shirt and a pair of my favorite jeans. Smiling at my luck, I head to the shower, where I let everything out before the day.

I let every emotion, every thought from good to bad, seep from my pores. Every piece of my broken heart, I let wash down the drain. Stripping down, I begin the process that I have grown to treasure. I look as the water swirls. It's relaxing to know that the simplest things have a system.

My dad has a system. I once followed it too. But as I did, I felt as if I was losing myself. I felt as if my soul was molding to what he wanted and not what I wanted. Not anymore. My heart told me to take a step back from him and everyone. It was a sudden change, but no one has seemed to notice yet. Sighing and running a hand through the cascading droplets, I let that entanglement work its way down the drain too.

The heat of the water smooths my stiff neck and back, allowing me to get a few clean snaps to break free. The soap that I'm running through my hair gives me a chance to think about my day, and what I need to get accomplished.

My business class has to be the most boring class a person can take at this college. We write papers and take notes. The professor speaks, and we fill in the blanks. It's simple and to the point. I should be thanking my professor, but I have been reluctant to do so. I feel like if I speak about it, he will change the system, and I already have enough studying on my plate as it is. But, my favorite part is the simulation. We practice being in a board meeting, and we all take turns being the boss making the difficult decisions. Then, at random times when there are gaps in the schedule, we watch financial videos and even movies about successful people. Frankly, I don't care about that stuff at all. Not anymore, at least. What my father has roped us into in the last couple of months has made me recalculate what I want to do. Seriously enough, I don't want to be a part of a company like what my father is doing.

Lowering my shoulders at the realization, I take one more final spin under the spray of the gradually chilling water. Seeing no more soap bubbles, I get out into the cold air that makes my skin blister with goosebumps.

Taking small strides to the mirror, I take a realistic glance at the person who is looking back at me. The figure resembles me, but it also isn't me. That man has sunk-in eyes, reddened from the wash of the shower, and has less muscle than what I had a month ago. Trembling, I lean on the counter to take a clearer look. My hair is flat against my skull, my eyes are sharp and dark brown, and a small amount of scruff is coating my face. Sighing, I scrape at my chin. I've let myself sink, and all because of a mistake that wasn't even mine.

Frustrated, I think about when I was happiest. When I was young, when I was free, but also when I could think for myself without my father's harsh breath in my ear. Back then, people used to think that I was boring as I grew up. I didn't have many friends like a lot of kids with money.

I couldn't seem to fit in with those types of people. They were rude and cruel to those who didn't have financial stability. Knowing my place and understanding that we can't choose what type of family we are born into, I made a vow with myself: just be kind.

Squinting at the memory, I pull on my pants and button them, and as I begin to remember the laughter of the children of my youth, I let the happiness fade as I shrug my shirt over my shoulders. But like a splash, the memory bombards me anyway.

As I worked up the ranks of age in school, I always felt accepted by the people who didn't know my father. I have always been drawn to those who are serious about their education. Those types of people are committed, but they also know when to enjoy themselves, know the basics of how to tell the best jokes, and are the most comforting.

When I ran with those crowds, I noticed that they tended to understand the challenges that come with life. Without knowing me truly, they still understood that we all have faults that can change our entire outlook on life.

Knowing that I am running out of time, I swing open my bathroom door. Above me, I watch as the steam leaves the bathing room and enters my sleeping area. Grinning, I enjoy watching the clouds of perspiration slide into a new space.

Stepping out of the bathroom and into my room, I see a silhouette in the doorway. Knowing who it is without even adjusting my eyes, my grin grows wider and holds. Just from the shadowed stance all the way down to the casual silence, I can tell that it's Lindsey.

"Hello." I pass her way, letting her know that I'm nearly ready.

I walk across the threshold of my room, gather my books, and put them into my bag. The silent protector makes me feel safe, like nothing in the world can get to me. For the first time, I feel calm in my own skin with someone looking over my shoulder. I've always had people to look after me, but I never felt safe before. The power of having hired help has been handed down to me, but I've never wanted to use it. But for once, I congratulate my father on his pick this time. "You did well, you old bloke." I smile to myself. I rock my shoulders back and my spine twitches.

After all, he might have just hired someone who can actually keep me alive long enough to see my father correct his ways.

Looking over my shoulder, I still see Lindsey's morphed shadow. "Would you like to come in?" I ask as

I continue to gather everything.

Glancing back again with my arms full of books, I catch her shake of rejection. Shrugging, I lean back into my task. As I shift around the room and set my book bag on my desk, the shine of glass blinds me. Already knowing the person in the picture, I cup my hand around the frame. Reaching out to put it face down, my eyes meet the gaze of my mother's frozen expression. My father keeps putting the picture of my mother on my desk, even though I hate to think and look at her. Dropping the picture, I don't care about the crack of the glass.

Wrinkling my brow and gnawing at my lip, I think about what she once told me as a kid. Her favorite saying was, "When you fall, you learn, and when you get up, you force yourself to be stronger."

It was a motto for her, but I hated how she would say it. She never said the memorized words with kindness. She would use them against people. I felt like she was judging me for not being strong enough; because I wasn't like her.

Stealing one final glance at Lindsey, I tell myself I will never be like my mother. The safety she would force upon me was something I never wanted. She and my father are opposites. In marriage, most people are, but these two never clicked like the others. My father went from rags to riches, and my mother was always rich and was always scared of being put into rags.

They divorced when I was twelve. They said it was mutual. They said it wasn't my fault. They said they would still talk. My mother said she loved me. My father said she would come by and visit.

That never happened. Ever. It's been over eight

years since I have even spoken to her on the phone. She is remarried and has too much to focus on, she once said.

"Are you ready?" A quiet voice speaks behind me.

Gasping at the intrusion of thought, I turned back to where Lindsey was standing. Dressed in dark jeans and a green sweater is Lindsey. I see a necklace around her neck, and that's when it dawns on me, when did she go home and change? And how long have I been stalling in the rabbit hole?

But forgetting about it, I just nod to answer her question.

At the overflow of memories, a wave of sickness washes over me for a moment. Grabbing at the wall in just the nick of time, I let the plundering dizziness come over me.

My head begins to pound, and my stomach lurches in a way that makes me open my mouth to vomit. I feel myself leaning all my weight into the nearest surface. Feeling overly warm and light-headed, I allow myself to drop to my knees. Just as my knees skim the carpeted floor, vise-like arms wrap around my torso, holding me up. Through my senses, I can tell it's Lindsey. The scent of coconut webs around her, always.

Panting for breath, I begin to plead to Lindsey. "This has never happened before, feeling sick at the drop of a hat." Worry laces my voice. "Help," I try to say, pointing, attempting to direct Lindsey to help me get to my bed. She crouches in front of my face and waits for me to speak again. Shifting my weight, she braces me against her.

Opening my mouth to find words, I can't. As my back arches on the soft cushion of my bed, Lindsey leans over me.

"Say something, anything. Just keep looking at me."

But I don't. I just close my eyes and lean back into the softness.

****

Heat is all around me as my eyes proceed to open. I feel tight and tired. My skin feels like if I move, it will rip from my tissue. Groaning, trying to sit up, the warmth seems to be holding me in place, not allowing me to move. Concrete, that's how heavy my eyes feel when I try to open them. Surrendering, I let them stay locked tight.

"Thomas? Can you hear me?" That voice so familiar but so demanding. Annoying, even. That voice has haunted me for years, but the concern always makes me come crawling back like always. Weak, that is what my mother always said about me.

"Yes, Dad. I'm awake." My voice is as rough as gravel and as thick as my father's ledger books. Nobody says anything now. Sensing the tension, I can tell that Lindsey is in the room. For some reason, I know I'm safe again. She won't let anything happen to me. If she can stop it, then I know she will try until there is no more breath in her body.

But as the heat shifts, I gasp. Sighing and trying to get my bearings, I feel like I am putting too much faith in Lindsey. Trust has to be earned, but I sense it in the way she looks at me. She will protect me.

If she is willing to protect me against anything, I should be willing to trust her wholly.

Finally having the strength to open my eyes, I take in the room. The sun is oddly bright, and the room is full of blank faces. My legs feel weird as I move them, and my head is fuzzy. All that comes to me is the look on

Lindsey's face. It isn't concern that is laced in her eyes or mouth. Concern is when you know what's happening, she is more scared. She is scared because to her, this has probably never happened before. Scared, because she has no idea what to do, or how to make sure that it never happens again. The Lethal Vasiliev is scared for me. She didn't know how to protect me from my own self.

I pull myself up into a sitting position, my core aching for a run or something athletic-based. The weight of my head is abnormal. Gazing with sore eyes around the room, I find Lindsey standing tall, her back straight and muscles alert.

"What happened?" I pant as I use my arms to shove myself into a sitting position.

"Son, they're coming. I know it and…and I don't want you getting hurt. Lucky for you, at this moment, you just have a fever." My father's eyes turn toward the only face in the room that I don't recognize. "The flu, the doctor thinks." That's it? Then how did it come on so fast? Why did Lindsey have a look of panic?

Shakily, I twist my legs over the end of the bed and attempt to stand, grabbing the post to my bed as I do so. I need my own space, my own area to think.

"Tom…" Lindsey says my name with caution. I have a feeling I'm not going to like what she has to say next. She comes closer. I can smell her intoxicating scent. Her eyes are like flames that draw me in, the frown that I so badly want to replace with her bubbly laugh and mesmerizing smile. Scolding the world, I swear at myself. Why am I like this?

"Thomas…Um, I think it would be best if you stayed at Ms. Vasiliev's place." Shooting my gaze in my father's direction, I nearly fall at how fast my head moves. "I think you are overreacting about this, Dad. Why do I have to stay with Lindsey? The weather gets to me, we both know that. This has happened before."

Nodding, but then shaking his head, he allows the paranoid thoughts to lead him. I can already see his next trail of thought. "I know. I know that, but something in my gut feels off. Trust me on this? Stay with your bodyguard."

Rotating my eyes in their sockets, I turn to Lindsey. Her body is solid and positioned at the doorway. Scuffing in a breath, I look at my father again. "How can I possibly trust you? But fine, get rid of me, like you always do when things get difficult. There is nothing to fear, remember? You said it yourself. No one can take you down."

"I'm not trying to be difficult," he shouts. Coming closer to me now, he points a meaty finger at my chest. "I'm doing this for you, so have some respect. Just go."

Snarling, he turns to Lindsey. She acts as if nothing is happening, but as my father steps closer, her eyes harden at his threatening stance. "She's trained in stealth, and she, let's face it, looks like she can kill."

Nearly touching her, my father grins like he's proud of himself. "Can you kill, Lindsey?" Not answering him, Lindsey stays still. As I look at her, in her eyes, I can see the hostility brewing.

Turning to face me, he smiles, he shifts on the balls of his feet. "I believe you will be better off if you stay with her. Until you get better. And while we try to figure out this threat." Frowning now, he whispers the last part, "I don't know how long it will take, though." And there it is, the threat that curses me to give up my daily life.

I just want to lie down, catch a few more Zs, and eat

soup or something that won't make my stomach cringe. But at the moment, everything makes my stomach settle into unpredictable knots. You are overreacting, my mind tells me. I've gotten sick before and far worse than this, but everything is about my dad when he's worried.

He fears these people that he made a deal with. He wants me out, so I don't take the blow. I know that. But internally, I know there is nothing he can do to stop them. There is always a price to pay, and this group of people is looking to collect.

Knowing that it will make everyone's job easier, I settle with a simple answer; "Okay," I whisper in a hushed voice. "I'll stay with Lindsey, Dad. You have my word."

And fuck, I hope my father knows what he's doing because once a promise is made, it can't be undone, very similar to a deal made at a crossroads.

Once a deal is signed, there is nothing that can reverse it.

Sighing and shutting my eyes, I cover my face with my hands and admit, "I hope this solves whatever you are fearing, Father."

Chapter 4

World's Come Undone

"Take the medicine every four hours," the doctor, who goes by Link, recites as he hands me the heavy bottle of capsules.

"What is it?" I ask, biting at my lip. Swallowing back any harsh remark that may live within me.

With the bottle in my hand, I tilt it down so I can read the label. It has my name and date of birth on it, and as I read the directions, I sigh. "This is for my headaches? Is that what I had to take when I was younger? The pills that Dad would try and hide in my food?"

Chuckling, Link smiles. "Probably. You have a weak immune system. We need to get that handled. But, for now, take those." He points with his ringed finger at the bottle. "When you need them. Only two at a time every four hours. Don't overdo it, get it?"

Nodding, I let the bottle fall against my chest. "Thanks, Doctor Link. If I need anything, I'll give you a call." I hold up his card.

Nodding again at his instructions, he turns back to me and asks, "Give it to the lovely woman too? Tell her the deal."

Standing from the bed, I walk Link out of my room. With it empty now of everyone, my lungs allow me to take a nice refreshing breath. The solitude is what I've been craving for the past few hours. I need a few minutes to myself, to take everything in. I knew that I had a weaker immune system, but the sickness came so suddenly, so forcefully. Sighing and listening to the rattling of the pills, my hands become clammy. As if there are still people in my room, I can nearly retrace my father's movements.

In and out, my father came and went. He gave orders and spilled useless commands. Lindsey hovered as the doctor ran my temperature again, and in the hall, she and my father shared a few hushed words. Lindsey hasn't spoken to me yet, and right now, I want to ask her how she feels about me invading her home. Her space. Her escape from work.

Striding to my desk chair and taking a plopping seat, I shove my book bag to the floor. The thud is alarming and looking over my shoulder, I wait for the choir of footsteps to come rushing back into my room. But after a few seconds of silence and with no footfalls meeting my ears, I lean down to pick it up.

"Is everything with you going to be this difficult?" Leaping from my skin at the sound of Lindsey's voice, I scold her for scaring me.

Reaching down to once again pick up my bag, I tell her, "You shouldn't be so pleased at scaring people. It's rude," I tell her.

Raising a brow, she stalks toward me, her eyes flashing.

Her feet move silently, and her body flows mesmerizingly. Strong, sturdy, and efficient, her form screams power, but her eyes showcase mercy. "I don't scare. People just don't listen is all." Smiling, she leans down and takes my bag in her hand. Effortlessly, she shoves it over her right shoulder.

"I'll get your things. You need to keep your strength." Humming, I wish to reject her words, but I can't. She's right. I need to get better and the sooner the better.

Hauling myself to my feet, I take one final look around the room. All my clothes are packed and stuffed into bags. My shower bag is full of everything I think I will ever need. Sweeping my eyes around the room, I try to remember what my room looked like when it was full, now it's just a shell.

No more posters on the wall. My desk has been emptied out. Everything of personal attachment has been stuffed into one bag or another, and even my bookcase has been capsized. My treasured stories have been piled into the closet.

Looking to my side, I ask Lindsey, "Do you think that by acting like I was never here, they won't come after me?"

Sucking on her lower lip, she just puffs out, "It has never worked in the past, but it's worth a try."

"They know he has a son, so if they want me, they can get me. Pretending that I was never here won't stop them from looking," I give voice to the truth for the first time. My father won't listen to me, but with Lindsey's calm manner beside me, I feel myself telling her things that normally I would never say.

Angling her head closer to me, she utters, "Do you have any idea who these people are? What are they really after? Or, what your father did to these people?"

I shake my head. "No. He hasn't told me anything. He didn't tell you either?" Lindsey roams the room, double-checking that everything of mine is packed or shoved away.

"Hmm," Lindsey mutters through laser-focused eyes. "No, I asked. I demanded to know, but he said I didn't need to know." Opening my mouth to challenge his ideology, Lindsey just turns to me and holds up a hand. "It's no use. When people are embarrassed about what they have done, they won't speak about it. We will just have to figure this out on our own, Thomas."

Rubbing at my eyes, I click my tongue to the roof of my mouth. "I'm sure no one at the company knows either. He likes things hidden. He always has, even when I was a young lad."

Pushing the thought out of my mind, I move away from the area of the desk and take one more look around at the walls and floor. "We should be heading out, yes?"

Crossing her arms, she nods and then locks eyes with me. "Once you are in my house there are a few rules that you will need to follow. Not just for my liking, but to keep you safe."

"What are they?"

Waving her arms around the room, she dismisses my question. "Let's just get everything in my car, and on the way to my house, I'll fill you in."

Casting a farewell look at my room, I pick up the last bag by my bed and usher Lindsey into the hall. She moves so quietly, with no effort. Thinking, I follow her down the stairs into the living center. As she looks from one side to the other, I watch her braid move from side to side. It's like a coiled rope.

I tap her shoulder. "I'll go find my dad. Will you take these to the car? I'll be there in a minute, all right?"

Meeting my eyes, she exhales a kind dismissal. With a fluid turn, Lindsey walks down the hall and then vanishes out the open front door. Out of my sight, I get ready to get down to business. Gently, I walk down the corridors to the kitchen, where I know I'll see Sally. Smiling as I see her, I nearly run into my father's empty dinner chair.

"Sally," I call her name, "have you seen my dad? Lindsey and I will be leaving soon, and I want to talk to him before we head out."

With her arms covered in flour up to her elbows, she frowns at me. "Oh no," she mumbles in a pout. "What shall I do with you gone? Your papa doesn't like my pasta like you do. But, I'll send you food, yes?"

Tightening my lips, and sighing, I tell the woman who has become like a mother to me, "No, Sal, I don't think you will be able to do that. But," I raise my left hand in a peace offering, "I'll check with Lindsey, okay?"

Still feeling unsteady and ill, my lungs seem to itch. Through labored breaths, I ask Sally again, "Where is my dad?"

Sally points to the door to the left with her flour-coated fingers.

Approaching her, I feel so sorry about leaving her here with my father's over assuming notions and downcasting comments. I have grown to appreciate Sally and her wise words, so with my voice low, I tell her, "If you need any references, I got you covered."

Sally's jaw drops, and I know she understands.

"I want you to be safe. If things start to get out of control, you head for the door." Without waiting for her words of comfort, I just carry myself in the direction Sally said my father was.

Stopping momentarily, I lean against the doorway.

"Take care of yourself, Sal." Smiling the best I can, I whisper, "I'll see you as soon as I can."

"No, no, young Thomas, the pleasure is mine." Stepping toward me but not touching, Sally smiles proudly. "Call me when you can, kid."

Shutting my eyes, I turn back to the task at hand. I need to stay focused. I need to get everything I can from him now before it truly is too late. And I need to let him know that if there really is a risk of danger, he needs to separate himself. I've watched plenty of television. If you have someone close to you, then the bad guy will use them against you.

The yard's plotted land is empty and smooth. Only a few dead leaves litter the ground. As I look around, I see parts of my childhood replaying as I search for my father. I walk along the patio as a breeze washes through my hair and makes it rise from my scalp. A curl falls in my eye, and with an impatient shove, I swipe it back in place. Through the shadows and dancing tree branches, I see my father with his back to me. I've gotten so used to seeing his back recently I nearly forget he has a face at times. Seeing him doing nothing, I see an opportunity to get the information that I need.

Rushing forward, I lock my hand along my father's shoulder and turn him so he can meet my eyes. "Who are they?" His eyes, dark and callous as ever, hold no answer. His mouth is shut in a firm line of knowing but not telling.

"You know me and Lindsey, just tell me. If we don't know who these people are, how is she supposed to keep me safe, Dad?" Biting at my lip, I try to steady my shaking hands.

With his suited body, my father leans in close, and

with his musty breath in my face, he says, "For your protection, you and she can't know anything. It's better this way, trust me. If you know the truth, you'll die."

Shoving at his puffed-up chest, I beat down his words. "Just because you're a coward doesn't mean I am." Pointing to where Lindsey is helping load the car, I tell him, "Maybe if you were sober enough, you wouldn't make deals like this. What do they have on you?" If I have to leave my home, my life, my routine because of this man, I damn well deserve some form of explanation. I need to know the truth. For once, why can't he just trust me with the truth?

"Come on," I plead. "Just give me something that we can work with here." My eyes burn with frustration as my father takes hold of my hand just to remove it from him.

"You need to stay in the dark on this one."

Snarling and licking at my chapped lips, I look back at where I walked from. Standing there in all her glory and rich demeanor is Lindsey. A deep scold on her face, and her eyes nearly translucent in the blinding sunlight. Seeing me looking, she stands a little higher and curls her arm inward.

Time to go. Bowing my head one more time, I walk away from my father. Taking deep breaths, I gather myself. As I come to stand beside Lindsey, I drink in her scent, and without a single word, we leave the house and enter the packed car that also smells like her.

Taking in the details of the car, I smile seeing that we are using her personal vehicle and not the one that my father gave her. We are one step closer to not being linked with him.

Leaning my head on the glass of the window, I roll

it down slightly so I can get some air. As the window buzzes down, fresh air rushes in and helps me clear my head. Shaking my head at the exhaustion within me, I take a deep breath. With Lindsey behind the wheel, I feel safe. And knowing she's on my side, I say with a mouth full of sour words, "He won't tell me anything."

Lindsey doesn't meet my eyes. "I'll protect you, Thomas. You have my word. As long as there is a sliver of breath in my body, I fight."

With those words ringing through my head, I turn to look at her with a wince as my head begins to pound again.

Reaching for the bottle of pills sitting in the cup holder on my side, I unscrew the cap and pop two in my mouth. With a woozy swallow, I choose to make another promise, a vow I know Lindsey might need one day.

"If you fight for me, I'll fight for you."

"All I need from you, Thomas, is to stay out of harm's way. Let me do my job so you can continue to live your life."

Exhaling and letting my head fall into my palm, I just watch Lindsey. In her strength I find shelter. She may not want to hear the truth about me willing to defend her, but I will keep reminding her.

As long as she fights for me, I will give it back. We will be evenly matched. She may be stronger, more skilled, and prepared, but someone needs to fight for her.

I may not have been raised to help others, but I always will.

"Lindsey," I say with determination. "we are a team and we will protect each other, no matter what happens."

Chapter 5

Unexpected

The front door is bigger than I expected. Her house is bigger than expected. Everything I see around me is so different from what I thought it would be. No matter where I look or what captures my attention, I'm able to see a new piece of my bodyguard. I'm able to see into her in the slightest of ways.

I'm looking from left to right and taking in the lay of the land. I'm left breathless in awe. And the pain in my temple is slowly increasing, but I have to take this all in. I have to know what she's like. I need to stay solid so I can see who Lindsey Vasiliev really is. For her and me, we need to understand the other.

Wincing at the light, I hold my throbbing temple. Right now, my head is like a heavy weight. My body feels stiff and weak. But while I feel useless, Lindsey keeps pressing forward. In only two days, she has been working here, for me, and I can already tell that she keeps things to herself. She never seems to let anyone in.

I don't. My life is always an open book. Since my father became so famous for his fifteen-million-dollar contract a decade ago, our lives have never been the same. He built the life he wanted with that money and never looked back. My father has never been a man of regrets, and he never will be.

With a flash of sun, it reminds me of the worst part of being the son of a famous man. The worst part? The constant cameras and secret photos being taken. But worst of all is the danger of doing and saying the wrong thing at all times for others to see. All it takes is one person to capture me doing something childish and then I'm finished. My dad would have my skin.

My life has always seemed like a big flash from a camera that leaves me dazed and confused. And I never seem to be able to get solid ground under my feet so I can fall gracefully. And no matter what I tell my father he never helped me. Still to this day, my problems are my own and his are his. We don't share. We don't help. We hide and hope.

But now, there is no waiting. There is no hiding. He brought Lindsey in, so he must believe that I need her more than ever. He must believe that we need her.

Sighing and turning back to the present, I skirt around the entryway. The air in the house smells stale and of dust. Smiling, the giddiness and butterflies fly at the satisfaction of knowing that she is so intimately human. Even the legendary bodyguard has a dusty house.

I slide my finger across the tabletop and hold up the prize to show Lindsey. "Dusty, it seems?"

"Stop touching things. Just sit, would you?" Lindsey's voice comes out heavy. Masked, her eyes drift to the closed door.

Lindsey opens the door to our right. I meander into the spotless kitchen, which does not smell like dust, just to defy Lindsey's request.

As Lindsey disappears, the back door leading to the porch opens as well. As the clean, crisp air seeps into the kitchen, I allow myself to look around the kitchen more in depth.

A single mug is resting on the counter, no plates or utensils are out in the open, but turning to the right, I see a jug of purified water sitting in the corner by the fridge. Curious, I shift my weight to see where Lindsey went, but not seeing her, I pull back the fridge door. Full, organized, clean healthy food, but there is a container of juice front and center.

Just as I lean my head into the fridge, I remember what Lindsey wanted me to do; she told me to sit down. Sighing, I mutter hopelessly to myself, "but I want to stand." I need to take everything in. I have to know more about the woman whom everyone fears. I need to see her in her element. Seeing her in her own home allows me to see what she's really like. I *need* to see the real Lindsey Vasiliev.

But seeing her differently doesn't last long as her strict voice pounds into my ear. "Get some sleep. Thomas, your body needs it. Use the guest room."

I don't want to go. When I'm with her, everything around me feels secure. With her, I feel like I can breathe and be real.

"Everything you need should be in there." Lindsey still doesn't look at me as she speaks. She's preoccupied with the pitcher of water in her hands.

As she pours the water, I begin to wonder how long I can stall her. Feeling the words at the tip of my tongue, I attempt to keep them glued down. "What if I don't want to?" Doubting and not listening to her seems like a terrible idea, but going to bed sounds boring. Needing to know her, I demand to stay awake.

Exhaling a breath and placing her hands on her hips, she mutters, "Just go, okay. You had a fever earlier. You need to get some rest. It's for your own good, Thomas."

"Fever-shmever," I ramble as she comes to stand beside me in the kitchen. Closer than ever, I can almost taste the coconut smell floating off of her.

Rolling her eyes at my comment, she just adds, "If you get bored watch some television."

Shooting my spine straight, I want to offer the idea that we stay together, but as if reading it in my eyes she beats me to the topic.

"I guarantee that you're safe here. Just sleep. It looks like you need it." Her voice seems clipped and on edge. I can tell that she doesn't like people in her space. Nodding to show that I understand about needing space, I just wish I could really dig my heels in and get to know her without there being a battle.

It's useless to try my point any further. I glare at her. "Fine. See you later. If I miss taking my medicine, can you remind me?"

"I'll do that." She pours one more glass of water. In a crystal-like clear glass, the liquid swooshes and swirls. Lindsey hands me the glass and then points to the bedroom at the far end of the hall.

"You'll know it when you see it. I'll bring in all your stuff in a little bit. Get some sleep. You'll thank me later." Choosing to pick an argument with her sounds deadly, so like a good boy, I choose to keep the peace and do as she says. Knowing we will have plenty of days to bicker, I decide to move.

Taking a final glance over my shoulder, I see it in her eyes—the fatigue. The dark circles rimmed below her eyes, those are from not sleeping well. Sighing and taking a greedy gulp of the water, I choose to shrug it off.

As I turn to leave, I remember she mentioned rules.

"Wait, Lindsey, what are the rules I need to follow?"

Lindsey swivels, and with large crystal eyes, she grins. With a threat edged in her eyes and a warning in her stance, she just gestures to the bedroom. "Get some sleep. The rules aren't important now. I'll tell you when you're better, Thomas."

****

The sound of a startling beat wakes me from my slumber. Choosing to obey Lindsey, I went to bed early at noon. Now that it's long past nine at night, I no longer feel tired. I feel curious. My head feels two times better. My limbs don't feel so much like jello.

Standing, I turn off the muffled television and open the bedroom door. The throbbing beat is coming from somewhere else in the house. My feet shuffle on the wooden floor as I try and find which room is Lindsey's. At the very end of the hall, I find it, but she's not there. Checking every room like a mad man, I still come up empty. Startled, I can't find her.

Just as I'm turning away from her room, the round of beating sounds stop.

Trembling a bit, I walk into the kitchen and pour myself a glass of water. Noticing the back door ajar, I take a hefty step closer to it. Then suddenly, the sound of beating noises returns. I set my hand on the open door, waiting for it to return a third time. Beginning to hear it, I choose to follow the sounds. I let the moonlight guide me through the darkness as I try to find the source of the noise that woke me from the peaceful sleep I hadn't had in a long time. After the one door from the off-side of the kitchen, and after sliding through a narrow hall, another door lays before me.

*What the...*my mind travels through a million

different thoughts a minute. Stiffening my spine, I lean on the door. Listening, I attempt to figure out what the sounds are.

Stepping through the darkness, I knock on the door between me and the unknown. My heart hammers in my chest, and I fist my hands, getting ready to strike. Sweat dampens my hair. Sweat and fear mix with my unsteady coordination. Just as I'm about to lean on the door and try to listen to what's happening, it opens, and I feel myself starting to fall.

My body rams into a solid surface, but hands keep me stable, and long, sweet-smelling hair is on my shoulder. As I look up, I see Lindsey. Sweaty, beaten, and worn. Her eyes seem dark and troubled, her body is tense. It all comes together like a flash. She's just training. Or doing a late-night workout. Lowering my head again, I curse myself.

"Shit, I'm so sorry. I thought…I just…Um, I thought someone was breaking in. I thought you left." The look on her face is dangerous, seething even with the red flush and haunting eyes. "I couldn't find you," Backing away, with my arms raised, I make a beeline to leave, but her damp hand clamps around my wrist.

I can tell I caught her in a bad mood. I never thought that I would see her like this. Closed off but so exposed. Her body, posture, and stance say open, but her fiery eyes warn me to leave.

As she helps me recover my footing, she moves to the side, and then I see all the weight equipment, punching bags, and a treadmill. Poking my head to the side, I take in all the other things scattered around the cushioned floor: dumbbells and free weights are scattered around the room, each screaming to be used.

There is so much stuff in one room that I no longer feel comfortable thinking that I can defend myself. *Wimp*.

I just feel pathetic now about my unreasonable panic and also knowing that I couldn't throw a steady punch if it meant me living or dying.

Looking at her in apology, I take in her appearance—all sweaty. Her arm muscles are exposed and threatening. Her hair is damp with slick sweat along the side part of her temples.

She has never looked that lethal to me before. But I feel so glad that my father picked her to defend me. This woman is no joke. She could probably take a bullet and keep fighting. Shit, I really smile for once. Lindsey is my personal bodyguard. Like a weapon, with training, anything can be used to take someone down. She is a blunt instrument that can wound someone with no hesitation. And this fatal person is all mine.

As suddenly as her touch came, it vanishes as she growls. "Thomas? Can you just—I don't know—be on your own longer than a few hours? I have training I still need to do." As if seeing my flinch, she adds nearly politely, "And I can't sleep." Looking at my widened eyes, she gives a false smile. "And by all means, enlighten me. Why would someone try to break into one of the most secure locations in London?"

Knocking my head to the side, I see her point now. It's a real thought that I missed. Good question on my part—why did I even think that low? I should have thought everything through a little better. Who would break into her house? People know her. They know her reputation. You say *Lethal Woman,* and your skin shivers. Lindsey's face may not be known, but the threats that hover above her, everyone can feel it. She is capable and not to be messed with.

I back up and walk back into the kitchen. My heart is beating rapidly as I try to relax. I totally messed up. She already doesn't like me, and now I'm sure she won't want anything to do with me while I'm a visitor in her house. Already, not even a day in fully staying with her, and I'm already fucking up. The word idiot rings through my head. *Great*, I think to myself, *you just pissed off the one person who can keep you alive.*

"Come with me," she starts walking down the hall. I follow suit, not wanting to be left behind. But from the long strides, I can tell that what she is about to say won't be pleasant.

"You should really learn something about me; I don't trust anyone. And I really don't like arguing, and I don't play games. So that makes this house one of the safest places you could be, trust me."

I don't trust easy, but by the tone in her voice, I have no hesitation or doubt about what she claims. You can't keep something like this to yourself.

"This house is the best place for us." Lindsey's claim makes me nearly stop walking. Trying to make my mind work faster, I think hard.

So what am I supposed to take away from this conversation, really? From the intensity of her voice, something is off. I wonder, did I stare too long? While trying to read and understand her, did I press too hard, push too far? Then it hits me like a plowing train. "So what I see is what I get?" I ask, not wanting to mix anything up or make her feel uncomfortable any more than I already have.

"Yes," she huffs. "I don't have anything to hide, so what you see is what you get." She darts a heavy gaze in my direction. "Now I'm going to check your room. Prove that there is no monster under your bed, then I'm going to take a shower and finally go get some rest." Lindsey turns her body, but her eyes never leave mine. Seeing the question building, she asks, "So shall I enter?"

Tightening my fist, trying to keep my face from burning with embarrassment, I mumble, "Oh, yeah. Go for it." Heat creeps and builds onto my cheeks.

Lindsey turns on the light and opens the closet. Taking small steps, she then gets down on the floor and checks under the bed. After rising, she looks over her damp shoulder at me, then opens the window and looks out. A chill settles over the room, and it's not just the draft from the open window. When she closes the window, she makes sure to lock it.

Heavily, she sighs and shuts her eyes before slowly crossing the carpeted floor. Lindsey doesn't speak as she walks out of the room. In the hall, I can almost feel the wave of ice slipping off her.

"Goodnight, Lindsey," I say, attempting an apology, and she simply waves.

"I'll see you in the morning, Thomas. If you need anything, you know where to find me, all right?" Nodding, I watch her as she leaves me standing in the hall. The small comment sends a smile to my lips.

How desperate am I for a friend that I turn to my bodyguard? She is the only person besides my father who is on my side. She's the last person I should be getting attached to, but as I ever so slowly get to know her, I feel my trust reaching out to her.

Pacing back into my room, I take hold of the door and twist the knob, I feel something inside of me come unleashed. Shutting the door, I can still see light from the hall creeping in. Sickly, I lay back down on the now chilled bed. Gently, my head levels out, and I start to think about what we are going to do tomorrow. From the look in her eyes, I can tell that she is brilliantly strong but so soft at times, and that softness almost comes through for all the world to see. Just barely, she lets it surface. It's like you have to walk through the fire of hell to see it. Once you see the gentleness within her, it can send you to heaven.

This is a person that I trust, she may not trust me or anyone, but I am willing to bet my life that she will protect me at all costs. After all, she did promise, and she isn't the type of person that breaks promises easily.

As I shut my eyes, listening to the rhythm of water hitting the tiles in the bathroom up the hall, I let myself get comfortable in my sheets. No matter what happens, this is a day worth remembering, and this is a life worth living. Being with people that make you happy, even if they just don't know it, is a great feeling that keeps me smiling as I drift to sleep.

My trust is strong with Lindsey Vasiliev. I know that she will lay down her life before she lets anything happen to me. If only she knew that I would do the same thing.

She's in my heart now, and she's become a part of my family. She walked into my life and now I don't want her to leave. I have very few people in my life, and I refuse to let her go. She proved to me that anyone can be strong. You just have to be willing to try.

For the short few days that I have known her, I can see the truth within her.

She doesn't lie.

She doesn't fake who she is.

She is being clear with me.

Lying in my bed, I know that I have fallen in line with her too quickly, but as I turn on my side and gently exhale, I know that I could be far worse off.

Lindsey will help me no matter what I do. She is a person that never seems to fail at her word. Lindsey doesn't know it yet, but she has somehow saved me.

In her simple actions and movements. In her quiet manners and silent commands, I feel safe and understood. "Thank you," I practice saying to her into my pillow. "Thank you for saving me when no one else was capable." Grinning at the chance of that day, I feel my heart flutter, wishing for that day to come.

Wishing for the day where I can breathe without the agony or the fear that I will be cut down, I slowly breathe in the chilled air and listen to the beating of the water hitting tiles.

"One day," I promise to myself. "One day, I'll be able to thank you for giving me a fighting chance."

Chapter 6

Life Isn't Fair

I wake up with a kink in my neck, and my head is pounding. The pain floats in and out like a needle that keeps getting pressed into the skin. The uneasy pain starts at the base of my neck, then swarms up to my temple. Not being able to stand the needles running through my brain, I simply conclude to get up and start my day—with a few Tylenols first. So now, I'm sitting on a stool with my elbows resting on my counter island, scrolling through my phone with the enticing aroma of coffee swelling through the shallow room.

Peering out the sliding glass door, I let the songs of the birds lighten my mood. This is my favorite part of the day, the harmony, the chirping of the birds, and the new fresh morning air. But oddly, the night is also my favorite, the time of day when the world stops for a rest and people settle down to recharge. It's a simple notion to remind us all that we need time to catch our breaths. "I wish for opportunities like that," I mutter as my hand wraps around the rim of my coffee mug.

I've learned that even when it's night, my alertness never fades. Sleep doesn't come as easily for me as it does for other people. My mind never fully shuts down, and when it does, it's always hard to wake in the morning. The memories that I have spent so long locking away summon me when I sleep. There is no escape from what I have done. The past can't be outrun, it will always find you, and when it does, you don't stand a chance against the very situation that left you hollow in the first place. The past lurks and never gives you a chance to breathe. If you miss your step, you fall, and it will get you.

Consequent to my dark mood, last night wasn't how I thought it would go. Thomas was supposed to sleep, stay in one room and not come searching for the source of the noise that I was making. Clearly, I thought he would stay away from me, not come looking. I thought he would sleep through the whole night from how he was snoozing when I checked in on him before heading out to the workout room. Thomas is a kind man. For the short time we've known each other, I've found him to be honest and gentle. He didn't deserve the hostility that I poured on him. Thomas deserves better than what he's getting. He deserves better than what I got.

For my whole life, I only knew one way of living because of my parents. My parents were simple beings, skilled but ruthless. I got plenty of fistfuls of anger that my father would shove my way. My mother's voice would cut me deep. Every memory can be used for your success or be the one thing that stands in your way. And, so as I work out, I let what they taught me, shoved at me, and released on me be the catalyst to who I unwillingly became. I took what they gave me and locked it within for only my viewing. What I endured and acted upon as a young teen, most would run from.

One thing I've learned is that no matter what, family is the fuel that keeps us going, either in a good productive way or a vengeful wave that just keeps moving and causing destruction.

Overall, I was hoping that Thomas wouldn't see me as a destructive force yet. I know deep down it would be impossible to hide my anger from him. I just didn't want him to see me at a breaking point this early in the mission. Not even a damn week in, and he might be afraid of me already. I know I have a personality that is not welcoming, but I at least wanted Thomas to have trust in me. Well, I burned that bridge.

Sighing, I settle my lips on the rim of my mug and inhale a simmering gulp of the rich dark liquid that keeps my blood flowing these days. Wiping at my eyes, I try to get the sleep out of them and get my head into a steady state before Thomas comes in.

But bitterly, my mind settles on something my father told me once: "When a person puts everything on the line every day, they learn that no matter how much they train or try to counteract what they feel, there is only one way to get it all out: use it. We, as people, need to use these emotions to stay mortal, to remind ourselves that we are not invincible. There is no way to run from what lives within you, so use it."

That day, it was foggy and past bone cold, but my father insisted that we go for a walk in the village before he left for another mission. As we walked, he talked, and I simply listened. My father's voice boomed through the fresh-smelling, bustling street. He didn't care about the volume he was speaking. As he talked and warned and gave me pointers on life, he never looked me in the eyes. I never asked what he would be doing, or where he'd be going, but that mission was the very mission that he disappeared from all those years ago. That was the mission where he left my family for good.

Without a final word, he left my family, and then he tore us all apart. "Life is full of regrets, and at times, they are used as a strategy to win something far bigger." Scowling at his weathered face, I remember that day; it was a bleak morning that he left and simply gave me those words as a parting gift with Jonathan hovering over my shoulder. "One day, you will understand." Looking at me and my brother, our father frowned. "It is something both of you will come to experience. Choice is equally as dangerous as action."

Sighing, my fingers itch to ring my brother, but with a glance at the time, I know to leave him alone. In the distance, I can hear faint footsteps, but ignoring it, I try to gather my father's features from that last encounter, but I can't. Just as I take another hefty sip from my mug, a voice chimes in.

"Good morning, Lindsey." A groggy Thomas walks into the room, and his dazed eyes settle on me. He startled me for a moment, but not enough to make me scold myself.

As I run my gaze over his appearance, I can tell he didn't sleep well this time around. His dark, curly hair is tousled in different directions as if he ran his hand through it every time his eyes opened in the night. When his gaze runs over the kitchen and lands on me, the crescent moons under his eyes conclude the theory. One eye looks so hollow it seems he was in a fight. I frown internally. Somehow it was my fault. Everything with me is a fight. Nothing can just be simple and clean. I always taint what's around me.

I ignore the bitter thought and continue to watch him. He makes his way into the kitchen and finds the coffee machine nestled in the corner. He pours himself a cup and walks over to where I'm sitting. He doesn't even put cream or sugar in his coffee.

Setting the cup down after taking a sip, he swallows intensely, as if he's scared that he will drown in the coffee, then with a rough ramble, asks, "What are your plans for today?" Roaming his gaze over my face, a slow frown settles along his forehead. "I'm getting this vibe that you're going to be alone a lot. Am I right?"

The question in his voice has me startled, alarmed, but somehow I know he is right. Overall, I don't feel like talking. I'm not really used to having people in my home this early in the morning.

I really have to train myself to be a people person again. I love people, I chide myself, just not in my home or this early in the morning. My home is my only port of reassurance. It's my safe place.

Wanting to prove him wrong, I suggest, "I was thinking we could go for a run. But you are welcome to stay here. My brother will be stopping by later, so I was thinking that you could be useful today." When I first speak, I shake my head. I don't want him to think that I'm a terrible person. Oddly, I want Thomas to like me, to respect me, and to treat me as an equal. Secondly, above all else, I want Thomas to know that he can trust me. I want him to know that I'm human. That I am breakable…That I'm just like him; flawed.

I wish I could overcome the cowardice within my heart and just say that having someone depending on me again is scary, that the last time I gave a vow to protect someone, I failed.

Just as I'm about to speak again about what I feel, Thomas beats me to the punch.

"So, we would go for a run, I would help you with

housework, and then sit down and meet your brother? Why does this sound like a date, Lindsey Vasiliev?"

I laugh then. The sheer laughter in his voice reaches through me for a second and draws out a chuckle. I've never been on a date, and that would most definitely be weird. Only Thomas can break the tension, even if it is for a minute.

My phone rings then, and Thomas looks at it, smiling, as if wanting to prove himself correct. "A gentleman caller?" Thomas queries as I reach for my cell.

The caller ID proves him wrong as Jonathan's name comes up. My brother isn't someone who likes calling; no matter what, you must call him first. Knowing that, what he has to say will be furious. I reach for my phone and swipe to answer. "Hey, Johnny, what's up?" My voice floats through the network channel, and it sounds different from my regular voice. Less serious and minor with a squeak.

Waiting for him to respond, I take another sip from the lukewarm coffee. I can already see my brother now sitting on his couch this decently chilled morning. A smile comes to my face as he begins to speak.

"Hey, Linds," I can hear the shuffling of papers on his end of the line. "I was wondering, are you cooking, or is takeout an option?"

Rolling my eyes, I bite the inside of my cheek. "Johnny, I'm cooking. Not *mama's* food, my own. Like from cookbooks and the television? Plus you will get to meet my boss' son. Trust me he's a handful. I swear, you two will get along just fine." Behind the conversation, I can sense that something is troubling my older brother, who hates small talk.

"I can guess what you are planning on cooking already. And somehow, I think this whole situation is awkward, but I'll see you later." Jonathan's voice pauses for a second, but then through the silence, he explains, "Work is calling. I'll stop by when I'm done with these last few clients."

"All right, I'll see you then, Jon." Content, I know there is something bugging him, but somehow, deep within, I feel like it's something he doesn't want to tell me. Both of us are secretive, that was how we were raised, and some habits we've both learned die very slowly.

Smiling, I think about one fact I adore about my brother. We always hang up without saying goodbye. Jonathan believes that saying goodbye is welcoming something bad to happen. He may be right, but not wanting to dwell on it, I shut off my notifications, knowing that no other calls will be coming. As I settle my phone back on the counter, glancing up, my eyes lock with Tom's. His face has changed, it's deeper, darker, and his eyes now are ringed with an emotion that screams jealousy.

"Who was that?" His voice comes out clipped and offset. A storm has darkened his already chestnut eyes.

Bluntly, I state, "No one for you to be concerned about. Now get something to eat, get dressed. We head out in an hour. On the dot." I want him to struggle for a while. It's wrong, but I have never been very kind. Vicious, controlling, and blunt, yes. But no one has ever claimed me to be decent with kindness.

I stand up from the island counter, and the pure shock on his face is rewarding enough. I'll tell him later, or depending on his mood, I'll let him use whatever he's feeling as fuel for his run. This two-mile run will help us both, I think. It will allow us to clear our thoughts and organize our feelings.

I think it's about time Thomas learns how to save himself if a time comes when he's all alone.

Striding through the hall, I can't help feeling trapped by this situation. My stomach twists with knots. I barely know anything about the people that are coming after Tom's father, and that bugs me. Most people would want those defending their child to know the dangers so they can be protected. Scoffing at the borderline hostility forming, I tensely shut my door.

Back in my bedroom, I let out a few roaring pants to calm myself. Settling back on the task at hand, I grab a few garments out of a couple of drawers and begin to change into my exercise clothes.

They are simple and allow my skin to breathe. My joggers reach my ankles, and I pull on a pair of foam-insole shoes that allow me to sail across the pavement and make me feel free as I run. Then, shrugging on a plain T-shirt, I look out the window to see what type of jacket I should wear. Seeing the overcast clouds, I decide to put an oversized hoodie over my shirt. The last thing I do is pull my hair back into a low ponytail, knowing the sweat that will soon be clinging to my hair will weigh it down and make it fall from the band holding it in place.

Ready, I grab my keys from the bowl by my door and head back into the kitchen to wait for Thomas. I have to teach him how to defend himself; there is no other way. If something happens to me, he has to know his limits and how to overcome them if need be. Thomas has to know that he can reach beyond his limits. If he wants to live, he will have to push himself nearly over that edge. At the brink of breaking is where we evolve. I learned the hard way and so might Thomas.

Exhaling the deep resentment at making Thomas uncomfortable, I peer out of the frosted glass paneled window. The trees sway in the wind, and some leaves break away from their branches as a cold front attacks the greenery. With my body and mind alert, I listen to the sounds around me. I hear Thomas moving around in his room, and I feel guilty about having him here. I know this is the right thing to do, to keep Thomas safe, but it won't be easy. I don't want to hurt the man that has to trust me, but at the end of the day, it might be a cost I'm going to have to pay.

By breaking him, Thomas may just make it through this. If I fall, he will have to keep moving if he wants to live. There are limits to the body, but if the mind keeps ticking, the body will soon follow.

I need to make Thomas capable. He doesn't need to be dangerous, he just needs to know how to play the game.

****

"Ignore what your body and mind are telling you. Just keep going. Turn up the volume, and get going!" I sprint ahead, just a little. Thomas needs to work for what he wants. At times that song or last beat can push you forward. I see him out of the corner of my eyes, his breathing is heavy, and sweat is gleaming on his forehead. The sweating will help expel the sickness that still lingers in his body. I know for a fact exercise will help keep him healthier.

He's working hard and defiant to give up, two very good signs to me.

"I've learned that when negativity knocks at the

door, you have to be the one to push it away, shut and lock the door." The wind carries my voice as I try to propel Thomas forward.

I clarify even more, "I've learned through running and all the intense training that you have to put every little piece of yourself into what you do. If you give up, there will be no progress."

Never stop working toward what needs to be done, I tell myself. Sometimes, that is easier said than done. I didn't get this composed, sculpted, or skilled by not having my off days. Even those that train every day struggle, and I'm one of the best procrastinators in this industry.

"How do you not stop?" Tom's panting breaths make me slow a little, knowing that he's giving it his all.

I can see how red his face is, how inactive he has been. "All I can say is that you have to promise yourself that you won't give up." I stop to breathe a little, and I take a sip of my water before continuing. "Because if you give up, you'll never know how great or how far you can go."

A refusing breath comes from Thomas, and glancing back over my shoulder, I know he doesn't believe me.

There is one more hill before our run is done. I slow my pace and place my hands on Thomas' back and slowly push him, his pace increasing slightly. I take the lead, and the last section turns into a race. As we stream ahead, I can hear Tom's steady but exhausted feet hammering the pavement.

Just as we emerge at the end, Thomas stops, drops to his knees, and begins to pant with sweat dripping down his lean columned neck. Thinking back, I beam at how impressed and proud of him I am. We were about a mile in when he began to slow, but I give him credit and my admiration. He never gave up. He swore and cursed all the way, but he didn't stop moving.

Maybe he is a warrior, after all.

Leaning down, I offer Thomas my hand to pull him back onto his feet. As he wraps his hand in mine, I inform him with a grin, "Well, I think you deserve a really good dinner." Clapping him on the back, I continue, "I'm impressed. You did great." Glancing back at the house, I begin to steer him back inside, knowing that I still have to continue my training.

As we march up the small concrete steps, I mutter through my settling breaths, "Right now, I have to continue my workout. You are welcome to watch some television, just don't set or record anything to my DVR." I continue into the house and enter my workout room, but I give Thomas one more final warning look. As I open the door, I add, "And don't leave the house. If anything feels off, come get me. Always come to me, never approach."

Thomas opens his mouth, then shuts it. He has his arms even at his sides, and his damp sweater has a wide ringed circle from his sweat. Still looking at him, I want to know what he was going to say, but he just shrugs. Slowly, he forms a smile, and biting his lip states, "Have a great workout."

Intensely, I roll my eyes and take a gulp from my water as I walk through the narrow passage to the workout room. Odd lad, I confess, but pure with his intentions.

Rubbing at my stiff neck, I set my things down and set my phone to some heavy music. Waiting for the beat to bounce from the speakers, I pull on my boxing gloves and square up to the punching bag.

Just as the coarse voice bounces out, I start the routine that I reconfigured a week ago.

Punch, breathe, step back.

Left hook, breathe, bounce.

Right hook, breathe, step back.

My pattern continues until I can't lift my arms without some form of pain. Rubbing at my throbbing right shoulder, I gingerly begin to unstrap the gloves that have been so worn down that my hands have made a permanent impression within them.

The throbbing beat coming from the speakers bounces in my eardrums. The song's rhythm also flows into my movements. Mechanically, I set up the weight set and begin to prep the bar for the sets.

Breathing with slow, shallow pants, I let my mind weave from thought to thought. Mildly, my mind settles on the memory of my mother; she was tall, curvy, but powerful with her stance and muscle tone. But, in her day, it was different than it is now. As time moves on, all things change.

She didn't have the ordered training as I do. She worked her ass off, but not nearly as much as I have to. I never imagined that so much work would have to be maintained while being a bodyguard. I knew that you would constantly have to be active and be able to defend yourself and those you are guarding, but damn, I have to work out two hours a day just to maintain and get an ache out of my body. With progress comes static so you have to keep upping the amount in order to make it a challenge.

I've been training for so long that my body can no longer achieve soreness. It gets weak and occasionally tender, but there seems to be no more ache that I would use as fuel anymore.

As I sip on my water, I set up the weight bench with adequate weights. Lowering myself flat on the bench, I begin my reps. Heavy weights with the same amount of repetitions. At seventy pounds, I do seventy bench presses. By the time I've completed that section, my hair is wet with sweat, and my breathing is heavy and unevenly paced. As I set the bar back in the holders and shove myself up, sweat rolls down the groves of my stomach and sides.

Wincing at the numbness in my right wrist, I chide myself to keep moving. No matter how tender my muscles become, I drink water and continue on.

Bench press with seventy pumps. Squats with a hundred agonizing fake sits. Pull-ups that make my shoulders snap back and forth with the movements, with only thirty completed. Crunches that, with a hundred done, make me flop down on the ground wheezing and wishing for breath to enter my lungs. After trapping some oxygen in my lungs, I repeat what I did one more time.

So in total, I completely exhausted myself. The two-mile run, the warm-up boxing hits for ten minutes, the one hundred forty bench presses, the two hundred squats, the sixty pull-ups, and then the two hundred crunches. Overall, I feel dead but accomplished.

There is only one way to see success, and it's by not taking the easy way out. Your body will tell you to slow down or stop, but don't. You have to keep going. Every time I walk into this gym, it's like a battle that I must win, but before I can win, I will lose countless times. Still, occasionally, I lose. Weakness is in the mind. I still have to fight my need to surrender. But this gym, the training, and the need to help others, it all forces me to keep moving. I don't have time to give up. No one does. So, with my body straining, I call it quits for the day.

As I pick up my things and make my way back into the house, I see Thomas with a bowl of popcorn on his lap, the television on, and an action movie playing. I silently try to make my way to my room, but Thomas catches my attention. "You look dead."

Looking away from the screen, he smiles at me and then adds, "I'm glad I didn't do that circuit with you because if you look dead, I know I *would* be dead."

Squinting my eyes at Tom's strange comment, I just wave my weak arm and go to my room.

Grabbing some clothes, I limp all the way into the bathroom. Twisting the knob to turn on the shower, I gently strip out of my completely soaked clothes.

After a training day like this, a shower is a relief.

Refusing to look at myself in the mirror, I step under the intense spray of water. As the water rolls down my body, my mind unravels.

Sighing, I think about what people give every day. People, including myself, my brother, Thomas, Tom's father, even my parents, we all must overcome obstacles to get where we are today. That achievement is massive. The power and strength it takes to keep moving through the agony of the unknown; it's relieving to know that I'm not so helplessly alone.

That's why when I saw how my parents put everything on the line; I knew my calling. I wanted to be brave and courageous like them. I knew what I would have to overcome. I knew what would be thrust upon me, but everything has a meaning.

Life isn't fair. At times you won't get your credit, and sometimes you don't even get what's due to you, but you have to keep working and getting better. You have to prove yourself, not just to the people around you but to yourself as well.

Running the soap across my chest, I soak the washcloth. Setting a trembling hand on my shoulder, I look at the scar that is still twisted there. When I took a bullet to my shoulder, I didn't get the credit for saving my client's life. It wasn't even a thought to them. To most, I am expendable. I end up being another hired help to their game. But to the Pavlovs, I hope I am more than that. Wishing to be more than a shield, I inch my head up to face the spray of water. Needing to clear my head, I soak my face. Wanting to silence my mind, I count my breaths.

Gently, after my thoughts have been silenced for a few minutes, my mind kicks back into gear. I can't help but believe that to be underestimated is the best advantage you can have. At least then, no one will see you coming as you rise from the shadows. No one can predict your will to fight. Then, no one can prepare themselves. With the higher ground, there is more of a chance of winning the fight.

Shaking my head clear, I demand a different topic. While rinsing off all the grime and dirt, I contemplate what to make for dinner and how Thomas and Jonathan will interact when brought together. But as I shut off the water and begin to dry my hair, I feel like I already know the answer to that. Two hot-headed and attention-seeking men meeting for the first time will not be smooth sailing, especially since there is only one me. Swearing, I already know how the situation is going to go. It will begin in a fight but end with them as friends.

While dressing, I decide to leave my hair dangling down the back of my shoulder blades. After I place my dirty clothes in the laundry bin, I walk back into my room to collect myself. My body and mind seem weaker today, but shutting my eyes and breathing slowly, I tell myself to just keep moving. "Always keep moving."

Sailing past the living room, I see Thomas still sitting there in front of the flashing screen. His head is propped on his palm, and his eyes are shut to the plot unfolding on the screen before him. A small hooked smile shuffles onto my face as I begin to head to the kitchen to get dinner ready.

Maybe this won't be as horrible as I think, but either way, I just have to keep myself and them calm. Both have egos that need to be fed, but I think it's time they feed their souls instead.

Sighing at my own exhaustion, I tell myself, *Just make it through this evening, and then you can take a nice break.* Getting to work, I begin to prepare for the possible battle that is to come.

Chapter 7

Respect is Earned

As I look out the kitchen window, I see that my brother has finally arrived. A grin comes upon me as Jonathan, in a dark suit and a bright blue tie, makes his way up the path. His stride is weighted and slow. I can already see it's been a rough day.

Looking out the window, I watch the older brother who never let me fall on my own or let me give up on anything that I strove to achieve. Memories of him pushing my hair back, getting close to my face telling me to get up when I didn't feel like it come swimming back to me. When I first started training, he demanded I see it through, and he was determined to help me get to the top of my game. And he still is. Never once has he given up on me. As kids, he was the soft and set one. I was the feral and unchained one. I was the one our father believed would carry the lethal notion. He was right, only because he was the one that shoved the title at me.

As the front door opens, I shout, "Johnny! Nice to see you. How was the meeting? That contract still hanging over your head?" Jonathan almost got a major deal to go through about a month ago, but one of the investors backed out, thinking that my brother was just lucky at his job. But to be fair, he fought for this house. Our parent's house, which is now mine. He is one of the hardest working realtors in London's business office.

"I don't really think it's worth it anymore, to be honest." Jonathan's gaze roams around the kitchen but never stays centered on anything. "If they don't think I can last with the big boys, I think I have no choice but to prove that prune of a man wrong."

"Don't take it too seriously, though. Remember what Dad used to say, 'People who speak of changing things have a weight to carry, while those who keep quiet have no risk.' Just think about what you really want. But listen to me, you don't need Mr. Andrews. You are great at what you do." There is no joke in what I say. We may fight and disagree, but we also have endless faith in one another. My brother is one of the best people I have ever known. He has the same power and legacy as me, yet he never lets it control him. Jonathan has the purest heart and best intentions. He wants the best for everyone, even if they've done wrong. It has helped him reach great rewards in life but it has also cost him great opportunities. At times my brother refuses to acknowledge that not everyone can be redeemed. Not everyone should be. Sometimes bad people are just bad.

Choosing to never lie, I tell my brother, "You are great at this. Just keep moving. Do what's best for the clients." It's always too much work to come up with a lie that works, so I never do it. Sighing and wanting the both of us to relax, I begin to head back into the kitchen. Now, all that is left before dinner is waiting for the timer to go off so we can all sit down and have a nice warm dinner. "Sit down," I tell my brother, and I make my way to the living room, knowing where Thomas is.

I can still hear the humming from the TV and the occasional dialogue from whatever he's currently watching. It seems like an older sitcom show that I used to watch. Grinning at the memories of the show, I turn my attention back to Thomas. "Dinner is almost done."

He looks up at the sound of my voice, his eyes full. A smile ticks to his lips. The smile almost reaches his eyes. *Almost.*

He takes the remote and shuts off the television, his eyes full of a strange light, and his body is tense. "Is your gentleman caller here yet?" His gaze darts to mine. He wants me to squirm. But there is one thing that I thought I made clear to him, I never give in, never give up, and I definitely don't back down to anyone's claims.

Ignoring the question, I turn away and continue to the kitchen. I can hear him stammering for something else to say, but I keep walking, we both enter the kitchen at the same time, and I decide to give him the answer he has been searching for.

"Thomas, this is my brother, Jonathan."

Thomas' cheeks grow a slight pink from embarrassment. He mumbles a quick and quiet sorry before he folds into a chair, ignoring me. Seeing the empty plates at the table, he begins to pick at the cloth that is covering the scuffed oak table.

Jonathan, too, takes a seat as I take the pot off the stove. Intently, I listen to my brother's rough voice as he questions Thomas. "So you're the one that my sister works for? I truly hope you're treating her with respect, for your sake."

Thomas and I both look at my brother with shock on our faces. Jonathan has never been a protective type, and he sure as hell never gets involved with my professional business. Opening my mouth to propel my brother's snarky mood out the window, I feel drawn into Tom's awakened eyes.

Thomas raises a brow as he looks at me. I shake my head saying drop it. But as if knowing he can push my brother's buttons easily, Thomas crosses his arms over each other and intertwines his fingers. "So you think I'm somebody that would take advantage of the one person that can keep me safe?" Shoving his plate to the side, Thomas leans inward toward my brother's sharp eyes. "I want you to know that I follow the rules, and I treat people with the respect they *earn.*"

I take the pot's handles in my hands and walk back to the table. Not so gently, I flop a loose load of chicken pasta on both of their plates. Trying to get some space from the tension that's growing in the dining room, I fill my plate but then head back to the kitchen sink. I set everything on the counter, and I lock eyes with both men.

I point to my brother and counter both men's words. "The fact that you two are arguing about the fact that respect must be present, but don't give each other a chance, is annoying. You offer people respect, and as you learn about them, that's when you make the choice to be kindly civil, or family civil."

Then, as if sensing Tom's casting brown eyes on me, I shift so I can read his expression. "Have enough respect for me, Thomas, to know that I can handle my own situation. Now, boys, grow up and be men for once. Get to know each other before you decide to dodge one another."

Placing my hands on my hips, I turn back to the counter and then grab my plate. "Linds," my brother's large eyes remain aimed at me, an apologetic look on his face.

Raising a hand, I tell him. "*Nyet.*" The Russian

dialectic rips out of me. Slowly with stern eyes, I demand from my brother, "Get to know him. Have respect for me to handle my own situation. Stay out of this, Johnny."

Deciding to let the two simmer, I decide to go watch some cable.

Foaming oddly at the two men's words, I know this, women always have to earn the respect they get. Women are always shadowed before anyone gets to know them. People's exteriors tend to always decide who a person is. If they are skinny or curvy. If they are glowing or faint. If you walk with confidence or not. Everything about a woman is tested and watched. Angry at my brother's simple question, I feel tense.

I decided a long time ago that no one could tell me who I am. I will make my own legendary story if I choose, and so should everyone else. We shouldn't have to worry about what other people think about us as much as we do. Have respect for yourself and know your own worth; that is what we all owe our souls.

Blowing out a steady breath, I know that these two are better than what they just did. I am not a piece of meat that doesn't have a voice. I am someone who earns what she gets. Every last bit. I don't need my brother to defend me to a client, and I don't need Thomas to throw shade. As far as I'm concerned, both men seem to be uncomfortable around one another. They are trying to see who has the higher ground, but I refuse to be in the middle of it. And I refuse to be the excuse of their bantering. All my life, I've been in the middle of all types of situations and that needs to end. I want Thomas and Jonathan to figure out some form of comfort with each other.

"I just want peace for once," I say as I approach the

couch. "I wish for silence." Sighing, and tired of having a mask on, I nearly drop it as my breath slips from me.

Stepping into the living room, I set my plate on the table and decide to go change. Making my way to my room, I change into comfy clothes, compression running joggers, and a plain shirt. Pulling my hair into a bun, I wander back into the center of the house.

As I enter the living room, I hear laughter. The sound of my brother's laugh is like music to my ears. I haven't heard him laugh in a while. Craning my neck, I look into the kitchen area, and I can see both of them smiling. Shaking my head, I know that those two are officially weirder than I imagined. Going from battling to see who can be top dog to getting along like old friends.

Turning back to the living room, I take a seat on the couch. The cold fabric seeps through me but as I settle in, warmth returns to me. Shutting my eyes for a short moment, I listen to the words that the two men are saying.

"…Lindsey is layered…" I hear my brother's partial sentence.

"Lindsey is like no one I have ever met before. She is scary but also protective at the same time." Thomas' voice is quiet and settled. Scared that I would hear, I think.

Feeling the heaviness strip me of all my strength, I shut my eyes. "If only I could be as strong as everyone thinks. If only everyone knew how heavy everything truly is." Whispering to no one, I open my eyes and swallow a whimper of despair.

Taking my fork in my hand, I take a long pull of pasta into my mouth. Turning on the television to drown out their chattering, I shift the volume up one block. Sighing at their change in demeanor, I can still remember the gnawing looks they were giving each other. The bloody murder stare that all of us perfected since a young age, and now they are laughing and talking about normal guy stuff.

"And people call me weird," I say to the TV.

As I enjoy the meal and occasionally chuckle at the bantering between the two friends on the television, I get pieces of Jonathan and Tom's discussion, the two are talking about sports, family, and the girls that they let get away.

Smiling at the sudden normalcy with my brother, I can't help but think that I'm just happy that my brother has someone else he can confide in because with this job, you never know what will happen. That is the one thing Jonathan refuses to talk about; what will happen if I slip up like our mother did? I wrote out a will and updated it just two months ago, but Jonathan still refuses to understand that he is the only person still in my life, and if my time comes, he will be handling the final wishes. Jonathan is my only family, and he's the only person I have left. If I go down, he's all that's left of the Vasiliev line.

As I focus on the screen and take another fork full of pasta, I hear Jonathan's footsteps coming in my direction. "Lindsey?" Jonathan calls me from the other room.

I sigh but don't get up. I know that my brother is leaving to go to his own home. Sadly, I look down at my plate and gurgle out a sigh of sudden distaste.

Jonathan has a client in Paris he has to help next week, and he's going a few days early so he can get acclimated to the time and to the city he will be staying in. When it comes to his work, he will go to long lengths to make everything perfect for himself and the clients.

Hesitantly, Jonathan steps into the living room, the light from the TV casting shadows across his strong features. His suit jacket is now resting in his arms. "I'm heading home. I'll talk to you soon."

He steps closer and places a hand on my arm. He glances at what I'm watching and then flickers back to what he's going to say. "Later, Linds. Just be careful. I'll be back soon." He steps away slowly but then glances back at me. "I'm sorry about earlier. I just want to make sure that you are in good hands. Thank you for dinner. Everything was wonderful." Peeling back a layer, he says lower, "I cleaned off my dish, so I'll be going now."

Sitting up, I catch his hand in mine. "You'll call when you land, yes?" I ask, as my eyes relay what the characters in the show are doing. Patting me on my shoulder, Jonathan chuckles out, "I always do. You two take care," Jonathan waves at Thomas and then goes out the front door. Sighing, I lean forward and set my dish on the table. This has happened before, where he comes over, we share a meal, and then he leaves right after, but this time something doesn't feel right.

Listening intently, I wait for his car to start. This is the first time in a while that I'm going to be without him. Ever since the last mission went up in smoke, Jonathan always wanted to be closer, but now, I guess he knows that I'm well again. After all, I do have a client to protect.

But still, my only family member still available has left, and my heart suddenly caves with the steady agony.

At the sound of Jonathan's car fading away, Thomas steps in next, and he acts like he's going to speak but then just takes a seat at the other end of the couch.

He glances at me, but he shuts his mouth. He repeats that rotation a few times, and I just keep my eyes centered on the show. Humming, I think, what could he possibly want to say to me? Waiting, I pull a blanket from the back of the couch and drape it around my legs as I settle into a comfortable position while watching an episode of the show I feel like I've seen before.

Nestling deeper into the warmth of the blanket, I feel exhausted all of a sudden. I didn't want my brother to go. I didn't want a somewhat of a stranger in my house. I didn't want to put my life on the line almost every day, so now that I finally have a day to relax, I realize how tired of everything I truly am. What am I supposed to do with my life?

Knocked out of my thoughts with the words, "I'm sorry," I peer at Thomas. He is looking at me with pleading eyes now. They are brimmed with tears that I didn't know men could create. That idea that grown men don't cry makes me suddenly furious. Not once have I seen my brother or my father cry. I was always taught that showing vulnerability is a weakness.

Choking on his words, Thomas pleads with me. "I didn't mean to just…blow up. I don't know if I ruined your night with your brother, but I want to apologize." Bellowing a breath of hesitation, he continues, "I know how untrusting you are, but do I have permission to ask you a question?"

I close my eyes. Now I really just want to sleep. "Sure. But nothing personal." He blinks at me slowly, a cascading smile spreads to his face. He slowly moves his right hand to the back of his head, resting now with a sleepy expression, as if mirroring my own.

"Why did you choose this path? Why do you want to put everything at risk?" Coaxing me toward the answer, he begins to speak with his hands. "You are a girl with nothing to lose but everything to gain. Why risk all that potential of a better future? You could have so much more if you were willing to work for it."

Too personal. Everything that he just asked is crossing a very well-seen line that I very well placed in the sand. How can I possibly answer that? My mom did it and for some sick reason, I want to make her proud. My parents never thought my brother or I were good enough, and I still want to prove them wrong. Or maybe, I chatter in my head, the adrenaline rush is what I live for? It makes me feel powerful even when I feel weak.

Biting the inside of my cheek, I give him the only answer that I can. One that he most likely won't be happy to accept. "I don't know…I just don't."

Sighing and turning away from me on the couch, he whispers, "Well, I hope one day you find something or someone that will make it all clear, and until that day comes," Thomas leans a little closer to my shoulder and smirks. "I'm going to keep asking that question because I don't want you to waste your chance at a remarkable future."

"You have a chance at a future too, Thomas," I say, keeping my voice low and steady.

"Hmm." He chuckles and gently pushes his back on the couch. "I suppose we both have some figuring out to do then?"

"No," I chant. "you are the person with the thinking to do. I'm all set." Locking my attention away from Thomas, I attempt to hush more words that wish to spill from me…

Feeling my tongue curl with words, I whisper, "We work for the future we want. If you want something badly enough, you will get it. And maybe…" Turning to Thomas, I fold my hands on top of the blanket. "Maybe I enjoy being a blank slate. It means then, I can build but can't go any lower."

"Naw," Thomas draws out. "That is a sad way to live. You have a chance at a workable future, so why are you doing this?"

Frowning at his tone, I take in Tom's expression. His dark gaze roams my face, trying to read me, but as he does that, he shows me something that I haven't seen in a pair of eyes in a long time: hope.

Thomas has hope for me. But not so much for himself. Biting at my lower lip, I offer him a gentle, but genuine smile. "How 'bout this, if I start living for the future and try to figure out truly why I'm in this business, can you do something for me?"

Confusion laces Tom's face, but he claims with a grin, "Sure."

"If we both make it out of this, you will start living your own life. No more listening to what your father wants you to do." Turning so I can see Thomas more clearly, I finish, "You have potential to help the world. I can see it in the way you move. Try thinking for yourself, and be your own person. If I have to open my eyes, so do you. I think that is a fair enough trade, Thomas."

Thomas angles his head to the side, and a lazy cascading smile rims his lips and meets his eyes. "We make a hell of a pair, don't we? You have a deal, Vasiliev. I live for myself, and you try to see a future where there is no more violence."

Faking a smile, I let my eyes look into his. "I'll sure

as hell try. But no promises. Old habits and rituals die hard."

"I know," Thomas says as his hands scoot closer to mine. Moving my hands back and out of reach from him, I lick my lips. Attempting to get rid of the chapped feeling, I lean forward and take a long sip of water.

"Sorry," Thomas moves farther from me. "I'll leave you alone now, Lindsey."

Before I can stop him, Thomas rises from the couch and like he's on a mission leaves the living room. Frowning and wishing to hit myself, I nearly call him back.

Let him go, my mind commands. It's better that everyone in this situation keeps their distance.

This way, when everything is done, we can all go our separate ways.

Exhaling, I click off the TV and slide my whole body onto the couch. Plopping my head on a pillow, I shut my eyes and ignore the lights that are still on.

"Stay strong, Lindsey." I command myself. "Remember what happened last time when you let a client make their own choices. Don't let that happen again. Keep them in line. Keep them independent from you."

Frowning and surrendering to the headache, I blow out a long breathe and allow my mind to click off. Tomorrow is another long day, and I will need all my strength for it.

Rest, fight, and rise…the never ending pattern of the Lethal Woman.

Chapter 8

Lethal From the Start

Her life isn't what I thought it was. Her brother isn't as dangerous as I imagined him to be. Both are just damaged people trying to make the best out of what they were handed. She is seen as venomous and unkind, but now I see her in a different light. She is crossed more times than not, but she always just wants to fight to see another day.

Her brother, Jonathan, let go of the past that his parents shoved at him. He didn't let them stand in his way. He told me that after they both left, he had to watch the only person he cared about in the world struggle just to breathe.

She wasn't always lethal from the beginning. Like all things, there is always an origin story. Their parents taught them how to survive to a point but after the initial training, Lindsey and Jonathan had to figure out the rest on their own.

I can still see the genuine smile that Jonathan gave his sister, and that makes me feel something I never thought I ever would. I saw the passion between the two, and that is something that I don't think I will ever have.

Jonathan barely even spoke to her, but he broke through that wall she built up. While me, I tend to spend every day with her but I can't seem to break her out of the jail cell she put herself in. I'm beginning to think Lindsey won't let anyone but her brother in. Maybe Lindsey wishes to stay confined? Maybe all she lives for is fighting for others...

On Sundays, she does take-down training sessions, so we have to go to a gym for that. She kills me; she really does. What Lindsey does, I have to do.

With the training and the skill and determination that she had from start to finish, she never faltered. She never stopped. Sweat would build on her forehead and ever so slowly slide down the side of her face, but never once did she stop to wipe it away.

We didn't talk. We didn't make eye contact for the first hour. She did her own thing and I did mine. I went for the weights when she went to the treadmill and stepper.

We went at it for that grueling hour. Finally, with thirty minutes to spare, she went to the boxing ring and did combat hits and sets of wrestling. It was scary yet amazing how she could take down someone twice her size.

Now, all I'm doing is watching and slightly trembling in my drenched clothes. A sweaty smile glimmers on her face as she shakily glides to the edge of the ring and grabs her water bottle. As she sips, she never takes her eyes off the hulk of a man standing before her. Lindsey is the only woman in the ring. Lindsey can swing as well as take a hit like no other. Wiping her lips with her thumb, she smirks as she sees the blood coating her hand.

"That was rude." She pesters the hulking man named Frankie, her trainer, as he pushes to apologize for the unprotected hit. But Lindsey stalks forward, looks at the people around her, then with a keen walk proceeds and twists around Frankie to bring him to the mat.

The other two men in the corner back away, step down, and leave. "Shit, Vasiliev," Frankie bursts out laughing. "That one was quick and steady. But we have to work on how you drag your right foot as you swing up."

"Figured, it's been bothering me lately." Lindsey continues to talk to her trainer as they both come to a standing position. I watch her in admiration. She's a sweaty mess, has a foul mouth, and a locked demeanor, but somehow, I feel myself reaching out to her, knowing that she won't offer anything in return.

As if she is in slow motion, sweat drips down her chin and onto the mat as she swings under the ropes and makes her way toward me. Her head dips low with steady breaths, her hands are red, her knuckles seem irritated as she uncoils the wraps.

"That was amazing!" The words flow out of me the second she stands an arm's width from me. "I can't believe that you can do that. Have you always been this brutal?" I whisper in awe.

She offers me a sly smile as she walks away. "Just get ready to head home. Be ready in ten minutes." At the beginning of our morning in the gym, her hair was pulled into a braid, but now it is so dangerously close to falling out of its weaves.

Hesitating as she walks in the opposite direction to the women's locker room, I try to get my heart to settle into a more even pattern. Once she's out of my sight, I take small but hefty strides to the polished wood door.

The men's locker room is empty when I enter it. The early morning sun is still shimmering through the high, thick-looking glass. As I change my clothes, I keep thinking back to when I was young, and my father would try and save me from things that could and most likely would cause me harm.

While I was being sheltered, everyone else had to pray and plead for assistance. While I never thought about my dad wearing a crown, I realize now that he had just as much power as a king, to the point where he never had to worry, until now.

That image just never came to me before until I started thinking about everyday people and from what I've learned by watching and learning about Lindsey. I understand now that my family seemed to have it all. The money, the looks, the attitude, but we never had what most families have: love and care for one another.

My family didn't have love before, but I might have just a little bit now. My father has opened his eyes and has finally been scared of the mortality of humanity. He truly understands now that he is not invincible. He sees now that our lives are in someone else's hands. I could die on this day, and I would die knowing that at least it ended on a good note. We are back on talking terms for the moment, even if it doesn't last.

But isn't that what most families are like? You get along, but as you grow older, you change and form your own opinion, and with that opinion comes the falling out that separates family members from one another. Some people, I clearly know now, can't offer an open mind to someone else's ideas. Some people, it's better to never fight against them. If you do, somehow you're the one on the tail end of an argument. Winning becomes impossible, so you're forced to drop your point or idea completely.

Scoffing at my own thoughts, I turn on the spray for the water in the corner. Shutting the curtain, I just let the water beat down on me. Staying under the water long enough to strip myself of the thin patches of sheen from my workout, I step out and wrap a towel around my hips.

Making small and stiff movements, I use my extra towel to dry the beads of water. As soon as my body is dry, I shove a shirt over my head and tug on my pants and shoes.

Just as I start to shove everything back into my bag, a sharp knock on the grained wooden door pushes me back to reality. With no more time to contemplate, I ruffle my hair, shake out my stiffening muscles, and throw my bag over my shoulder as I begin to walk to the knocking noise.

As I'm walking, something comes to me; the sanity of my life is literally like my gym bag. The bag is used only when I need to become sweaty and beaten, and right now, my father is doing the same.

He just uses me, the company, and its employees because he has to hide away the secrets of his filthy mistake. He uses everyone around him to hide the mistakes he has made, and now he isn't the one living with the consequences of his mistake, I am.

He has put a bounty on my head because he used the wrong people to make a nice little nest-like profit. A profit I might inherit if we both aren't killed by the end of this ordeal.

Cracking a few knuckles, I throw myself back into reality. Knowing that Lindsey is waiting, I whip the door open. Everything negative and corrosive is set straight, I tell myself as I take in Lindsey's features. The woman that stands her ground is sitting on the bench. I know what she is doing. I tend to these days. She is giving me space to breathe and still be normal. But like an angel, I always know she is close when I need her.

She's like a shadow that I'm dearly thankful for. Without her, I would be sitting on the couch in my father's living room, just wasting away my life, the only set of days that we have to live, and I mostly just let it wash down the drain.

Damn, how pathetic I truly am, right? Without her, I would be nowhere. But now, as I stand before her, she makes me feel stronger somehow. Maybe it's because I know she will do all that she can, and that alone is good enough for me. At least someone is willing to fight for me.

Rubbing at my neck, my eyes trail at Lindsey's normal clothing. Lindsey is now dressed in a pair of old, worn jeans and a bright red sweater that screams 'I'm Free!' but from her expression, she feels anything but free. Her lips are chapped, and her hair is neatly combed back and slightly damp. But, like always, it is uniformly braided again. She is put together in a way that reflects her personality and the notion that nothing slips by her.

But as I look at her, it's almost like nothing took place at all. Like she didn't just fight beefy men, and win. Like she isn't dangerous…

"Do you wanna get something to eat? We didn't eat before leaving the house, and you went pretty heavy on your workout drills." Her mysterious eyes gleam at me. I've never seen anyone with her eyes before, blue but so gray in low lighting. Somehow, they remind me of a stormy sky that refuses to let the world know how heavy the clouds are becoming.

Striding beside her, I see a slow smile stretch across

her face. Her features are strong in a way I've never noticed. As we walk through the doors, her body looks so small compared to the bright light coming in. Her bag is hanging against her as she walks, always beside me and always alert. At times, I forget that she's there, but it reassures me that I'm never alone and always safe.

She won't let me go down without a very dangerous and bloody fight.

I sneak a glance at her, the braid bouncing on her shoulders as she walks. "Where do you wanna go for brunch?" Lindsey asks, seamlessly ignoring the normalcy of the conversation.

Brunch? Do people still say that? "Brunch? Really?" I ask with a chuckle growing in my throat. Lindsey just glares daggers at me.

She offers a wave of dismissal. I chuckle at the scolding she is giving me at the moment. Confidently and casually she and I just walk side by side, like two people who have become great friends. Sighing, I can't help but think about when this is all over will Lindsey still be willing to know me?

Steadily walking to the passenger side of the car, I glance in through the windows, noticing a dog collar. But I've never seen a dog in her house. Squinting at the collar, I notice she is already in the black sedan. She sees me looking and signals me in. I sigh and get in, thinking about why she feels like she has to keep things from me.

But as soon as my legs slide in and my arm heaves the door shut, Lindsey's voice melts into my ear.

"Shadow had to get surgery a day before I met you and your father. He's been at the vet since. They want to make sure he will make it through the treatment. He's supposed to be released in the next few days."

"Shadow is your dog?" I question, making sure that I have the correct type of animal.

"Yes." She starts the ignition. "He's the best friend I never had as a child."

Shadow, that's ironic. She's like my shadow, and she has one too. Lindsey backs out of the parking spot and turns the wheel so we can enter the main road. Refusing to allow myself to speak, I can't help but think this is a woman who has many demons, and all I want to do is help her.

I've lived in my head too. I know the dangers that come with it. Being stuck in your own head with no escape. It's far too dangerous.

Just too dangerous.

For me.

For her.

For anyone.

****

It takes me a few minutes to realize that we aren't heading to her house. We passed the entrance, and when I saw the main highway, I knew where we were going immediately.

I frown. I don't want to go home. My father hasn't even called me. He hasn't checked in to see if I am even still alive. I don't think he has even called Lindsey either.

Above everything else, I would rather go to Lindsey's place and sit on the couch with her and hopefully coax her to talk again. The sound of her voice, talking and telling me stories about her family, makes me feel at home.

I like her home, not my own. That estate has never been a home. It's been a prison with fancy rugs and heavy furniture.

As she glides the car through the curves, dances between lanes, and once hammers the horn, Lindsey never once explains why she's driving me to my father's house, my house too, but my heart isn't there anymore.

For most people, going home isn't this weird or uncomfortable. The chewing on my bottom lip gets deeper and harder as we get closer. Seeing my dad could be the end of me. I've been able to step out and have a taste of real fresh air, and now I don't want to go back into the muggy chamber of that house.

Just as we are a few streets away, Lindsey speaks. "Your father wants to check on you. I can understand your hesitation. I sense the tension between you two but hear me out for a moment. You only have one father, no matter how crappy, pathetic, or absent he is, just…give him a chance." Lindsey sighs and locks her fingers around the wheel. "This whole situation has opened his eyes, and he wants to keep you safe. That's his whole priority now. I think he's trying to change, Thomas. For you."

Bullshit, he wouldn't give me the time of day when I was younger. My heart forgives many people, all but him. I can't bear it. No time that passes will help me forgive him, hate him less, yes, but forgive him? Never.

Feeling the need to draw the attention away from myself, I ask Lindsey a question. "Who was your dad?" The squeaky tone of my voice has me shocked, but I just keep going. "How do you even understand what I'm going through? Do you even understand, or is this another part of your job?"

Maybe people are right; I am a selfish, self-centered brat who, when times get hard, tears everyone else apart. But that's how I tend to handle things. I become rude as

I grow uncomfortable. I never had role models to show me the correct course of action. All I've ever done is lock myself away and hope that no one noticed my remarks.

Sometimes I just need understanding from someone I respect. And the last person that can offer me that is Lindsey Vasiliev.

Watching her now, with my sore eyes, I listen to her cracked words. "My dad…He was a sniper, and he killed innocent and guilty people." She cuts herself off for a second as she prepares to make a right turn.

Making her face emotionless, she continues, "He would come home for a short time, and even as a little kid, I could see that his eyes were dark. There was murder behind his eyes. He wasn't a good man. But he fought for us until the very end." Lindsey holds her gaze completely and utterly on the road, hiding her expression from me. "He was killed in action, and after that, my mother lost focus on a mission, and she was also killed. My parents had their own skills and their own flaws, but in the end, I knew their job titles would always put us in danger."

Sighing and releasing something that can only be described as pain, Lindsey explains, "That's why I take everything so seriously, Thomas."

Military sniper for a father.

A battle-ready mother.

Now that I look at Lindsey Vasiliev I see a woman I would be proud and willing to stand beside. It's too bad that we met because of a job. I would love to be able to call her mine until the world fell apart. But some things, I completely get now, can't be held by some.

"We're almost there. Just look at me and hold out one finger when you want to leave. That will be the signal." Lindsey shoots me an awkward expression. "But remember, he just wants to talk. He loves you. You are the most important thing to him." Her hands are so tight around the steering wheel as she pulls into the estate that, for a second, I thought she would pry it off completely.

As we pull into the lot, I notice her hair is hanging over her shoulder. I so badly wish she would talk to me more. Her advice and confidence help guide me. Lindsey somehow always offers a new perspective that I can't help but feel myself always giving into.

She parks the car, and she offers me a gentle, reassuring smile.

I step out, and before I have time to shut the door, I see my father marching toward me. He never moves above a stroll. A smile is on his face. His arms are outstretched as he comes in for a hug.

Like a basking storm, he knocks the wind out of me as he collides into my right shoulder and torso.

"Tom," is all he can whisper before he starts crying. All I can do is hold him and pray that this is a sign of better days to come. And that the mistake he made can be overcome.

Chapter 9

One Way Street

Lindsey said that her dog, Shadow, would be released from the vet's care today. She said that she would be back in about thirty minutes to an hour. But what Lindsey didn't say was anything about her friend coming over for a visit.

Slightly sweating, I try to keep my thoughts clear and not try to make any conversation with the woman who came barreling into Lindsey's house like a hurricane.

I choose to not listen to this woman standing before me, claiming to know Lindsey. Something about her is off, from her unnaturally dark hair to the small scar across her upper lip. Lindsey doesn't seem like the person to make friends with. And to be honest, from what I've gathered about Lindsey, I know she has no friends. And certainly, none of them would be as stupid as this woman and break into Lindsey's house. Everyone knows the Lethal Woman's house, and no one would dare enter it without permission. Everyone in England knows the Lethal Woman has one rule and for some reason, it's always followed. No one dares to break it. Until now…

I've listened to what Lindsey has said before. It was something like, in this line of work, you can't afford to make friends because friends can easily turn into enemies. And that is a risk not many bodyguards can take. So that honestly seals the deal about this woman being an old pal of 'Linds,' as she keeps calling her.

The mysterious woman's devilish dark eyes turn to me as if sensing my train of thought. "You could tell me your name. Make this tension a little more bearable." We lock eyes for a moment. Nope, Lindsey is the only one that I have come to trust. I can't turn my back on her now, and I sure as hell can't trust this strange woman Lindsey has never mentioned before.

Lindsey was the only person outside my immediate family to see me at my weakest. I trusted her with what I had to say to my father. I trusted her with my intoxicatedly emotional mind. I hold my silence.

"Oh, come on!" Devil woman turns her eyes to me, glares, and steps closer. "Talk, or I will end you." Her threat goes on deaf ears. Talking to her seems like the worst idea at the moment.

That and I don't want to face Lindsey's wrath.

But shivers run up my spine as she continues to step closer. Her eyes grow wild as I begin to back away and out of her reach.

She wouldn't dare lay a finger on me in Lindsey Vasiliev's home, would she? That just seems like a death wish that she is handing straight to Lindsey.

But just as she collided with me, and we ended up ramming into a blank wall, a groan stiffly seeps from my throat. Pawing at my chest, she shoves me even harder into the wall. "Tell me your name, now?" the woman asks but still doesn't let me off the wall.

Frowning, I shut my eyes for a blow that she may land. Bracing for it, I feel my body becoming tense and drawn in. But as I open my eyes, a voice ripples through the room like a booming explosion. Soft but then fierce, it suddenly blows everything apart. "Amanda!"

Amanda, that's her name?

Trying to shift so I can see who called out to her, I'm blocked. Amanda keeps her stance in front of me, and with my knees bent, I'm stuck.

"Amanda, I suggest stepping away from him." Dead straight, an emotionless voice is sent our way. Gasping with relief, I nearly fall to my knees, knowing that I'm not alone anymore. Slouching down, I loosen my muscles.

Shifting my eyes up off the floor where they were staring at my gray socks, I see Lindsey's poised posture. She is standing in the doorway, her fingers curled around Shadow's dog leash and her other hand balled into a fist, ready to strike. Amanda looks me dead in the face and uncurls her fist from her side, and she takes a step back from me.

"Lucky," she swears as she continues to take three large gallops backward.

Lindsey cocks her head to the side. She looks at me, drops the leash, and steps closer to Amanda. Shadow, Lindsey's dog, comes running to me, and I instantly feel more at ease. Shadow's a dark-colored Pitbull with white markings along his muzzle and chest. Like a speckled cookie, his fur is unique.

Grinning, I busy myself with focusing on the dog. Shadow's eyes are pure and shining as he looks at me. His tongue is hanging out of his mouth, happy as can be while I'm nervous about what's going to happen next.

"Thomas, what did she tell you?" My mouth goes dry as I try and remember if she even really told me anything. Standing from petting Shadow, I open my mouth to speak as Amanda shifts so she can glare at me again.

"Would you chill for once, Lindsey? Seriously, I just asked him his name." She cockily beams at me and then turns all her pent-up rage onto Lindsey. "Now, what should I have not told him? There are so many things. Like that mission that went wrong." Lindsey's jaw ticks, the muscle bobbing, and then as long as it took for me to blink, Lindsey had Amanda by the hair.

Slowly Amanda ends up on her knees, her head being held up by the strands that Lindsey grips. Her eyes are like venom as they bore into Amanda's pain-ridden face. "You should know the truth about that mission better than anyone. You are the reason it failed! I suggest you keep it to yourself or…well, I feel like you know the outcome." Sneering, Lindsey makes one more move that makes Amanda pitch out an ear-piercing shout.

Lindsey lets go of Amanda's hair suddenly. The woman falls to the floor and stops screaming. I step away and cover my actions with the excuse that I'm petting the dog. Shadow follows Lindsey into the kitchen with a fish toy in his mouth. After one more look at the woman on the ground, I too follow Lindsey to the kitchen.

Taking my place on a barstool, I try and will myself to be calm. Lindsey takes a pot full of meat and vegetables out of the fridge and places it on the stove. The homemade meal looks so good that I'm ready to dig into it. Just as I lean my arms on the counter, a groan sounds from the floor.

The sound is Amanda getting to her feet and coming in my direction.

Startlingly, Amanda still has that odd look of pleasure on her face. "Wow, Lindsey, you still have your touch." Amanda begins to run her fingers through her hair, and as she does so, she states, "Now," she asks. "Is that how you treat your friend? Would Harrison be happy with how you acted just then, dear?" Angling her head dangerously to the side, Amanda brings a smile to her face as she takes in Lindsey's pale, bitter expression.

"Lindsey, dear, you really shouldn't threaten the one person that knows about your rarely failed missions. Did she tell you, Thomas? How she got tricked, and her employer got killed?" Inching her smile up a little higher, Amanda then adds, "Brutally. And she didn't do a thing to stop it."

I don't look back. From Lindsey's tension in the room, I can guess that some of what Amanda says is true if not all of it. Did Lindsey really make a mistake, and it cost her someone's life? Is Amanda trying to scare me away? Lindsey steps out from the counter, her long thermal sleeves pulled up to her muscle-laced elbows.

I saw what was coming, and I ended up shocking myself by stating: "I think you should leave now." There is a feeling in the air around me. Lindsey is looking at me with wide eyes while Amanda just glares. With one foot in front of the other, she steps closer, her breath labored and her mind set on ruining someone today.

Getting ready, Lindsey clenches her fists. I can see the anger growing intensely on her face. Amanda takes one final glance at me before she locks eyes with Lindsey. As if asking for a challenge, neither woman steps down. The deafening silence makes me shudder under the pressure of not knowing what's going to happen or the fact that danger might be right around the corner, and I'd never see it coming.

"You have no idea of the damage that I could cause

you. The things that I could share." Amanda's whisper doesn't go on deaf ears, and she is counting on Lindsey to react. "I know so much about you and the pain that you caused because you failed to get the information right. Or have you forgotten? We were a team. You said I was your friend!" The pulse in my neck spikes. But Lindsey, beside me, seems unfazed by all the words and threats being spilled like blood.

Lindsey takes a step forward. The two are now almost within touching range. The splinter-like shivers travel across my spine again.

"You thought we were friends? A team? You ran away the second the bullets started flying." Shocking me, Lindsey begins to spill the truth. "You left me with Harrison. I couldn't protect him and take out the people wanting to hurt him. You had to be my cover. Last time I checked, friendship isn't a one-way street." Reeling forward, Lindsey snarls like a rabid dog. "You left! Vanished the second the compound was swarmed, I was arrested and tried for second-degree manslaughter," Lindsey isn't raising her voice very loud, but I can almost feel the blistering anger building under her skin as she keeps taking steps forward.

With cold gray eyes, she looks Amanda dead in the face and continues, "The files freed me, but you left me when I needed you the most." Hitching her head to the side, a feral and vicious tick ran through her eyes. "I was always there for you! So spill my secrets because you can't ruin me any more than you already have." About to head back to the kitchen, Lindsey swivels back to Amanda. "And also remember, I hold some of your darkest secrets too, but me being a better person than you, I would never share them." Right then and there, her voice rose. The second she stopped talking, she turned away.

As if forgetting about the kitchen and the beginnings of a meal, Lindsey took a water bottle out of the fridge and simply walked to, I'm guessing, her bedroom. "You should know about secrets, Lindsey. You have more than the fucking queen!" Amanda shouts after Lindsey.

Deciding I'm not having any more of it, I decide to step in. Lindsey has demons, and I know that deep down, we all do. It pisses me off that someone that you once trusted wants to use part of your secrets against you. If someone wishes the worst for you, they were a snake in the weeds all along. Never to have been trusted. There is always that one person you let in that injects you with venom the second you make a mistake.

Amanda is just standing there, almost afraid to move, but I want her gone. Something is off with her, and nothing at this moment will stop me from sparing Lindsey just a few more fractions of pain; if I can, I will.

"Leave," I point to the door, keeping my voice low. "Now," I repeat when she just looks at me with glazed eyes. "Go!" I shout, raising my arm and nearly ready to escort Amanda to the door.

I don't hesitate to step closer. She looks at me with wide eyes now. Amanda turns around and heads to the door.

Nothing. No emotion, nothing comes to her face. From the look in her eyes, I can tell that this won't be the last time we see her.

"You be careful with her," Amanda says through clenched teeth. "Nothing about her family is right. You keep your eyes focused, don't fall into the trap. Nothing is what it seems."

"Get out!" I shout. Feeling my hands ball into fists, I let my anger coil out of me. "Just get out!" I say more forcefully this time. Shutting my eyes, I know that Amanda will leave this time. I don't know why she came here or why she outed Lindsey's secret like that, but this I do know, I trust Lindsey. Nothing can change that.

I have made my choice; I stand with her.

As the front door shuts, my head turns to the way that Lindsey went. Sighing, I try to decide what to do. I want to so badly be with her, tell her it's all right. Anything to calm her racing mind, but I can't.

I know I can't. To her I'm just business. But to me, she's something so much more.

With a bleeding heart, I turn my attention to the food left on the stove.

Chapter 10

Run or Fight

I just stare at the coffee pot. The events of yesterday evening still have me shocked. The anger in Amanda's voice to the secrets she wanted to spill about me sounded so evident and overwhelming.

She had no ounce of hesitation either. Why did she choose to return to London now? What could she gain by tossing me into the flames of self-pity and doubt? She just wanted to make herself feel better. I know Amanda. For years, we worked together, and she has a tendency to cross a line to make herself seem more righteous.

Oddly, inclining my head up, I think about another factor. What made it even weirder was the fact that Thomas stepped in and silenced her pathetic cries. He stepped up when I didn't expect him to. He defended me when I no longer had the strength to help myself.

Folding into my hands, I allow my head and mind to collapse. The pounding pain in my cranium has me leaning on the counter for support. The twisting and turning all night has left me with a kink in my neck and a festering pain along the front and back of my skull.

Shutting my eyes to try and block out the pain, I register what needs to be done today. I have training, and Tom's father has him on online courses due to all the possible dangers and threats that would most likely be missed. Thomas' father just thought that in the long run, it would make the most sense to have him do his courses at my house, where I could keep an eye on him at all times.

Which, accurately, gives me some free time of my own. He's busy, so he won't be leaning on me with boredom.

Sighing at the intolerable solitude, I can't help but wish Thomas was here. Thomas hasn't spoken or even checked in on me once. I don't blame him. I am a person that rarely shows emotion, it's in my job description, and I'm the best at what I do because I can be brutal. I'm only the best because my father made me so, I can't help but bitterly throw out to myself.

My actions tend to speak for me, and I have a fear of letting someone in because what if I fail again? Harrison wasn't supposed to die. He wasn't supposed to be there when everything went down. I was supposed to take his killers out, but in the end, Harrison went with them. Like a captain going down with his ship, Harrison sank.

And that night never leaves. Not in the daylight, and sure as hell not in the nighttime.

The memories of that night have been haunting me, but Amanda has made the nightmare into a full-on possessed haunting. When everything replays, I have no control, I panic, I want to scream, I want to hide, but I always know that it's just a nightmare. I always pray that it stays that way. But I know that at times nightmares can become reality if we spend too much time dwelling on them. So when I have nightmares, I get up so I don't dwell too long.

Knocking my head back, trying to relieve some of

the pressure, a voice makes me nearly rock out of my seat. "How did you sleep?" Thomas is standing on the other side of the kitchen island. He seems innocent to the knowledge that he just scared me. But as I look him over, I notice that his hands are evenly spaced, his weight is balanced. He seems ready to take a blow by how tense his muscles are.

I would never land a blow on him, but as I rub at my brow, I try to ignore his sudden growing fear. "I've slept better, but I've also slept worse. How about you?" I ask, not wanting to indulge in my issues. As the words bounce through the room, Tom's eyes are staring deeply into mine. The brown of his eyes seems to shift in different lights, from chocolate to black. The beauty of human eyes sometimes catches me off guard. I'm still looking at him when he speaks in an early morning voice: "Miserably…terrible? I don't quite know the word." Sighing and rubbing at his dark eyes, he pipes up with a question, "Tell me that we have something to get my mind off of my inner thoughts? I need to do something different."

The look on his face made me shift from my seat onto my feet. I have to do training, but I can always do that later, so sticking to my guns, I decide that maybe something different is the best thing to do. After all, I feel myself growing dimmed out of my mind with the same repetitive actions.

Not knowing what to do yet, I just target my words to Thomas. "Um…Get something to eat, and I'll explain what we're going to be doing today. I think it might help." I pick up my cup of coffee that has long grown cold, take a sip, and slowly proceed to my room to change into a new set of clothes.

"Wait? Aren't you going to eat something?" That stopped me. I never think about my health like that, I tend to forget about myself, and it never registers until it's a little too late. The fact that Thomas cares enough to ask me that question scares me. He's growing connected to me, and that alone is a dangerous action that I must end.

Ultimately, the question that eats at me is: What happens if he thinks that we can be more? What if he does something stupid? I know for a fact that I can't hide him from the people that have a price on his head. No matter what I do, what his father does, nothing can hide him from the fact that in the end, if they want him, they will find him. But I won't let them hurt him. They can find him if they want, but they won't be able to take him. That is a vow I created all on my own.

Sucking a breath in through my teeth, I just tell him, "Tom, don't worry about it. I'll grab a granola bar or something before we leave." Turning to leave, Thomas catches at my solid arm. "Just relax. I'll be fine." This time, I stride farther from him. I turn away and walk quickly to my room. The burning of Thomas' questions freaks me out. He's beginning to care about me more than I would like.

No one ever truly asks me questions. Growing up, there was a rule in my house: Attend to your own business. None of my other employers ever asked me questions. They just wanted someone who could handle dangerous situations. That's what most people care about. But Thomas…He just cares. He cares about what I feel, what I do. It makes me glow to finally see someone who cares about me besides my brother, but something inside of me swears I shouldn't trust him.

If I trust him, I may get hurt.

If he trusts me, he *can* get hurt.

And that alone is a vicious cycle I refuse to let him enter.

Shaking my head, I steady my thoughts. No matter how badly I want to open myself up, a part of me is hesitant. The hesitance within me comes from years of trickery and abandonment. Having broken and self-centered parents can do that to a person. Trust isn't given; it's earned. Always, even if it's someone you know won't hurt you.

My parents made my brother and me withdraw from the world. We only had each other we were taught, and that made us into perfect soldiers but horrible civilians. For a long time, I felt under attack. I felt like if I didn't make connections, and if I stayed distant, everything would work out. Now, it's all a mess. Everything I ever thought I was, it's all changed. I don't want to be the most dangerous person in the room anymore. I no longer want to be the quiet woman in the corner that everyone steps away from.

I'm tired of people knowing my reputation over who I really am. Thomas has helped me see so much more. Knowing him for this short amount of time has helped me become something more. I know that I can still be powerful and lethal, but I can also be content and patient outwardly rather than just burying them deep within myself.

I think it's time that I become the image of what everyone sees when they hear *bodyguard*. Now is the time that I lock down my image of danger for hire and become a person that no longer hides behind a mask. I think it's time that I step out of my shell and forget the ghost that once lived inside of me.

Bodyguard or not, dangerous can stay my middle name, but I think it's time that I stop guarding my heart. But with one rule, my gun still has to be loaded and aimed at all times. Always prepared but also willing to give the world a chance.

I need to be willing to give myself a chance. I need to live, to fight, to defend, but also be open to a new future.

****

"Are you ready to hit the road?" The cold air hits my face as soon as I step outside. It seems to be a bitter slap for what I'm doing. He should stay inside and be safe from the world, but to be honest, staying inside has my nerves twitching. I think he'll like the plan for today, or at least I hope so.

"Yeah, just because I knew you would forget I grabbed you this," Thomas holds his hand out to me, a fiber bar wrapped tightly within his slender fingers. "You have to eat something." He doesn't look back as he makes his way to the black car parked in my driveway. To make a point, I unwrap the bar and take big bites to rid myself of the distraction.

Cinching my belt tighter, I ensure that my holster is tight and concealed. As a fierce blast of wind comes in, I zip my overcoat and let it fall around my waist to hide my weaponry.

Ready now, I take my place in the driver's seat. Starting the engine and shifting the car out of park, I begin steering the car from the wide driveway.

As my foot clamps down on the gas, Thomas says lowly, "You shouldn't eat that fast. It isn't healthy." Thomas seems…unsettled. From his tense posture to his locked jaw.

As I turn the wheel, rain slowly slides down the windshield. The bitterness in the wind should have been my first clue that it was going to pour. Just as I perch the car on top of the hill fog rolls in and casts the road into a haze of uneasiness.

"I'm sorry," Thomas interjects. He glances at me with a sad smile. "I just get cranky without sleep. Forgive my intense tone, but I just want to make sure you remember to take care of yourself."

Muffling a groan, I roll my eyes in his direction. "Really, you don't need to worry. I'm fine." Thomas makes a scoffing sound, so as I emerge on the main road, I state, "But thank you for the bar. I did forget."

I glance at him. His hands are curled together as if he's cold. His hair still isn't brushed, but he seems comfortable in his dark jeans and hoodie. Right now, he has dark-rimmed glasses perched on his nose. Oddly, Thomas seems so much more mature for his age. Behind his dark eyes is more pain than he lets on, and he seems to have more understanding than most could infer. Attempting to ignore my thoughts about him, I up the volume on the radio. Noise is seeping from the speakers, a tone made so long ago but still familiar.

"You have to take care of yourself, Lindsey." Thomas mutters. "You are my bodyguard and I need you at your best."

Skipping my attention back to him, I hum in response. Keeping my eyes on the road, I think of the perfect thing to say back to Thomas. Suddenly, it comes, "Don't worry about me, Thomas, worry about yourself." Simple and clear.

With my point spoken, I listen to the music coming

from the speakers.

Keeping my mind focused on the roadway, I can't help but notice the gloom settling over the small countryside. The road is dark with rain. A bittersweet chill overcomes the world when rain enters, but right now, all that comes to mind is the harmony of the song that Thomas is now singing along to, drumming his fingers on his thighs. Traffic is light as I pull the car to a stop at a red light. The trees along the road are wild in the rain, making me worry about when the winds become stronger. This might be one of the biggest rainstorms in London's newfound town's history.

Booming through my settled thoughts, Thomas questions, "Are we there yet? I'm bored, and you're not talking." His hands are sprawled across his knees. His eyes focused on me, but I refuse to offer a look at him. At the moment, I choose to stay on the road and get to our destination.

"Almost. One more light crossing, and we will be there. I told you before that when you live in an isolated area, it may take you longer to get to some places." I feel Tom's beady eyes on me, so I add, "Especially when you don't go to this certain area that much."

The car glides through the green light, and before my very eyes, a huge building with reflective glass windows towers over us. Going up the ramp-like concrete expanse, Thomas gets a full view and an understanding of what we are going to be doing today.

The rain has caused people to seek shelter at home, so multiple parking spaces are left vacant. Claiming the nearest available one to the mall, I decide to pull into it.

Thomas looks at me with a giddy smile. "The mall, thank God! I was getting *so* bored."

His smile immediately sends a grin to my lips. "I figured that you might need a place to go and feel like everyone else." Shrugging at Tom's gobsmacked expression, I reflect, "And this was the first thing to come to mind."

Blowing out a long breath, Thomas looks out the passenger window at the slanting curtain of rain. "Wow, this isn't what I imagined we would be doing as I lay awake all night."

"If it helps," I begin. "I didn't plan on this."

Taking one more final look at me, a sly smile of joy grows on Tom's face, and his white teeth flash as a flicker of lightning slashes through the sky, "Let's go then!" Thomas shouts and shoves the door open.

Before I can say anything else about staying close to me or keep your eyes peeled, he's already darting out of the car and down the ramp to the entrance of the mall. His hands are in his pockets as he crosses the small street that divides the mall from the parking lot. I jog to catch up to him, almost whacking him over the head for dashing ahead of me like that.

I tell him, "We stay together. We stay in each other's sight, and if anything feels off, we split, all right?" Talking as we enter the warm air of the mall, I insist that Thomas understands. Thomas nods along, signaling his understanding of my words, but that cheeky grin is still woven on his lips.

"Thank you, Lindsey. You did listen to me." Nodding and peering through the little stalls and small shops, I listen to Tom's words, "Thank you for trusting me." Nodding again, I look at a nice necklace with a gleaming opal on it.

"I just want you to know that, however the last

mission ended, no matter how tragic," Thomas lays a tense hand on my shoulder, forcing me to stop in my tracks. "I feel like it somehow brought you to me, maybe fate." His brown curls flop over his eyes as he speaks to me, and he turns back to the gold necklace I was looking at as he finishes his sentence. "The panic that is left inside you, just some advice from someone who deals with that: Leave it in the past because you are no longer alone. You have me, and I understand fear. Trust me, it's a horrible way to live. To be scared of everything, it makes you cautious. And you can't live like that. There is no life in constant fear." Seeing where he slipped, he adds on, "More than you already are, and with that, it must be a horror in your head."

Silence is all that comes to me as Tom's brown pleading eyes search mine, "Lindsey," he turns to me with his hands zoned in on my shoulders. "You have a choice in life. Run or fight, and from what I have seen from you, I know you are a fighter, so let go of the things holding you back."

Thomas drops his hands from my shoulders and returns them to his trouser pockets. "Don't let whatever Amanda said get to you. Remember what you told me? You can't afford to get distracted." I smile as I acknowledge the fact that he remembered what I said. "Lindsey, I need the most capable you. I need the unstoppable Lindsey Vasiliev right now; because deep down, the only person I can trust right now is you."

Opening my mouth to respond to all of his words, Thomas just raises his hand in a gesture of dismissal. "I'm not telling you to be the best for selfish reasons. I only trust you, Lindsey. I'm not even sure if I can trust myself, but there is one thing I'm sure about, and that's you, Lindsey." Shaking his head, his eyes stay glued on a flower pendant that screams beauty. "My dad can think whatever he wants, but this isn't the time where I am willing to let anyone just walk into my life."

He then takes my hand and pulls us into the warmth of the small jewelry shop. "And," pulling his wallet out, he flashes me a smile that makes me draw back by the glint that is in his eyes. "My father shall be buying you that necklace today."

Raising my hand and opening my mouth, I try to stop him. "Nope," he waves me off in a way that no one else but my brother has. "I'm getting you that necklace." He lowers his chin, and his chocolate eyes sing with affection. "I want you to have something as beautiful as you are, Lindsey."

Left with no words, I let him buy me the necklace. With the receipt and little box shoved in my pocket, I continue on with a lavish smile on my face that refuses to die.

Shop by shop, we look, he buys, I scold at the prices, but overall I feel myself sink into the skin of a normal twenty-three-year-old woman.

For the first time in a while, the hours that passed felt like minutes, and the minutes felt like seconds. A carefree side of myself escapes and doesn't want to be put back in her cage.

Once this is all behind the Pavlovs, I might just consider Tom's words and find something else to put my skills into. Maybe the once spoiled boy is right. I shouldn't be wasting my opportunity-filled life if I never truly gain anything from it.

Maybe, once this is done, I leave the Vasiliev legend where it truly belongs, buried with the people who thrust it upon me from the very second I drew my first breath.

With so much over the horizon for me, I think after this mission is done, I should retire. No more Lethal calling card, no more guarding people who just want a shield. It's beyond time that I build a life. No more danger for me. I want a longstanding future where I can build and grow.

Shocked, I understand what I want.

Nearly stopping in my tracks, I almost forget to breathe.

I want the Lethal Woman within me to die.

I just want to be Lindsey Vasiliev. I want to be a woman with everything to *lose* and not everything to *gain*.

I want to have something to lose, then I would fight harder and better.

Thomas is right, he would be the one to help me come to my senses. He was right all along. This isn't who I want to be anymore.

Once the Pavlovs are safe, the Lethal Woman will be extinguished.

It's about time the woman my parents wanted me to be is ruined. And how good will it be to be done by my own hands?

If you have to kill who you were there is no better way than to cut the cord. Be the soldier willing to make that choice. Change for the better.

Freedom of a past self always comes with a price, but the present you will receive waits on the other side.

To be free, a sacrifice must be made and like never before, I'm willing to make it.

I'm ready to earn my freedom from this shell I have become.

For myself and those I have lost, it's time that I move on.

Chapter 11

Don't Waste Your Breath

The cracking of my knuckles on the bag sends vibrations throughout my whole body. The wraps around my wrists to the gloves covering my whole hand, the vibrations just seem to seep in and drive me even harder.

The memories of earlier this morning keep flashing back, the calm in my soul to the determination to get through this training session. I never thought the one thing that could bring me down would be stolen. The very thing that has everything about me in it, it was lifted right from the hands of the man that is controlling me now.

I got a call before I came out here from Tom's father, Anthony. His voice was hushed and uneven. He warned me that someone got into the company without clearance and stole a file. He kept rambling and droning on that he was sorry and that the time to flee might be upon him.

Like a coward, Anthony thought of himself before anyone else. Before his own son. But before he could skip off, I had to get answers.

Once I was able to calm him, he told me that the file was one of the most important in his office. It wasn't a business contract affiliated with his company. It was a personal file. Whoever broke in stole my file. They stole the only thing that could bring me down.

In that very file is the contract of this deal, the file that sets me apart from just a hired gun. That file holds the records of my innocence, just in case anything goes sideways. But as Anthony dribbled on, he told me he recently acquired the Vasiliev file that was created when my father went rogue. That bundle of papers holds my family's darkest secrets and records over the years of what we have done, whom we hurt, and whom we even killed. In that file, it tells whoever holds it the only thing that I have never told another soul. Whoever possesses it holds everything the world knows about the Vasilievs.

Punching on, I thought I was over that stage. I am to be paid for my work, fairly. There is always something that has to be kept when you make a deal like this. Just in case trouble comes, or if I don't live up to the expectations.

But, we had to leave the Pavlov estate before I got to make any copies of the deal and of the terms and regulations. That was my shitty mistake. I trusted them when I shouldn't have. And most importantly, I should have known that Anthony would have my family's file. I mean, after all, I am the Lethal Woman who he hired.

"You are a soldier for hire," my mother would recite these words before she left my brother and me every night. "You do as you are told. You do what needs to be done. You don't hold back. You rise even when you fall. And if need be, you never look back." My mother, very much like my father, never let us see her weak. We were heirs to the throne, and we had to fight if we wanted to see the world around us. My father was the king of violence, and my mother, she was just as deadly. A feared king and queen fell, and as the next ones in line, my brother and I had to cut a few cords and lash a few rules. We were monsters before we kneeled to the regulations given to us. If we wanted to stay together, we had to bow. So we did, and with that, we thought the file died with us.

But as the daughter of a skilled killer, I should have known nothing stays dead for long. Not in this world or this industry.

The *what if's* are haunting me. The sound of the creaking of the bag hitting the back of the stand sends me into a frenzy to release more flying punches. I should have known that these people wouldn't stop. Why would they? I'm so foolish to even think that they would just suddenly swoop in, and I could take them down easily, without too much of a fight.

One can wish, but it never seems to work that easily.

I've been in this situation before, all the way down to the shady characters of these thieves to the sudden appearance of those whom we thought would never show up. Hell, I should have known to expect them at some point.

Distracted for a second by the bright lights above me flickering, causing me to throw a wide punch and my knuckles connect with the metal stand behind the bag. Moaning at the impact, I huddle my fist close to my chest and pucker out my bottom lip at the pain.

Casting a glance at the door once I hear the hiss, I see Thomas standing there with a frown etched on his face. He waves his hand in a gesture for me to come, but all I want to do right now is stand here and pound on this bag like it can solve all of my problems.

Due to all this stress that shouldn't be on my shoulders, I can't help but feel like the darkness is closing in. Normally, yes, there is loads of stress and worry, but never about my own truths. I am supposed to protect Thomas. I shouldn't have to worry about myself. I shouldn't have to worry about the whole of England knowing that I've been living a lie.

Wheeling forward, I feel like I'm about to come undone, and then there might be nothing left inside me worth fighting for. Sighing and using my sore hand to rub at my tired eyes, I just decide to call it quits on destroying the bag.

Giving in, I know Thomas will continue to stand beside me, refusing to just give up and leave me be. Sighing, I can see the disturbance lined between his brows, and that's when I know that I can't just cast him into the shadows. Knowing that if I don't stop now, he will just follow along with me, so I give up on releasing my anger.

Taking a shuffling step away from the doorway, Thomas raises his arms, his hands angled and in line with his shoulder in a sign of surrender. "Lindsey, please," he says with so much force, I pull my boxing gloves off and set them aside. Looking down at my knuckles, I can see the bits of peeled skin and bruising red splotches.

Refusing to leave me to my demons, Thomas keeps coaxing me into a settling mood. Gently, he takes the initiative and grabs my shoulder. "Come inside, get warm and let's just think this through."

A tidal wave of emotions crashes down within me. My day was going so well; great even. Now all I can think about is the fear of screwing up and having no safety net to catch me when I fall. "What is there to think through, Thomas? They have *it*." If I go down, I know Thomas will too.

It's not an if anymore. It's just a matter of time, I

know it.

"Thomas." I breathe. "You have to understand. These people will know everything about me. I, you, *we* need to be ready when they come. I just know that they will be coming soon." I sigh and bow my head in my bruised hands. "It's only a matter of time now."

Oddly, Thomas whispers in my ear, "We are not so different, you know." Moving his feet, so they are close to mine, he continues without meeting my eyes. "We both have something on the line. But I can trust they won't see what's truly coming. You said it yourself." Tom's eyes are covered by the blue ball cap that is upon his head. He's no longer looking over my shoulder but at his bare feet. "You have a track record that no one can live up to. You have a face of innocence but an attitude of danger." Holding my shoulders, he does a little shake to make me take in his words. "No one is as skilled as you, at least no one that I have seen. So trust me when I say you may not know what is coming…but they have no clue of what is about to rain down upon them."

Thomas shifts from one foot to the other, his feet having exposed veins that make him look ridged. His few strands of hair poking out from his hat remind me his hair is still un-brushed. Thomas carefully removes the cap and looks back into the hall of the house.

"What?" My voice is sharp. "Thomas, what is it?"

His smile is gone now. It's replaced with an angry expression. He moves away from me and goes back into the house, causing me to be alarmed.

Pushing after him, I propel myself forward, not allowing Thomas to take the first steps in. Speeding to the entrance, I keep my body ready. If this is them, then this fight is about to begin. Rounding on, my feet keep marching. But, as I plow through, my eyes are sickened by the man standing in my house. The very man that allowed this all to happen.

"Dad! You have to call," Thomas bellows, with a vein in his throat throbbing. "You know you are supposed to call before you just walk into someone's house." Thomas shoves his hat back on his head and cockily adds, "Especially if that someone could have literally killed you!" Tom's shout has a creeping vexed edge. He's done. I can see it in his posture. I can feel it in the air. Thomas is fed up. And, I don't blame him. Nothing with us can just be still. There is always a fire brewing to burn us down.

Anthony Pavlov, the man that started all this drama, is standing in my hall. A bottle of whiskey in one hand and a peach-colored folder in the other. His face is covered in dirt, and his suit is crumpled, even ripped by the designer's logo. A scuff of blood is on his lower lip and peppered on the collar of his white suit shirt. Taking in his appearance and seeing the destruction causes me to spare a glance outside the window.

No guards, no men in suits, no one. Terror runs through my whole body in the absence of his men. What did he do? What did this selfish, careless man do now? What has he been doing?

"Mr. Pavlov." I get his attention warningly. "Where are your guards?" But then, remembering the beatings from my father, I add, "And what are you doing in my house with a bottle of whiskey?"

His son never looks away. The pain in Thomas' face makes me suddenly think this is normal, yet I refuse to accept it. I've been through it, and I don't want Thomas to be hurt in my home. This home will no longer see acts of violence.

Maybe Thomas and I have another experience in common, drunken fathers with no cares in the world but themselves. All we ever truly wanted was a family to stay together and fight for us, but even now, that seems like a dream that will never come. All it has become is a nightmare. Everything beautiful eventually turns ugly.

Looking down and stepping closer, I choose to stand here and offer support. As if remembering that I'm there, Thomas looks back at me, his hair has curled on his neck, and his fists are clenched. With his knuckles white and his nails biting into his palms, I rub my hands along his back. I vowed to myself to help Thomas, even if that means taking a step back and surrendering the control I once had. For Thomas, I will gladly step aside so he and his father can settle this fight.

"Now," Anthony Pavlov's speech slurs. "Now, there is plenty of time for questions later. But where is the kitchen and some glasses for this splendid whiskey, dear?" He starts moving around the room without my permission to enter. I remember when Thomas said that if I ever wanted answers, his father had to have a few shots in him, maybe this is my chance. It may be my only chance.

"No!" A shout booms out. Anthony and I both look at Thomas. "You can't just come in here like this! I'm done with your games, Dad. Get sober and fix this mess!"

The sway in Anthony's stance makes me guess that he has already had enough to drink. But as he looks at his son, his next words are aimed right at me.

"For your information, I did fix my mess," His eyes are black as coal, and as he locks eyes with me, I can see a glint of red in them. "Here, I believe this belongs to you, Ms. Vasiliev."

Pumping his arm up, he sends the file flying. The file dances through the air. I don't try to catch it. All the contents scatter onto the floor. Pictures, letters, charts, medical records, witness statements—it's all there from my past to my present. I can see how I have changed through the ages. Nothing inside this file makes me wanna jump and hide it; not anymore. I think Thomas already knows the basics of the horrors I have caused. And I know that Anthony has read it, and the only other person in this room that would care already knows in his heart of the pain that I have caused and faced. They both know, so I feel no need to shield it from their eyes.

But there is one ache inside of me that refuses to dissipate. Who collected all of this? Some of these things I have never even seen, and most of the papers in there are mainly articles about my parents. About my mother's death and the vanishing act of my father. It's like whoever made the file took everything that happened personally.

Slowly and almost in a daze, Tom lowers down to help me pick up the remains of my file. A file that almost gave me a heart attack when it was taken but now no longer seems so important. It seems worthless suddenly, even though it has all my client lists over the years. Shuddering at the fact that I have been watched for so long, I want to vomit. Who would do this? I ask myself as I collect the previous report. Harrison Perry, the one I couldn't save.

With shaking fingers, Thomas hands me what he retrieved and ever so slowly heads in the direction his father vanished. Sighing as I watch him go, I never wanted a family to fall apart like mine, from the yelling to the terrible lies that destroyed us all. With my file in hand and a plan in mind, I refuse to let this remainder of a family disintegrate.

"Thomas, do you remember when your mother left? Do you remember when she said that she wouldn't just disappear from our lives?" Anthony hums with the bottle still in his fat hand.

"Well, now that you are a man, do you understand me now? What I did, what I do now? The cold rain that would fall upon me, there was no mercy on me. But son, the heavenly light saved you." The senior Pavlov glances back over at me. "You found love and memories that will forever grow. So I am a hopeless man," Anthony doesn't look up from the empty glass he took from my shelves. Pouring generously, the brown liquid swishes back and forth as he moves the glass around, the ice cubs tapping the edge of the glass. The ice hitting the sides is the only noise filling the room as we all hurt in the silence.

"Dad, really! Snap out of it!" Thomas has moved forward, a sharp glare on his face. A growl formed in his throat. "Put the glass down and be a man, I get that you have a lot on your shoulders right now, but you can't drink your problems away." The man on the stool simply shows no interest in what his son just said. I step into the room a little farther. Thomas gives me a murderous glare, but from the look on his face, I can tell that it isn't aimed at me but at the man that no one can reason with.

Stepping forward to ease the tension, "Thomas," I murmur, placing a delicate hand on his shoulder, "Go in the living room, blow off some steam. I…I think I can reason with him."

Thomas opens his mouth, ready to speak, but I hold

up a hand. "Go." I tell him and look toward the living room. "Give me a few minutes."

The pressure that was bothering me earlier just keeps coming back with even more force. Slowly, I bring a hand and press it onto my temple, my brain squealing into my ears. With one foot in front of the other and my hand on the table, I go to the other side of the kitchen and start to make tea. With no words, no look, I already hate the man that has cast his son aside. A person should never hate or dismiss their children, no matter how wasted they become.

"A girl like you cannot reason with a man like me, haven't you learned anything?" Anthony teeters on the stool, his hair broken free of his normally finely brushed scalp. "People like me just don't care about people like you." With steam coming in contact with my face, I look to the living room. Thomas has one hand on the top of his head, and the other is on his hip. This is the only reason why I'm doing this, right? I am here for him, and that's it. It's in the contract. I am here to keep Thomas safe. It doesn't say anything about the selfish man that fooled me that's sitting in my kitchen.

With my teacup in my hand and my back to the counter, I speak my mind for the first time since I have known this man. "A girl like me has no limits. We do what we have to do." Setting my cup down, I let my gaze roll over Anthony. A generous smirk wedged on my lips. "You, sir, you're just pathetic. I'm here to do my job, while you what? Just sit on your ass and lead them to us? A man like you will never understand what people like *me* go through." I feel my temper rising, the blood in my veins heating and beginning to boil.

I try to pull myself together. "You will never see the

horrors that we witness. The devastation that we carry with us. So I have one thing to say to a man like you: if you want to get yourself killed, go for it. But not here, not now, not with your son so close and so broken. If you care, you will get him out of this."

Glancing back to make sure Thomas isn't listening, I finish my claim. "If you want your son to survive this, just stay out of his life until this is over. Consider him and what he needs for once and not just yourself. Be a father."

"You have a mouth on you," Anthony slurs, but there is a rich edge in his eyes. "You have no idea what you were pulled into, do you?" A slow laugh builds, and amusement grows in the eyes of the messenger. "You have no clue what you are about to step into. For your sake," he smiles, and his red lips shine. "I hope that you ascribe to the same methods as your father."

"Maybe explain it to me?" I say, crossing my arms, ignoring the nagging chatter in my brain.

"No," Anthony offers a crooked smile. "No, I don't think I will. There would be no fun in it then, now would there?"

Curling my lower lip between my teeth, I suck in a shaky breath. He wants us to fail? Scrunching my face up in realization, I suddenly understand. Slapped with the knowledge, I feel my face wince with the imaginary blow. "This was the deal you made?"

"What?" The older man gasps. "I made a deal that was supposed to help my company grow. They were supposed to protect me and keep me on top of the board. To keep me untouchable."

"Looks like it's not just me now left out to dry, now is it?" I say, shocking myself with how calmly the words flooded out from me. "What did you do to betray them? I know you crossed them, Anthony." Leaning down, I face the man that sentenced not just me to death, but his son.

Leaning forward, Anthony flops his head down on my counter, and he continues to sway his glass back and forth. "If one loses, we all lose."

"No," I state, shaking my head. "You hired me to protect your son, and that is what I'm going to do, Mr. Pavlov. *You* will fall. *He* will not."

"You will never win," Anthony whispers, still swirling his cup. Meeting his eyes, his sad but cold eyes, I just shrug. I have never been considered a winner in life. "You're right," I admit to him. "But I'll survive. I always have, and I always will."

Leaving the kitchen with a loaded gun of a man, I now have to speak with Thomas. I didn't mean to say all that. But as Anthony said, a man like him shouldn't even be bothered by what I just said, but a part of me knows he will be. "You failed him, but I won't." Edging my voice and leveling my eyes, I get him to back down.

Rounding the corner, I nearly collapsed at the sight of Thomas. The living room is quiet as Thomas sits on the couch, one leg on top of the other, his hands resting on his knees. I know that when he sits like that, he's bothered. He's shutting down. Thomas, I know, had to have heard some of that conversation, but how much, I'm not sure.

I clear my throat to let him know that I'm in the room. "I spoke to your father," his eyes never meet mine, but his head is to one side. Knowing that he's listening, I continue, "But I don't—"

"Lindsey, it's fine." Thomas cuts me off, still not

meeting my eyes. "He does this a lot. More times than I can count, really." Ramming his head back on the couch, it shocks me to see the seeping anger within him boiling out. "It pisses me off, but he is still my father. Under all that ego and ignorance, I nearly feel sorry for him. Don't waste your breath trying to reason with him. It will never work. It never has."

"He needs to sober up and then—"

"Don't bother. He won't give you anything. He's loyal to them. I think he was all along. He didn't cross them, Linds. He bargained with them."

Angling my head with sympathy, I stride forward, "He wouldn't—"

"Oh, Linds." Thomas shuts his eyes. "He's been doing this my whole life. Makes a deal, sells his soul but never asks what it will cost him *before* he signs. They want me or you, and since we are a team, I'm guessing they get both now."

Sticking my arms out, I fold on the couch beside Thomas, his eyes opening as he pats my shoulder. Knowing and seeing his agony, I offer him a way out. "If you leave now, you may still have a chance."

Squinting his eyes, his brown orbs brim with sudden anger. "They know I'm with you by now. I'm leverage. We both got caught in this trap, darling." He sighs and curls his slender fingers into his shirt by his chest. "It could be worse, you know?"

"How?" I offer, still not comfortable with the silence.

"Hmm." Thomas leans closer to me, our eyes sharing a conversation just like our lips. "I could be alone. And so could you."

Sadly grinning, I offer no more words. We both just

lean into the comfort of the couch and hope the drunken man in the other room is somehow wrong. That he messed up with wording, but I already know he didn't. Anthony Pavlov isn't that type of man. A jerk, a coward, a fool, yes, but he wouldn't dare lie about the whole thing. The contract was a hoax, and now, Thomas and I are both the collateral in the fool's dealings.

The house has gone silent now. Shadow is lying on the floor, holding his sacred toy between his paws. He knows that Thomas isn't happy, and knowing Shadow, he'll try and get a smile out of him. One way or another, Shadow will stick beside Thomas, knowing that he needs a solid form to lean into.

I choose to relax, forget about the drunken man's words for the evening. Tomorrow is another day. We will get everything out into the open then. Thomas is right. I can't waste my time with a person like that, nowhere is the only thing you'll get.

Needing something to focus on, I turn on the television and plan our next move, to try and stay ahead of those who might be heading our way.

I know I have to start now because they are coming, I can feel it, and we are running out of time. Anthony's whole plan was to steer us in the wrong direction. He played us, and now, he's in my home. He won't bring harm to us, but he did betray us. He sold his son for a profit. If Anthony is here, they will be too, soon.

"Can you save us?" Thomas looks at me with clear eyes. "Will we be all right, Lindsey?"

Hearing my name come out with a sad tone, I feel my anger dropping. I want to save Thomas. I *need* to save him. This isn't just a job anymore, this is for true survival.

Honestly, I look into Tom's eyes. I reach for his hand. "I will make sure we make it through this. You have my word, Thomas. These motherfuckers will pay."

Frowning, Thomas clutches my hand tighter. "Together?"

Nodding, I wish I could lie to him. If one has to make it out of this alive, Thomas must be the one. I just need to stay strong and fight like never before to save him.

Finally finding my words, I whisper, "I hope so."

And hope is the key. Hope is something I'm short on.

We are running out of hope.

And if there is no hope, then there will be nothing left to fight for.

Chapter 12

End Game

The snoring from the other room drifts in from where I'm sleeping. This has to be the second time that I've fallen asleep on a couch since Lindsey has come into my life. And still, my mind continues to drift back to her. Lately, as I lay awake at night, I see her. In my dreams, she floats on a blanket of white, and during the day, she is lured into the darkness.

No matter how hard I try, all I see and think about is her. Lindsey Vasiliev, the force that many shy away from, is simply a woman with a ghastly background that would have killed many. I see her as a person. I see her as a vengeful angel. Lately, even through the haze, I just see Lindsey. No lethal tactics, no legacy, *Lindsey* is all I see.

Sighing and levering myself up, I can hear the tapping of the rain pellets on the roof. Clenching my side, I advance to the paneled window and push the drapes to the side. The rain is falling heavily as I look outside the bay-like window. The only sounds that can be heard are the snoring and the slow, calm beats of my heart, along with the rain pellets. Scratching the fluffiness of my hair, I roll my eyes at the continued ramming noises of the snoring that my father is releasing.

No matter how old I become, his snoring continues

to annoy me.

Looking around the room, I try to figure out what to do about my dad. For some reason, I can't get the nerve to go wake my father from his slumber. No matter how annoying he may be or what he has done, I don't know what I would do without him. I don't know anything about how to run a crumbling company. My father has blocked my independence, and now I feel like I am embracing the very things that my father wants to keep me away from. The danger he signed up for, he has unleashed on me, I think as I try to reason with my loathing thoughts.

But, rolling my head on my shoulders, I know that he asked for this to happen. He sold himself just so he could stay rich. He never once thought about the consequences. Ramming a hand through my mussed hair, I ask myself, how can I love when all that I have ever known is how to make someone *not* love you? My father taught me well. A bitter snaking reminder lingers within me. "Love isn't important. It's just a weakness," he would say while mixing one of his cocktails.

Nearing a breaking point, I let my mind clear. Looking around the room to block out the thought, I noticed the papers that were in Lindsey's file, the ones I only glanced at. Something inside me is drawing me to the very noticeable bundle of papers. But now they are no longer in the folder. They are stacked up in a heap on the table.

Feeling nervous, I look at the bundle again. A stream of light is coming through the window from the moon. It's almost like the world wants me to investigate Lindsey's past. *She wouldn't want you to read them...*

But, biting my lip, I feel the itch to see them. I want

to know about the broken girl that turned into a warrior. Sighing, I know I shouldn't. I shouldn't want to know. But like an itch, the need grows stronger the more it gets ignored. We have chosen to trust each other, and looking at her past without permission like that, I would break the bridge that we built together. I can't lose the bridge, but the need to understand…it's winning.

Shoving myself closer to the papers, I feel the early morning chill as I remove the blanket that is wrapped around my shoulders. Slowly and quietly as I can, I make my way across the room. Curiosity happened to get the best of me this one time.

The moonlight gives the room a starlight feeling, only small pockets of features can be seen, and the chill sends goosebumps all along my arms. The light guides me as I find the papers. There are pictures, articles, and contracts. I caress my hands across the stack. Every bone in my body goes cold. The blood seems to stop traveling to my heart as I see Lindsey as a small child.

She looks so small, pale, and fierce. I see what she meant now when she described her childhood. She looked revengeful then, but now, there is this lingering look in her eyes always. *Distrust*, my mind rings up for me. She has no trust now.

Moving on, a choking sob racks out of my body. There is a picture of us, her at our estate. The picture is of her, the very first night that my father and I met her. Dressed in simple gear, and her hair in a fury of being late.

God…my mouth goes dry.

There is a second one as well, just beneath the one with Lindsey. This one is of us at the mall with her looking at the necklace I bought her.

No…clutching a hand to my heart, fury builds.

The chills don't stop coming as I begin to flip through more pictures. They have been keeping tabs on us, haven't they? Shocked and on edge, I started to read one of her contracts. Not just any contract, the contract that cost her more than just a life…in a way, she lost herself and her confidence.

The name printed on the top in the main right corner: *PERRY, HARRISON.* Fearful, I toss it back down on the top of the file, scared to see what else it says. Racking my hands through my hair, I shut my eyes and try to get the image of a dead man out of my mind.

But as soon as the image came, I saw another one. Lindsey bloody and cowering on the floor. Trembling, somehow, I know what she's feeling.

I understand that feeling, letting someone down and not being able to trust yourself. Gasping for air, I settle my hands on the back of my neck, scared to move my train of thought. I don't want to see any more blood, violence, or dead people. I don't belong in this world, I keep telling myself. You are going to be a dead man.

Misguided by my mind, it travels on. There are just some people that can't trust. Lindsey is that way, so I can't judge her for that. Now, I really do get it. I can't even trust my own father. I can barely trust myself, as it is at this moment.

Shifting, I can imagine the pain it must have caused her to trust someone and then get betrayed, as well as blackballed from the world for something that wasn't even her fault. This file, it doesn't make me hate her or lose faith. If anything, it makes me understand her anxiety even more.

Shutting my eyes again, feeling the ache of

exhaustion settling in, a voice emerges. "Thomas?" Lindsey's hazy voice comes from the darkest corner of the room, just out of reach of the moon's rays. A simple outline is all that I can see. But from her tone, she's not angry, not shocked, but worried. Worried about what I would find? Worried about what I would think? It's a mystery to me. She should know by now that I can't judge someone else when I've done many wrongs myself.

Willing myself to explain, I begin, "Lindsey, I'm sorry. I just—I…" There are no words to explain why I feel the way that I do. I just want answers. I want to be able to connect with her on a deeper level.

"I just read one thing and looked at a few pictures." Lindsey nods and comes into the faint light in the room. Standing in front of me, her eyes seem to go translucent. "I trust that you will see the truth that lies within those words, Thomas. But I won't answer any of your questions, at least not yet. I don't think I can." The silence that unfolds into the room is unsettling. I ask so much from her. Things have gone too far.

She is my bodyguard. She is my protector, nothing more. But she is. She is a friend, a companion. She isn't just someone. She's the one that keeps me sane in these strange times.

Movement stirs me out of rhymed thoughts. The overhead light makes everything far too bright. Suddenly I can see Lindsey, and she can see me. Her hair is evenly in place, rimmed glasses on her face, and a tight sweater that shows her broad shoulders encases her body.

"Thomas, it's fine. Really, what else could I lose? You need clarity of what I have done. This is the best way to get it." Peering at me through thick lenses, she grins shakily. "Stop looking at me and just read everything." Hugging her arms around herself, she turns her back on me. Knowing why, I don't bother to push her any further, but with a lump in my throat, I pester her. "Why can't you just tell me?"

With her back on the wall, her rim-framed eyes shower with light. "If I tell you who I really am, who I have been raised to be," she jabs her finger in my direction, but her loosened shoulders show no defense. "If I tell you, then, if you refuse to believe me, just know that I can't be blamed for your disappointment. I can't tell you because of the disappointment I have for myself and because you would no longer trust me." Horrified, I raise my arms up, and as I reach for her, Lindsey sidesteps. "You could never disappoint me, Linds," my voice trembles in the bright room. Seeing Lindsey standing tall, straight-backed, but blank in the face, I wish to hold her. "You don't disappoint me. You scare me." Pushing her back to the wall, I trap her between my arms, and she doesn't try to get away. "No matter what is written in that file, it won't change how I feel about you. From the first time I saw you, your appearance screamed danger. You have skill, power, and strength, but your will is what throws people off." Leaning in, I can almost taste her scent as it invades me. "You have a will to you like no other. You fall but never stay down. You are lethal, Lindsey, just like your report promised."

"That isn't what I was talking about, Thomas." Shoving at my arms, she escapes. "In that file lies the truth about my parents. The real truth. I'm not what I've been saying I am."

"What haven't you been, Lindsey?" Leaning my head on the wall, I watch as her body remains loose.

Loose like she is bracing for a blow. "Innocent," is all she says before walking away from me with my mouth gaped open. Why would I refuse to believe that she isn't innocent? She's a person for hire. She is supposed to protect her clients, so by reports, I know that she can't be innocent of her actions. But, with her intentions, I know that deep down, she is innocent there.

Truly do I really need to know what she meant by that? It's her life, her mistakes, her lessons to learn and not repeat. I have already given her my trust. She doesn't need to explain herself. We all have some things that we want to keep in the closet. I know I do, but…if she's going to share this part of her life, then maybe it's fair if I share a part of my shadowed life.

"Lindsey," I beg for her to understand, for her to know that it's okay for me not to read this part of her life. But her eyes are far too intense as she turns back to me, her stance too guarded and dangerous. "Okay," I say through a yawn. "I'll read the papers. But to make it fair, I think I should share a part of my life with you."

"No," Her jaw clenches as she says that word to me. "That's not required. I don't want you to do that. I need to do this. It's what's right, Tom."

Not backing down, I say to her with pure warning. "It's not your choice. If I read, I share." Taking the large bundled papers in my hand, I return to where I was sitting minutes ago. The warmth is gone, but it slowly cascades back. Lindsey claims the "Main Chair," as I call it, the chair that is open and exposed to everyone and everything.

At least she didn't say no to me again. I smooth out a few crinkled edges of the papers.

Taking the first paper into my shaking hands, I can

see a picture of a much younger Lindsey. In the images, a strange old typing font spells out Vasiliev. What is that supposed to mean? Why no first name, why no other information? A crease forms in my brow as I try and figure out if the answer is in the picture itself. But nothing catches my eyes. I'm starting to overthink everything I see in these images now.

Taking page two from the bundle, I look at Lindsey again. She seems comfortable, but a muscle in her jaw stays rigid and locked.

The second page has words that I don't understand. Another language, it seems. But below the typing is another picture. It's pretty much the same thing. She's just older. She's lost the baby face chubbiness and innocence. I look up. Was that what she meant? Her cheeks have become sharper, her hair longer. To me, she looks lethal, like she promised. So far, I haven't seen anything that has made me hate her like she fears.

Flipping through the stack, trying to save time, I see something that makes me stop. A new name is printed on the headlines, Stepanov. Did she go by different names during each mission? Was she working with her parents when she was young? I can't bring myself to look at Lindsey now as I flip through picture after picture.

I can feel her eyes burning into me, but I can't give in. I've still got papers to make my way through before I can ask her questions. Questions that I hope I get the answers to.

Now it's another page's turn. There is no image with it but a letter of some kind. In a language that I don't speak or read. The script printed on the paper is super elegant. Time and energy were poured into each and every word.

Wanting to know what it says, I flip to the other side and see a translation that pulls me in. From code names to blackouts to finally, a name that pulls it all together: Vasiliev. But that's it. That's all that makes sense to me. I don't get it. Nothing makes sense, nothing illegal, nothing out of the ordinary.

But what's creepy is the way the images of Lindsey and people I don't recognize are taken. The images seem to have been taken at a distance. Some of the images look like they were in the middle of their everyday life. One woman is carrying groceries, Lindsey is caught mid-word while talking, and an older man is dressed in a black suit looking angry.

Now it's to the very last piece. I decide to move past all the unnecessary pages like her medical reports and her client rosters. People are entitled to their secrets, and I don't feel like reading anything about her old work, or seeing what she and Jonathan were doing in their younger years. It's not my right. It never will be.

The final big document looks the most worn and aged. It seems to have endured long, hard years, water stains, and it has even begun to turn a pinch yellowy at the right-hand corner.

Running my hand across the top, I take in the words that are boldly printed on the weathered page. The final page has headlines, and attached is an article that seems so fragile in my hands that I barely even breathe as I hold it.

I read each word like it could be my last. I slowly comprehend the meaning of the words. Looking anywhere but where Lindsey is sitting. Through the side view of my eyes, I notice that the sun is coming up through the rain clouds. The orange glow peeks through the thinning fluffiness in the sky, which happens to be giving me more light to read the headache-causing font.

My eyes meet Lindsey's for a moment. That moment causes me so much pain. She so badly wants me to understand what's in this file. Now I feel so bad about when I first met her. I acted so arrogant, so stupid, and rude. But things change. I thought she would judge me, so I judged her, not realizing she was simply doing her job.

Taking my eyes off the wall, I settle back to my reading. About a paragraph in, I hear noises that pull me out of it again. Lindsey stands and begins walking away.

I'm struggling to decide if I should stay here or go after her. "Wait? Lindsey, where are you going?"

She doesn't turn back around and face me like I thought she would, but she stays facing the other direction and utters, "Thomas, I'll be back. Just…finish going through that stuff. I need air, that's all." Why do those words make me feel so hollow? Why does everything bother me? Leaning my stiff neck forward, I try to locate where I left off.

The document that resembles an old news article reads:

A dangerous soldier was lost in Moscow yesterday evening as of four. He is known to be armed and dangerous. As of this moment, we only have a limited amount of information. Some which is still considered classified under the Federal Bureau of Investigation (FBI) ruling.

We know now that Volkov "Wolf" Vasiliev vanished from his post by the border that was kept secret and known as 'Classified' only he and six other people from Moscow knew of the Check and Release procedure.

Currently, the procedure is now under investigation due to one of its most crucial members' disappearance.

At the moment, no other person related to or associated with the procedure is allowed to speak. All have been cleared of helping 'Wolf' Vasiliev, but it is still an ongoing investigation that continues to prove problems.

This is all that is known, Wolf was about halfway through his final military service tour. So it is even more important that his service team finds him. He (Wolf) decided to retire and spend the rest of his days with his family, and we hope that he gets his final wish. The cause for his change of heart is unknown. Or if he is in danger. No charges have been filed, but he was/is one of the finest snipers that worked on classified missions. He lived in North Carolina while between tours, but he returned home to England to visit his family from time to time. It is quoted that Wolf would reside in North Carolina to help restore his mindset before returning to his family.

Wolf is married to Stepanov Vasiliev…

I ram my eyes shut. The beautiful older woman in one of the photographs was Lindsey and Jonathan's mother. Shaking out the kinks in my arms, I continue reading.

He (Wolf) has one living daughter Lindsey Vasiliev and one living son, Jonathan Vasiliev. Private information has been released, and permission has been granted to speak about this man's personal life.

We know that Wolf was born in Russia but moved to America at the age of ten. He enlisted at the age of eighteen into the military. While on patrol, he met a woman who is now his wife. Stepanov was born and raised in Moscow in the eastern region. She moved to England with her husband about a year before their marriage, and once she gained citizenship (which was issued a year before the couple's first child was born), she and her children found a home in London.

Their firstborn child is Jonathan and then followed by Lindsey a year later. They were born and raised in the skills of their parents (Wolf and Stepanov). Lindsey showed interest in her mother's field: Protection of others, while Jonathan paved his own path.

I try to breathe as I look up from the multi-page article. I feel tense and unsure. So far, I don't see anything that makes Lindsey a bad person. Her father possibly, yes, but Lindsey and her brother, no.

Taking a deep breath and then letting it loose from my lungs, I dig back into the reading.

...The continuum of article 22: Wolf Vasiliev's Disappearance

Both children (Jonathan and Lindsey) have reached their teen years and now both their parents are lost, both in different actions.

Their father, lost at the border, has never been found. An investigation was held, but no headway or knowledge of his whereabouts have been confirmed or released. He is declared deceased, but hope still remains that he is simply Missing in Action. A funeral was held for the missing soldier two years ago. Both children and his wife attended.

Their mother was killed by an employer (but if it is true, or confirmed, we do not know) just this winter. Her case is private and there is no other information that we can share at this moment. All that we know at this delicate moment is that she was declared deceased when police came to the scene. A private funeral was held, only the children and a lifetime friend of the family attended.

Stopping, my heart sinks. First they lost their father then their mother. Lindsey warned me, she even freely explained, but I wasn't ready. I wasn't ready to hear that what she told me was the truth. Counting to three, I continue.

The children left behind are of the age that they can decide to stay in England or live with their last remaining family in Moscow, both children refused to return to their mother's homeland, and as of last year, all information and details on them have been lost.

There is no further information that can be offered about this now ruined family.

Jonathan is now estimated to be seventeen years of age, while Lindsey is sixteen years of age. Nothing has ever publicly been released of the children. Both children are lost, and no further details are preventive to what they can do. We know that both of them are known to be armed and dangerous. Both have combat capabilities and have weapons training. It has been rumored that both helped their father in their younger years with missions, and both got professional tips from their mother before her death. Both children have experience with ending missions, and they will do as they are told. Be careful, and be warned, the Vasiliev's legacy lives on. After all, they are their parent's children.

What does that mean? Having dinner with the two, they seemed to be like normal siblings. Dangerous to whom, those that intend to harm them or someone who can't defend themselves? And after all these years, how could they not find them, or do Lindsey and Jonathan never want to be found? Everyone knows the legend of the Lethal Woman, but does no one really know who she is?

"Find anything interesting?" Jumping almost through my skin at the sound of a voice, I turn to look.

Standing there with his hair a mess, his white dress shirt still splattered with blood, and his face a pale mass is my father. "Dad, what are you doing up so early?" He doesn't say anything as he lumbers to a chair and continues to look at me with an odd expression.

"You are trusting her, the girl, I mean?" Tilting his head to the side, now I can see the cut on his collarbone. Sympathy isn't what I feel at the moment when I look at him. It's a bullet of anger that rips through me.

"Son, how many times have I told you that you can't just lay everything down and expect a perfect outcome?" Leaning forward in the chair, his bloodshot eyes peer into mine. "She cannot be trusted. You should know that better than anyone else. Lindsey Vasiliev isn't who you think she is."

Did he know? All this time that I've been trying to secretly dig deeper, he knew about it...all of it? And if so, why did he even bother hiring her? What was the point of doing that if he didn't trust her?

Pulling my lip between my teeth, I think of something to say, "What are you talking about? Her parents raised them this way. They didn't ask for it." Twisting my back so it is at an even angle, I finish, "She is my only option. You betrayed me. And her. All this time, you were just yanking on us."

"Naw," he says through swollen lips. "There was a deal."

Humming, I just say through dry lips, "And I'm guessing you didn't read the fine print." Rising from the couch, I gently tuck everything back into the file. No images, articles, medical records, or client lists will stop me from siding with Lindsey. I have faith in her, and nothing can steer me off that path.

Nothing will ruin the laughs and rare moments that I've seen Lindsey happy. I know that it wasn't all a game. Setting the pile of papers on the small glass coffee table, I begin to walk in the direction I saw Lindsey disappear. I need clarification. Someone needs to explain, and only one of them knows the truth.

Shaking my head to clear it and loosen it from its stiffness, I glanced up at my aging father. "Dad, would you lie to me even now? Now that I know the truth about this?" He says nothing as he keeps staring ahead as if the answer is behind me.

"Son, I would do anything to keep you alive, no matter the risks or lives I would have to destroy." He inches his chin up higher. "You matter to me, not some stranger." His face is flushed, and he looks sick as he lowers his voice, "Don't you see it now? She can't save you. She's in to save herself. Why else would she show you all this? Out of good character? She's using you!"

I feel like those words cut deeper than any knife could. I suddenly feel robbed. "Why would she use me? Has your brain begun to rot? She can't gain anything from me." He rises from his chair, raising a hand to silence my words because he hears footsteps coming in our direction. The silence that is surrounding us is suddenly broken when Lindsey walks into the room in her normal bodyguard attire.

Pointing her words at my father, her voice fully addressed to him, I step into the background. "You say that I'm a fraud of my word? You say that I'm giving

149

him that…that very private information to gain his trust? I was taught to be dangerous. I did everything my parents ever asked of me, and this is what they created. I wanted Thomas to see that. I wanted him to see that beyond the veil, I'm still human. That I have weaknesses."

Lindsey briefly stops to make eye contact with me, almost begging me to listen closely. "You would be right. You wanna know why? Because right now, I have to have his trust. These people aren't going to just drop something this important."

Stiffly flopping her hands at her sides, she whispers, "They won't stop hunting and waiting. Look at you, for instance. They have the ability to do so much worse." Shocked, I look at my father. He came here because the people he made the deal with got to him. "And you should know by now, Mr. Pavlov, no matter how dangerous, nothing can stop me. So buckle up because from this moment on, it's going to be a bumpy ride."

"Vasiliev, you better know what you are doing. If not, I will have your head." My father's cruel words don't seem to even leave a dent in the armor Lindsey has made. She looks directly at my father, a challenge that he has never invited or willingly let anyone do before.

"I'm well aware of what I'm doing." Hitching her voice a decibel higher, she states, "Now, do you remember what you said? That I am here to protect your son and no one else?" Lindsey steps closer to my father, so they are almost face to face in the living room.

"Well," she begins, "I hope that you know how to shoot a gun because I sure as hell am not helping you." Rotating her eyes over my father's face, a smirk plasters onto her face. "Get ready for war, sir, because you just cheated them by coming here."

Leveling a step back, Lindsey says curtly, "I hope you know how to stay alive when the end comes crashing down, sir, because right now, it's the end game." A challenging chill settles over the room, and for once in my life, I see someone rise above my father and make him almost bow in fear and truth. For once, he doesn't question the words that someone offers.

Lindsey looks one last time at my father and then glances at me, and proceeds to stalk out of the room. Knowing that I have questions I want answers to, I follow her out.

She's right, this is the end game, and it's time that we are all on the same page.

No matter what my father tells me, I no longer trust his words. My faith, unwavering, is with Lindsey. If there is a person that can get us out of this, I know that it is her.

She is the woman who spoke to a man who gets everything he wants down. She made him bow, and with that, I know we can win every fight as long as we stay together and focused.

With her beside me, I know I will be protected. That file, in its vagueness, changes nothing. She is the heart of this operation. She is the skill. She hasn't lied to me. My father has. He was the one that has confined me to hell, and it's time that I learn how to walk away.

It's time that I listen to Lindsey's words—I need to build the life I finally want.

It's past due. I owe this to myself. I need to move on. But first, Lindsey and I need to survive this battle.

For Lindsey's honesty, I wish I could give her back something. Wishing I could help her, I make a vow. I will fight alongside her no matter how this goes down.

She gave me her trust, which she never allows, so I refuse to surrender.

We are so close to victory. We have the knowledge of knowing that these people are coming. My father unexpectedly gave Lindsey and me a head start. Now, all we need to do is survive the battle.

If we survive this, I will do what I promised Lindsey.

I'm going to finally be the person I want to be.

I owe this new chance to her, so I will fight like mad to achieve the goal of becoming a better person.

For Lindsey, I feel like I will do anything.

I want to make what she is putting on the line for me worth it. Lindsey deserves a chance to step away and be able to breathe.

I will do anything to make sure that Lindsey and me walk away from this…together and all in one piece.

She saved me and now I need to save her.

The Lethal Woman is just a woman, and she is worth so much to me.

Chapter 13

Royals Fall

My whole world is falling apart. Piece by piece, I see the world that I knew shatter like glass. My heart, I'm not sure if I can keep taking these hits. I feel like Lindsey and I have been left behind for good now, like the world no longer sees us. Like the world doesn't even want us.

Now, it seems to be getting worse. We have to leave my father behind now. I'm left listening to his slurs and kicking as he thrashes in the chair that Lindsey pinned him to.

"Where are you going?" My father bellows through yellowed teeth. "You have nowhere else to go!" He keeps reminding us, but Lindsey just kept packing and making phone calls that she never let me hear fully.

"That is my son. You have no right to keep me here!" My father kicks out at Lindsey and summoned every last legal threat he could as we walked away from him. "You can't just leave, Thomas!"

Reeling back, with a bag in my hand and Shadow cowering beside me, I let my flaming eyes settle over my father. "I should have turned my back on you long ago, Dad. I stayed for you, yet I also longed to leave. You've destroyed my last chance to have a normal life. I hope you are happy now." Shifting away, I settle my eyes on Lindsey. Her scolding face, tight muscles, and angled jaw make me want to attack my father even more, but knowing we have to leave, I let my boiling blood settle.

Continuing with the little bits of packing, I ignore my father's continued chatting. His anger grew after I packed the few belongings that I wished to take with me and started to follow Lindsey. She's right. In the end, a man like him must learn. A man like my father deserves whatever comes for him. I can't keep trying to bail him out. It's long overdue that I finally walk away.

But no one claimed walking away would be easy. Leaving behind the only person you had, it's a painful blow he just keeps making worse.

His boisterous yelling is heard throughout the whole house. The noise is causing my ears to ache and my stomach to turn to knots. My hand is shaking while I'm waiting in the car.

Lindsey thought that if I waited out here as she finished getting everything ready that it would spare me some ounce of pain. It's not. If anything, it makes me desperate to just vanish and never look back.

I know I've heard my father yelling before, plenty of times, but never like this. Pure fear embodies me. From my place in the car, everything feels so faint, feels so distant. Hollow, like I never had a heart at all.

This is a crossroads I never thought I would have to face. The passion of staying alive; or the threat of extinction from a man that I once thought so highly of. I can almost still hear my father's threats ringing in my ears. Long ago, I learned the hard way that when he's like this, it's best to keep my mouth shut and back away.

But that was then, and this is now. I no longer have a feeling of dread. Even with everything going on, I feel so much…stronger but weaker at the same portion. I want to leave and never look back, but I also have the fight in my soul to keep fighting the man that gave me life.

The deep river of blood pumping through my veins all the way to my heart centers me and reminds me when I feel my pulse that I can do this, that I can keep fighting.

As long as I have confidence in myself, then I can do what needs to be done. I can help Lindsey, and I can help keep myself alive.

Momentarily, guiding my eyes to the house and the walkway, I see the emptiness. Lindsey has still yet to return.

I can hear my father still yelling, but the words are unintelligible. I know that she has to be moving around within the house because of my father's relentless chattering. Lindsey left the car running, and the warmth of the heater keeps me operating. But because it's operating, my mind keeps wandering.

The idea of what will really happen to my father hits me, the threat of Lindsey and me getting caught, to the fact of what if she can't keep me safe from these people. I feel like they aren't questions but statements that will soon rise to the boiling point.

Suddenly the yelling grows louder and louder, and the one-sided fighting seems to end when the front door closes. My father must know that it's over, that I've made my choice. I just pray it turns out to be the right one.

Looking out the window, looking at the house that made me feel at home for one final time. But it's time to grow up and fight for what you want, and by doing this, I think that I'm finally acting like an adult.

I try to calm my nerves as my eyes follow every

move Lindsey makes.

With strong, rippled arms, Lindsey opens the door. With one foot after the other, she takes her seat in the car and fastens the belt.

"Are you buckled in? Thomas?" I hear her, but I so badly don't want her to see the tears that are brimming in my eyes.

A soft hand loops over my shoulder. "Thomas, I understand this is difficult, but this is for the best. He is in no condition to be trusted." Putting the car in drive, she gently jerks the wheel. "Trust me, these people are ruthless, but they won't dare go into my house." Her house? Why would they obey the rules if they know she isn't there? They'll catch on eventually.

More realistically, why would they fear Lindsey? Granted, I have read the papers, and I've seen the pictures of some of her most brutal moments as I skimmed over *all* the pictures again, but why would people like *them* fear someone like *her*? One against a whole group.

Glancing at the rearview mirror, all I can see is the rolling fog that slowly swallows us. I couldn't pull my eyes away from how Lindsey holds the wheel. Her knuckles are white, and her arms are tense. I can see the pressure that she's forcing into the gas pedal. How are we going to get out of this stupid mess? How is the light ever going to shine on us again?

Will life ever be the same as I knew it before?

No. Those days are long dead. The second my dad made a pact with those people, my glory days were over.

I already know that I betrayed and disobeyed my father, which can't be forgiven. So there is no going back to that life. But, overall, I can tell that that will be the best choice to make. He's already surpassed his three strikes.

Now, because I have Lindsey, I know that there is a slim chance that I can continue to live. No matter what Lindsey does, she lives in my thoughts, and I can't just forget her like she was never with me. I feel my heart tugging to side with her always, and that makes my pulse jump and throb as I get a flash at a hopeful future with her still with me.

Without thinking, I ask, "Lindsey, what's going to happen to us? To Shadow? Can't we just give them what they want and stop running?" There is nothing to say. Her lips are sealed, and she doesn't even try to mask the tension and creases on her brow that enlighten me of the fear of this situation.

"No," she nearly whispers through ashen lips. "We have no idea what they might want."

"I think they might want me," I whisper, looking at my reflection in the passenger window.

Lindsey jerks the car to a sudden halt, twists in her seat, and asks with a tone of no remorse, "Enlighten me, what would they possibly want with you?"

"To use my father?" I ask as a question and not so much as a statement.

Scoffing and smiling oddly, Lindsey just glides back to her original speed. "Oh, darling Thomas, they already have him. They don't need you."

Then she hums, and with a gentle tap on the wheel, she informs me, "I have a kennel worker coming to get Shadow. He's in his crate. I informed her of your father in the house and to ignore him."

I can't help but admire her. "Why would she ignore him?" I ask, picking at a thread of my jeans.

"Because." She mutters and turns the wheel. "I told her to. She trusts me. She's gonna take care of Shadow. That's her job." Raising my shoulders, I believe her. When someone like Lindsey gives you an order, you tend to follow it.

Looking at Lindsey's blank face, I know the fear must be consuming her just as much as it is me, but she just chooses to mask it with rude remarks. But, there is one thing I do know that is weighing on her, she never lets the conclusion of failure stand between her and the end of this deal. But, even with her confidence, I know there is doubt.

Everyone has doubts. It's what makes us human. We, at times, have to walk away, not to just save ourselves but those we value the most in life.

Sighing in union with the terrible voice that keeps whispering to me the number of infinite things that could and most likely would go wrong, I watch as the world folds in with the arriving storm. This one, I heard, is supposed to be harder than the one a week prior.

Out of nowhere, Lindsey speaks, "Thomas, I want you to know something. Running isn't always cowardly. Right now, it's the only thing that we can do." Lindsey points between us, and I watch her finger dance in the air. "At this moment, you have to do what's needed for survival, and running is in that category."

For a split second, she draws her right hand up to her left shoulder and lets it rest there. A shiver of emotion peaks through her eyes before she addresses me again, "Think of it as a food chain, okay." She bites her lip and locks eyes with me for a brief second. Rushing her words, she thrusts out, "Now remember we are on the bottom of this chain, so everyone will be coming after us. We have to keep moving and think wisely." How can we possibly keep moving when everywhere we go, people find us?

I mean, those pictures, right? They knew when we went to the mall, they watched her when she came to my family's estate. Gasping, I grasped her arm, "They are watching your house!"

"Yes," she drones out. "That occurred to me too. If they are tailing us, they are going to be going for a very long, confusing ride."

"Why?" I question, feeling my stomach roll at an odd angle. Biting down, I clench my fists and try to keep my mind clear.

Oh my, my mind whimpers, *what have I been sucked into?*

As my stomach goes through a series of flips, I keep my eyes on the scenery outside. Counting the trees we pass, I get my breathing to even out.

About to say something, I stop.

"Lindsey," I say her name softly, nearly afraid.

Peeling her eyes off the road for a second, she offers a sickening smile, "Where we are going, if they follow us, it will be a rough go. Twists and turns, many branch-off roads, the list goes on."

Clamping down the bile rising in my throat, I ask, "What if they just search every road?"

Lindsey turns her attention to the radio for a second, and she then just pats me on the shoulder. "It's a possibility," she offers, not reassuring me one bit.

My head begins to throb again. The nervousness makes my stomach twist again. "Linds, could…can you slow down? I feel a tiny bit sick." Her eyes venture from the road to my face. Her hand tightly grips the wheel as she looks at my face. Her eyes darted over me. "Do you feel sick again, like before? Maybe the flu?" She momentarily looks back at the road. Her eyes read the signs in front of us. Her hands work wistfully. My eyes are growing heavy. I'm not sick, I know that. It's the stress. The stress I can't face. The stress that just keeps building.

"Thomas, open your eyes. You need to be alert." Ramming my head back with extreme force, I jar my eyes open. Lindsey's voice drowns out the wince on my face as she murmurs over the radio, "I know that the pain is vicious, but you have to...have to...just keep calm. We're almost there."

With my head against the headrest, I slowly turn my stiff neck to look at her. "Has anyone ever told you that you have to make every wrong right? Somehow, everything that you do wrong, there is a way to make it all up?"

Without a glance, Lindsey reaches out her hand and claws at my jacket sleeve so she can reach my forehead. "I didn't know that," she says as she makes a tight right turn. "Are you sure you aren't coming down with something?" Lindsey's deep blue eyes dig into my soul, and for some reason, I smile. Her eyes alone have more soul than anyone else that I have ever met.

Chiming in with my thoughts, my voice spikes in the car, "Do you think anyone will ever love me?"

"Thomas, why did you ask me that? Are you sure that you didn't hit your head? You keep jumping around." With wide pupils and clammy pasting of her flesh, I can see that she's worried about me.

"No, no, I'm fine. I-I just wanted to have a real conversation with someone." Yearning for Lindsey to see my thoughts, I just offer, "Whatever happens, don't blame yourself. No matter how this ends, I know that you have tried your best."

Honestly, she's the only person I have come to show my true self to in a long time. She is one of the only people that I can clearly think around, the only person that sponges up my voice and listens to what I have to offer.

She doesn't respond after that. The car ride is just silent. Knowing that I alarmed her, I chose to stay silent too.

In the silence, I can't help but think about my father. Is he okay? I know he's mad, but is he hurt? Will I ever see him again? Just as I pull myself out of my thoughts, Lindsey is pulling off the main road. The normal paved path now turns to dirt and gravel. The woods and landscape around us are dark and thick with overgrown foliage. The trees seem like the only living things out here besides us.

Moaning at the darkness, I question Lindsey for a second, "This is where we will be staying?"

Rubbing at her hooded eyes, Lindsey warns, "This place is not a home. It's not a place that most people would dare ever go." The tone in her voice worries me. What does that mean? Lindsey's eyes are shadowed, masked even in a way that I can't read. So badly, I want to pull her into a hug and tell her that she's not alone. That this isn't the end, that there is still so much fight within us.

That we can overcome this episode in our lives.

Pulling up, I'm captivated by the scene and the slightly odd smell of the stale water.

Wrinkling my nose, I turn to Lindsey. "Linds, what

is this place?" A long expanse of small buildings and a road are in front of us. They all look old and water-logged. Moss is growing on one of the old shacks that are nearly about to fall into the water. As Lindsey drives closer, I can see old wooden planks that were once a bridge of some kind. Pieces are missing, and some parts look so soggy they couldn't even hold a bird. I wouldn't walk on the planks for any reason other than escaping.

"Thomas, this is the original concept of the Royal Docks, but this site was never used. This is where an empire began and where an empire fell. It was abandoned when I was a child. Now, all that's left for this place is decay." Sighing, and pulling her coat tighter around herself, Lindsey pushes open her door. "Very much like my life, this is where I found out the truth of my future. This is also where lives were ended or defined. This dock has seen it all, and I think it has one more battle in it, don't you think?" Her hands are deep in her sweater pockets as she emerges into the awaiting storm's winds. As I step beside her, the wind picks up, and her hair is sent whipping behind her. As I look out into the water in front of us, I feel my pride trickle in, and this is where my fate shall be decided. But at the moment, all I could think about was winning my life back.

"I believe that this crumbling dock can take one more beating. Let's just hope that its bones don't break beneath us." There is nothing that can clarify what I feel. Looking at Lindsey, I know that there is power within that sweater. Strength, knowledge, compassion, but not ego, ignorance, or cowardice.

Watching her and coming to stand in her line of sight, I can see the painful memories replay within her eyes, but I stand my ground and let the evening air bite at my exposed hands. As if the atmosphere around us couldn't get colder, a slow sprinkle of rain began to seep from the heavens.

"Take this as a warning, Thomas." Lindsey's steel-blue eyes meet mine as she speaks. "I am hired to do one thing, and that's to keep you safe. So when the time comes, and trust me, you'll know when it does. You have to do as I say." She steps closer, and the breeze slowly blows her hair in my direction.

Locking eyes and taking in her windblown features, I let her words roll over me. "Thomas, don't be a hero either. Do as I tell you, and you will have a chance to get out of here."

Licking my lips, trying to gather some moisture, I tell her, "I trust you, Linds. You give me the order, and I'll obey."

Knocking her head back, she allows the wind to dance around her, "Remember this, I may not always be strong, but everyone, if they choose, can save themselves. And that's what I expect you to do. You should too. Be ready to save yourself."

I know what she is trying to say.

Trust the fact that she is going to keep me alive, and if she can't, then I must do everything in my power to save myself because I have the strength within to finish the job if need be.

"The only person who can save you is yourself?" I ask her, knowing her answer but wanting to still hear her voice.

"Someone can help you, but first, you must be the one to take that leap. Changes are coming, Thomas, and I think it's time that you've been taught how to save your own hide." Smiling at her cruelty of words, I follow along as she begins to take shelter among one of the only sturdy-looking warehouses in sight.

Chapter 14

Fall To Your Knees

The fall of an empire took place beneath my feet. It's a tingling feeling to know that someone else possibly had a secret battle in this very spot. Looking around, I notice how calm but dark it is, and I think that maybe if Thomas would just embrace the silence, it might calm him.

Solitude has the ability to help people find inspiration and guidance in the darkest and most troubling of times. I used to be so strong, so empty, but now as the tide turns, I feel nothing. Nothing breaks through to me like the chance that I might not be able to save Thomas. I promised not to fail, and now, being in the dark, I feel like I have no way of getting him out of this.

He doesn't deserve this. He's been able to make me feel a little again. After so long…maybe all my life, I've run from what was chasing me, but now, I don't feel the need to run. I need to stand here, take the blows, and take the force of the hit so Thomas can survive. After all, he finally gave me something to believe in.

Kicking at the pebbles that line the small shore, I feel Tom's presence. He has wanted to be alone for the past few hours. I know that he has spent his whole life dashing after one dream or another, and now, he must feel the helplessness of feeling his heart caving under the idea that we, too, might fall here as well.

One dream dies, and another begins. But now, he's probably fearing having no dreams at all…

It was here, in this fake dock, that my father lost his battle all those years ago. It was here that he told me his official goodbye. This dock that he loved, he told me the history of how it was built but then left to rot. It was here that he trusted me with the family legacy. My father left my life that night, and ever since then, I've been drawn back to this place.

Standing here, I just watch the water run down the channel. Knowing that Thomas is in the more settled warehouses on the lot, I at times let my gaze fall in his direction. Looking out for him always, I wish I could just take the weight on his shoulder upon my own. Knowing that he wants to cry out for help, I wish I could take the brunt of his pain. He is a good man, worthy of a good life, a soulmate, and a family. All he wants to do is help people, and yet now he is the one paying the debts of his father.

Blinking up at the wrinkled gray sky, the wind meets my face as I take everything in, the blistering wind holding no hesitation in where it goes or who it hits.

Maybe I should just take Thomas far away from here, but at the end of the day, I know that will solve nothing. Saved for a day but running all his life. That, I refuse to allow Thomas to experience.

Nothing surprises me at this moment. As the sky opens and the wind beats down at all those who are in its path, I nearly embrace that sorrow as my companion. Thomas is avoiding me, and if I were in his shoes, I would hate to see the person who might have brought this upon me too. This world is relentless. Once someone is on their knees, they continue to be beaten down, even further than they could ever imagine.

Exhaling into the breeze, I watch as my breath matches and lingers in the air. My gaze follows the tangles, and as it swings around, I take one more final look around the embankment. Remembering Tom's hatred for being here, I can't help but reminisce about what I told him, "Being off the grid is the only choice we have at the moment. The longer we have to rest and recover, the better the chances of warding off these people that have made it their job to kill us will be."

Knowing the truth in my words, Thomas just stuffed his hands in his pockets and stalked back to the warehouse, muttering how he wished Shadow were here. We've been here for nearly a day already, and somehow it feels like we've been here for longer.

Glancing at the bank, the water is getting choppy, and the air becomes colder by the second. It seems I can sense the storm that is settling in. Looking up at the sky, I can tell. The dark, thunderous sky and the swirling clouds seem to blend together to make the sky above look like it's going to cry along with me. Darting my eyes at the warehouse with Thomas in it, I mutter, "I miss Shadow too." Sighing, remembering my call to the boarding kennel, I feel my eyes sting. "I wish you were here to help me."

"Trust me, he would be if you let him." From the sky to the ground, I turn around to see Thomas. His foot cracks a twig, giving him away. His eyes hold a playful glint that makes me chuckle. He wanted to surprise me and lighten the mood. He tried so hard. "Shadow is your truest love," Thomas whispers as his eyes remain on the ground for a calm second, keeping his arms stiff at his sides.

A slow smile spreads across his face. His face, God, I can see where the stress is getting to him: his eyes, the dark bags under them, his hollow cheekbones, and his raw lips where he bites them and runs them through his teeth. The worry is evident in the way he holds himself, one arm locked around his torso, his head slightly bowed, and the fact that he keeps running his hands through his already messy hair.

"You know that legally this was supposed to be an easy job. I thought that by now, all this," I turn to face Thomas and stretch my arms wide to make my point of where we are, "would be over. I guessed terribly and horribly wrong."

He doesn't look at me. His face is tilted down, and the wind ruffles his tan jacket. His pale face is in the shadows due to the clouds, but he can't hide the fact that he is clenching his jaw, keeping from saying something.

Needing company, I beg him to speak. "What? Just spill it. There is nothing else that can shock me now." Again he looks down, his hands stretching to his pockets. There is something in his eyes when I look at him. His face is a clear giveaway that he's hiding something. As the wind picks up, he inhales deeply.

"Tell me, or I'll make you." Threats have always been my go-to force when I need answers, and right now, any tension between us could cost us our lives. We need everything out in the open.

We have to be on the same team and share information that might save the other.

"You don't understand." Thomas pleads, his voice cracking as the breeze tangles in his hair. "I told my dad that something bad was going to happen, but guess what, he didn't listen to me. Now you and I are paying that price, and where is he?" Locking eyes with me, I read the hatred in his melted brown eyes. "He's safe at my bodyguard's house."

Nearly leaping toward him, I breathe deeply. I keep my feet grounded. "What was I supposed to do, Thomas?" Beating my voice over the harsh noise around us, I try to get Thomas to explain everything to me. "What did you want me to do? What options did I have?"

Wheeling at me, Thomas snarls. "I don't know! But we are *here* while he is *there*."

Turning my head, I incline my chin, so our eyes share the glare. "I called the police, Thomas. He won't get away with anything."

"Don't you see it, Lindsey? He used us. My father set us up." Knowing his anger, I shift so we are closer.

I've been there, betrayed and left to my own devices, but as time goes by, he will slowly learn that being put in this situation may have just made him who he truly is. Being put in these situations makes you realize that life and death make us want to show who we are deep down. What we will do to live and what we will do to ultimately survive.

Hoping to make Thomas feel better, I add to the statement, "In the end, there is only one person I have to protect and that's you. Your father? He would be the first person to not listen to me and make things much worse." Placing my hands on Tom's wide-set shoulders, I beg for him to understand. "I get you're angry, but you have to stay calm. For you and me, we have to think long before we take action."

"No, I'm not like you," Thomas says, backing away.

"I-I can't just think of battle maneuvers and jump in. This isn't my job. I run away from danger." Hitting the wind back, Thomas bellows, "I am a coward who runs from a fight!" Guilt is something I have felt very little of in my past. But since I've known Thomas, I have felt guilt more than ever before. He shouldn't even be in the same location when the bullets start flying. I have to have a plan. An escape, I have to have the upper hand in this.

Looking at the man in front of me, I can see the agony all over his face. "You will make it through this." I let the truth bleed through my cracked voice. "Just don't give up or give in. Keep moving." The red puffy eyes, his peach skin that is peppered with dew from the settling clouds, I command him, "Just breathe. I will guide you through this. Every step of the way."

Everything is on repeat with us. At this moment, surrendering might be the right thing to do. I don't know who is in control. Knowing the person behind all of this might be the only chance we have. The brutal truth lies in his face. Thomas has been subject to so much.

Sighing, I speak to the storm, "We are not going out like this."

I can't ignore it anymore, and he can't hide it. I see it in his eyes, his lips, the posture of his limbs, and the way he reacts. I can see that he wants the truth but fears it.

That happens when you are lied to for so long. You can no longer pinpoint what is a lie and what is truth.

Looking at him and taking in his expression, I whisper, "I hate the fact that you always look sad." Bending my neck back to look Tom in the face is a struggle as the wind beats at me.

The sound in the back of his throat seems to be like

a whisper. He slowly steps closer so he's in front of me. His emotions are exposed openly. The wind whips through his hair, sending it into his eyes, but his jaw is still locked from what I can guess is anger. His eyes are still as vibrant as ever, though. Slowly he looks at me, and his voice becomes a whisper again, like he fears the world will hear something it shouldn't. "When I first saw you, did you know what I saw in you?" Reclining his posture, he says with a tight jaw, "I saw anger, so much hate. I still see it deep in your eyes. What made you this way? Why do you have so many secrets that you fear sharing with me?"

Swallowing the saliva that coats my mouth, I try to figure out what to tell him.

What am I supposed to tell him?

That I hated myself for so long?

That for so long, I have been living a lie?

Shifting my weight between my feet, I try and contemplate what to say. His cold hands touch my face, but his eyes are boring into mine with warmth. Something is different about him, something fierce and powerful. The stress has made him a different person. He's become a man willing to fight.

I can *almost* see it in his soul.

"Do you want to know what I think?" Shifting between his feet, Thomas rambles on. "You live from job to job. You always have to be strong, always have to be prepared, and I'm starting to think that you aren't as dangerous as you claim to be." Leaning closer to my face, he gracefully finishes, "To me, you are human, you make mistakes, you have your bad days. Be honest with me. Why can't you just trust me?"

"Do you really think I like who I have become? I

have a job, an unforgivable one, and in this job, I have to stay focused. Security is what I have to focus on. You," I point between him and me, "and I can't keep fighting like this. You trust me, and I trust you. It's settled." Battling through the thickness in my throat, I barged forward, "I have to hold up my end of the deal. I hate having to be the bad guy that ruins lives!"

I turn my back on the man that keeps making painful memories come back to bite me. I so badly wish to tell him everything. But, to tell them you have to experience them all over again, and some wounds, those should just remain as scars.

"Do you want the truth about why people hide from you?" I hear Thomas shout behind me. "It's your eyes, Lindsey. When you look at people, and when they look back at you, you see into them. You can see through all the bullshit." I can hear the ring in his voice, and the exhale he releases into the air. "When people see you, they move away because they know with your eyes on them they can't lie. They can't avoid the truth or the brutal honesty you force others to take upon themselves."

Barely turning back, I continue to listen to him. "In your eyes, they see all the wrong they have done. Like a soul on fire, you make others see the worst parts of themselves. That is what makes you lethal, Lindsey. Your eyes tell a story of unforgiveness, and when people see that, they know that it's time to run."

"You're wrong," I tell him as my legs carry me forward. "No." I can hear him chuckle in the breeze. "We both know that I am dead-straight on that fact, Lindsey. You can't hide from me, not like you do with everyone else."

With my boots hitting the gravel with more force than necessary, I continue to walk away. Thomas doesn't follow, but he keeps watching me. With one final look of defiance, I see pain is edged into his features. As I walk around the building, a thought comes to me.

A plan forms in my head, and it builds like a wildfire. Suddenly it all comes to me like an explosion. As angry as I am at Thomas for calling me out, I still feel this building firefly of a thought glowing in my brain.

The back door in the largest structure has an overhang that leads to the second building. Thomas can use that as an escape when they come for us. He would be covered, at least, and people in front wouldn't be able to see him. I have to build the rest, but at the moment, as I look out the window to still see Thomas standing there, his hair tousled and his face red from the cold, I know what I have to do.

My heart goes out to him. I so badly want to try and make the best of this moment. He seems to get me every time. I know that it will start to rain soon, and I know that the only way I can get him back inside of the compound is to give him what he desires.

Taking a breath and rubbing my face fiercely, I open the door and let the air hit me like a hard blow. The stabbing pain in my heart continues as I know that I'm about to change everything. The secret I promised can no longer be kept. Right now, the only thing I can do is tell the truth.

Walking out the door, fighting against the wind, I make my way to where Thomas is standing, facing the channel of water that looks bitterly cold. His expression seems to scream, wanting to jump in the freezing water.

Shuddering at the cold, I shout above the howling,

"Thomas, please come inside. I'll tell you everything you want to know, but please…just let me tell you everything before you say anything." From this distance back, his eyes glow.

Pleading outwardly, I holler, "Please just hold your judgment." My eyes are large and watery. I can feel it. The cold is biting at the tears. It's almost like a punishment for finally opening up and telling the truth.

Ambling closer to me, his pleading eyes find mine. "I can't hate the woman that is going to save my life, now can I?"

Pausing at his words, I answer, "You have no idea what I'm going to say yet." Worry laces every inch of what I'm doing. If he loses his trust in me, we are good as dead.

"I don't need to," he chants, "because I know you." He takes my hands and folds them into his. As he takes my cold hand in his equally frozen one, his lips curl up into a bright smile.

"I think it's time that we spill our guts. At this moment, it's the safest choice to ensure that they have nothing to hang us with," Inching his lips into a frown-like smile, he murmurs calmly, "Lindsey, you up for it?" He asks the question in the most understanding way.

"If empires can fall here, then so can our walls that we build around our secrets." Looking at him, I feel the confidence in knowing that I'm not alone. He will have secrets as well that will bring us both to our knees.

Come to think about it, both of us have built lives on false hope and secrecy. Maybe it will be for the best if we let everything go and drop everything that we have been hiding inside. With that, I can go into this battle with a clear conscience and a lighter heart.

I know that through the truth, we will re-emerge as better and stronger people.

I have hope in us.

I have hope that we can save each other.

We are the only people that can end this. It's in our hands to take this one. I know that by speaking the truth, at least if we die, we will go as light as a feather.

Chapter 15

Tell the Tale

The memories of the past tend to cast us with a haunting remembrance of who we once were. People that we have run away from and the very people that we refused to ever become.

Some memories are meant to be left behind. Resurfacing them is just done to open the wound again, knowing that it may never heal or scar over.

At the end of it all, we are all a part of glossed eyes that no longer see the present. The breath of choking lungs as sobs erupt from the human body, and the speeding heart of someone who can't calm down.

As we choke on haunting pieces of ourselves, we all become broken bodies that no longer function. While in pain, all we feel is the memory, nothing more, nothing from the present.

Looking at Thomas now, his hair has fallen across his face, and his mouth is set in a grim line. Taking my shaking hand and placing it over Thomas', what we were once hiding from each other wasn't as serious as we originally thought. His life was miserable, but Tom didn't judge what I had to say. He listened and frowned all the way through.

Through each of our painful stories, we understood what the other went through.

Rather than judging, we embraced and chose to understand each other.

The summit of our hesitation was something I never saw coming. What he said, what he felt. Everything expanded at an alarming speed, from our childhoods to our secrets that have raised us to be who we are to this day.

As our wailing increases, so does the wind. It hits the side of the compound with an extreme force that leaks through the cracks in the walls. I can almost remember my father's angry face as the cold wind bites at my face. The chill resembles the bark in his blue eyes.

This anger that I hold inside, I soon learned from talking with Thomas, is what I have been holding for him. All these years, the tears, the revenge plots. Knowing now all the roads that I never crossed and the roads that I will never get to travel, it was all because my anger was being held inside because of one selfish man.

As I speak, I can almost remember the yelling matches, the simple conversations that soon turned dark and spiteful.

My voice came with a cost. No one was allowed to challenge the beast, not in its territory. Growing up, I would cower, and I would be still and silent and take the blows that I caused, but in the end, I knew. I knew that I had a voice, and in order to be seen, you sometimes had to start wars.

A war was exactly what I got in the end. The slamming, the yelling, I took it all in. I took the poundings knowing what it would cost, but in the end, that was the origin story for the lethal calling. Through the survival acts as a child, I became the very person that most people know. Through the challenges of my family, the legend of who I would become was born.

As I speak, Thomas keeps reminding me that it was preparation for what I would have to do later in life. But that pain, I realized, will never leave. The pain of my father's cursed voice, to my mother's muted mouth. It was never enough. My life never changed. Somehow, I am back at the very beginning. Hiding, cowering, plotting, and still not knowing what actions to take. I no longer know what to do. Being lost, I'm scared to face this battle.

I deserved what I got. I started the war, and I had to become the casualty of it. My parents made me into this person, but after speaking for God knows how long, I learned that all the silence I got, I brought it upon myself. I'm the soul that would never stop, would never back down.

I just have to keep reminding myself of that.

As my story about my father's violent rage comes to an end, Thomas loops his hands behind his neck, lets his arms hang, and then his dark eyes glower through the darkened corner of the warehouse.

"We all get to a point where staying silent isn't effective anymore," Thomas mumbles in an aching voice as he reaches out to take my hand. "Sometimes what you say turns into a bullet, and at times the outcome of it, I think we all at times wish it would kill us."

"I was twelve." I cast my eyes to the ceiling, focusing on the water stain that looks like it's going to explode. "Rarely, when my dad would come home, if anyone spoke out, there were consequences. I loved him but feared him at the same time. It got to the point where I simply did as he wished. The missions, the late nights, the training. My brother and I took it all, just so we could live a little."

Picking at my nails, tapping my fingers together as they are in a fist, that's the only thing that keeps me from crying. To be so little but be so strong meant taking my heart and ripping it in half. For so long, I kept my life a secret, but with Thomas slowly spilling his guts, it no longer feels so shameful. Every once in a while, my voice will crack, and a tear will spill. With every drop that runs down my cheek, I start to let everything go. All at once, every wall inside of me comes crumbling down. In Thomas' arms is where I find myself as I relive every single painful memory.

Watching my father turn against my mother, watching my brother become a man far too young, watching my friend die before my very eyes and not be able to do anything about it. It comes flooding back like it was never gone at all.

Nothing feels worse than having time stop as you look down at the casket that should hold your lifeless body and as the music rings in your ears as if it's trying to find a heartbeat that will never come again. The noticeable pain makes it to my face, and shivers run down my spine as Thomas brushes a hand through my hair to silence my cries.

"Nothing can stop you from feeling this pain, but," Thomas vocalizes slowly with velvet eyes, "maybe this is a sign that you came this far, and you have to let this stage of your past go. It's time to bury the past and march into the present with your head held high."

Thomas held my hand but continued to look at the ground as he re-sighted what he was going to share with me. From what I have gathered so far, he came from a well-rounded family, or so it seemed.

His mother and father divorced on ugly terms. His mother never kept her promises. Anthony Pavlov never wanted to raise his son alone, and he turned to drinking to suppress his flaring mind.

Thomas would run away to the river close to a bridged highway. He would walk through the river and show how he felt. He would scream and hit the water until there was nothing left inside him. Remorse, that's all I feel. Pity, I know he doesn't want that, and he's past sympathy. Neither of us speaks for a while. The only thing that comes to my mind is wanting to drive far and fast. But as Thomas speaks about his father's cruel remarks, he flawlessly finishes with, "People always say that through the passage of time, wounds will heal, but what no one tells you is that the deeper the cut, the deeper the wound." Cutting off, Thomas sets his eyes on mine and bites his lip, seeming to change his direction. "The deeper the loss and the deeper the failure, the deeper the cut truly is, and the more time it will take to heal."

"It will become a scar," I tell him, knowing that by speaking about our family's issues, we have reopened wounds that once didn't bother us. "What we experience, what we lose, what we fail at, it will always remain. Scars don't leave. They just fade."

Pulling my knees up to my chest, I focus on breathing, so I don't suffocate. "Do you think we will ever find peace, Thomas?"

Slowly—too slowly, he turns his head in my direction and frowns through red-stained lips. "We have not had a picnic of a life, so I have a feeling that this won't be the end of our troubles, Lindsey." Letting his hands fall flat on his knees, he waves his fingers in a slow arch.

"I just want to be free," Thomas mutters with his rich eyes closed.

Letting my eyes travel over his body, I feel my breathing hitch as his eyes catch at mine suddenly.

"I want us both to be free," he says with a clipped voice but a hollow expression. "We just have to get through this."

Nodding, I offer Thomas a small smile. "We will." I wish for a more honest promise, but one doesn't come. So badly, I want Thomas to be free. I may never get the chance, but he can. He will. Thomas is braver than he thinks and stronger than he believes. If I can get him started on the survival plan, he can finish it.

All it takes is one small step. No matter how small...

Suddenly as an idea comes to me, and before I can process what I'm saying, I suddenly announce to Thomas, "Get your coat."

Thomas looks at me with a wrinkled brow and raises his eyebrows, but he has no worry lines on his forehead. His eyes are even, and a sly smile makes it to his lips.

"What do you have planned, Vasiliev? If it involves training in the rain, I will pass." Pulling my upper lip through my teeth, I try to figure out what to tell him. Should we go for a drive? We should just escape for an hour? Be normal twenty-somethings for once?

Slowly, I let the hesitation roll over me. "Just get in the car. I'll be there in a moment." He stands and kind of hovers by the chair that he was sitting in moments ago, his hands resting on the back of it.

His hair is flat from the lack of brushing. For a moment, I see a person who so badly wants to live for himself. And as I turn my back, with four long strides, he walks out the door to the car that I parked at the back of the largest structure. I keep it there because I know those people will be coming soon, and I want him to have an escape. That path in the back will be the only way for him to get out, and I will hold off whoever these bastards are until he gets as far as he can. He deserves to have a life, even if I don't get to see it.

With that thought lingering, I pull the closest hoodie over my head and let everything fall away. As I raise my shoulders, I can feel the soreness throughout my body. I can feel the icing pain in my bones that is almost willing me to cry. But it's a simple dull ache that will soon fade, knowing now that Thomas can see right through me. I will soon have to hide all forms of pain. We opened up to each other, but at times, a person must choose to live completely open or have a few moves hidden.

As I rub a long scar along my back, I look for the car keys I placed on the table a day ago. I run a frustrated hand through my hair as my mind screams for me to move faster. I find the keys a second later, but I just end up staring at the wall.

I feel like this is the end. I will put that car in drive and then everything will come crashing into place. I badly want to reach for my phone, turn it on and dial my brother's number. He can help. We've made a plan before. That's how I made it out alive last time. But this time, Jonathan can't be brought into this. Not until I know more. Jonathan deserves to live his life, not be sucked back into mine.

Turning on my heels, I briskly make it to the door, turn the knob, and walk to the black car hidden behind the building. I can just barely make out Thomas' shape in the tinted windows.

Everyone deserves a chance to live their life…and

it's time that I cut through the fog. I need to free those that I care about. Make it through this mission and we can all walk away.

For them, I will risk everything.

For Jonathan.

For Thomas.

Even for myself.

I will face this uncertainty like my father showed me. I will rise above the fear.

Pulling open the driver's side door, a harsh wind comes and almost makes me lose my balance. Before I can fall, I clutch the seat and hoist myself up. The muscles in my shoulders tighten, and as I look at Thomas, his lips are raw, and his fist is close to his mouth. I know what he's feeling: worry and possibly anger. I know because, underneath the surface, I'm worried too.

As I start the car, something inside me screams. Putting the car in reverse, something inside me breaks. Someone will die during this mission, and I made a deal with myself at the beginning. That person will not be Thomas. I would rather lay down my life for someone instead of standing by that casket again. I refuse to stand by and let that happen again. Everything will come to an end the moment they come for us because I'm done with the games this world wants to play.

It's time that I officially start fighting back, harder and fiercer than anyone ever imagined.

I need to show England that I am still the Lethal Woman. I will use the tactics one more time. Give the Lethal Woman a proper sendoff…with a victory.

Just as I roll my shoulder back, a beat full of sorrow fills the car but listening deeper, it's a beat that makes you long for peace. Taking in the melody, I allow my breath to release. One more drive, one more break. What is the chance that they have been watching us this far? I mean, after all, we have been squatting in an abandoned dock center that hasn't operated since before I was born. That dock was left to rot, and it was never even given it's own name; so as the car sails, I wish to give that location a proper send off.

It's not royalty.

It was never a real dock.

It was a savior to my father and now for me.

"Savior Port." I say. Thomas dips his head and gives a look of confusion.

"The dock," I explain. "To us, it will now be called Savior Port."

"It's not a port, Lindsey." Rolling my eyes at Thomas, I smile at his honesty.

Keeping my hands steady on the wheel, I do a quick once-over of Tom's posture. Seeing his tense structure, I want to offer comfort. "Maybe not." I attempt to keep our conversation going. "But that location gave us salvation. That dock was never given a chance to live. But now, it's helping us live."

"Yeah," Thomas frowns. He touches his reflection on the window. Then his head darts in my direction. "Savior Port it is then, Lindsey."

Jostling me around, the car dips through the muddy patches, and as if Thomas knows what I'm thinking, he whispers something I know he's not just saying for me but also for himself: "We'll make it out of this alive. No matter what it takes, we'll be all right."

Everything comes back to that sentence; we will make it, we'll be all right. I'm sick of it. But for Thomas,

I keep my thoughts to myself. I need him to be square with me and we need to be on the same page. Now and until we walk out of this nightmare.

Shifting my seat, I ignore the gnawing feeling in my gut. "Do we trust each other?" Asking, needing, pleading, I wait for Thomas to speak.

"I always have," he whispers. "And I always will." Turning, so he is angled to face me, Thomas peers into my eyes. Gently, his hand skims my coat-covered shoulder. Casting a feather-like grasp on my arm Thomas pulls me in closer.

"We are in this together. Where one goes, the other goes. I'm here." Taking a pause, Thomas shifts his chilled hands on my face, and he stares into my eyes as he says confidently, "No matter what people say or do, you, Lindsey Vasiliev are the truest person I have ever known."

Smiling, I place my hands over his. "You don't know everything."

Grinning widely, Thomas doesn't bat an eye. "I know enough. And that is all I need."

Letting his hands drop from my face, Thomas sweeps his hands through his hair gently but seemingly teasingly, making me question our conversation for a minute. "There are secrets. There are things I have done and things that my parents have done, that…that, it's not good."

"You've shown me who you are." Boosting his shoulder back, Thomas melts into the seat. "It will be fine, Linds. From what I told you and what you told me, I know that you are the person you say you are."

"And what is that?" I ask, scared to know what Thomas has figured out about me.

Flawlessly, Thomas leans in, and his muggy breath fans my cheek. "You are brave." He comes an inch closer. "You are kind. Fierce, honest, loving…" Drawing out his words, Thomas settled his eyes on mine, but they dip lower as he casts a longing look at my features.

"No matter what happens, my trust in you will never fade." Smiling, he turns back in his seat properly and points at the road. "We should move along now. We've been sitting here for a while."

"I'm sure it can wait," I murmur as I long to understand the words shining in Tom's eyes.

"No, darling," Thomas chatters. "I think it's time that we face what the road holds ahead." Propping his head on his hand, he offers a smile that I know is somehow false. "Together, we will face that road together."

"Okay," the murmur in my voice isn't convincing, but right now, it doesn't need to be. Thomas sees me for who I am and not for my title. "Let's enjoy the road while we still can."

Chapter 16

Vasiliev

The stern expression on Lindsey's face as she looks straight ahead makes my stomach twist. Most of our time together seems to be spent in a car. From the first time I warned Lindsey about my father's grim ways to our shared moments of secrets that have very much kept us in line, we've shared the confined space of a car or warehouse.

But the slow rhythm of the radio and the once in a while glances that she thinks that I don't see seem to make us grow more connected. Our broken hearts keep on beating with never-ending strength to keep us going. Even on my darkest nights, my first encounter with her, she brought a light so small to help guide me.

She was the one that showed me the light.

The moment I saw her, I knew that she would be the one that would guide me. She would be the one to protect me. I knew that she would do anything to honor her word, even if that promise became her last words.

But looking at her now, all I can see is a woman who wants to protect people. Not just me, but everyone. This complexity within her wants to correct everything she and her family have done wrong. Seeing through her rough patches, I just accept her as she is and what we will have to do.

As the car lurches, my stomach dips, and I think it's because Lindsey said that she just wanted to go for a drive, and therefore I had to come with her. I don't mind normally. Anytime I'm with her, there is less fear than when I'm alone. But now, in her stiffness, something seems off. There is power in her stance, her shoulders, and the way she plans what to say. I admire that, but now that she knows I can see through her, she seems to be hiding something. Lindsey radiates power and modesty with strength, but I can still see the agony reflected in her eyes. What we said to each other—about my parent's divorce and her shitty circumstances with her parents—created a connection, but somewhere along the last turning point, we seemed to have lost the ability to reach each other.

Unfamiliar with where she is guiding the car, I set my left hand on the door handle and twist my fingers around it. "Lindsey?" I say her name as a question. My own lips seem foreign to me. As I watch her guide the car, I seep back into the silence.

Falling back in my thoughts, I can't help but remember the picture I saw of her when she was younger. She looked happier then, carefree. I can't help but think about losing all of my family. I lost my mother, but I still have a lost-minded father. But Lindsey's father is either dead or a prisoner. All she has left is her brother. The one person who has had her back.

And now, I think she fears that once this is all over, that's the way it will always be. She and Jonathan against the world. Reeling, I can't help but feel myself wanting to hold her hand and tell her, "It's not over." But it's not my place. People that meet and bond during extreme circumstances, the relationship doesn't last. It just tends to stumble along until the levee breaks. Extreme circumstances pull people together but then, without the pressure, there is nothing left when there is no danger. The attraction dies.

"I've been thinking of a game plan. You might not like how it ends, but I think I know how these guys will act." Lindsey looks at me for a second before continuing to focus on the road. Her voice just floats through my head as I keep my eyes focused on the road along with her. "They will charge, they will try to overpower us, but what they don't know is that there's a back door, which you will leave through." Appalled, my eyes overcast, and all these questions and comments want to spit out of me. As I look ahead, my mind swamps. All this silence, all this leaving me out to dry, and now? Now, she chooses to speak, to basically just tell me that I will be leaving her behind. With hostility on my lips, and the words forming, my mouth opens.

But stopping me, Lindsey claims, "Then you will call my brother, but I'll give you a code word the minute the cowards show themselves." Her face is rigid as stone, but her eyes give her away.

Looking at her, I know that she won't tell me the whole plan. Some people never give all the details, and to me, that was once all right because we had faith in each other, but now, by her keeping me in the dark, she's losing me. I don't want to trust her because I don't want to leave her. "How will you know what to say? The code word, I mean." That, to me, seemed like the only question I could ask without pushing her too far. I know that she shared everything with me now. I know that I simply have to trust her judgment, even if her silence pisses me off.

Her eyes dart to mine. One hand tightly on the wheel and the other resting on her other shoulder. Her eyes are dark, her hands clenched. "My brother and I rate situations by code names. When I needed his help last time, the code word was *Smert,* which means death in Russian. I thought I was going to die that day." She takes a long breath, her body rising and falling, "but I guess I was wrong." A scary tone lies underneath what she just said. Looking at her, I can almost see that broken little girl that is lost and all alone with gifts and talents that no one can know about. All I can think about doing at the moment is staying silent, but I so badly want to comfort her, but she's not that type of person.

Changing the subject, I turn to facts and theories. "Who do you think is behind all of this?" Struggling, then another question springs up. "And why my family? I get my father is a total piece of work, and he might as well be made out of money, but why now of all the times?"

Her hands twitch on the wheel like her wrists are getting tired. Her head tilts as if to make it easier to see me. "Thomas, these people have probably been planning this for a while now. That's their edge."

Feeling anxious and tense, I try to listen to Lindsey thoroughly. "Right before I had my meeting with your father, both of you were part of some headlines in the United Kingdom. If they wanted something, they knew when to strike. Like at this moment, your family's company is in debt, making deals to survive." Leaning to the side, she rubs her shoulder. "They knew where to make you hurt. They wanted your father and you divided, but guess what?" Lindsey aims her gaze at me, forcing me to pay attention. "They probably didn't plan on me stepping in, now did they? Because of this curveball, they had to rethink their strategy."

"Maybe they knew all along," I tell her. "I mean, they went after your file. They knew where my dad kept it. My father said that this was about *all* of us."

"I almost forgot about that," Lindsey says as she locks her hands around the wheel even tighter. "What do we *all* have that they could possibly want?"

I so badly want to know who these people are. What are they looking for, and why are they after me officially? Suddenly, it occurs to me that I don't know where we are driving to, but the silence is what I'm grateful for. Lindsey rarely speaks any words, her hard expressions are how she communicates, but right now, she just seems like she's shutting down.

Not dropping the question, I ask again, "Linds, do you have any predictions of who these people might be?" She presses her lips into a thin line, her eyes focused deathly hard on the road.

"I might," she groans. "They might be former clients or clients that just recently signed on with your father's company. But I'm not entirely sure yet. Time will tell, won't it?" But I don't want to wait until it's too late. I want to know now. I need to know who we will be facing.

I want to be able to stand tall and take the punches that come my way. I want to be a man and fight my own battles, but I think we both know that I can't do this alone. The woman next to me has taken a bullet. She has taken multiple punches. She is so much stronger than I am. She's stronger in so many ways. I feel like I owe her this chance, a chance to get away. I want her to be able to live her own life.

"You should disappear. Get away from me. You don't deserve this; any of it." There has to be another way to defeat these people. But, there is no evidence to give to the police, and Lindsey's family's name isn't very popular among the authorities.

Lindsey turns to me, her left hand rubbing her forehead. "Thomas," she speaks to me in a tired sigh. "I was hired to protect you, and that is what I intend to do. Face it, I'm not leaving. Now just be quiet and listen to the sounds of the road. In the silence, we might find the answers we need."

"Or a real plan will emerge?" I say, not wanting Lindsey to get the final words in.

But when Lindsey doesn't say anything back, that's what I do. I stay quiet and let the sounds of the tires turn wisp into my ear. The whispers of the wind draw my attention and even cool my body. It makes me feel free and safe with the draft billowing around me.

"Do you want to stop and get something to drink or eat?" Lindsey's sudden rapture pulls me from my own mind. "I think it might be the calm before the storm." The small moments when we act like real people are when I feel most alert and separated from the world.

I have gotten used to hiding and sheltering away from the world. But the small moments when Lindsey and I can be normal people, I will fight for those moments to be able to know that after all of this, there will be a continuum story. Every time my brain drifts from one thought to the next, I always end up looking at her. My heart beats a little faster, and my eyes become a little more alert. I wish I could see and know so much more about Lindsey. Like a lurker in the night, she still has stashes of herself left in the darkness.

These are the moments I can't live without, the calm and peaceful. Or maybe I just can't live without her. My own mind seems to scream at me.

"Sure," I answered her question about food. "What are we gonna eat?"

Her smile, her average complexion that I could spot in a crowded room, and her dominating stance that pulls me in makes me smile. The way she holds herself, there is authority and maturity in her stance. The build that she put years into, the skills that you won't know about unless she was tested, that alone makes me refrain from my own cowardly acts.

Together we stand but divided we will fall, that even a person who has never seen true actions of violence knows. You do, or you die.

"I was thinking about maybe grabbing a sandwich at the stop ahead. Then we can go back to the dock and try to get it, so it's not so gloomy." Lindsey rambles on, but my mind keeps trotting forward.

I have no intention of leaving Lindsey at any point. We will fight this together. Lindsey may not know it yet, but after this fight, it will not be our end. She doesn't know it, but I'm willing to work to get this job done. Nothing can keep me from the life that I want to live.

Lindsey's head tilts again, and her lips become tight. Her hands grip the wheel. And the shift in her loose body to tight makes me stop rambling instantly. Panic floods in, and all of a sudden, with a jerk and tight turn, the car is sent into a narrow ditch. But she corrects it and pulls the car back onto the street. Bile rises when I think about what is to come.

Our moment of solitude and normalcy is ruined. Just like that, something comes in and slices through our harmony.

Clutching my seat, I turn to face Lindsey. Her face is calm, but the fierce biting on her lower lip tells me otherwise. She's focused but nervous. Looking at her at this moment, I know that if I die today, I know that I spent it with someone that means the world to me.

If I have to die beside my bodyguard, my death won't be miserable.

Sad, but not horrible.

Closing my eyes, I speak the words that I never wanted to say, "Did they find us?" All I get in return is the squealing of the tires and the gravel cracking under the weight of the vehicle. Panic settles in the lowest part of my gut. I thought I was prepared for this, but the sight before me is something I never thought I would ever have to witness.

Lindsey looks at me for a moment, panic strained into her features. "Has to be. Who else would be trying to ram us off the road?"

A clear twist of panic, wide eyes, awed mouth, and pale flesh remind me she may be powerful, but she's mortal. "Lower your head," she tells me, not even sparing a glance.

As the car swerves, she adds, "Buckle in tighter. This is going to be one long ride." The sheer honesty and underlying tone have me pulling on my seatbelt and pressing my palms into the cushion of the seat.

"Will we make it?" I say, locking my eyes shut, trying to find materialistic objects and feelings to focus on. Without a single missed beat, I can feel Lindsey guiding the car, forcing it along as she tries to lead us to safety. "I will make sure that you get out of this," she states murderously.

"Whatever they do, I will wheel it on them tenfold, I promise." Not looking, I plead for her words to be right.

I believe in her. I do. Really, I trust Lindsey but now that the problem has arrived, my faith wavers. Not intentionally, but figuratively. I want both of us to make it.

Lindsey, my mind whispers. With my eyes sealed shut, I can still see her. I can feel the warmth of her body close to mine. Gently, I squeeze the seat under me, and my mind screams again, *Linds*.

"Shit," I curse audibly. "Linds, I don't think I can do this."

Without looking, Lindsey presses her hand into my shoulder and squeezes. "Just do what I tell you, and you will make it. Just once you start running, don't look back. Just keep running."

"I'm not running," I say, not wanting to leave Lindsey behind to fend for herself.

"It's either you run, or you die." Clenching up, I can feel the impact of the moment. This is it? I run to save myself while the woman that my heart pleads to be with is left to die. No, I can't leave you, I want to tell her, but I know it's as useless as trying to dodge a bullet.

Nodding along, I promise nothing. If she fights for me, I fight for her. That's the vow I made, and that is the only promise that remains. If one falls, we both fall.

"All right," I whisper, misleading her. "What you say goes."

Chapter 17

I Will Return

Everything was forgotten as I tried my best to get rid of the people in the black car behind us. They exposed their guns to me once. They don't want to kill me right now, I don't think, but once they realize that I won't let them near Thomas, I'll be the enemy too.

And they won't hesitate to take me out.

That or it's a warning. No one else is supposed to get hurt. And if we stay on the main road for too long, then these people will have no problem taking out the people who get between them and us.

Looking at the traffic ahead of us and all the exit points, I know that I won't be able to get out of this. There is little room to move and no time to get a head start on outrunning these people.

Racing past cars, I try to get past people without much conflict. They keep getting closer, and there is this fear that if they flip this car, we are as good as dead.

Thomas closed his eyes a minute ago, his lips quivering. I want to promise him that we will be okay, but there is no point in lying to him. Trembling myself, I wish the car to move faster or for people to get out of the way so I can just sail ahead.

Making a hard left and pulling the clutch back, we skid onto a dirt road that I know far too well. Looking behind me one final time, I step onto the gas harder than needed but damn it, we need to get a few seconds of leeway if we want to get into the warehouse in time.

The speedometer keeps spiking higher, and it's at the point now where I have never seen it. My hands tighten on the wheel as the front right tire hits a rock, my mind shifts, and swearing plays on repeat as my hands begin to sweat. "Come on, come on," I will the car on, needing to get Thomas out of this.

"We will get out of this," I state outwardly. Not knowing who I'm speaking to, I just keep letting the words spill. "Thomas, get ready to run." A shaky breath slips from his lips, and I can't offer him any remorse or consoling at the moment. I have to stay focused on the speed we are at and just the right time to make the turn. My world becomes dusted out due to the dirt from the road sailing along behind us. It's not a cover, it's more like a trail, but at this point, I know the truth; we can't get out of this. We will have to fight.

Up ahead, I see a broken bridge that is a death trap, but there isn't anything else in our favor. Pulling Thomas out of his state of panic, I turn the car too quickly, and he opens his eyes, and a scream almost spills from his lips. I can see the bridge better now. It's missing pieces but not too many, the metal beams are rusted, but we will live to see the other side.

Alarmed by the speed and the creaking of the planks, I shout, "Close your eyes again! Thomas, please close them." I beg him, his dark eyes landing on mine for a second, but then they slowly shut. My heart beats rapidly as we cross. I haven't prayed in a long time, but something inside me breaks, and I whisper a prayer of, "Lord save us," that I so desperately beg will help us.

Just this once, I plead that God hears me.

Answers me.

Will help me… just this once.

As I close my eyes and rest my head on the steering wheel, a jerk comes from behind, pulling me out of my own mind. Hesitating only for a second, but then an idea comes to me. I make a slight left, and now both cars are side by side. I can see who's in the driver's seat.

Just as the windows line up, my mind breaks. Questions flood through me and then they just break loose.

Do we really want to know who these people are now? When should we call Jonathan? How can I save Thomas? I close my eyes and listen to the sounds our cars make, the dirt crunching under the wheels, and the sound of a horn.

Turning the car once again, my face tense, I can't see their faces too clearly. They can't see us perfectly clearly either. Screwing my eyes, I see a tattoo edged into the driver's skin. My stomach sinks, and with the seat belt around my chest tight, I barely breathe. "Papa." My voice shakes as my eyes land on the rough tousled silhouette of the driver.

Trembling, I remind myself, if we can get back to our hideout, they won't ever know it was us. I can ditch the car, and we can be done with it.

Lies. All lies. They know it's us. They've been watching Thomas and me, possibly even before I signed the contract. Swearing, I know that we will have to face these people. Correction, I know that I will have to face these people. Thomas just needs to get the hell out while there is an opening.

"Lindsey," Thomas whispers. I look at him with

wide eyes. "Don't worry. Don't think, just do, get us out of here." I turn back to the road, my heart rate leveling and my mind releasing. I know what I have to do. It's time to cross safety off my list.

I nod to Thomas and step on the gas pedal even harder. I stiffen. There is a chance that there will be another road, and I need to be ready to take it. Patience is all it takes before I see my getaway. Shifting to the left and moving forward, I notice that it looks familiar. Fear clenches within me. These people know what they are doing, and they know exactly where they are taking us. I ignore the turn and pray that they get fooled. The lump in my throat seems to grow as we get closer. Panic is settling in with every passing mile. Knowing that there is only one way to get the word out, with one hand on the wheel and the other pulling my phone from my pocket, I decide to do the unthinkable.

I dial my brother's number. The car tailing us is getting closer, and the fear of who's in it makes my hands twitch.

"Lindsey, what's going on? You never call me. Are you there?" My brother's voice makes a tear fall. There is a cover he took over when our mother died. He no longer wanted our father's name. I kept it as a reminder of what I am capable of. If I blow my brother's cover, we will both be dead. Dead by the hands that vowed to kill us years ago. Dead by the hands that made us who we are today.

It is connected now. I should have known. How could someone have the Vasiliev file other than another Vasiliev? Sobbing, I begin to hate myself. I should have fucking seen it when Anthony confessed that I could never win.

"Johnny, he's here. It's him. I can feel it." Pausing, I flash my eyes in the direction that we are going. "I don't know what to do. Please, Thomas has no part in this. I thought it was about him, but I was wrong." His line is silent. Then there is a click, and I know what is to come.

I hear his breathing before I register his voice, "Get to the safe house. No matter the cost, do as the plan says." Jonathan's voice is clipped but elegant as he breathes me a reminder. "Linds, remember this is not the end. You know him. Use his weaknesses. Tell Thomas where to go. I'll help you when I can. Go!"

The line goes dead. I know that he's lying. This is the end. Looking up, I allow Thomas to see the fear that is eating me alive. What do you do when you find out the man trying to kill you is your own father? The man that taught you everything you know? That knows your skills, your tactics, and even worse, your weaknesses? How do you hide the fear and anger from your own father? How do you play the man that wrote the book of getting fooled? This was a person I thought was dead years ago. He left, and then he vanished.

Steadying myself and blocking out the fear, I pull on the mask he demanded I use. Now it's time that he claims that grave for good. If I go down, he will too.

Keeping the car steady, I turn my attention to Thomas. "Thomas, promise me that no matter what happens you do as I say. You need to trust me and don't look back. Don't ever look back. Just head through the back, up the hill, and follow the path to the homes that are ten miles back." Seeing his eyes, I know what he's thinking. "I know it's far, but you need to just move, don't think. Don't worry about me." Stripping myself of my confidence, I let Thomas see the real me, the fearful me. "And don't give in. Don't worry about me." Knowing that I need to cut the cord from Thomas, I set my mind in the mode that my father always wanted me to use.

Unclipping my gun from the holster, I raise it, preparing for a fight. A fight that I might not come out of. The holster on my hip feels hollow now. This will be the most vicious fight of my life. I never thought that what I had already experienced would be a cakewalk.

"I'm not letting you do this alone," Thomas says, confidently.

"I'm sorry, Tom. This…t-this, it's not your fight. It never was." Thomas doesn't look at me for a long time, his head is low, and his lips are being bitten by his teeth. Leaning forward in my seat, I rip my sweater off and let the air bite at my flawed skin.

"Okay, but you have to promise me something, then we will have a deal." Swallowing hard and closing my eyes, pulling my left hand as tight as possible on the wheel, I try to keep myself from crying. I fail, and as I look at him, he knows that I can't make any promises. He nods, but he speaks with a calm demeanor.

"You have to come back to me, okay? I know we haven't known each other long, but I feel like you are a part of my family now." Gulping down a breath, he holds my gaze momentarily. "You promise me that you will come back, right?" I hit my head on the headrest, the tears are too much, and my jaw aches from the violent tension.

I can't look at him. All that I can say is, "I will try, but this is something that you can't make promises about. These people are dangerous. It's worse than I thought. These people will pull us apart. But when we get to the compound, I will distract them, you will go out the back door, you will get out through the back and get to the trail. If you think you are being followed, go into the foliage. Don't look back. Leave the rest to my brother."

My eyes never waver, and my hands never leave the wheel. My heart rate doesn't change. There is a plan, and all I need to do is follow it. Looking at my wrist, a cross is dangling below a scar that I earned from the very person that is trying to take my life right now. "A lesson will always come to you in the disguise of a risk, Lindsey. Remember that when the world around you begins to fall." Hearing the words of my father in my head clear as day, I growl. He won't win. He can't. Not this time.

Suddenly, I see a paved road up ahead, and I do the only thing I can.

I turn. Harder than ever before, and merge the best I can with the remaining traffic. Fast and dangerous is the only way. My hands shake, but this mission is to do or die, and I will be undefeated at the end of all this. Cars honk, and I know that this is the best chance we have.

I knew that deep down, I would return to this place. This road, passing by that house. He knew it was going to be me. Closing my eyes, I can see everything before it all goes wrong. Before I take a vow like my mother. Looking up, I see Thomas shaking. A scowl digs into my eyebrows.

We have to win this.

I have to win this.

I keep switching lanes, giving us some distance, then out of nowhere, I turn. The road that leads to the docks has seen many things. This will just be another added to its very long list of encounters.

The uneven terrain jostles the car, but with determination, I make sure to make it to the warehouse on the property. The dock's emptiness and gloom are welcomed as I pedal harder and faster.

Just as we get close enough to sail through the warehouse, I clamp the brake. Not waiting for the car to come to a stop, I pull the keys with me, screaming at Thomas to follow me, and everything starts to unfold.

I jerk Thomas into the building, telling him the plan quickly again, but he raises a question I almost forgot he would ask.

"What's the code word?" Blinded by the name, I lose my voice. "Lindsey! Focus, the code word, what is it?" Panic rises when I'm forced to say the name I so badly wanted to forget.

"Wolf," I whisper, not being able to meet or explain to Thomas what is fully going on. But, I tug at his sleeve, clamp my gun in my hand and begin to move to the warehouse. It will be dark, and nearly empty, and Thomas and I already know the layout well. We will have the advantage of location, but my father, he will have the advantage of numbers.

Swinging back, I clamp my hand around Tom's wrist and shove him in front of me. But with his hand on the door, he stops, turns to me, and with pleading eyes, he whispers, "Come back to me," as he plants a hard, brief kiss on my lips.

No warning, but I felt the fear. I could taste the hate. I could sense the emotions that he is suppressing. Just as I open my mouth to speak, cars start rolling in. Guns get drawn, and men begin yelling. But I have no time to count how many.

I push Thomas in front of me and force him to keep

his word that he will listen to me. With sharp fingers, I push my hand into his back and force him to open the door.

Before he could even get through the door, they started firing at us, and all I can hear is the bells tolling of the fate that lay before us. And, as my hand takes hold of the knob, a searing pain bites through me.

Chapter 18

Kings Never Die

I could feel the bullets whizz past my ear. The pull of the terror inside and the heat of the bullets drive me back into reality.

Just as I reach forward, I feel Lindsey's hand on my back as she demands me to open the door and get to cover before they get to us.

I almost forgot about the plan, but Lindsey's cries ring in my ears.

I need to get a hold of myself. I need to get my shit together.

With my sweaty and slick palm on the thick, paint-chipped door, I shove the door forward with my shoulder. It sticks and makes me freeze. But when clanging noises connect with the door, I shove harder, knowing that the men's aim will only get better the longer we stay here. I ram the hinges and get the door to release.

Just as the door releases, Lindsey's cold hand is upon my upper arm, pulling me along. I think it might be the shock of this moment truly happening, but I can't move. I feel frozen, dead on the spot. But what catches me off guard is the fact that the warehouse is bigger than I remember, but I can see the back door in my sights. But then everything seems to break through the surface.

Just like a swollen bubble, everything explodes in a matter of seconds.

"I can't," I pant. "Linds—" Lindsey folds her body close to mine and shudders her words out, "You need to go." Vising her hand on my elbow, she plants a hefty kiss on my cheek and shoves me away from her. "Go!" She shouts as my world explodes.

The metal door opens, and bullets hit everything in plain sight.

Lindsey pulls her gun to her chest, forming an "L" pattern with her hands. She has her left under the gun, closest to her chest, while her right holds the gun.

Her general motions feel so fluid, posed even. I try to remain calm, she is trained for this kind of stuff, but a deep cry is forming in my throat.

Without thinking, I turn back. I hold onto Lindsey's shoulder, letting her know that I'm here but mainly reminding myself that I'm not alone in this situation. Lindsey's eyes turn to my deer-in-the-headlights expression, her eyes are emotionless and sleek, but I know she is giving me a silent command.

She rises slightly, just enough for them to see her. She knows that I'm covered, but she no longer is. A man with slicked jet black hair with a few strands of gray turns his gun on her. She doesn't drop her weapon. She stands her ground. Her foot taps the floor twice. She's signaling me. Now it's just a waiting game.

Keeping myself covered and low to the ground, I crawl toward the door. Every time my knees and hands come in contact with the concrete floor, I get closer to my freedom…but farther from her.

There is a mass of men who could kill her on the spot, yet she doesn't waver. As I crawl farther from her, all I hear is the hammering of bullets slicing the air and shouts as people fall. One of these men might be her undoing, my mind keeps telling me. Crawling as fast as I can to the door, trying to stay covered and silent, but no matter how fast I go, this barrier inside slows me down.

I so badly want to make it out that thick, cold door and call her brother; I need to be able to save her. Rising from my crouch, I dash for the door, my only chance to escape and Lindsey's only chance to survive.

Jiggling the knob, I realize that it won't open without a fight. Bracing my shoulder against it and whacking the knob, I hear it crack. Just as my wrist begins to turn it, and a triumphant smile forms on my lips, I stop deathly still in my tracks.

Something cold and metallic smelling is pressed into the left side of my face. Slowly I turn to see a graying male. He's a tall, muscular man with slicked-back hair styled as if he doesn't bother to brush it and a beard that has seen better days. But his eyes are what make me paralyzed. The blue-gray tint with a dark shadow cased deep within. His body is curved at an angle, and the black pistol is pointed directly at me.

He's a stranger that wants to kill me, yet something seems so familiar about him. Shuddering, my eyes begin to water. Lindsey, I sigh. I failed her, my beloved. I let her down.

Locking eyes, a menacing smile lingers on the man's face in front of me. "Let go of the handle," he taunts. His voice draws shivers down my spine. As he looks in the opposite direction, he speaks again, "do as I say, and you'll both live." With wide eyes, I look in the direction he is now facing.

Lindsey is on her knees, her hands clasping the

ground to hold herself up. Blood is dripping from her scalp, and it slowly travels down to her bruised jaw. The man with the unsettling voice turns back to me, holds his gun closer to my chest, and directs me across from Lindsey.

As my legs wobble as I walk, I nearly stumble as I approach Lindsey's battered form. Meeting my eyes, I nearly read the words she is asking me: I guess this is it, then?

The man with haunting blue eyes waves over another man, who points a new gun at me, right between my shoulder blades. With a forceful grunt, he orders me to my knees. Crouching down, I let my knees hit the floor. From my bowed state, I can see Lindsey better now, the bruise has a ring of blood around it, and her eyes are glazed over with tears that make me so angry. But, the way she is kneeled, weakened, and held in place, I can still see that she is as unforgiving as the day I met her.

"You let me down," the man says with his back to me. "Yet as I look at you now all I see is a soldier conflicted. So I ask myself, why would that be, Lindsey?"

Lindsey's eyes meet mine, a single track of tears run down her left cheek, and a cruel shadow falls over her face as the man steps in front of her, pointing the gun at her chest. A look passes over Lindsey's face, and then suddenly, the man turns to me and places his gun against the side of my neck.

"I see now," a sinister growl grows in his throat. "You fell, my darling, didn't you?" A vein throbs in his neck, and as he looks at me, he marks his words to Lindsey. "My daughter, the lethal force that never stumbled, has finally set the family crown down."

Daughter? Daughter! My mind shouts, but soon, I feel myself shutting off. Fighting the fit of tears, I nearly fall completely on the cold hard ground, I am so stupid, I tell myself. How could I have not known? The eyes, the name, the gentleness, the force…. Lindsey and I have to fight her father.

But, bracing, I remind myself: Show no weakness. Do this and you might live.

Men pace back and forth. I just watch them, and I try to determine what they are saying, but every time someone looks over, I bow my head and lower my eyes. *Be obedient,* I tell myself. *Don't raise suspicion that you may put up a fight.*

Seeing guns everywhere, I cower. Nothing is as scary as watching the truth unfold with a gun pointed at your head. Lindsey is silent as she looks at her father with horror. Her eyes are dark and masked with anger and confusion. The only noise in the cold, drafty, and dull compound is the heavy and rapid *tap, tap, tap* of the rain hitting the metal roof.

Marching away and yelling out orders, Lindsey's father, Wolf, I remember from the article, appoints a young man to watch us.

The young, scared man pointing his gun at me is watching Lindsey. As I look around the room, all the men watch Lindsey with their guns aimed and ready. They know something about her; she isn't some girl trying to play the hero. They know she is the heir to the lethal legacy. She is the daughter of the man they, too, seem to fear.

They did their research, and they came prepared. She was right all along; this was never about me. It never was. It was a ploy to get to her. These men know she won't allow herself to fail. Now they know how to use that against her.

With a heavy, haunting sigh, I understand they will use me against her.

The leading man, her father, who is standing in front of everyone, walks closer to Lindsey as if he has no death wish at all. But with that simple move, I can see a slight limp is prominent in his left hip. His clasped hands are rough and wrinkled with age, but a gold band encloses the third finger on his left hand. His face is friendly but clearly full of warning. But his voice is even more chilling. It's deep and almost fatherly. He steps in front of Lindsey, and he slowly runs his right hand through his messy, graying short hair.

"Lindsey," he smiles. "Look at how much you've grown. Your mother would be proud. I would be prouder if you would walk away and leave the boy with us." Crouching down, he touches Lindsey's blonde hair. "Please do as I say. I can't hurt you. Not now, not ever. But I will if I must, and I won't give you a second chance." I try to stand slowly, but I'm forced back onto my knees. This won't end happily. Somehow, I just know it.

Someone's life is going to be claimed tonight.

As I wait for someone to say something, the cold continues to seep through my jacket. The thin material doesn't keep me warm. It just tends to keep the cold raindrops from seeping into my clothes. With my knees aching on the concrete floor, I can't help but shiver from the cold.

Lindsey glances at me as I shake, and I pray that she says something that will help with my boiling rage.

Watching her father, I wonder, what does he want? As we continue to look at each other, the gun keeps getting closer to my head. It's almost touching my drenched hair. Sighing, I accept what is about to happen to me, but when Lindsey sees this, panic ripples through her delicate features.

She goes still and then seems to explode.

She stands, forgetting about the guns that are ready to kill her in an instant, and she walks forward. She is face to face with the man that claims to not want to hurt her. She stands there and looks into the eyes of the man that so badly wants to ruin my father and me. Lindsey locks eyes with me, and with a demanding nod and a shade of her eyes shifts. She is demanding that I listen closely.

"Father, you can't force me to break a promise that was made. Promises can't be broken." Her eyes are no longer dark with anger but icy without emotion. "Should I remind you of the damage I can do?" Her threat seems to go on deaf ears as the man that she called father steps closer.

Raising my eyes, I watch as Lindsey's father lays a hand on her shoulder and whispers something that I thought I would never hear. "I don't want to kill you like your mother. I can't do that to you. Please be the daughter I raised you to be and listen to commands." His booming voice doesn't even make Lindsey flinch. Her eyes remain stone-cold, and her jaw clenched. I know the look she is giving the man I now know is her father, and it's not a good one. That is the look of someone wishing to have a chance to do something to cause pain.

Lindsey doesn't reply to her father's commands to back down, and as he grabs her roughly, my blood begins to boil. His hands claim Lindsey's shoulders, and he quickly knocks her down to her knees and then lowers himself to speak to her again.

"Listen to me. You aren't as dangerous as you think. You don't have a reputation. I do. I made you what you are. I gave you the reputation that people fear. You aren't the Lethal Woman. You are just a wrinkle in my story." Her father glances around the room and then locks eyes with me before looking back at his daughter. "And you know that you can't stop me. I have an army. What do you have? A selfish boy who can't even defend himself?"

As he finishes speaking, he strikes her across the face. The force knocks her sideways. Her hands fly forward to try and catch herself. Lindsey ends up failing, and her head hits the concrete with a startling *thunk*. As I watch her eyes close, my heart seems to stop. My breath follows suit. This can't be the end, can it?

From the articles I've read, the pictures I've seen, I should have known. Deep down, I think Lindsey knew all along. The pain in my chest spreads and is almost about to explode when the man pointing his gun at me turns toward Lindsey. She is still unmoving, her head turned toward me. I can see the blood still dripping from her face. The new wound on her lip is wide, and the crimson blood is trailing down her chin.

I force myself to look away. My eyes trail on the man that is threatening to take everything that I have ever loved. As he paces back and forth, my eyes follow him, and they never waver.

"Why did you come back after all these years? You ruined everyone's lives. If you wanted out of everything, why didn't you just leave? Why did you have to kill

Mom? She did nothing to you." I turn toward the voice, Lindsey's bloodied face is touching the ground, but her eyes are open now.

Lindsey's voice is filled with pure agony, and it breaks my heart. Lindsey lost her mom in an extremely brutal way. As I look at the monster in front of me, I know that my mother is alive somewhere, having a great time. I can live without her, but Lindsey and her brother were ripped from their mother's semi-loving arms. I can live on knowing my mother wants nothing to do with me, I can live with that, but this…is and must be hell in Lindsey's mind, finally knowing the truth about her mother's death.

Lindsey slowly pushes herself onto her feet. She wobbles a tiny bit as she directs her shaking yet angry voice to her father, "You are no man. You are a coward with no heart. You have destroyed everything that our family has ever created. You are wrong. I am dangerous. I still have what she taught me. And you are no soldier, you are weak and selfish, and I will kill you when I get a chance. Mark my words, *otets*."

Wolf laughs. Deeply and wholly, he laughs at his daughter's threat.

Her father pulls out his gun. His arm sags under the weight, and he points his weapon directly at Lindsey. "I should just kill you now." Wolf's lips thin and become tense like wire. Lindsey doesn't even look away. It's a challenge to see who's weaker. Neither one wants to stand down, and I know that someone will have to take a bow.

"Then do it already." Lindsey spits, her eyes wide but confident. She quickly looks at me, and I can see the sorrow and regret in her eyes. As we look at each other, my heart shatters.

"No. No, no, no." My words spill out, but no one is listening. Lindsey keeps looking at me. A friendly face is the last thing she wants to see, and I am the closest thing to that. "Kill me, but let him go, Dad." Bargaining for me, Lindsey smiles sadly and calmly at me.

"What are you suggesting?" Wolf limbers toward Lindsey, their equal eyes blazing.

"Give him mercy." Lindsey doesn't miss a beat nor does she step back when her father is a minor inch from her face.

"Turn it off, Lindsey. Turn off the human side of yourself. Trust me, it will make what I'm about to do so much easier for you to bear."

"No," striking her hand out, Lindsey slaps the gun to the side. A bullet is fired, and it hits the metal framing of the warehouse. No one looks because all eyes are on the father-daughter duo. "Give him mercy."

A meticulous smile forms on her father's face, seeming to know that this is one thing that his daughter won't stand down from. "For you, Lindsey," Wolf licks his reddening lips. "I will give him mercy, but consider this the only deal we shall make." Lindsey nods, accepting the blow that is about to come.

But noticing the movement of Wolf's index finger, I prepare myself. Just as Wolf pressures back the trigger, I bounce on my feet and launch myself. I didn't think about what was going to happen. I didn't have to. I knew that if nothing was done, he would have pulled the trigger, and with it aimed at Lindsey's head, she'd be dead before she hit the ground. Skidding to a stop, my body bounces off of his. But as my eyes dance with observations, I notice his finger pull in completely.

A fierce cry of panic slips from my lips, and I watch as Lindsey's body crumples to the ground in slow motion. Her eyes are wide open, her mouth sealed shut. I don't remember how I end up on the ground, with a throbbing head and a bloody nose but as I look around in the chaos, all I can do is see her.

Pale.

Still.

Silent.

Propping himself up, Wolf bellows at me, "I warned you both. I am not a bargaining man, she had her chance, and I was willing to do as she asked, for you! And Thomas, don't you know? Kings like me never die."

With a racing heart, I watch as Wolf strides over to me. "I'm invincible. No mortal can ever touch me. My legacy and story will live on forever." His voice is a simple buzz in my head as I crawl closer to Lindsey. Towering above me as I crawl, he grabs my shirt. "I am the person that lesser men and women fear. I am a man who has become a monster." Plowing his feet into the concrete by my neck, he leans down closer to my face as he drops me. "I'm not a beast, Thomas. I'm just a legend that comes and goes."

Letting me go and watching me crawl, Wolf looks down with pity at his daughter. "Lindsey, you deserved better," his eyes lock with mine as he looks down upon his daughter. "But I warned you. I didn't want to hurt you. But," with a sick laugh, he just shrugs. "I never said I wouldn't, though."

I rest my hand upon Lindsey's arm. She is deathly pale and clammy. Blood is pooling under her, and I know I should have done what was promised. As I look into her eyes, I make a vow that I will fully act upon. No more half measures. I chose a half measure when I should have gone all the way.

With my blood boiling and tears spilling, I whisper: "It's time to end this."

Chapter 19

No Half Measures

Looking into her stormy eyes, there is this empty feeling inside. It hasn't loosened its hold on me, and I don't think it ever will. Stuck forever, I feel like my heart is giving out.

I know that something isn't right.

I know that deep down, this is what these people wanted; they were never after the Pavlovs, just the last Vasiliev that everyone knows about. All along, they wanted the one person who could stop them to bow, and they finally got to her because they used me. From the beginning, I was the pawn used to bring down the queen. Lindsey had no idea. I had no idea.

My father knew, though. And he let them hurt her. He allowed them to come for us.

Dropping, my body gives out.

Sinking down, I cradle Lindsey's upper body in my arms and try to soothe her agony. Lindsey is in pain. It is evident all over her face.

The wincing, the drawing of her limbs into her body, and the vast amount of times I've seen her shut her eyes and swear.

The silence is the worst part for me.

The fact that they are so sure that this is the end.

Shading back to the memory, I can see them through

my dreary eyes. Everyone vanished as her body hit the floor. Her father spoke his words and left, his gun still pointed to the floor as he strode away from Lindsey and me. By leaving me behind, is this his form of mercy? Let me forever feel the regret and knowing that I am the one that brought Lindsey to her death?

He didn't even bother to finish the fight he wanted so badly. He left me standing, and he just allowed one bullet to hit Lindsey. His cockiness, I hope, will become his downfall.

I can still see it; clearly, I watch as he stalks away. He doesn't even bother to glance back once. He just leaves his only daughter to die. It's a loose end that he doesn't bother to tie shut.

"He should have made sure to finish us both." I say, grinding my teeth together.

A chill settles over me, and my body rattles to no end. Every noise or jostle of the wind sends my nerves into fight mode. Ready to defend us both.

But looking down at Lindsey's withering form, I know that she won't make it much longer if she doesn't get medical attention.

So…I set aside my fear and assumptions and kick myself into gear.

I take her hand like I've been doing for the past five minutes. I can't bring myself to let her go. But her eyes are glazed over in agony, and her body keeps shaking. The wound is wide, and blood is everywhere.

It pools around her in a way a thoughtless man like me can understand.

I can't tell how bad it truly is, but I know that it can't be good from the look of it.

I take her hand, knowing that I have to do

something. "We have to go. You made me promise you to follow the plan, and I will. He won't get away with this." The unbearable tears start to roll down my cheeks, and I frown deeply. Making sure that Lindsey is semi-comfortable on the concrete, I pocket her keys and watch as her blood smears onto my jeans.

Not taking any more time, I stand from my position, her body gently hitting the concrete below her. As I'm about to turn, her hand grasps mine. Blood is all along her limb, her fingers dark from trying to stop the bleeding. Her eyes are no longer vexed, her body no longer shakes. This is the Lindsey I know. This is the woman who *claimed* her title. This is the woman that makes my heart leap.

She doesn't let go, but she struggles to swallow, and then she speaks, "Take my phone. Te…tell Johnny the code word. And no matter the cost, stop my dad. He needs to be stopped. Otherwise, he'll keep destroying this world." With every word, her voice gets weaker, and as soon as her hand drops from my arm, I shake.

"No, Lindsey, come on. I can get you to the car."

Her eyes open, and my fear diminishes when I see the starlight blue. "Stop them," is all she says as she turns away from me as much as she can.

"Lindsey, come on, we can get—" She shakes her head and claws at the wet fabric of her shirt. "Just go. Find them, and get Jonathan." She smiles, and her reddened lips shine, and it makes me forget about the cold. "I can hold on. You just need to go. They will be back. You can't be here when *he* returns."

"Lindsey, no—" I try to get her in my arms, but she slaps at my chest.

"They will be back, so I can stop them when they

do," with a cough, she sets her eyes on mine. "Go!" And my body begins to bolt for the door.

"Stay awake, all right?" I shout as my legs carry me forward. "Just hold on. I'm going to get help." I hate myself for this. This is stupid. I can get her help, call her brother, and track her father simultaneously.

But, as the cold claws at my lungs, I run and run. I run until the door is in front of me, and I run even after I claw my way up the steep incline of dirt that the assholes must have done. Just as I peel outside, the world seems to stop. The hollow, mourning sounds of the forest in front of me offer no calm. Everything inside of me is screaming, pleading, growling. This can't be over. I made a promise, and so did she.

I scrabble up the incline, and as I do so, I begin to cry. I never thought that I would full-blown weep at any point in my life, and in the past forty-eight hours, a lot has proven to me that things change. Images of Lindsey's smile, her laugh, her scolding, her strong look flood me. Images of her flash as I search the car for her phone that I know she left in here. My hands brush over something cold and rough as I dig under the seat.

With a fierce tug, I pull the simple cased phone into my hand. A small picture of a dog is pinned to the bright screen. A smile crosses my face as I remember Shadow. But as soon as the good memory comes, it's gone. As I put the car in drive, I make a claim that it's for them.

I'm not letting another single person down. Not again. That is something I promise to myself.

"Not again," I whisper to myself. "Never."

The mud clings to the wheels and makes the chance of getting down this hill harder. As the car pushes forward by my blind eyes, I keep thinking of her. All that keeps coming to me are images of Lindsey on the ground and her eyes completely blank of life.

The thought is too much to bear, and with my eyes focused but full of tears, I continue to try and see through the pelting raindrops. I keep my left hand on the wheel and grab Lindsey's phone from my lap. It's so fragile to me. It might be the last memorable piece of her I will have left. As the car slows and the light turns red, I dial Jonathan's number. He is my last hope, our last chance. He needs to answer.

My fingers shake as I tap the screen where she once did as well. Fingerprints are almost nowhere to be seen, but I can see where she last touched it. With a strike of confidence, I tap Jonathan's name and press the phone to my ear.

As it rings, I become so cold, so numb, and my shoulders wobble as a clean sob leaps from me. "Lindsey? I was worried. Where is Thomas? What happened to the plan?" I shake my head and refuse to let the tears fall…again.

I take a shaky breath and attempt to explain. "Jonathan." My voice cracks as my voice forms his name. "Lindsey is wounded. We need to get help as fast as we can. I will go to the safe house as she planned, and can you get her help? Can you get to her? She refused to leave with me." I breathe softly and wait for what Jonathan will say next.

"Wait, slow down. She was hurt? How bad?" His voice breaks as he speaks the words he probably never wanted to hear in this mission.

"It's bad, but she made me promise to catch her…your dad." There is silence on the other end. I know that he is trying to figure everything out. This was not part of the plan. I was supposed to escape, get to the safe house, and signal Jonathan's cue to swarm in and help defeat the bad guy trying to destroy lives.

I should have known. Nothing goes according to plan.

At least not when I'm involved.

"Thomas, listen to me. He will come back, he always does, and I need you there when he comes back to finish the job."

Squinting through the fatigue in my eyes, I question Jonathan for a second. "How am I supposed to handle him? Lindsey is on her deathbed, and…I-I-I can't take Wolf out. Lindsey wanted me out of there—"

Stopping me, Jonathan continues, "I will try to get there in a few minutes. It sounds like you are in a car right now. Turn around and get back to her. Keep her safe until I can get there. And no matter how much she fights you, stand your ground. Don't let her be alone when they come back. She can't do this on her own."

Hold my ground against her? Hold my ground against a murderous father? My heart beats a little too fast as I turn briskly. I try and listen to what Jonathan will say next. But no words come through.

"Jonathan? Please, tell me what to do! I'm freaking out. I can't stop this psycho dad of yours without you. Lindsey also told me to go. She will be so angry when she sees me walk through that door." Panic trembles through me. There is so much agony and fear inside of me. My heart feels like it will explode. My head feels so flustered. Questions and worries won't leave me alone as I go back to her.

"Listen to me, Thomas. You are her only hope." I can hear slamming and clicking in the background, and then Jonathan's voice comes through again. "Believe me, I am almost there. Just get back. If they come, you have to stall. If they aren't holding her, don't leave her alone, and when I come, we can get her all the help in the world." Jonathan cuts himself off, seeming to need a moment to collect himself. "But catching Wolf is important. He is a wanted man. It's because of him that Lindsey and I are feared but also hated."

Nothing he just said helped me. As I pull up to the last red light, I figure out what has to be done. No more twists. It's time to finally do something that will actually work till the end.

Just as the light turns green and I pull onto the backroad, I realize that I wasn't as far away as I once thought. Knowing that Jonathan is right, I floor the gas but also try to get my mind clear to come up with a plan.

I can see the warehouse in front of me. I pull up to the front and find no cars or people. Jumping from my seat and slamming the door shut, I run to her. I run to Lindsey, the one person who has ever had me feel this fear of losing someone, but also this sheer amount of joy by just seeing her smile. She's the only person in so long that has made me feel alive.

I can finally say that I'm running to the one person who has my heart fully, and she is completely unaware of it. Pulling my arm back, I open the heavy metal door and stop dead in my tracks.

What I see before me makes my heart stop. My pulse jumps in my throat, and I nearly choke on the image.

I bring my hands through my hair, and I open my mouth to scream out of complete frustration. But no matter how much I want to, I can't seem to look away.

With my eyes still watery, I weep out a plea that I hope will be heard, "Please, put the gun down."

Chapter 20

The Burdens We Bear

I can see him, and he can see me. His eyes rack me, and my eyes watch him carefully. My eyes are blurry and unfocused, but my arm is still steady and calm as it holds my gun trained on the figure.

As I stand there, my heart flutters. My heart has been leaping for what seems like hours, even though I know it has only been minutes. My body aches in ways that only could come before death. But now, with a heavy breath and an enormous headache, I lower my gun.

Seeing Thomas standing there with the door open, his hands and arms covered in my blood, I only know at that moment a heart is on the line. Thomas looks at me with shielded eyes and a dependent frown, but he doesn't step any closer.

I close my eyes, and with the last ounces of strength I have left, I move to try and find somewhere to sit, my hands resting on things in front of me and my boot-attired feet ever so heavy. The pain in my lower abdomen is starting to fester, and the blood is still not clotting in any way. As I look at the wound, I know it will need surgery and recovery time, but deep down, I'm panicked about how bad it might be.

With a hiss, I lower myself upon a crate, and with the audible noise ringing through the warehouse,

Thomas makes his way to me, his hands ringed together and shaking. His hair is puffy with curls but matted with sweat. His hands hover over my shoulders as if he doesn't know where to place them.

My whole body aches, not in a satisfying soreness after a workout is completed but in an aching way of your body telling you something is wrong. Thomas takes my hand and presses his free hand's palm to my forehead. A river of sweat is slowly cascading down my temple. My legs and arms feel unstable, and with the amount of blood that is traveling its way through my black shirt, I know that time is running out.

The air has become cold and stale. The adrenaline that was once keeping me warm is gone. With shivers running through me, I try to stand, but nothing wants to work, and my vision has become clouded. How can I protect someone if I can't even see straight? Swinging my weight forward, I try to find an easy way to stand, but suddenly strong arms keep me locked in place.

"You need to stay down. You are using too much energy, and I promised your brother I would keep you safe no matter how mad I make you." Pulling my hands up to my matted hair, feeling suddenly exhausted and just tired of it all, I give into Tom's words. "Are you all right?" I ask Thomas. Not sure what happened after I blacked out for a minute while everyone streamed out.

Sighing, Thomas runs a hand through my hair, soothing an inch of my pain. "I'm well. I'm breaking. I'm scared." His list is noticeable in his stance. Faintly, I will a smile on my face. Trying to keep Thomas calm, I offer, "Everything will be fine."

Thomas scoffs but then pushes my drenched hair away from my ears. Toying with it, he pulls me back into his chest, so I'm leaning on him. "I hope so. I couldn't live with myself if you don't pull through."

"Thomas," I try to say through my cottonmouth. "Nothing here was your fault. You tried. You listened."

"I got caught," he chokes on his words. "If the door wasn't so stiff, I could have gotten out of here in time. I could have gotten help. I would have been able to save you."

Shakily, I brush my hand along Tom's stubbed jaw. Stroking his cheek, I feel him lean into the movement. Grinning, I comment, "You did save me."

"I got you shot," Thomas scolds through a thick voice. "I tried to take him down, and he pulled the trigger. I got you shot." Brushing his cheek even harder, I get him to listen to me. "No. Thomas, he had that gun aimed at my head. I would be dead right now if you hadn't done what you did."

Nodding numbly at my own words, I just feel so worn out and used to the bone. My body pleads for rest, and as I shut my eyes, I feel myself falling. But Tom's chest catches me. His arms loop around me.

"Stay awake, darling." His command comes out in a cooing voice. Slowly, even his words fade as the pressure within me becomes too much.

The weight that has been carried on my shoulders for years and the burdens of what I've done ultimately keep me grounded to Earth right now. Closing my eyes for just a second longer than normal turns into the worst idea possible. Now they don't want to open to see the broken world around me.

With my eyes closed, I place my hand on Thomas' arm and softly whisper a strange request. "Do you know any poetry? Can you tell me something? Just speak to me, please." All I can hear is his footsteps moving from my side to in front of me, his hands resting on my shoulders to keep me from falling any farther. "I have a better idea."

I can't answer, so I just nod. I need to focus on something other than the pain rippling through my stiff body. Thomas clears his throat, and he slowly speaks in a heartbreaking manner. "Just let me do this," His hands on my shoulders are strong and firm yet reassuring. My eyes drift up to his, and suddenly it is over. Slowly and gaspingly, his lips caught at mine. Slow and then hard, he drives my lips apart with the force of his need. The fingers that cling to my shoulders lean me in closer to him. Every thought in my head vanishes into a pure, pounding white, and as soon as I saw the light, it darkened so quickly that a gasp of fear ripped through me.

With the fear of the darkness inching in closer, I push at his chest. "No," he says, growling in the back of his throat. He brings my lips back to his. And just like that, as it was before—with the light and the darkness, I cave in to Tom's chest. Looping my hands under his jacket, I pull him close, finally admitting what I fear the most. As he chooses to part this time, a small, needy whine slips from his lips.

Slowly opening his eyes, Thomas swallows deeply. "You aren't leaving me," is all he says as he loops his arms around me and tries to get me to my feet.

Thomas holds onto me tighter, and I feel his breath fanning my sweaty face. A thin layer of sheen coats me, and I know from the way Thomas is looking at me that I look as if I'm knocking on a door I thought I wouldn't be so close to.

Breathing slowly and grasping my sore hand, Thomas stutters the rest of the words. "We will get you out of this." The rough, gravel tone in his voice still lingers deep in my mind. All this time, the hiding, the acts of being a jerk to others, I wish I could take it all back.

He comes from a rich family, and therefore I thought that he would be smug and slap everything that goes wrong in my face. But he never did. He always keeps himself in check. My heart pounds as everything starts to spin around me. The room that was once still continues to shake as my eyes keep collapsing closed.

Feeling my body sway, my body stumbles. Hands catch me. They hold me still as my body trembles. "Relax," Thomas says as he rubs at my back. "I've got you, Linds."

Reaching out, I classp my hands around him. Feeling sick to my stomach, feeling the knots spread, vomit crawls up my throat. "Thomas," a groan spills from me.

Letting me lower to the ground, he holds back my hair as a dry cough climbs out of me.

Thomas clears his throat to begin to speak again when the metal door directly in front of us rattles as if someone is trying to fist their way in. Within a second, my mind and body go from pain-riddled to fight mode. I know that can't be my brother; he's quiet and planned. That only leaves one man, the man that swore that this time he would finish the job.

Forgetting the pain and the lingering invasion of Tom's lips on mine, I get to my feet. Standing and claiming the floor, I prepare myself for another round of bullets, but the only thing that hits my pale skin is the dancing reflections of the stars and moon above.

Fear, fear is what locks me in place.

Fear is the four-letter word that has determined my life for the past twenty years. Looking at the night sky above me, I notice movement by the window. But it is quick and almost unnoticeable, *almost.* Moving one foot in front of the other, I start to investigate. For as long as I can remember, my father has always loved to play mind games. Games that mess with your mind and send you into a frenzy to try and solve.

"Gun," I whisper to Thomas. With a demanding look, he picks it off the ground and places it in my bloody hand.

I motion to Thomas to stay down. I begin my slow travel to the opposite wall of the door. Keeping my movements low and slow, I listen. But as my feet inch on, silence lingers in the air. Knowing my father's tactics, I pick the perfect place to wait for him. I plant my body so when the door opens, he won't see me. My gun is positioned by my thigh with both hands ready. Now it's only a waiting game of when he's done trying to trick us.

Standing there waiting, memories of when he used to play this game with my brother and me come swimming back to me. As little kids, it was so scary yet so fun, but as we got older, he made every move and every action into a tactical situation that would determine which one of us died, my brother or me. Jonathan wasn't that good at the game, but he always won. I didn't want to win against my brother or my father. I only cared about my father's actions. He thought that I wasn't paying attention or that I just didn't care; he had it all wrong. I was preparing for this very day. I was preparing for the day I knew he would turn against me.

I was hiding myself the way he taught us. I seem to be always playing against his game.

Just behind this door, he could be standing there waiting for one of us to be stupid and open that door. But I'm not stupid, and I refuse to let him do any more harm, and in between the heavy winds and raindrops plowing the roof, I swear I can almost hear his footsteps.

Looking to my side, I can't see Thomas. He has packed himself away behind the metal cabinet in the corner. Smiling, knowing that he is out of sight, I prepare myself. I plead with the heavens above for one more chance, or at least for Tom's safety. That is all I want. I want Thomas to be able to get out of this. I want him to survive this. I want him to move on, have a life, have a family. I want him to help people like he wants to.

I just want Thomas to survive this night.

With the rattling of the doorknob, I come out of my thoughts and brace. And with the slow creak of the hinges, I prepare myself. The door opens, and I slowly raise my gun to a pointed position.

I wait a few calculated seconds, and then I swing the door closed, drawing my father's attention squarely to me. With my gun pointed out and ready to fire, I say one final prayer through foggy eyes, but I'm met with a collapsing amount of force that knocks me to my knees.

Cracking down to the floor, a shudder of panic runs through me.

A pair of matching eyes meet mine, and there is no mercy in them, so as quickly as I pull the trigger blindly, my eyes close for what feels like the final time.

As quickly as I pull the trigger, I feel like there is resolution.

And this time, my eyes close without the aid of pain but with the help of peace that swarms my mind and cleanses my senses. Unconsciously, my mind clicks off. There are no more movements to be heard, no more actions to be completed. In my mind, this is it. I did it. I harmed the man that planned to end me.

I don't know if I killed him, but I hope I did. I feel myself sprawling out along the cold floor. Now, I remind myself before I fall any deeper into the darkness, Jonathan should be here soon. He can handle the rest. He can guide Thomas out. He can make sure that our father is done with his reign.

Smiling faintly, I can feel arms pulling at me, but the movements are useless. My body no longer feels. My mind, empty of worry for once, clears. My eyes shut tight, don't even register the darkness. My limbs, slightly tingling, have no ounce of strength to move.

Thankfully, I begin my count and list my needs. One, keep Thomas alive; two, tell my brother I'm sorry; three, give me peace no matter where I go. As my brain travels over three, a faint sigh is audible to my own ears, and just like that, everything all at once goes dark.

Just like a light clicking off, at first it's alarming, then suddenly, you adjust. And then…you just float away.

Chapter 21

Words Left Unsaid

People say that what doesn't kill you makes you stronger; bullshit. People say that failure can teach you a lesson; but only if you know what you did wrong.

There is so much pain in this world that in order to mask it we're told to learn from it. Sitting on the cold concrete floor with the moon just barely rising I'm left to wonder what I did wrong.

There was a plan, there was a course of action but yet I'm still holding an ever more wounded Lindsey in my weakened arms. Everything was flipped upside down in a matter of seconds, I realize now that once a bullet is fired it can't be wished back into the chamber, and the damage can't be undone either. No matter how hard you try, you can never take back what has already been done or said.

That bullet that her father fired can't be taken back, and neither can hers. With her still body in my arms, I can't help but replay what happened the second the door came flying open. It was like any other horror film, the bad guy almost always knows just the right place to look. The second he stepped through the threshold he turned and fired. There was no time for me to jump forward and hit him or anything; he just opened the door, then fired.

The rain and wind stopped and now I'm left with the

silence that is eating me alive. Jonathan said a few minutes, he swore he would be here but he's not. *He swore…*

Lindsey was right everything went to shit when I found out the truth, I only wished that I told her how I feel earlier. In order to calm my racing mind, I rock back and forth. As my body shifts, I watch Lindsey's feet, the thickness of her boots skid on the concrete but her legs stay bent at an awkward angle. This is what's left of the soldier that I first met, and the only reason why she's crumbled on the floor is because of me. I wouldn't pick up the gun, didn't run fast enough, I got scared. And now she might die because of me.

Everyone I've ever loved leaves one way or another.

Maybe I'm just not supposed to love anyone.

Shaking, I plant a kiss on Lindsey's temple. Clammy, I mutter, "I should have taken that last bullet. Why do I always feel like you purposely do these things?"

Silence. No words, just the slight howl from the wind outside.

Taking Lindsey's hand and linking her fingers through mine, I tell her, knowing that she can't hear me, "I think I've fallen for you."

Chuckling, I nod to myself. "It's stupid. We haven't known each other for long, but when I'm with you all the pain that I felt disappeared. When I'm on my own I don't do so well, but you taught me how to find strength within myself, Linds."

Crying, and clutching her even tighter into my body I set the world around me ablaze as my hands rack through all the blood that is clotted to Lindsey's clothes. "Please don't leave me," I murmured into Lindsey's filthy hair.

Inhaling deep breaths of loneliness, I try to find the small things that remind me of Lindsey's flawless character, but her scent is nonexistent. It's just blood, some bile fills the air and sweat. Lindsey's coconut scent isn't around me anymore to calm the storm that is swelling in my heart.

"Thomas!" A scream of a voice startles me from the depths of self-pity. "Thomas! Where are you?" The voice doesn't resonate with me until the face floats into my line of sight. The slicked-back hair and scruff of a beard almost makes me leap back out of fright. Clutching Lindsey closely to my heart I move backward with the last bit of strength in my legs.

"Tom, hey, listen to me." Jonathan settles on the ground beside me for a second. "Stay still, she's losing a lot of blood and every time you move it might make things a hell of a lot worse." Jonathan's voice just floats toward me and then vanishes. Focusing isn't an option for me at this moment. But when he sinks down to my level and I see his eyes, I try to focus.

"Lindsey…" My mind goes blank, unable to recall what I wanted to tell Jonathan. "… she will be fine, right?" I ask him, knowing he can't give me an answer.

Jonathan's intense eyes make me want to break down, my heart is screaming with fear and everything around me seems blurry. His footsteps head in the direction in which his father's body lay. I'm too far to see, and I'm too far to even care. My heart is set on getting Lindsey medical attention first.

Letting go of Lindsey, I command myself to release the woman that I feel myself beginning to love. "I did this," I tell Jonathan, not knowing if he is listening to me or not.

Watching Jonathan as he checks his father, I feel bitterness swarm within me. Wolf Vasiliev can rot in hell for all I care. I want Lindsey to live, not the man that enjoys killing his own family.

"He's still alive, and knowing him, he'll make it. The bastard heals just fine." A part of his voice is full of silent hate that I almost missed. Jonathan comes up to me and crouches down on his feet, close to my face he whispers, "I have to move her so I can see the wounds, okay? Thomas I need you to let her go, all the way. I need to help her." His words take a while to settle in and connect with my brain. I raise my arms from her shoulders and slowly scoot away so I won't be in the way.

As Jonathan goes silent, I flip my hands over and stare at all the blood. Shaking, my fingers wrap into fists. "What have I done?"

Jonathan looks at the first wound, the recent one that penetrated her thigh. He takes a strip from his shirt and wraps it around the wound. He ties it as tight as it can possibly go. He stops and looks at me, dead in the eyes, "You didn't do a damn thing. This isn't on you, Thomas." Reeling back at the harshness in his tone, I feel my heart leap to my throat.

Sinking to look at the extent of Lindsey's wounds, a sob rips through me. The wounds are deep and now I understand why she passed out as quickly as she did. Between the trauma that she has already faced and now with the bullet in her leg, that's a lot of blood to lose and still stay conscious.

Watching Jonathan as he works on Lindsey I pay close attention from my place on the cold filthy floor. His hands slowly raise the hem of her blood-soaked shirt. The flesh is red and sticky as he tries to separate the cloth from the laceration. I can still see the blood seeping onto the floor and pooling around her. Jonathan and I both look at Lindsey's blank, and empty face. She is so pale, so colorless. This shell isn't Lindsey.

But the examination doesn't last long as we both hear a groan from a short distance away.

Their father is sitting upright, his knee covered in blood, but besides that, the man remains untouched. His eyes hold an emptiness, and his spine-chilling smile remains on his face as he looks at Lindsey; his own daughter. His eyes travel from his son to me and back to Lindsey. His eyes blazed with anger as he stares at Jonathan.

"I thought you were dead. She lied to me, you lied to me. I didn't raise liars." Jonathan doesn't stop from what he's doing. It's as if his father's words don't even cause a dent in his armor.

His hands are now covered in his sister's blood, very much like mine are. Without turning to his father he speaks words that I never thought the suit-wearing man would ever say. "You're right you didn't raise liars, you trained killers. Now tell me, how does it feel to kill your own flesh and blood?" Stopping, Jonathan points a bloody finger at his father. "Do you feel remorse? Do you see the life slipping away from your daughter!" Jonathan stands and in a few stiff steps, he is right in front of his father. "You betrayed us all and I hope you can live with that."

The man's face wrinkles into a crooked smile and he chuckles a reply that makes my blood run cold, "I found a way to live with the blood on my hands, but what about you? Both of you?" Wolf's eyes land on mine. "No one is truly good and no one can rewrite the past. My heart is something that never settles. I made my sacrifice, but are either of you two willing to surrender what you love to make your destiny worth it?"

Jonathan looks at me with a scold on his face, but his eyes hold a secret. I think both of us are thinking about the true answers to the twisted man's questions.

"Killing those that I love for my destiny will never be worth it. If I have to destroy to get what I want, then kill me." Jonathan's bright eyes never leave his father's. "I will refuse to become like you."

My heart races as I think about my father. He sacrificed so much for me, but what did I ever do for him? Left him to die? Lindsey, she is bleeding to death because of me, and how can I ever repay her for that? How can I possibly repay her for being willing to walk through fire to save me?

"Cat got your tongue?" Wolf's voice makes me want to cower and hide, but as I sit on the floor and wait for the paramedics to arrive I tell myself to hold strong because Lindsey did. I know that if she can face her past, face a man that killed God knows how many people then so can I. But the silence doesn't last long as a wail of a siren blares through the building. It's faint, but at least the wait is over. I stand from my sitting position, my body tense and alert once again. Jonathan stays crouched next to Lindsey with his head almost touching the ground, his hands keeping pressure on the major gunshot wound.

"Thomas..." Wolf says my name in a sing-song way. Not meeting his eyes, I ignore him. But as I do, Wolf's voice begins to make my skin crawl with unease.

"I warn you now, Thomas, the world will never be safe. People will betray the ones they were once allies with. The traitors will be named, blood will still be spilled." After he says the word 'blood' Wolf looks at a paling Lindsey. "Lies will still be spoken and sacrifices will continue to be made for the greater good. Once one challenge is defeated, another will take its place." Chuckling, Wolf just leans back on his hands, not even bothering to put up a fight. "Mankind will fall to its knees and beg for mercy. But you wanna know something? Mercy won't come. Nothing will come because nothing can save you. This is not the end for you." The sirens are getting closer but my eyes are getting foggier. My heart continues to hammer in my chest making it hard to breathe. Pain spreads through my arms, and my soul seems to rip away from me.

"The sacrifice of my daughter can't spare you from the debt that must be paid. The only reason why you are alive right now is the fact that my daughter took your place." Wolf laughs mechanically. "But one day someone will come and there will be no one standing in their way to end you. Be warned everything comes with a price and one day you're going to have to pay your own debt with the cost of your life."

As the sirens narrowed in, my knees buckle and my hips shift. "You can't run from this," Wolf keeps talking, but I don't feel the impact when my body collides with the ground. All I can feel is regret choking the life out of me. And my heartbeat is slowing for the first time in what feels like a decade.

I just let myself sink under the weight of what I've done and those I have failed. Shutting my eyes, lightly touching my throbbing head, I press myself harder against the ground.

Wolf's right. The bastard is right. Everyone ends up paying the price for me. Never have I ever faced a situation on my own, but now as my mind clicks and shouts rings out throughout the space my eyes become glued shut.

The darkness behind my eyes is similar to that of the warehouse. Hoping that my eyes stay shut forever, I clench my teeth together and ram my head into the concrete floor with all the self-hate that I have gathered throughout my life.

Shouts, screams, and hands claw at me as I do it one more time for good measure. An eerie and oddly familiar laugh cuts through my final thoughts and the icky *thunk* as my mind shifts off from the blow.

Chapter 22

Far From Okay

The fluorescent lighting above my head makes me squint my eyes. The antiseptic scent hits my nostrils like a brick to the face. Everything aches, body, mind, and soul. But my heart hurts the most. It's the guilt keeping me pinned to the bed that hugs my defeated body.

Like barbed wire cutting at my skin, I feel the need to stay still. To not move. To not breathe. Closing my eyes again, I feel the weight of the drugs running through my veins keeping me slow and unmannered. Gasping as I attempt to rise, I ram back down and bury my head in my pillow.

The tube in my nose tickles, and the wires connected to my chest feed my heart rate to the machine. The rhythm of my broken heart is the only sound found in my room. The silence around me seeps into my bones, making my head and heart even heavier.

I don't deserve to be here. It should have been me who took the bullet. I understand it now; she was willing to give up her life because, in her mind, it was a call to redemption. I don't know much about her last mission, but the way it ended, I should have known that she refused to let a client get hurt again. As my thoughts continue to stir, my head hurts even more. Gently trying to tug the tubes from my nose, I stop when I hear movement in the hall. No one comes, but the sudden realization that I'm watched makes me leave the breathing nubs in.

"Lindsey," I croak her name, wanting information. "I need—" Starting to speak, I stop when the dryness in my throat makes me cough. God, it's my fault. It's all my fault. If I never met Lindsey, she would probably be fine right now, on another mission and guarding someone else, someone more worthy than me. Someone they couldn't use against her. Someone who isn't such a coward.

I should have known she would do something like this. When Amanda made that guest visit to Lindsey's house, and part of the truth came out, I should have known…Harrison. She loved him, and he got killed because she couldn't save him. Now it might be my turn to lose someone I love deeply. I refuse to let that happen. I can't lose her. But her life isn't in my hands. There is nothing to be done but wait on God.

A groan slips from my lips as I try to get into an upright position. My fingers fiddle with the white plastic railing along my bed. I try to level myself up a little, so I gain some ground to see my surroundings. As my head rises from the pillow, my head spins, and the cotton feeling in my mouth and throat makes me gag as my eyes fog over. As soon as my eyes regain some form of level sight, a desperate sigh seeps from my cracked lips. "Lindsey," I repeat, trying to get up so I can find her.

The gray hallway is staring at me. The emptiness of it makes my fear grow. What if Lindsey didn't make it? What if Jonathan hates me? Where is their father? The heart monitor is screaming, but it only makes me panic more. The unanswered questions rack through me.

Everything seems to make me worry. I know that everything that has happened is because of me. My father may have started it, but I shouldn't have been so blind to it. The taps of heavy footsteps silence the commotion rambling inside me.

A pale and wrinkled Jonathan steps through the doorway. My heart rate speeds up as his face remains blank. He strolls into the room, and his eyes hold a wattage of silence. Looking at me, Jonathan gives a small nod as if to himself.

He walks closer and leans his body weight on the foot of my bed. His exhale worries me to the point that the monitor sings the truth of what I'm feeling. Jonathan looks at the rising lines for a while and then looks directly at me for the first time since walking in. He sighs and bends his head low, and pulls his shoulders back. Gently, he just rests his hands in his lap, unmoving.

With his head still hanging low, he speaks for the first time since walking in. "She's weak. And pale and so damn stubborn." Jonathan stands straight, walks to the corner, and pulls a chair closer to me. With force and exhaustion, he flops into the chair and runs his shaking hands through his very mussed hair.

He looks worse than I probably do. At least I got some sleep, even if it was forced. Jonathan takes in the silence and shuts his eyes. As he does, I watch him. "It's good to have you awake, Tom." Jonathan's voice is low, mournful, but tender. He lays a hand on his head, smoothing down some loose hairs. His hair is still, but the wisps of age seep through and the bundles aren't held back by gel anymore. But as I long to hear more about Lindsey, I just let Jonathan accept the silence. From his hunched shoulders, wrinkled shirt that is rung with blood, and his pants creased from all the sitting, I know that Lindsey and I both left him wondering on his own.

Looking up at him, our eyes meet. "I'm sorry." I mutter through a thick tongue. "I didn't—"

Holding up a hand, Jonathan cuts me off. "Again, Thomas, none of this was your fault." Blinking rapidly, Jonathan offers a gentle smile. "She fought to save you for a reason, so be worthy of that saving. And stop apologizing to me, you didn't bring this upon us."

Locking my fingers together on my stomach, I mutter, "My father did."

After the confession to Jonathan, we both fall silent.

Not knowing what to say, we listen to the sounds of the hospital. I can hear footsteps and the beeping of someone being paged. In this bed, in the silence, I wish for Lindsey.

I plead for her.

Itching to be beside her, my mind attempts to find a way to ask Jonathan the question that has been eating away at me since he walked in here.

Not being able to take it anymore, with wide eyes and a racing heart, I ask the question that has been weighing heavily on my mind. "Did she…Will she make it?" Jonathan bows his head, and his eyes become a bright blue as they fill with tears. He doesn't look at me for a while. He closes his eyes again, not letting me read through him. Hiding what he feels, he doesn't allow me to see his hurt.

"In all honesty?" Jonathan touches the air with his voice. "I have no idea. She crashed once. She lost so, so much blood. She's in surgery right now." Flipping his arm over, Jonathan glances at his watch. "God, Thomas, what if she doesn't make it? She's always been the strong one. She knows how to help me. What will happen if she doesn't wake up?" His tears cause tracks along his cheeks, and for the first time since I've seen him, I see a man full of so much hidden pain.

His shoulders shake from the rocking cries that echo from his mouth. The muffled and silent scream coming from his mouth makes me look away from his face. He deserves a cry. As his tears travel down, his body slumps in the chair, leaving him like a shadow of who he used to be. He is no longer the strong man with a stiff business suit, his hair is no longer set in place, and his clear eyes are clouded.

His strength has been chipped away, and I never thought it would. But I understand it. Being the only person awake and conscious during the first few hours of concern, I would not be willing to trade places with him. Going through the worry, the lecture of the doctors saying they will do their best, which is something I would have broken under the weight of in an hour.

"She'll make it," I say with confidence as I attempt to pat Jonathan's arm. "Lindsey…She's strong. A fighter. A survivor. She'll get back up from this." My voice was nearly inaudible due to the continuum of hiccuping cries. I just let Jonathan have this moment, I feel weak and just as worried, but I want him to have his time to break. Everyone needs to break from time to time. It is what keeps us healthy and in our right minds.

We all need a moment to ourselves without judgment or harassment when we break under the pressure around us.

Turning my eyes away from Jonathan, I focus on the hall that I can see over my white blanketed feet. No noises could be heard from the hall, no nurses, no doctors, no one moving throughout the corridor. I feel lost knowing that I'm lying in this bed because, being weak and stupid, I couldn't handle the pressure, so I passed out and crashed my head into the ground out of guilt. My body has the dull ache of agony, but I feel like I don't deserve the care that is coming my way. Lindsey took two bullets in order to save me, and at this moment, I don't feel like I'm worth saving.

Seeing Jonathan full of pain, the pain that I caused makes everything even heavier. Watching a powerful man crumble in front of my very eyes makes me realize that no one is truly invincible to the true forces of nature that run this world.

Silence drips into my veins through an IV that links into my arm. Jonathan stopped crying, and his eyes are closed now. My body is rattled still to the point that I can't close my eyes and rest. I listen to the monitor that reads my heart rate. I feel the rise and fall of my chest every time a breath leaves and enters my lungs.

I watch the clear morphine drip down the tube and enter my body. As my eyelids grow heavy, I continue to try and find answers in the silence. I close my eyes and think of Lindsey. Her smile, her eyes, and her strength. As I remember what she looked like lying on the dirty, cold compound floor, that's when I let the first few tears slip from my dry eyes. As the sobs rack through my body, I bring a fist to my mouth to try and muffle the screams of my torment.

The anger, the sadness, the emptiness, it all leaves me hollow as the tears fall. With every drop that slips down my face, I let a new prayer follow. Every prayer goes to Lindsey, to her safety, to her survival, and to just have her in my arms one day. Alive and well.

She has to make it. She has to recover. She has to know how I feel before it's too late. She has to know what she means to me. With all my tears out, I feel the weight lift from me as the squeak of rubber sole shoes starts to head in my direction. Without bothering to wipe my face free from the discarded saltwater, I allow my eyes to fall closed, and I begin to drift to a much safer place.

I don't want to be conscious when the nurses come in and check on me. I don't care if they see my tears, but maybe if they see me falling back asleep, they won't help me. Maybe they will all go back to focusing on Lindsey.

Truth is, I don't want to be saved unless Lindsey makes it. I don't want to live without her.

I can't face her brother's pain, they have always had each other, and if she dies, that's on me. I will be the cause for the last two remaining Vasilievs' downfall.

Now that is a weight I cannot carry.

It's a weight I refuse to hold.

I don't want to be awake to see Jonathan break down in front of me again. And I don't want to be awake while Lindsey is in surgery.

I'm too weak to face this world. My father always said so, and it is now that I truly believe him. I don't belong in this world. I don't deserve it.

I've always been weak, and now I see it.

I am not a fighter. I'm a runner. But with Lindsey, she offered me a chance to prove myself stronger. She brought a new side of me to light. She saw something in me that no one else has.

Bowing my head back, I sink. "Lindsey," I whisper in my haze as my eyes glue shut to the darkness, unable to fight without her beside me

Chapter 23

Head Above Water

It's been three days, and so far, nothing has changed.
I was released a few hours after waking up, but I didn't
leave. I can't leave. This is my world now. These people,
Lindsey and Jonathan, are my family. They need me, so
staying is what I'm left to do. No matter how much
Jonathan and I talk, everything just spins right back to
Lindsey. Lindsey, our savior, unwilling to wake up.

And now, Jonathan and I have been taking turns
sitting with Lindsey and telling her stories and just
speaking to her. Just yesterday, after the doctor
announced that all the surgeries were complete, Lindsey
could breathe without the aid of the tube down her throat.

Her main doctor smiled as he told us, "It's a sign,
boys. She's gonna keep fighting." As he turned to leave,
his smile dropped. "Now all Ms. Vasiliev has to do is
wake up."

Now, as I sit here, I feel the shift in the room. I'm
still in the same clothes from yesterday. Old faded jeans
and a button-down shirt that sags off my skinny body.
Sinking into a wakeful slumber, I look at Lindsey
through my bruised eyes. She's beautiful as she always
has been. Even while broken, Lindsey still screams
dominance. She's calm and delicate, not fragile like a
flower but like a loaded gun.

Lindsey was my *bodyguard*. She was…but she will always be my *protector*. I trust her and her alone. She shielded me. Guided. I don't want to lose that. Lindsey is more to me than a body willing to take a blow for me. She taught me to fight for myself. I owe my life to her.

But all she needs to do is wake up so I can show her how much my heart has come to crave her. How much I *need* her…

Drawing in a long breath, I shut my heavy eyes and lean my head on the side panel of her bed rails. The warm air in the room makes my already exhausted eyes sink even further against my cheeks. The heaviness of my exhaustion came after a long and extreme crying session that Jonathan and I recently shared. My tears dried up a while ago, but Lindsey didn't seem to notice. Her pale and still body makes hiccuping coughs rise from my soul. Looking at her lying on the white bed makes my heart sink to my stomach. The thick blankets are pulled tight around her torso and legs. I tap my foot as I bow my head to help me breathe, the faint noise of the machines aiding in luring me to sleep.

As I rest my head on my hands, I close my eyes and imagine what it would be like if things hadn't gone this way. I could be home, resting, clean, and not have everlasting shame hanging over my head. I could possibly have Lindsey resting beside me, with her head on my chest and my hand in her hair, but life never works the way we want it does it? We as people can never have all that we want in one moment, and if we do, it never lasts.

Shifting my eyes open, I drink in Lindsey's appearance. Lindsey's features are the same as they always are, but with extra cuts and bruises. It just seems to add to her strength and beauty. Everything is still about her. Her eyes don't even move as if she's dreaming. I find myself just sitting here, pleading for a miracle to happen. Pleading for her stormy-sky eyes to look back at me and want me as much as I want her.

I need her to be okay. I need her to keep fighting, to keep her head above water just this once. Jonathan made me promise that if she woke up, I'd call. That was four hours ago. He went back to Lindsey's house to gather her things and take them back to the new apartment that I had just bought. I read all the reviews and got all the information, and it was great. Not a lavish house, but a place where two people can heal together.

Jonathan also volunteered to go to my father's company, the company I just got legal custody of, and gather all the paperwork on the bodyguard transaction. Jonathan gathered the few personal items that I had there, and I told him to lock the place up after he left. I don't think anyone working there will be allowed to go to work for a while.

I know that everything must be in order when this case goes to court. Lindsey and Jonathan's father is finally being tried for all the wrongdoings he has done over the years, and Jonathan is choosing to tack attempted murder onto the list of crimes because of what he did to Lindsey. But the most important thing is that I need proof that my father hired her, so she won't get in trouble again. I won't let her go to jail for the shit that her dear old dad did. I won't let him run her name through the dirt. Not again and not ever, she fought for me, and now it's my turn to stand up and be a grown man.

I know that there will come a time during this case

when people will question Lindsey's motives, but as I watch over her, I just know I'll protect her, as my life depends on it. As I continue to sit here, I watch people walk up and down the halls, I sense panic stir through this restricted level for very wounded patients.

Sitting here, I've noticed that a hospital can be the best or worst place to be. The best, in a way, is like the good news of your child coming into the world, or if the diagnosis is a good one, or if that scare was a simple mistake that can be cleared up with a new medication. But the worst part of the hospital sends frightful images into my head. Images of a child's lifeless body lying on a table, or the ones you love being taken away on a stretcher, the doctor telling someone that there is nothing else that can be done. Images like that are what haunt my dreams lately.

Every time the images stir inside me, I look at Lindsey. Even with her body still, I can see the power hovering within. It's not the physical structure she has but her mental capacity and the way she thinks.

When she just looks at you, you can't help but remain silent. She demands people's attention without even knowing it. Her strength gave me the power to do something my father would be disappointed to hear. But it was the right choice. With everything that has happened, I removed myself from school. I'm far behind, the online classes were great while they lasted, but I have far more important things to do now.

I have to help Lindsey get better, and I have to take over the company that was left to me after my father was arrested at Lindsey's house by the police for fraud. I knew that he was doing illegal work, but I never thought it went this deep. He left me a money pit that has a fractured reputation. But I choose to think that I can make it better and legal—that I can get more real customers without putting everyone in danger. I believe that I can make the company run without the help of terrible people. Or deals that will come back to bite me.

As I turn my head in the direction of the sound of clicking footsteps, I'm startled to see Jonathan back so soon. His hair is spiky and messy. He is dressed in dark jeans and a black T-shirt. But what hits me like I've been slapped is that he has dark-rimmed glasses on, just like the ones I saw Lindsey wear once. I look back at Lindsey's bruised face as I try to calm my emotions. I hear Jonathan move a seat onto the other side of her bed and take her hand.

I haven't gathered the nerve to hold her hand yet. I only touched her once when her hair fell into her face, and I knew she would have hated that hair for disrupting her sight. There are just no guts left in me, I so badly want to hold her, but every time I get close enough to gather the courage, the images of what happened at that compound hit me in the chest like a brick. As I pull my chair closer to her bed, I can feel Jonathan's eyes on me.

"How long?" Jonathan asks, and confusion is evident on my face. "How long have you had feelings for my sister?" My face burns hot with embarrassment.

"Awhile," I say under my breath. "Ever since she put me in my place when I was being a royal ass." Looking at Jonathan when I say those words, I choke out the rest. "But Lindsey has always been striking to me. She just has this will about her, you know?" I know her brother could whoop my ass if he wanted to. I just want to make things clear to him while I still have the chance. I want Jonathan to know that I have the purest of intentions. Lindsey may be the Lethal Woman, but he is still her older brother.

He clears his throat and brings Lindsey's left hand to rest between his. He looks me directly in the eyes as he holds her hand. "Why her?" Pushing my head back, steady on my shoulders, I'm forced to think, knowing that Jonathan wants a real answer. "She challenges me," I begin. "She is ice while I am fire. She is calm when I am wrecked. We balance one another, and she forces me to only be myself."

Frowning, Jonathan runs a circling finger over Lindsey's scarred hand. "She wears her strength as armor. She won't let you in easily," he shifts his eyes so they fan Lindsey's pale face. "This girl has half heaven and hell in her." Jonathan leans his elbows on the bed, almost seeming to reach out to me. "You don't grow up the way we did and love easily. She will fight you, scare you, and may even hurt you, but remember, no one will be as scared as she is."

"I don't intend to hurt her, Jon." My hair falls in my face, and I let it remain as Jonathan's stormy eyes read me.

"No one ever does, Thomas."

"But I mean it," I say with enough confidence to scare myself. "I will wait. I will bow. I give her all the time she needs. She fought for me, so I will fight for her."

"It won't be easy." Jonathan drops Lindsey's hand and tucks it beside her side. "Lindsey has always withdrawn from people. She hides, and no matter how fierce she is, she always holds true fear in her heart. But you already know so much about her. I have a feeling that she will be willing to give it a try." Biting his chapped lower lip, Jonathan runs his fingers along the tip of his thumb. "Just be careful with her. Be patient. She's been through a lot. Don't make me change my mind, you got it?" I nod. There may never be another chance for me to get permission to ask her out, and I refuse to have both Vasiliev assassins on my ass.

I look with longing at Lindsey but then turn to Jonathan with a question that has been weighing heavily upon me, "Do you think she likes me too? Like, do you think she will accept my request?" Jonathan shrugs his shoulders and looks back at his younger sister with a smile on his face that I haven't seen in a long time.

"Right before the gunfight, I kissed her," I admit to Jonathan. "I kissed her twice, actually."

His eyes glow, and an assumed grin shimmers on his lips. "And she didn't kill you?" Jonathan rests his head on his hand and looks at Lindsey patiently.

"She didn't have the time to get to me. I'm sure if we were alone a little longer, she would have given me a well-defined bruise."

Chuckling, Jonathan directs his eyes to me and smiles. He speaks the words that take the weight out of my body, "Only Lindsey knows what she feels about you." Jonathan takes hold of his sister's hand again. "But my sister doesn't volunteer to take a bullet for just anybody."

Jonathan pauses as he looks me straight in the eyes. "Thomas, I know she likes you. Now make her happy and fight for her every day that follows."

Heat creeps up my neck onto my cheeks, and I attempt to tell Jonathan that I don't know if I'm there yet, but he just holds his empty hand out.

"Love her with all your heart and make me proud. Love her like no one else can. She deserves the best kind of happiness."

I can feel the heaviness in the room lift. There is no longer worry that Jonathan wants to kill me. He sees the intentions and smiles, knowing that I only have the purest motives at heart.

As I look at him, I see how much he loves his sister, and I see a little bit of her in him. He was raised by the same man, and they both experienced a crazy childhood yet still have that unbreakable bond that only siblings have. They are completely different yet remain the same.

Setting my gaze on Jonathan, I whisper with gratitude, "Thanks, mate. I will try my best to be the best man I can be."

I smile as I think about the future that I'm willing to fight endlessly for. Nothing can stand in my way now. Lindsey will never be alone because I'm going to be standing beside her and always offer my support. She saved me, and I'm willing to do my part in saving her now.

I smile wide as I take her hand and whisper three words that I thought I would never say in my life. "I love you." The words seep from my lips, and I press my lips to her forehead and close my eyes and begin to dream of the love I have for her, hoping she feels the same.

Sighing contently, I lean back and prop my head on my fist and let my eyes linger on Lindsey's face. With love showing through my whole body, I let the warmth of the room seep into my chilled bones.

As my eyes drift shut, I gently grasp her hand and rest my head on her bed, close to her heart, where I hope my love for her will be held.

As my body winds down, I feel Jonathan touch my shoulder as he leaves the room. "See you later, Tom," he says as his footsteps fade. A smile is still imprinted on my face as sleep invades me. For the first time since waking up in this hospital, when I shut my eyes, there is no violence on the other end. Now, I see a bright light. Hope, I see hope.

Allowing my brain to calm down, I listen to Jonathan's disappearing footsteps. Like a slow tapping, my ears track his footfalls down the hall.

He is a good man, and I hope that one day I can make both him and Lindsey proud. I owe them that much. I owe them my life. Without them, I wouldn't be here.

Lindsey might have been the one to fight alongside me, but Jonathan was the one who answered the call when we needed him the most. Without him, both of us would be rotting away right now.

I loosen my muscles and choose to think good thoughts as I descend into a restful sleep for once.

Chapter 24

At Peace

At first, everything was calm. In the beginning, no pain could be felt, but then everything came in waves. Slowly, then all at once, my bones began to ache along the surface, making me want to cry out.

In the beginning, it was the dull ache that spread from head to toe, then it was the heaviness of the drugs running through my pummeled body. At first, my body wouldn't move, and my eyes felt far too extreme to lift any higher than a flicker. But then I knew I was waking up by the rotten taste in my mouth.

Ever so slowly, I found the strength to lift open my eyelids, and the movement of my feet followed. The room was uncomfortably bright. Closing my eyes a couple of times didn't do anything to lessen the pain when I opened my eyes. When I open them again, my eyes drift to the heaviness that is weighing my hand down. I follow the hand to an arm and the arm to see curly brown hair. Everything inside me jumps. He's alive. My mind and heart cheer at the same time.

Thomas Pavlov survived the mission.

I did it.

We did it.

With as much power as I can conjure up, I run a caressing touch along the back of Thomas' hand with my thumb. It's calming to see the once stressed and panicked man in front of me relaxed as he sleeps. I watch my hand as I trace a small scar that runs down his knuckles. As the motion continues for a few minutes, I feel the weight of his hand shift. I stop tracing his veins and remain still.

Like the quick pull of the trigger, sudden panic rips through me. But then I calm myself. I remind myself that we made it. We deserve a moment of affection.

Thomas tightens his grasp and engulfs my hand, his grip shifting as he begins to wake up. My eyes begin to itch, and the only way to cure the problem is to either blink or use my unoccupied hand, but that would simply take too much energy. I think rapidly to try and bring relief, but it's not until Thomas opens his eyes that I have something else to focus on.

His brown orbs lock onto my eyes. His melting brown eyes focus on mine for another time. Widening my eyes, I take in his appearance. I take in the fact that he's alive and well.

As I look into his eyes, I see something living in there. As I try to figure out what emotion he is holding by looking into his eyes, his head continues to rest beside me. Thomas finally raises his head, and his messy hair sends a painful smile to my face. He grasps my right hand between his and presses his lips so carefully to the ridge of my knuckles.

The silence in the room is something that both of us find comforting. The knowledge that we are both here, at this moment, and breathing, seems to be a shelter that was worth building from the ground up. As he inches closer to me, I want to pull him into a hug. His hand never lets go of mine as he leans over my shoulders and lightly grasps me into a powerful hug. The wires and tubes attached to my body seem to remind him of where we are, and he takes a step back. Before he lets go of my hand, he plants a kiss on my forehead and looks me deeply in the eyes, and then slowly leaves the room.

"Doctors," Tom explains as he strolls out into the hall and signals people over.

So much has changed, yet everything remains the same. As I wait for doctors and nurses to swarm into the room and do a mandatory checkup, I think about how far my life has evolved.

No words have been spoken yet, but in a way, I didn't need them. I know. I can't help but realize the look in Thomas' eyes when he first saw me. The look of affection couldn't have been missed in any way.

As I wait, I think about what I want out of life. Thomas was right in the very beginning. He would be the first person to know why I chose the path that I did and why I put everything at risk. He would be the reason why I figured it all out. Everything seems so clear now as the wires, tubes, and machines continue monitoring me. I wanted to save the world or at least a part of it.

Just as the realization hits me, he comes back into the room with a heart-melting smile. He moves the chair out of the way to make way for the doctors that will soon fill the room. The sound of marching and rushed footsteps rings through the hall. I can't help but fear what they might say or what still needs to be done. The first person that comes through the doorway is my brother, in the most worried state I have ever seen him.

Jonathan barrels in and stands beside Thomas, mouthing the words, "Thank the Lord," as a nurse comes up to the monitor and begins to write. With a flick of her hair, she turns around, leans into my brother, and whispers something that I can't hear. Jonathan's arms are crossed tightly over his chest, and his lips are clamped shut. He nodded in my direction and follows the nurse out, leaving me with an overly joyful Thomas.

Thomas takes a hesitant step forward and folds his arms into each other, "I'm so relieved to see you awake, Lindsey." Thomas says in an almost breathless state. His hands ring together as if he's uncomfortable. I can see the reasoning behind it. I should have known. That kiss wasn't an in the heat of the moment thing. He meant it. Exhaling and fluttering my eyes shut, I smile knowing that at least my senses on that weren't wrong.

"It's good to be back," I say, my voice rough and choked.

He came back when I told him to run, he stayed when he should have gotten to cover, and he distracted my father when he was about to kill me. But I know that the moment he speaks those words, there is no way of taking them back. Once those three words are spoken, they will have to be acknowledged and acted upon. And deep down, I know that when he says them, he'll mean it. Knowing Thomas, he will love early and fiercely. I don't want him to make a mistake.

I know what Thomas begs to say, it's clear in his eyes, but I refuse to let them come between us. In time, those words can be spoken, but not yet. Neither of us is ready. If I know that, I'm sure Thomas does too.

Letting the tension go, I tell Thomas, "It's all right." My voice comes out in a rough and patchy sentence again. Suddenly, the question hits me, how long have I been asleep? Why did the nurse want to speak to my brother alone? As everything wrong runs through my head, Thomas takes a step closer and takes my hand.

"Everything's all right. You're okay."

I shift in my bed and give Thomas room to take a seat. To my surprise, he does, and it doesn't feel uncomfortable. I can hear people talking in the hall and the sounds of heavy, tired footsteps. Jonathan's hair is rough as if he's been running his hands through it, and his face is pale. He holds his right hand on his left shoulder, but he walks into my room with a smile on his face.

"Hey," he murmurs as he strides up to me.

With a couple of weighted strides, Jonathan stands beside me, opposite Thomas. The ache in my head returns, and I close my eyes for a brief moment. I can feel someone smooth down my hair with a delicate hand, and I slowly open my heavy eyes to see Jonathan with worry on his face.

I smile at him to reassure him that I'm okay, but it comes on so weak that I don't even buy it. I hear Jonathan and Thomas exchange a few hushed words, and the weight and warmth beside me vanish, but I know Johnny is still there.

The two men have different energies, and my brother is calm and quiet, but even as children, I could feel his restlessness within him.

His voice comes out rough when he speaks, "I didn't think you would wake up, you know that?" Smoothing a patch of my hair down, Jonathan lets his hand hover on my head. "I've been speaking to the doctors and nurses, and they kept telling me how each day you would get a little better." He angles his head as he speaks to me, his tea breath fanning my face. "That's why the nurse spoke to me. She told me that your recovery process won't be easy." Sighing, Jonathan ducks his head down as if scared to speak the words.

"Rehabilitation?" I ask, my voice still raspy and uneven.

Nodding, Jonathan states, pushing his hair out of his face, "Your core and abdominal wall were damaged when you were shot, and the one in your leg will leave you with weaker muscles. It will take a while to get you back to your full strength." Rolling back his shoulders, Jonathan offers a light pat on my head. "The nurse, Jeannette, said that physical therapy is the best alternative."

Slowly, I let my brother's words roll over me. I knew it, and I can handle it. If I could face my father again, I believe that I could handle anything. But, as my mind wanders and the soothing touch of my brother's pats, his words come to me again.

"Linds, have you noticed anything different about Thomas?" Jonathan's question makes my cheeks burn red. He and Thomas had to have spoken about this already...I can feel it.

Jonathan wouldn't be speaking about this if he wasn't sure that both of us shared the same bond. Jonathan, he reads through situations, and he reads through expressions.

I nod my head, but before I speak, I clear my throat. "Yes. What did you tell him, Jonathan?" My brother pulls back, and the bed creaks as his weight shifts on the mattress.

"Johnny! Seriously, did you get his hopes up? You know that I don't date, *ever*. I've never been on a date. I've never had a normal life. What am I supposed to tell him?" A pouting frown forms on my brother's face, and he does an angry turn.

"Linds, you can't live in the past. He cares about you, for Christ's sake. He knows what you've been through." Jonathan lowers his voice a notch, and then he explains, "Thomas is willing to help you through your recovery. He is determined to help you every step of the way." My brother looks back at the doorway, waiting to see if Thomas is coming back. Not seeing or hearing anyone, Jonathan shifts his attention back to me.

"Lindsey," my brother sighs, and his fingers twitch. "Thomas is a good man with a troubled past. The two of you together can help right each other. Give him a chance, and be brave. You've been through worse things than going out on a date. All right?" I nod my head, knowing what he said is right. I can't keep living in the sorrows of my parents. As I watch my brother leave the room, Thomas takes his place minutes later.

Like a rotating door, one comes, and the other goes.

Slowly, Thomas enters the room. He just stops and looks, his eyes showing the few hours of sleep he has gotten. A smile is on his tired features, and his curly hair is unkempt. But I barely even notice because there is so much happiness within him I know what he's about to do. With steady steps and even breaths, he takes my hand. "Lindsey, I hope you know that I care about you a lot…I—um, would you like to go out with me?" His nervousness brings a smile to my face. I never thought I would be this happy after what we went through. Like a teenager, Thomas seems so intent and scared.

There was no way that I would have predicted this. I knew that I was growing closer to him, but I didn't think he was doing the same. With a wide smile on my face, I squeeze his hand and confirm his request.

"Yes," I whisper. With the words open in the air, we

just remain together. Thomas is a man that I would have never thought I would need in my life. For as long as I could remember, I swore I was going to be alone for the rest of my life. But now, as Thomas folds his hand in mine, I see clearly now that there might be hope after all for a normal life.

Thomas continues to stay with me throughout the day as I continue to wake up and fall asleep. He took his post by the side of my bed and would offer comfort every time a nurse came and went. Blood samples and tests continued to be run periodically throughout the day, and by the end of the night, he was still beside me. He didn't leave like I expected him to, and as I closed my tired eyes, he was still beside me. With a smile on my face, I know that I finally experienced what peace must feel like.

With most of the wires removed, I can move more. The heart monitor patch and twists of tubes still remain. With great effort, I turn on my side and face Thomas. As I drift asleep, for once, I'm without worry knowing that everyone I love is safe and that I won't be alone when I wake up.

Before my body shuts down, I feel Thomas take my hand in his, and with a smile on my face, I finally fall into a deeply peaceful and painless sleep.

And as my mind clicks off, I no longer fear what I will face on the other side. Gently, a hand touches my cheek and then roams into my delicately cleaned hair. Slowly, a murmur meets me in the chamber of sleep, "I will never leave you," the voice promises.

I know who it is immediately, and with a gentle reminder, I know that I am not alone. I don't need to hide. I don't need to be dangerous. As my mind goes blank, I promise back, "I'm with you too."

Brown eyes will always meet blue. Together, we will rise and face the days that lay ahead.

Like the moon and the sun, we may be opposites, and we may shine differently, but always, we will need one another. And we will pave the path through the unknown just so we can see an equal light of joy and hope.

Chapter 25

Future Chances

Being able to walk on my own for the first time in about three weeks; feels like a major victory. I no longer have to hold the rails of my bed or the metal rod of my IV. I can freely move now, knowing that the final touches to the healing process are underway.

With the lack of constant movement of my muscles, overall, my body feels weak. The doctors have told me that it's normal. That the static feeling will fade the more I move. They keep telling me that over time I can rebuild and be good as new. But from walking from one end of the hallway to the other on my floor, I get winded. And Thomas holds my elbow the whole time, whispering kind words as I chide myself.

As I go through physical therapy, my core muscles scream in protest to exercises that were once easy. The leg movements to help repair the three damaged thigh muscles are the worst. I tend to lay in bed at night, remembering what it felt like to be strong at all moments. I tend to itch with excitement to hit the gym again and be at full top capacity. But I know that deep down, it will be a while, and I will have to have patience.

My days in the hospital tend to slow down by four in the evening. Thomas would stop by and check in by then, but he never can stay long. Jonathan likes to visit in the late hours of the night, long after work, and after people retire for bed. He told me one night when I heard him walk in that he likes to come here at night and stay for an hour or two and just relax.

That's all he said; he likes to sit in my dark hospital room and relax. Sometimes when I wake the next morning, I find a letter or a card, or if I'm lucky the book he just got done reading during the night will be on my small bedside table.

We don't speak that much anymore. He went back to selling and helping people find real estate. He works long hours, and, at times with complicated clients. My brother is a dedicated man, and I know that he likes to stay busy. When you are busy your mind doesn't get to ruin you. And with everything about our parents out in the open, we both have baggage to work through.

But Jonathan did say that he scaled back on traveling to be home for a while. "I want to be here for you if you need it. We're a family, and I want to make sure you're all right." He says as if he's planned what he was going to say to me in his head. "If you call, I want to be able to make it to you."

I wouldn't blame Jonathan if he did go back to traveling. He needs it, he enjoys it, and it gives him time by himself. I know that being here, surrounded by the healing and the dying is a heavy situation that does take its toll. I, myself, at times wish I could just check myself out so I don't have to listen to other people's cries at night.

I am defined as strong, but hearing someone in pain wrenches my heart out. When I hear it I end up covering my ears with my extra pillow and shoving it over my face, so I don't hear the crying directly, and so no one hears me as I break at night. Strong is what I am seen as, so strong is how I have to stay.

As I lay here after training, after my hour and a half of sweating, cursing, grinding my teeth, and crying, I find myself wishing to be at my house, being able to hold and pet Shadow. I still, at quiet moments like this, miss being able to lead my own life. I miss the sweet sound of the birds chirping from my kitchen and the sound of the wind when it rattles the screen door. I miss being at home and just being alone and being able to do what I want, what I need to recharge.

Now, I sit, and the overhead TV plays in the background. The smell of the hospital's cleanliness tickles my nose. It's around three in the afternoon, and Thomas should be coming soon and saving me from the extreme amount of boredom stacking up around me. "Don't let him see you break," I tell myself as I see my reflection on the overhead TV.

But at the moment, the mumbling of the voices on the TV drives me further into madness. As I look out the window and see the wind blow the tops of the trees, I feel my feet twitch for a run. Everything seems out of focus as everything chops together in my brain. Nothing seems on point anymore. The energy in the room shifts as I hear a knock on the door. I see a mop of brown curly hair, and a set of people in white coats enter the room. I turn to face them as I pull my hair back from my face and brush invisible dust off of my black sweatpants. Thomas comes to stand next to me and places his hands on my shoulders as the doctors form a line in the room. They are all smiling, so I can tell that my time staying in the hospital is coming to an end.

Glad but reluctant to leave the room that has become

my home, my skin begins to prickle with excitement and fear.

The line of four doctors, three men and one woman, glance at each other as if seeing who should speak first. Shifting, and after a few waves, they all silently know who will deliver the first part of the news.

The woman speaks first, offers a quick smile, and begins. "We all have great news for you, Ms. Vasiliev. But first the bad news, or the news that you already know about." Reading the name tag, I listen to Sara's cheerful voice. "Your body will need time to recover, and life will be difficult for a while. But we," she points to her surrounding teammates and then to Thomas. "Believe that you will have all the support you need. But with the great news, you're being discharged within the next few hours! Congrats, you truly are a soldier." Shocked and alarmed, I don't say anything.

Thomas grabs my shoulders to pull me into a hug as soon as he hears the news. "I don't feel like a soldier," I tell him. My head rests on his chest. I can feel how his heart beats a little faster when I wrap my arm around him. "To us, you are." Is all he says as he pulls back but keeps his arms around me. But as I process the news about being able to leave, panic stirs down deep. Where will I be staying? What do the doctors mean that life will be difficult?

I want to pull away all of a sudden, but Thomas' arms keep me glued in my position. His chin rests upon my head again, speaking in a low tone. "It's okay. I have everything under control." With every word Thomas speaks, I can feel his jaw move. It hurts slightly, but it…brings me back to reality. That I'm not alone anymore. That there are people willing to support me. I no longer have to act strong, and I don't need to fake being all right anymore.

"What did you plan, Tom?" He ever so slightly pulls back, but he holds my shoulders as if he wants to keep me steady. His dark eyes soften, and a small sly smile comes to his dry lips.

His eyes find mine, but then they travel beyond me to see Jonathan. I'm slightly startled that I didn't hear him come in, but even madder that he interrupted me from getting the answers that I needed, hell wanted even.

Thomas' smile widens as he shakes Jonathan's hand. They both seem to be on great terms, and as I begin packing, the men talk. It's hushed, and they seem worried. Once in a while, Thomas looks at me and gives a small smile, but then he turns his attention back to my brother.

"Can you please just tell me?" I speak with frustration. "I deserve to know if it's about me, so just spill it." My brother eyes me for a moment and shakes his head, but Thomas stalks toward me.

His kind eyes seem conflicted, and he pulls me into another hug. "I got us an apartment to share until you get better." He whispers almost out of fear. A smile floods my face, and I pull Thomas closer to me. Ever so slowly, I plant a kiss on his rough, stubbled cheek. "Next time, tell me," I warn him.

Feeling Thomas' tightening, I continue. "When?" I ask, already knowing that Thomas and Jonathan have already worked everything through without me.

"Uh," shifting his weight, Thomas tangles a look at Jonathan over his shoulder. "A couple of days after I woke up."

Shocked, I pulled back from Thomas. "You were

checked into the hospital? Why?" I stammer, not connecting anything. As the words slice through the air, I track my eyes over Thomas, not seeing much of a change in him but his more slender weight.

As we pull apart, Jonathan catches my eye and nods. "Both of you were brought here. You with your injuries, and Thomas had a head injury." Thomas holds my hand as he leans down, so our eyes meet. "I whacked my head on the concrete." He says in a child-like manner.

"But everything is okay, right, Thomas?" I lock my arms around him until he finalizes the statement.

"I'm fine," he says with an odd grin. "We both are." Tom presses a kiss on my temple.

Jonathan taps Thomas on his shoulder, the signal I get to confirm that they want to talk things over. Thomas squeezes my hand before reluctantly following.

"Buh-bye," Jonathan chants as he and Thomas leave the room.

Exposed and confused, I shouted after my brother, "We will talk about all this later!"

After they leave and the door is shut, I begin to shove everything I have on my bed so I can finish packing. As my hands fold and tuck the last remaining items left in the room in my bag, I feel exhausted.

As I wait for the information and paperwork that state I have been cleared, I feel my eyes closing. For the past few days, I have lost my appetite, endurance, and strength. All I feel is tired, vulnerable, and weak. So much for being London's Lethal Woman, huh? I amuse myself.

My body gives into the tiredness that has been haunting me, and the last remaining medications I'm required to take slowly seep into my system. As my pulse slows, I can almost still feel Thomas' hand in mine, and a smile finds its way to my face thinking about what he did for me, for us. But at the moment, all that seems appealing is rest.

As my eyes close, so do the lights that have been blinding me for so long.

I finally feel free, knowing that the next chapter in my life may be complicated, but I know that I have people beside me, willing to help me through all that has happened.

I feel at peace holding onto the life I am now getting, a comforting life that I have always wanted.

Slowly, as I allow my body to recover, I let myself wind down. I still have time to rest before I check out, and I know when that time comes, either my brother or Thomas will wake me.

But, needing a few minutes of rest, I curl back on the bed and shove my bag to the side.

Chapter 26

Burning Silence

The sight of seeing Lindsey standing in the kitchen makes my heart leap to my throat. I still can't get used to the fact that she moved in less than two weeks ago. All her belongings barely filled up the back of my truck. She said she only wanted to take the main things, like clothes, toiletries, and a few objects that she is connected to.

The rest she said can wait. The rest she promised didn't mean that much to her. All she wanted to do was get the important pieces and leave her family home for good.

But I still can't get used to the sight of her around me, for real, no more client and boss relationship. She and I are one, and there isn't this looming threat over our heads.

I just tend to find myself watching and waiting for her to vanish from my life in a dark, gloomy cloud. But, as I push a hand through my hair, I tell myself that I won't let that happen. She is with me, and we will continue to battle whatever comes our way together.

Right now, though, her hair cascades down her shoulders, and her eyes focus as she mixes batter that I presume is for pancakes, one of her favorite breakfast foods. She hasn't noticed that I've walked into the room yet; my heart skips beats seeing her so comfortable and happy.

Being so normal.

She could be doing nothing, and my heart would leap to her. Literally, I think that she broke me. I can just walk into a room after waking up, and somehow, she beckons to me.

Smiling, I enter the kitchen and journey to the coffee maker. Lindsey notices me, and a slight blush creeps to her surprised features. She moves to the side to allow me access to the coffee, but catching her arm, I can't help but whisper, "This is your place too." A flicker of a smile forms. "By the way, I love seeing you smile, love." Turning to pour the dark, bitter liquid into a mug, I still watch Lindsey out of the corner of my eye.

So far, I've been trying this out as a couple. Oddly, we still act the same around each other, but there is this closeness we didn't have before. So far, Lindsey doesn't care much for the nicknames, so I stick to strict compounds.

Slurping at the coffee, Lindsey asks, "What do you have to do at work today? I was thinking after physical therapy I would stop by and hang out." Her voice is timid, and Lindsey is not a timid person, so it makes me nervous. Placing my cup down, swallowing what's in my mouth, I walk closer to her. Her eyes meet mine, and I notice the emotion in them right away; fear.

Shocked, I reached out to soothe her. "Hey, it's all right. I can stay home with you. I know it's hard, but we will get through this." Ever since we moved into the apartment together, she's been having nightmares. The nightmares leave her wrecked, and sweat always drenches her delicate features, and there is nothing I can do to help her. She swears that having me with her helps, but all I feel is helpless. When I hear her screaming in her room at night, I run to her. All I can do to soothe the pain is hold her, but even then, she continues to shake and cling to my arms.

"No, please." Lindsey waves her arms out as she flips the final pancake. "I want to go out today. Maybe hit the gym. But I don't want to be alone." I close my eyes and pull her against my chest. "It will get better." There is this pull between us. We don't fight. We try to understand each other. We don't get angry often. We work it out as a team. But having her in my arms, having her confess her fears, I know that we love each other. We don't need to speak the words to know it. I take a deep breath. "Have another nightmare last night? I didn't hear anything?"

Feeling her head move back and forth on my shirt, I can't help but sigh as I loop my arms around her back. "Why didn't you call me?"

Again, she shakes her head. "I don't want to bother you every night, Tom."

Sucking in a hefty amount of air, I let it inflate my lungs, then exit. "You aren't, Linds. I'm here for you, no matter what you need."

Clinging tight, I feel Lindsey pull back. Her eyes flash as she pushes a strip of loose hair behind her ear. Offering a smile, she rubs my shoulder. "Thank you." I pull my bottom lip between my teeth. I can't seem to find the words.

Rubbing at my eyes, an idea clinks in my head, "After I drop you off at therapy, you should come by the office. I'll bring a change of clothes to work, and once I'm done, we can hit the gym if you're up for it." Having Lindsey in my arms, with her sweet scent filling my nose, I can't help but cling to her. I so badly want to rid her of the memories that rob her of sleep.

"That sounds all right," Lindsey flutters her hands into my shirt. "I'm done with therapy around noon. I'll get a cab when I'm done."

"Oh, um." Pulling back, I catch her attention again. "I'll pick you up when you are done."

"I can handle a cab ride, Thomas." Frowning, I don't know how to respond to her. I want her safe. I want her centered. The doctors warned that anything can be a trigger at this stage of the healing process. I know that Lindsey has faced things like this before, but reluctantly, I know she is hiding how scared she is.

Knowing that I have to let go of her, I sigh. Clearing my throat, I begin, "I know, but I want to make sure you are safe."

"I will be," Lindsey says slowly. "I have to start doing things on my own now. It's time, honey."

"Whoa," I say, placing a heavy hand on Lindsey's shoulder. "You have that look on your face."

Lindsey frowns, but a slow smile blooms on her face. "What look would that be?"

"It's the look you get before you are about to fuck somebody up. Badly" A smile plays on my lips.

"If that look is aimed at me, give me a heads up. I want to be out of reach of that blow, Linds." Laughing, she taps my chest with her right pointer finger. Her eyes shine and she takes a step closer.

Lindsey leans in and plants a heated but somber kiss on my lips. Tugging away from me, she takes a seat at the counter. "If you don't start letting me do things on my own, you'll be the one getting the beating."

Doubtful, I think. "Eat, get dressed, and I'll take you

to therapy, Linds." I think maybe it's time that I show her something. Lindsey unwraps her arms from around my waist, and the moment she lets go…I dread it. Having her close like that makes me feel safe, needed even.

She quickly sets two plates and adds a few fruit slices on the side. Retrieving my coffee mug, I take my place at the small kitchen island right next to her. The silence between us is different today. It's more tense than normal. She doesn't eat much of her food. I thought we were past that stage, but I refuse to press on it today. Win the war, not the battle.

In time I know she will get better. She will get her weight back. Soon, I pray, Lindsey will start taking better care of herself.

But something is nagging at me. She seems off this morning, almost disconnected. Watching is all I do, analyzing everything she does. But like always, her quick and sudden movements leave me confused. Before I even finished eating, she rinsed her dishes and went to the back bedroom. One step at a time, the doctors and Jonathan warned one step at a slow ass time.

Choosing to shrug it off, I restfully enjoy my coffee. I can hear the shower running in the distance, and for some reason, I can't help but want to walk into her bedroom and wait for her. I refuse to live with the tension, but I also don't want to settle into my temptation. Overall I know that we promised to work through things together, no matter how uncomfortable they may be. I just so badly want to settle things between us. But I know I can't push her. She can still beat me to a plump if she wishes.

Settling to not give in or comfort her, I clean the dishes and go to my own room to get dressed for the long day ahead. As I walk into my room, I quickly pick up my phone and check for any notifications.

Nothing. Just a blank screen displaying the time.

Sighing, I rest my head in my palm and a sudden wave of tiredness strikes. I flop back on the bed and listen to the beat of the water hitting the shower tiles. I shuffle a tired moan and crawl back under the covers. The boss can miss a day. I can say that I'm not feeling well, but that's not very adult-like of me.

I hear the water turn off, and with the rhythm gone, there is nothing to focus on to keep me from falling back asleep. Stuffing my head under the pillow, I make a prayer that involves me being able to take a today off. Maybe spend some quality time with Lindsey, figure things out between us and just sit at home and watch a movie.

A man can wish, after all.

"Get up, or you'll be late for work." Raising the pillow from my head, my heart almost stops beating at the sight of the woman in front of me. Her damp hair is tied back in an elegant braid, and a very formal blouse fits snugly against her torso and shoulders like a second skin. And the tall, knee-length boots give her more height and make her look more…bad-ass? There are no words to describe her at the moment, maybe confident, but that doesn't justify why I can barely breathe.

Slowly rising from my flattened position, I run my hand through my already disheveled hair. Humming a response, I watch as she exits the room, leaving me with a clouded brain and a fit of disrepair at the silence in the room.

But as I scold the wall, an idea comes to me. "Lindsey!" I shout through the apartment, hoping that she'll agree. In the kitchen, I can hear her pattering footsteps. They come closer, and the next thing I know, she is standing in the doorway, her eyes bright and a slight smile on her face. The sight of her glowing eyes startles me for a moment, but they also propel me to speak.

"I will go to work, but not as the boss—okay, I will still be the boss, but I want you to meet my team." Lindsey steps closer, her smile gone and her eyes shadowed. Like a switch, I spring from the bed and enclose her in my arms. Her rose-water and coffee smell tickles my nose.

"What about physical therapy?"

Hesitant, I let my arms loop around Lindsey. "When you are done, I will show you the team."

Lindsey wraps her arms tighter around my torso, the heat of her breath fanning my thin cotton shirt. Lindsey worms closer and whispers, "You won't leave me, will you? What if your team hates me?"

No words could silence her, so I settled for a shushing sound. Unclasping her arms from around me, I sink down to look deeply into her eyes. Those stormy orbs tell a million stories, but she looks at me with a newfound fierceness.

Placing my right hand on the side of her face, I rub circles into her cheek.

Smiling again, she steps away. "Never mind. Get dressed, Mr. Businessman. You got a team to show me, remember?" Rushing out of the room, she once again leaves me to my thoughts. Huffing, I pull my closet door open and pull a pair of dark slacks out along with a dark blue shirt.

What can I say? Lindsey is the most confusing yet

bravest person I know. To be willing to do something that she is unsure of takes a lot of heart and courage.

Rushing to the bathroom connected to my room, I ease a brush through my tousled hair and wash my face. My features are more pronounced due to living a healthier lifestyle, and my hair has been cut shorter recently. Despite knowing Lindsey for only a short amount of time, my world is now shaped around her.

She is the light that I'm constantly drawn to, and she is the one that keeps the fire burning inside. Shuffling a smile and sharing one last glance with my reflection in the mirror, I depart from my room and make my way to the kitchen to gather Lindsey's things for therapy for the day.

She always keeps her to-go bag by the door, and with it now resting on the counter, I can't help but think about how far she has come. From intense muscle movements to slow and steady weighted bands to help build her strength back. Clasping the dark green bag in my hand, the memories of helping her walk up the stairs that first day we moved in came swimming back to me.

We had our first argument as a couple on that day. Trying to be thoughtful, I wanted to take the elevator, thinking it would be easier for her. But she refused, stumbling over to the stairs, grasping the railing for dear life. Lindsey attempted to hoist herself up each step like it was a mountain. At that moment, Lindsey proved something to me.

She is invincible.

That day made me reconsider something inside the company. Who would be the lead security commander? Who could make me feel safe when I'm at my most profitable? Only one person came to mind when I asked questions like that: Lindsey Vasiliev. Checking the time on my phone, with a start, I realize that Lindsey will be late for physical therapy if we don't leave now.

Glancing into the living room, I can see Lindsey, her phone in hand and a smile on her face. Keeping Lindsey's bag in my hand, I advance in her direction. The smile grows wider when she sees me.

"He can finally come home! Thomas, he's coming home." Her eyes water as she speaks of her trusting companion, Shadow. When the heat rose and Lindsey and I had to go into hiding at the compound at the simulation of the Royal Docks, we had to leave Shadow behind. It tore Lindsey to pieces, but Jonathan got Shadow not long after we left, and he's been safe in Jonathan's house ever since. Just from guessing, I can predict that we finally got our request to have a dog in our apartment approved. Lindsey beams at me, and with a limp that is still noticeable, she takes her bag from me and begins to head out the door.

"Wait, slow down," I plead with her. "Don't go so fast down the stairs, please!"

Lindsey looks back at me with a grin that almost lights a dangerous fire inside of me.

I speed after her.

"Come on, Tom, the sooner therapy is done, the sooner I get to see Shadow! Oh, can we bring him inside with us to meet some of the colleagues you mentioned earlier?" She looks up from the stairs, and I'm met with something I can never resist.

Oh, God, the puppy dog eyes. I can feel my pulse race, and my brain becomes fuzzy. For being labeled one of the most dangerous women in the world, she looks at me with the eyes of an angel. I nod. I've missed Shadow as well. I'll do anything to make the love of my life happy. Lindsey slows to a normal pace, and we walk side by side, hand in hand. I can't help but remember the first day we met.

Her eyes stole my heart then, and they still do. If only the old me knew that after all the hell we would go through, in the end, it would bring us closer together. If only the old me knew I wouldn't be alone after everything came to a close.

But the old me doesn't need to know anything because all I care about is that the present me has her by my side. The present me finally has something worth fighting for.

The present me finally has some peace for once.

This present me, the new me, has a ray of hope the old me never thought would ever come.

Chapter 27

It Always Ends in a Fight

Sitting at the head of the table, with my hands clasped together and my face structured with no emotion, I sit in front of my security team. An array of old and young, male and female, intimidating and strict people clutter the small conference room chairs. But there is one thing that every person in front of me shows, respect. I can totally envision Lindsey leading, training, and working with them all.

I can see it now, Lindsey at the head of the routines, barking out orders. But right now, I have to get everyone on board with the idea of someone else leading and commanding them. I may be able to lead this company, but I can't do this. They deserve someone who knows what they are doing.

I give everyone a curt nod and a brief glance before I speak. "Thank you all for coming here before heading to the locker rooms." Taking a breath, I watch everyone. "I have called this meeting because I believe I have found the leader of this squad."

Silence, shimmering eyes, and a few brisk smiles. I hope no one in this room thinks it will be them, if so, what I'm about to do will be awkward. For me and that person. But as I look at everyone, no one says anything.

Clearing my throat, I lick my dry lips. Configuring

my words, I praise Lindsey. "She is one of the best I have ever seen, so give your full attention and respect to the woman that I will be bringing in." Rising to leave the room to gather Lindsey from my fairly large office, I see strange reactions to the news I just delivered.

As I walk to my office through the halls, I can't help but glance at all my employees. They are all hard at work, typing, answering the phones, or working on their computers doing their assigned tasks. I give them all my respect. Neither my father nor I are easy men to work for. And seeing that most of these people have been here since the beginning makes me inwardly smile.

The open door to my office makes me stop dead in my tracks. I never leave it open, but the figure leaning in the doorway immediately keeps me walking. Lindsey is scanning the people clustered around the room. Smiling, I know I made the right choice about signing her onto the task force. When Lindsey's eyes land on mine, warmth spreads from my heart to my toes. She steps closer, meeting me halfway.

"You ready?" I say, searching her face for any uneasiness.

"Maybe." She smiles and begins to walk in the direction I just came from. Her pace is calm, but her stony face of authority slips back on.

Lindsey, I hope you know that at times you scare me, I chant in my head as I walk beside her.

I step into the room first, and Lindsey trails behind me. I take my place at the head of the table. Lindsey notices there are no open chairs close to me. I notice the mask she put on moments ago slips. No one seems to have noticed but me, and everyone looks on in silence as Lindsey claims the long rounded edge, opposite of me.

Both of us are in front. Both leaders, both holding the power.

Every man needs a queen, my father's voice hisses through my mind as I watch Lindsey limbering down in the chair.

Lindsey clears her throat and gives me a quick look before speaking. "I am here today to inform all of you that I will be taking over as head of security. All commands and or questions will have to go through me, and we will all be working together so we can all be an effective team. Thomas Pavlov," Lindsey sends the spotlight back onto me, and I argue the closing portion. Easily, I lean my head on my palm and register all the faces waiting for me to speak. Gathering my words, I clear my throat before speaking.

"Ms. Vasiliev is here at my request." Gesturing in Lindsey's direction, I bat a smile at her. "I've seen her in action, and let me tell you, she is not a person to second-guess."

Lindsey's and my eyes lock before I continue. Within her misty orbs, I see so much emotion, but shaking my head, I continue. "Lindsey will be acting under my command, and since it's in everyone's interest to ensure I stay alive, I want the best people to help keep me and everyone in this company safe."

Pausing to glance around the room to make sure everyone is listening, I send a flicker of a smile to Lindsey. I don't bother hiding it. People already know from the magazines and articles that Lindsey and I are an item.

I clear my throat and begin again, keeping my voice calm and steady. "So I insist that you all learn everything you can from Ms. Vasiliev while you can. I know this is a difficult change in circumstances, but it is something you all will have to get used to. Lindsey Vasiliev is here to stay, and everyone will soon learn what I mean when I say she is the best at what she does." Clearing my throat, I try to decipher what to say next.

I realize I have nothing valuable to say, so I send them on their way with, "Now, get into uniform, and get to work. Meeting dismissed, have a great day, everyone. Thank you." As everyone scatters, I shout above the clambering, "Ms. Vasiliev will be joining all of you tomorrow bright and early! Good day and cheers."

The last remaining few still in their chairs roll back, look at each other, sigh, and then there is a little bit of small talk as the rest of the team leaves the room.

I keep my face stern, and my hands remain clasped as I watch everyone clear out of the room. Feeling tired and drained already, I lean back in the rolling chair and close my eyes. The sounds of a busy office give me something to focus on. I know that the security team will need a few minutes to get ready so there is enough time to relax and brace for the storm that will invade my day.

"Thomas?" Lindsey's voice makes me groan, knowing I have to open my eyes. "You look exhausted. Do you just want to go home and rest? You don't look well." My eyes open slowly, and Lindsey sits in the chair directly next to me. Her hands sprawled out on the table, waiting for me to hold them.

Taking her hands, I try to figure out what to tell Lindsey. "No, I'm sure it's nothing, and we can't just go home. You did your work for the day. You went to therapy, and you helped conclude this meeting. I want to stay and do more work, but I feel so tired lately." Ruffling my hair, I lean closer to Lindsey. "I'm starting to understand why my father never had time for me; everything is just exhausting by the end of the day. But don't worry, Lindsey, we will go get Shadow from your brother later. I promise you that much. And don't worry, I will be fine." I lean in, hoping that she will too, but she doesn't. I'm sticking out my bottom lip in a pout, and I see what's coming.

Lindsey looks at me with an odd expression, and for a moment, it almost makes me panic, but when a smile lights up her face, my heart rate slows down to normal again.

Lindsey stands still, holding my hand. She forces me out of my chair. With us standing flushed together, I take hold of her mouth with my own. Gently at first, but then an aggressive pull threads through my heart. Groaning as we pull apart, I let my hands linger on the side of her face. Lindsey's complexion is even but flawed. She has a few freckles from the recent sun, but her blonde hair is as soft as ever. Smiling, I tease another kiss from her. But Lindsey just gently shoves my chest away. Rolling my eyes, I lead her from the conference room, and we walk out to the main office locations.

We walk side by side again, like always. Lindsey's mask is back on as we walk by others. When we pass into a hallway where no one is, she reaches out and grasps my hand. "You know, at work, we can't act like we are dating, right?" She asks in a tone I have never heard from her. All the times we went through hell, I heard Lindsey speak in anger, hate, hurt, happiness but never true dread.

Looking into her eyes, I admit something I thought I never would. "You and I are a team. I don't care what anyone thinks, and neither should you." Tightening my fingers around hers, I thread our hands closer together.

"Lindsey, you are capable of handling this job. No one will or should doubt you or your actions." How can I convince her that she didn't get this position because she is my girlfriend? She saved my life, and she faced a murderous man. She fought a team of men with guns. She knows more than most that I would have ended up interviewing.

"Trust me," I whisper close to her face. "When I said I'm done hiding, and I'm done denying what's important in my life, I meant it. So no, I won't deny myself from you, Lindsey." Shrugging off Lindsey's laser eyes, I continue. "Let's make a deal, shall we? I won't be with you twenty-four seven. That would be impossible to do. And, we won't kiss in the middle of a group of people either." Lindsey's cheeks blush when I say the last part. We haven't kissed in front of anyone before, and to me, that doesn't matter. Just holding her allows me to feel the love and feel loved. Love, I understand now, is only as complicated as we make it. There are setbacks, challenges, and drawbacks, but if the two people are meant to be together, those challenges should mean something.

An adult relationship takes work, discipline, and understanding. I'm learning as I go, and so is Lindsey. But, ultimately, I think that if we want something bad enough, we can get it to work.

Slipping back into reality, Lindsey is tugging at my sleeve. "I just don't want people to think that I got this job because we are in a relationship. I want them to see my skills, not my dating card, you know?" The sea gray eyes meet mine, and grabbing her hand, I pull her close. Lindsey hesitates only a little but then gives in. Our bodies collide, and her breath fans my neck.

I can feel her tense muscles bunching. "You have nothing to fear. We are together, united by the truth of our love. No one can take that away from us…plus," I draw out, "If anyone says anything, all you have to do is show them your skills, then they can't deny why I hired you."

As I speak, Lindsey stays wrapped around me. The embrace is long and thoughtful. "I can't just beat up every person that doubts me." Lindsey chuckles as she allows me to still hold her.

"You're right. That would be a long list." I start out saying. "And," with a fake wince, I finish, "that would be far too much paperwork."

I never thought I would say those words to her. Being able to joke and buzz around with strange confessions is a rewarding feeling. As my mind clears, I bring Lindsey close to me again. "I'm happy you are here…with me."

As we let go of each other, Lindsey's phone begins to buzz, and I know that tone. It's the emergency line that I thought would never have to be used, or at least not this early in time. Lindsey's hands shake, and her eyes go wide.

Turning to stone, I take the phone and answer the call.

"Hello?" I say, with a layer of venom in my voice. Who or whatever caused our small moment of peace to shatter better have a hell of a good reason.

"Yes, Um. Is Lindsey Vasiliev there? I'm so sorry, but it's important that she gets this message. It's regarding her father." The man on the other line has a thick voice, an accent that I can't place. But from the rushed and panicked tone, I know that something is wrong or will be soon.

I'm understanding now that our fight is never over, and it may never be because, with my and Lindsey's bloodline, it always has to end in a fight. There will always be a fight brewing that one of us will be a part of.

"She's not here at the moment, but this is Thomas Pavlov. You can pass the message along through me. I will ensure she gets it."

"I'm not sure if I should—"

Running out of patience suddenly, I snap. "Please, just tell me…"

The silence on the other side is frustrating. Lindsey and I both need to know, to prepare for the worst, yet again.

Muffled voices and hurried footsteps drift through the line. "Sir? Hello? I'm Julian Thorn. I'm the main guard in cell block C. Wolf Vasiliev has made a request to speak with his daughter. He swears that it's important for an investigation, and he has been causing a lot of chaos, so maybe it would be a good idea that he at least gets to speak."

What the hell? Can he not let his family rest? Can he not leave them alone and accept his own fate?

Seething and rolling my fingers into a fist one by one, I try to calm myself. "Does it have to be in person? Can she possibly be behind the glass? They can see each other, but he won't be near her?" Plowing my hand through my hair, I try to think of a way to keep Lindsey out of Wolf's grasp.

"What options are there, Mr. Thorn?" I look to the side and see Lindsey sitting on the floor, her head in her hands. Her hair falling out of the braid along the sides by her ears. Panic grips my heart. I don't want her to go through this. I completely thought everything was over. How truly naive of me.

"I'm sorry, but I don't know the options or his terms at this time. He doesn't have many. But I think it would be best for her to come in as soon as possible, but I know that she will be safe no matter what, Mr. Pavlov. I really do hope you do pass this message along. It's important. Urgent even, maybe." Breathing slowly, I keep my eyes on Lindsey. A man like Wolf doesn't beg unless it's worthy of his time. Wolf must have a plan, and I wish I could make the final choice, not Lindsey. I wish I could rid us of him completely.

Trapped, I say, "I'll see what she says, mate. We'll be in touch soon."

Julian exhales a long breath and I can hear a muffled exchange. Then, "I bid you farewell and thank you for your time, Mr. Pavlov."

The call ends with a crisp silence. It seems that the world has gone silent in our despair. Anger flares through my veins. We both have a life. We both have something grounding us in place. Lindsey has finally moved past the dangerous life she thought she had to live. I know that it will never fully be over, but I also know her father will never let his family be. A man like him doesn't know when to let go. I don't think he knows how.

"Thomas." Lindsey's hair is now fanning her back and right shoulder, giving her a warrior aesthetic. God, how I wish we could have a normal life. "We have to go. He wouldn't demand to see me over something silly. That's not how my father works, please. Please let me do this? The sooner we know the truth, the sooner we can let this live in the past. Our past."

Dropping my head, I try to hide my face, not wanting to show Lindsey my anger. My jaw remains clenched as I speak, "He doesn't deserve this. He shouldn't be allowed to make any demands at all!" I begin to walk back to my office, not wanting everyone to hear this conversation.

As soon as I'm at the door, I usher Lindsey in and shut the door firmly. "He killed people for sport Lindsey, God! I hate the fact that even when he's behind bars, he still thinks he can run the world."

Lindsey's chilled eyes meet mine, and for a quick moment, I see a part of her wall be built back up. And I can see a part of strength return. As my vexation grows, a part of me knows that if I keep yelling, Lindsey will snap back into the lethal woman she is and rip me apart.

"I understand that, but in the end, we have to know as much as we can. I know his ways. I know how to get into his mind." Lindsey gently lays her palms flat against my chest, and she adds pressure as she speaks. "I'm not stupid. Now you can come if you want, but you will not stand in my way." Lindsey comes forward and lays a feathery touch on my lips. "If you swear we are a team, then you will stand beside me, not behind or in front. Thomas, you have no idea what my father or I can do. You have no idea of the dangerous skills that run through my blood."

The leading side of her returns, and she begins a quick pace through my office. With anger still raging inside me like a wildfire, I pace after her. As long as there is breath in my body, my fight to protect her will never be over, and at this moment, my anger seems to act as a shield around us.

Wolf better have something good because if he

doesn't, I won't have a problem ripping him in half, and if he thinks he can play us…he better think again because I'm tired of playing weak. It's my time to rise and accept the call to help Lindsey end this fight.

It's time that the Vasiliev children and I finally finish this battle with a royal gut-twisting ending…that the people on the right side of the law ultimately get to claim victory for once.

I think it's time the royal Wolf Vasiliev falls off his blood-stained throne.

So nodding my head, I promise Lindsey, "Fine. I'm beside you all the way. We take him down, once and for all."

Chapter 28

You Have My Respect

The drab gray concrete walls feel like they are closing me in. The sounds of footsteps don't help distance the thoughts plaguing my mind. With each click and chime of dangling keys, I can't help but think if it's my father. I can't help but leap up with each clang or clunk of the metal door. Sighing, I chide myself. I can't let my father know that he has gotten under my skin. He can't know. If he does, that will be another notch he can add to his belt.

But with each passing minute, worry laces its way through me, and my heart is hammering so fast it aches. In moments like this, I would normally reach out for Thomas, but my father would quickly figure out that something would be going on between us. He would use our connection against us. And right now, I have to be the strongest version of myself. My father can't know about my fear, my fear of him, or the ultimate fear of what he has done to me and my brother.

Footsteps echo through the hall and then two figures emerge around the corner. One I recognize immediately. His hair is the same color, a dirty blond mop of curls, and his stone-cold eyes lock with mine instantly. But the orange jumpsuit looks odd against his broad chest. A shadow of a thick beard highlights his strong face. He only breaks eye contact with me once to get a once-over glance at Thomas. The look in the eyes of the man that raised me, what feels like a thousand years ago, is haunting but more intimidating than ever before.

As the visiting cell opens, I inhale and exhale my breath orderly. Staying calm is the only way to find out what he has to say. Staying calm is the only way Thomas and I can leave here without my father's presence haunting us.

Laboring my breath and shutting my eyes, I tell myself that when I open them, I will be the woman that faced that man in the warehouse. That I will be the lethal woman that people have come to respect. The woman that some have come to fear.

Just as I'm opening my eyes, the guard places Wolf Vasiliev roughly in the chair directly in front of me. My father already has handcuffs on his wrists and ankles, but the guard places another pair of handcuffs to link him to the table. Hollows are under my father's eyes, and I only feel sorry for him for a moment because when I look back into his eyes, I can fully see the monster that lives within him. This isn't the man that raised my brother and me when we were very little. I have no idea what made him this way, but he isn't the man I remember looking up to as a child.

Once he was my hero, but then like all daydreams, my memories of my father turned into a vivid nightmare.

I take in my father's appearance as I wait for him to say something, and as I watch him, the guard remains standing close, and when Thomas takes my hand under the table, we make eye contact. He gives me a silent message in one look. He then stands and leisurely makes his way to introduce himself to the man that led my dad into the room.

Feeling impatient, I ask, "Why did you want me here today?" My father shifts in his seat, explosively pulls on the cuffs once, winces, and goes oddly still. His deep blue eyes blankly stare at me. It's blank when I look into them, and he seems to just be a shell of the man that I would use to beg to not go on his military missions.

As we closely watch each other, he skims his tongue over his very white teeth. A cocky smile emerges onto his face. "I want to offer you my help." I should have known. Everything is about him. Everything with him is just a sick game. But, I've learned how to con him into giving me more information before, and I know I can do it again. I just need to focus.

Glancing at Thomas, who is now coming back to our table, I lean forward and whisper to my father, "You have to tell me before Thomas gets here, before he hears us." Biting my tongue, waiting for my twisted father to take the bait.

His eyes widen as he takes in my lie. My father's head turns to Thomas, and with a sick growl, he leans his heavy chest onto the table. "What did he do? Lindsey, has he threatened you?" I look at Thomas with a look I've practiced a million times already. He knows the look because he was the one that came up with the idea. With a cold stare, he turns back to speak with the guard.

"We don't have much time, please. You have to tell me. Am I in danger?" *Of course I am. I'm sitting with a hired killer.*

For a moment, I can see his eyes shift into a soft hue of sapphire. He's buying my worried face. Tugging on his cuffs, the small amount of slack gives him some mobility. With my hands close to his, he touches the tip of my fingers. Seeing I'm in reach, a venomous smile forms on his face. With a quick sudden move, he grabs my hand, and ever so gently laces our fingers. Ready to rip away from him at any given moment, I wait.

Clicking of keys sound, and Julian, the guard steps closer. "Wolf, remove your hands from the visitor."

My father inches his chin up, growling. Dropping my hands, he smiles flashily. "Happy now, mate?"

"No," Julian states as he takes a few more steps back toward Thomas. "Don't touch her again. If you do, this meeting is over."

Waiting for Julian to step back to his post, my father looks on at Thomas. A red tint slides over his face. Shaking his head, my father says, "As long as you have my blood running through your veins, you and Jonathan will be hunted…hated even more so." He cuts off to make sure that the other two aren't looking before he continues, "But that's not why I begged you here. You and Jonathan know the risks. No, this is so much bigger than anyone ever thought. The people that put the bounty on Anthony Pavlov's business are back. They want to bring down every business and take London as their own. They want to bring all of Europe down, starting here. They will kill, steal, do anything to make the whole of London fear them. A deal has been struck, my daughter, and the first person standing in their way will be you."

Understanding now, I see the full circle. "That's why you had to go after me?" I ask, a chill hovering over my spine.

Bowing his head, my father sucks in a breath. "You are a threat that they foresaw. They knew you would step in. They know the legend about us Vasiliev's. No one else would be crazy enough to stand in front of you. I took the deal. I took it to end you."

A cold shiver runs through my spine. I drop my hands from him, causing a thud to erupt through the concrete and metal corridor. My father's face drops as he takes in my facial expression. Real panic explodes in my chest, making it difficult to suck in air. Now I get it. My father was willing to kill me so no one else could. In a way, it was his abnormal way of protecting me.

"You would kill me to spare me?" The ache spreads, and my eyes shift. Clutching my hands to my jacket, I feel my head spin for a second. But then, even more so, questions begin to erupt. This isn't completely about me. It's about my home. These people want to destroy my home? *Why*?

"So these people are willing to put London in ruins so they can live in luxury?" Clutching my head in my hands, I feel my father's eyes fall around me. I understand now that my father was expecting me to laugh, to not take him seriously. But how could I not? This is a huge plan that takes skill and inside jobs. I know that London, the United Kingdom especially, has its fair share of corruption, and it's safe to say that some of the most illegal activity happens within my country, but not everyone should have to face the consequences of illicitly run companies.

I just can't believe there is a gang of people out there that want to bring a country they live in down just for the fun of it. Taking my head in my hands, I try to soothe my pulsing brain.

Tapping on the table makes me look up. My father's vast eyes pin me down to listen to him. "I'm warning you, child, that even the most corrupt businessmen have hearts, but in the end, money is the winning factor.

People listen to wants, not needs." His glossed eyes match mine in a tangent of worry. "Remember, *dorogoy* Linds, this is and will be a war between powers. You must know that death will follow, and no man shall surrender their heart for the greater good this time. *Bud' ostorozhen Lindsi.*"

Clasping my hands between his own, my father's eyes hold me still. "Not everyone gives into greed," I mumble.

"Oh," my father scoffs, knocking his head back a tad. "Really? Because I'm sure you took that job for the Pavlovs for two reasons; one," my father raises one finger, "you needed to fix your reputation. And two," raising another finger, he aims them at me, "for the money."

"You see, baby, not everyone is as willful as you. People cave. It's natural." Clinching the cuffs tighter, my father continues to tap the metal table. One rap, he ignores me. The second rap, he looks at Thomas. Then, by the third, he shoots a heated look at me.

As my father ignores the words he gave me, I replay what he told me. My fathers' hands remain clasped around each other, and his words ring loud and clear in my head. *Be careful, Lindsey.* Wolf Vasiliev is warning me now but not offering any more information.

Twisting through all the thoughts, I let my eyes travel to Tom's sturdy figure. Thomas remains by the guards' side, looking at my father's hands. My head rotates back to my father's heavy gaze. His mouth is in a thin angry line, and there is a snarled question held in his gaze.

"Tell me, *Lindsi,* what do you fear the most?" Folding my legs over the other, I cross my arms across my chest, no longer wanting to have this conversation with my father. "Tell me, Lindsey, do you fear lying to your father or betraying the one you love most?"

My father waves at Thomas. "I can see the love in that pathetic boy's eyes. I can see his anger as he looks at us. I'm telling you now that I told you the truth because I am your father and you are my daughter. That boy," he stops to glance at Thomas with a poisonous glare. "He will die knowing that he cannot compare to a woman like you."

Anger floods through my body. I rip my arms from their crossed position and stand with enough force to send the chair back a few feet. He knows nothing. No one does. No one ever will. Thomas has been through fire with me. No one can take that away from us. Especially not my father, the man that would rather kill his family rather than just help them.

"You know nothing." Standing straighter, I take a step back from him, to gather space. "You left, you killed Mum, you have no say in what I do anymore." Bowing my head, I clasp my hands behind my neck, willing my lungs to work through the hollowed, aching pain in my chest. "You have no idea what is right for me anymore, Dad."

"Don't turn away from me!" My father's roar pours through the room, and the guard steps forward. Raising a hand, I tell him, "Leave him be. He's just a monkey in a cage. He can't do anymore harm."

Pulling a breath in through my nose, I level my eyes over my father's heated ones. "As a child, I knew we weren't normal. You made us do things that no one else knew about. You were the worst. At least Mum had a heart."

"I have a heart, Lindsey. Why do you think I wanted to be the one to end you? I love you." Shaking my head, my teeth come out in a truthful sneer. "No, you don't. You feel obligated to care about me." My muscles twist tighter, and my stomach clenches as I step forward. "I'm not the warrior that begs for the scraps of your affection any more. I'm better than that."

Leaning down, my eyes read his face. I smile at his growing anger. For once, I feel like I'm winning with him. "All I ever wanted was for you to be my father. Not a soldier. Not a hired killer. Not a man who runs when things get hard." Clenching my jaw, I try to keep it from quivering. "All you needed to be was my father," feeling the tears coming, I turn away from him. As my back turns, and as my eyes glaze over with tears, his voice floats back, "What we all became was for the greater good. Your mother and I had secrets to keep, and we did the best that we could by you and Jonathan."

"You made us keep your secret. Jonathan and I were the ones that had to face the outcome of your treachery." Wiping my nose, I look over my shoulder and skim my eyes along his poorly aged face. "Like poison, you wanted it to kill us. The secrets about you and Mother destroyed us. That was the burden we were forced to carry."

"No one asks you to carry it, Lindsey." Shutting my eyes, I swallow my own regret. And with one more look at Thomas, I shift back to my father completely. Seeing him now, cocky and knowing, I let my face slump. I let him see my hurt. Showing emotion isn't a weakness. It takes strength, strength that my father will never understand. "Jonathan and I did what we needed to do in order to move on. If you can't remember, let me remind you; when you left, we only had our mother. Then you killed her. You took her from us. And because of you, we had no one. We had to cut all ties from weakness. *We had no one*, so we shouldered what we had left. We had to hide what you did, what you still continued to do. We had to rid ourselves of the world that you demanded we live in."

Tired and ready for something to drink, I level my eyes with Tom's. Looking at him, I feel his worry. I can almost feel the anger as it ripples off of him. Taking a step forward, my father clears his throat. His voice floats out, "I tried to lead you the best way a man can," his voice lowers, and slowly, his eyes rise. "A man fights for his family. I passed on what I knew to you and your brother. Remember, I came to the call when I knew it was you. I answered your call for mercy."

Shutting my eyes, I fold my head in my hands. "I don't care," I croak. "I hate this! You made me this force that won't just shut off. You made me into your lethal prodigy, and I don't want that weight anymore." The tears fall. My body remains still, but as my voice shakes, I feel myself losing my edge to keep up with him. I'm so tired of the games my father has played. I just want to go home, pet Shadow, and relax with Thomas. I wish there was a way to just forget about my father. Forget about who I was. Forget about the Lethal Woman title. I wish I could just leave her in a hole, six feet under.

I've decided before and it remains the same, I don't want to be that woman anymore.

I look at Thomas, and he looks on with an exposed expression, with a drawn-in brow and tight eyes. But my face stays neutral as I look back at the man that raised me to be who I am today, an *istrebitel,* a fighter. My anger loosens as I think about the truth. "You lost, Dad. That alone will suffice for Jonathan and me."

"No." His voice is breathy, loose, and free. "Hold onto this. You can't win a battle without a few calculated losses. No matter how much you may regret it later, every loss is a piece closer to winning. No matter how much it may hurt, with every loss, there is a gain. With each step back, you get a few more seconds to think." Stopping himself, my father's eyes shine with misery. "I lost, yes. I lost you and Jonathan." A smile cracks through his misery. "But I also won, didn't I? You are here, right?" Cocking his head to the side, I wish to smack that smirk off his face.

Looking down at my father, I understand what needs to happen. "A war or a battle will always come upon us, but *Otets,* I am not on your side. You are a traitor to what you once taught me. You are not a man, nor are you a fighter. You lost. I don't care how much you try to mess with me. I know you lost. Fucking face it like a man. Accept the defeat."

As the words slip from my tight-lined lips, my father stands from the chair and yanks the cuffs that are binding him brutally. His eyes are full of clouds of darkness and pure vexation. Coarsely, he spits, "You know what they say; the past we create will always lead to our future. It's up to you which side to choose, but choose wisely because there will be no going back." Looking at my father's tall and muscular frame, my first instinct is to draw back, but I hold my ground. Face to face, and full of venom. I'm never backing down from this man again, I owe myself that. I have the strength to take the blow, and it's time that I admit that.

I watch my father. I watch for vulnerability in his

stance and posture. His head tilts down, and his jaw remains clenched, but his eyes are what scare me the most. Cold, dark, and menacing...he's promising that this isn't over, that it never will be between us. He knows that everything will come back.

No matter what, we always end up coming back into each other's lives. It connects then that it will just be something that I will need to embrace, so I don't bother to step back before speaking to the man that has threatened many lives. "I will not choose a side. No matter what you say, I'm done." With a fraction of an inch between us, I spit my last words out as if they are poison. "I will simply do what's right. And this time..." I clench my teeth together as I speak the next few words. "...everyone will know the family name for what it is, a curse that binds everyone with it into the shadows."

"You can't just lay down the title you were given."

Angling my head, I smile through the ache. "I earned the Vasiliev name and the lethal title. You gave me nothing but pain." Baring my teeth in a snarl, I give my parting words. "I am no bitch that lies down. I gave everything I had to this family, and now, I'm done. I'm not that woman anymore."

My father's once-raging face now lacks its fight. He drops back into the chair, his wrists bloodied from the cuffs. I remain standing and look at the defeated man before me. A man that has now fallen from the mountain that he made from greed and ignorance. He is a shell of the man he once was, a lost soul that will never be able to rest in peace.

I look at my father for the final time and begin to walk away to correct the mistakes that will soon take my life captive when he speaks for the first time in a century in a language I haven't heard in full for so long: "*Vy uvazhayete moyego rebenka, no doroga vperedi nebezopasna. Bud'te ostorozhny, eto ne konets.*"

His eyes meet mine. What he says stuns me. It was a saying my mother used to say, "*You have my respect, child, but the road ahead is not safe. Be warned, this is not the end.*" I ignore it and keep walking. I'm about to light the people that destroyed my turning-the-page life on fire. But I turn back once, and it ends up being a mistake. I should have listened to my head, never turn back because that's when the guilt bites.

The image of my father slumped in a metal chair, handcuffed and wearing a sad expression burns its way into my mind. "You will always be my daughter, Lindsey." With patterned eyes, my father snarls out, "I can't ever imagine you not being the Lethal Woman, Lindsey. Whether you like it or not, that is who you will always be."

The look in my father's eyes breaks my heart. But I walk away anyway. I can't help him now. He did this to himself. It's time that I live by my own morals and forget the words of my past. I turn my back on the man that stabbed my family in theirs years ago and walk toward my chance at a new future.

As I approach the open metal door, I grab onto Thomas, knowing that one way or another, this battle will end with us. My father's words ring deep, but my need to withdraw from it clings steadily.

Clasping his hand and linking my fingers with Tom's, I allow myself to sink into him. He gave me his trust, and in return, I shall give him my full devotion. My father is wrong about one thing. I'm the one who doesn't deserve what I have. I don't deserve Thomas. He is too kind, too gentle, too sensitive, while I am completely closed off to the world. Like an iron box, no one can enter and see my true heart.

Maybe this battle that is rising, maybe it will be a call to the new world. Greed is the fuel. Greed is the force. But there are two types of greed, the one for selfishness and the other for the aid of others.

These people want to tear down my home, then I will use my own form of greed as fuel. For Thomas, I will do anything. He welcomed me with open arms, and he embraced me with a gentleness that many can never master.

And, as our hands remained linked, I make a promise. A promise that I will honor in this life and in the next, I will lay down my life for this man. Thomas Pavlov is too pure for this world, and I will do anything to protect that gentleness. I may be broken, but I refuse to allow Thomas to experience that.

Tightening my hold on his hand, I tell myself to never let go. If I can hold on, then I can do anything. Lindsey Vasiliev and Thomas Pavlov against the world.

Forever and always.

Today and tomorrow.

We will fight side by side until both of us are put in our graves.

And, that is a truth I know for certain no one can take away from me.

Chapter 29

Anger is Far More Dangerous than Despair

The scent of coffee wakes me from my dead sleep. All I remember from last night is coming home, changing, and sitting on the sofa, not wanting to be a part of the world. The conversation between my father and I wouldn't let me rest; distress still races through me.

Groaning and rolling back my shoulders, I sit up in bed. The bare walls of my bedroom stare back at me, making me wonder what I want in life. Still to this day, I have no idea. I have thoughts and wants, but no clear path. Thomas? Yes. Peace? Yes. My brother? Yes. But people like me can't have it all. There is always something that stands in the way of our harmony.

Glancing at the clock, I know that Thomas is already awake and probably dressed and ready to head to work. Sighing, I try to clear my clustered mind by trying to figure out what to wear for the day. But, no matter how much I command my body to move, it won't. Stuck still and defeated, I feel the shell I made last night slip.

Commanding my muscles to work, I stand and get to the closet.

But one thing keeps kicking me in the gut; how will this problem be solved? Going to the authorities won't do any good. My father is a criminal, and no one will believe him.

But before I can start thinking about the sacrifices that I might have to make, a quick knock rattles my door. I drop the blouse that is resting in my hand on the dresser and slowly open the door. A scattered-looking Thomas fills the entryway, and his dark eyes lock onto mine. His face is free of any emotion, and his dark suit makes him look different…uncomfortably different.

I back away from the door and continue to get ready for the day, getting my clothes laid out and shoes shined. Thomas takes a seat on the edge of my bed and closes his troubled eyes.

Just as I'm about to leave the room and get a cup of coffee, Thomas speaks in a hushed tone that startles me for a moment, "I'm sorry. I didn't mean to ruin the plan. He's smarter than I gave him credit for." Regret bubbles up in my stomach. I've been so worried about London, as well as mine and Thomas' lives, that I forgot what he would be feeling.

Turning to look at him, I reply, "Don't worry, deep down, I never really thought he would buy it for long." Giving Thomas a weak smile, I turn to walk through the hallway when Thomas grasps my elbow, locking me in place.

"What did he tell you? You looked…troubled when we left the waiting cell." Our faces are so close together I can feel his breath on my face. My heart breaks knowing that there is a side of me I don't want Thomas to know about.

"He warned me. And he might have mentioned a saying my mother used to say to Johnny and me all the time." Backing away, I shrug off the tears. "It's no big deal. We need to focus on the task at hand. How are we supposed to stop these people?" I try to rip my arm from his grasp, but he pulls me back, and we end up both hitting the wall by the door.

Anger flares onto Tom's face, but it's a tamed flame this time. "Don't hide anything from me. How are we supposed to resolve this situation? We don't, Lindsey. It's not our problem." Vising his hand around my elbow, Thomas guides me away from the wall. "We will inform the authorities and let them handle it. Not everyone can be saved, and it's not your job to try either."

"We have to do something," I banter back. But Thomas just levels his eyes and says tonelessly, "No, we don't."

I flinch back. Never has he ever been this painfully truthful to me before. But what hurts the most is that he's not even worried about what might happen next. What if these people target him and the company again?

"Thomas, tell me, what exactly would you do if the company possibly got put in any danger?" Thomas looks at me with so much aggression in his eyes I begin to back away.

"The company," he dishes out, "is not as important to me as you." Stepping back, Thomas backs out of my room, ready to enter the hall. The suit he is wearing tightens as he folds his arms across his chest, looking like he might actually fight with me.

Appalled by his reaction, I have nothing else to say but: "You can't use our relationship as an excuse, Tom."

"Uh," Thomas humorlessly chuckles out. "I thought looking out for the woman I love was what I was supposed to do. I don't want you getting hurt *again*, and I don't want you put in a dangerous situation like that *again*."

The light from my bedroom casts a shadow into the

hallway, leaving Thomas in a creepy glow. For a moment, I see an image of my father coming toward me. "I know," I plead out, reaching out to Thomas. "Trust me, I know, but I can't just do nothing. That's not who I am. I fight. I don't concede."

Taking my hands, Thomas settles the flames in his eyes, but his argument doesn't end. "This isn't your fight, Linds."

I try to step away. "Don't," Thomas demands and holds me in place with his hands on my shoulders. "Don't think for one second that I don't want to help, but shit, Lindsey, we can't do this. Not again. We don't have what it takes."

"You're right," I shout. "We can't, but *I* can."

"No!" Thomas wheels and clamps his hands around his tie. "We aren't going through this again. We can't." Thomas steps forward, wanting to touch me, but I back away deeper into my room, wanting to leave Thomas in the hall.

"I should have seen this coming. You are…" I stop myself from saying the rest knowing that what I was about to say would be crossing a well-defined line. But from the look on Tom's face, I can tell that he caught on to what I was going to say.

Raising his hands so they are level with his shoulders as if in a gesture of surrender, I see the pain evident in Tom's pupils. "Don't compare me to my father, or yours for that matter." Then, as if a switch was hit, Thomas continues to explain, "My dad may have started this investment firm cleanly, but he opened the doors to corruption that I don't dare go down. So don't you dare compare me to him. And don't ever accuse me of running everything I have worked so hard for through the dirt." He looks at me with a face twisted in resentment. "And…please don't fear me as you do with your father. I love you, and I would never hurt you. So please, don't do this. You did your part, now let the rest go, Linds."

Looking down at the hardwood floor, he releases a mighty breath, and with a shove that springs him back from me, he walks a few feet back. Leaving me suddenly, I let myself lean against the wall, but he doesn't leave me alone in my pity. I look at the leather band around his left wrist, and I let a pent-up cry escape from my throat. I can feel my shoulders shake as the tears trail down my cheeks. Just when I thought I couldn't look any weaker or more foolish, I feel my knees buckle. But I never collide with the floor. A strong arm holds me close.

"I'm sorry," I murmur. "The words just slipped out. I was angry. I shouldn't have—"

"Shhh," Thomas whispers into my hair. As I listen to his cooing, I clutch and claw at the fabric of Tom's shirt. My knees remain bent at an awkward angle until Thomas picks me up and carries me back to the foot of the bed. Gently, he sets me down, but he doesn't let go.

Everything that I've been holding inside is screaming for an escape, and at the moment, my emotions are getting the better of me. The anger inside seems to be seeping together with all the hurt causing me to cry even harder.

Thomas runs a hand through my hair, trying to calm me, but I push it away. Misery grabs at my heart and demands my full attention. "Shhh," Thomas coos into my ear. "I'm sorry. I shouldn't have reacted that way. I trust you. I love you. Linds, I just don't want you to get hurt." A low echo of a sob escapes, and Thomas pulls me in closer.

Raising my face to meet his, our lips touch. He stays still for a second before he reacts. The saltiness of my tears gets wiped away by his callused thumbs, and a warm smile is perched on his lips. "Darling, you are strong but not invincible. If you go down this road, we go down it *together*."

With a lowered head, he comes to me again. His lips are as soft as feathers but capped in a manly appeal. My hand comes to rest on the side of his face, my lips dance along with his. When we break apart, I look into his melancholy eyes. I so badly want Thomas to know that in the end, he didn't hurt me, that at times people just…break down. I want Thomas to know that at the end of all this, I know he is right, but I can't help but feel the need to help all those who are in trouble.

Thomas keeps his face level with mine as he breaks the silence. "Please tell me what's wrong? I can't stand seeing you in pain…and again, I'm sorry for my outburst. It's not who I am."

I run my index finger along his scruffy jaw. The whole time, his eyes watch me with tenderness and care.

"My dad said that you weren't worthy of me, but without you, where would I be?" I admit to him. Without Thomas, I wouldn't be happy, free, or alive. He saved me, and no one can change my mind.

Rocking back, I stare into his eyes. "My father just expects me to take this whole organization down, but what if I can't. I'm human, nothing more, Tom." I place my hand on his chest, feeling the rhythm of his heartbeat. "I'm sorry for what I said. Anger isn't my best feature. It just seems to cause more trouble than good."

He hums a response, lets go of my arm, and flops back down on the bed. His suit jacket wrinkles at the edges, causing his dress shirt to become too tight for his torso to fathom.

As I watch him fiddle with the bracelet on his wrist with his eyes closed, he comes up with a suggestion. "How 'bout we take today off and take Shadow for a walk and come up with something nice to do for the day?" Pausing, Thomas picks at a thread that is loose on his shirt. "I understand your need to catch these people, but we are also citizens. I vote that we both double-check every employee. You are head of security, and you have power…we can both take very cautious steps to keep the company safe."

I sink back onto the mattress beside Thomas. Our hands find each other. He closes his eyes and sighs. "I don't want to break your heart." Thomas almost looks ashamed after he speaks. I smile at him, knowing that the only thing that could break my heart now would be to lose him. "You won't. I made a vow to keep you safe, and I will honor that until I stop breathing."

"Don't ever stop breathing then," Thomas mutters as he presses a kiss on my temple.

As he wraps up his statement, Thomas reaches into his suit pocket and pulls out a thin, dark blue and black card. The words *United Forces* are edged in red print. My breath hitches for a moment.

"What is this?" I ask. Thomas turns onto his side so he can face me, and he laces our fingers together. A small smile printed on his pink lips. Pride evident all over his face.

Thomas looks at me deeply with his soft brown eyes. "I changed the name of the company. It's not my father's anymore. It's mine…and you saved my life, and you continue to do so. It's only fair to change the name to something more fitting. Two separate forces came together, and we are a force to be marveled about."

I respond in the best way I can, I pull Thomas in, and we get wrapped up in each other. Peace won over the anger and despair that was caging our hearts. As I look into the eyes of my other half, I know that I'm willing to do anything to keep him and my family safe. My ruthless heart may have been tamed, but it will never lose its fight.

As Thomas holds me in his thick arms, I forget about all the troubles around us. I only focus on the warmth around us and in the apartment. Nothing else matters at the moment. It's just about us.

As my eyes close and my arms wrap around Thomas, I understand that it's time to let go of the person I once was. Worming my way into Thomas' side, he groans but pulls me in closer. I'll do anything to ensure his safety, I remind myself. As the darkness of peace pulls me under the waves, I finally accept my present and future…I found my calling. And now it's time to move forward.

I forget the words of my once loving father and decide that it's time to surrender the information to the police.

Thomas plays with my hair as I drift peacefully into the embrace, and I murmur, "It's going to be okay. I'll let it go. It's time."

Holding me close, Thomas whispers, "I love you too."

Smiling, knowing Tom's affection for the words, I just hug him. We can lay here for a while, and then we can show Shadow the park that is close to the apartment. Sighing and smelling Tom's earthy tones, I know that the peace won't last forever, but I also have the faith that we can work through anything that troubles us.

Together, I know we will try our best, and together we will continue to grow and learn about each other.

Together, we will build a life.

Together, Thomas and I can have the things we never could as children. As a team, we will become the better versions of ourselves.

Together, we will let the battle go.

Together, we will face this cruel world.

Chapter 30

Some Things are best kept in the Dark

The quick pace of the training room makes my heart rate elevate. Lindsey completed physical therapy a few months ago, and ever since then, she's been working with the security team full-time. Already, there is a routine that the team follows. She has them run two laps around the room as a warm-up that also includes ten push-ups and crunches. Sometimes when there is nothing to do in my office, I like to come see her. No matter how stressed I am, if I see Lindsey my body melts with comfort.

She's my destructive angel.

Lindsey is my guardian...now and forever.

As I make my way around the room to speak with Lindsey I can't help but notice the beautiful bright smile that lights up her face. Her smile seems to glisten when she notices me. And I hope mine does the same when I see her too. Strolling to her side I can't help but notice the sweat that rolls down the curve of muscle on her arms. Slowly, but surely, my lethal force is making a comeback.

She's worked fiercely hard to get to this point, and it always makes me proud to see her healthy and strong again. Smiling, I remember all the hard days, and all the long hot baths I would run for her. I can recall the sore muscles that we shared together. The long nights in bed, trying to get Lindsey to relax. None of it stopped her. She kept training, fighting, and recovering so she could be the best version of herself possible.

All these months later, I still can't help but light up when I see her.

Stepping forward I plan on addressing the current issue that has been flooding through the London business grapevine. Things have gotten worse. Almost every company so far has been accused of wrongdoing in one way or another. Evidence always pops up, and it brings that company down. Slowly, my world has been rising but also falling apart.

Thinking about it all, Lindsey is the only good thing that has been keeping me going. But, as I stroll across the shining floor, I notice the business that Lindsey has adapted to.

There are currently fifteen employees that Lindsey has been working with, and each team of two people is stationed with different priorities. So far United Forces has escaped any accusations that have been floating around, but I can't—the company can't—take another hit. Since my father's arrest and the whirlwind of the trial and everything that came out, it brought us down. It almost ruined most of the investment plans that came our way. Many clients backed out, and many escaped once their term was up.

But overall, we dodged the bullet that could have sent us to the morgue. Lindsey's testimony explaining everything she did to protect me hit the headlines, and it left people wondering why a highly demanded bodyguard is working as security. I have to admit as I watch her demonstrate what she is asking of the team, that she is far beyond perfect for me, and this company. She makes my life so much more bearable, and livable.

Looking at her now, laughing and joking with the people around her, I thank God that she didn't leave. That she stayed, and that she fought every rumor and shot it down with a very clear scope. Lindsey never lost her edge, and it's been a few months since we heard the news of the people that want to bring down all the companies in London. Lindsey and I came up with a name for the bandits: *Privideniye*. Lindsey calls them that, I simply call them Ghost. To me, they are the Ghost Crew.

Lindsey is directing a new member of the team through the first set of fighting and defense training. Lindsey's face is twisted in concentration, and sweat slowly drips down the side of her face and falls down her slender neck, and the young woman she is working with doesn't look any better; she looks like she's about to collapse.

Casting a silent look to Lindsey I whistle, causing all the attention to land on me. "Listen up everyone!" I shout into the fairly large crowd. "Things are escalating and Lindsey and I believe that most of you are fairly ready to start patrolling soon. But…" I pause glancing at Lindsey to confirm this is what we want. "…every person that checks into this building, every day, day or night will be checked twice, when they enter, and again when they leave. You all should understand why regarding it's on the news almost twenty-four seven. I expect the best out of all of you." Clicking my tongue to the roof of my mouth, everyone takes that as a sign that the lecture is done.

Short and sweet. I've never been one for long

howlers but lately, I feel myself wanting to offer support and guidance to the people that work here. I want to make their work here easier, but lost myself, I don't know how to help anyone. Everyone is lost, and simply trying their best to make the deadlines that are in place.

Every day, someone falls under the pressure. Under the accusations.

Rubbing at my sore eyes, I wait for the finishing remarks from Lindsey but she just waves them along as she wipes sweat from her hair.

Once everyone has left the training hall, Lindsey comes to stand beside me again. Lindsey peers along, looking at her cadets as they walk out of the room with strained muscles. Looping her arm with mine, she shoots me a smile that almost makes all my worries vanish.

From the angle her arm is I can clearly see the tattoo that spreads through her forearm. A detailed arrow with a sharp head and small but unique threads seem to soar from her elbow to the middle of her arm, heading for two shining stars that edged into her strong wrist.

"Linds?" I say with a delicate edge. She simply hums a response. "You know I love you right?" Her matted hair swings from one shoulder to another when she turns to step in front of me, getting so close there is no space between us.

"Of course. You only say it every day." I smile, and take her sweaty hand, not caring about the sheen that coats mine. All that matters is the fact that she looks and feels healthy again, and the fact that she remains in my life.

Our hands remain joined together until she has to step into the locker room to get cleaned up before we leave for the day. As she opens the thick wooden door. I get a final glimpse at the beautifully detailed tattoo that we designed together before the door closes. Turning away from the door, and heading up the hallway I notice the silence in the building.

Everyone that works here, hell, lives in London knows about the advancements the Ghost crew is making on local businesses but no one knows the dangers that United Forces is facing except me, Lindsey, and the select few people part of the security team. The walk upstairs to my office is slow and thoughtful, my hands in my trouser pockets and my mind clouded with worry.

Lindsey and I are going strong, and we even talked slightly about moving into a real house together. Shadow shares the bed with Lindsey and me, and he seems to be glued to my side. At night when I wake his dark eyes are always there to meet mine. And the worst of Lindsey's nightmares ended; or at least what's what she claims. But it's not just my worries about her that keep me awake at night, it's also the worry of if I can keep this company afloat. I don't know what to do. I can only hold out for so long. One day, I fear my time will be up. Then, what would I tell Lindsey and all the people that depend on me?

I never thought I would fail this soon. I never thought that the business I tried to save might just die, once again, and maybe all together.

As I walk the sounds of a busy workday crowd my head, and I almost sprint to my office in order to reach the silence. Once in, I almost collapse with relief.

Plopping onto the couch, resting my head in my hands, I try to remember what needs to be done before I leave for the night. Taking my plain cased phone from my pocket I check for any meetings. None this week but two on Thursday for the upcoming week. Placing the phone down I open my laptop to try and answer some emails and fill out a few reports that go along with two new investment products.

A rap of four knocks echoes through my office when I'm almost done with the final report. Looking at the file one last time I sigh and shout for whoever it is to come in. The thick paneled door shuts with a groan and glancing up I see Lindsey.

My breath always gets stuck in my throat when I see her in uniform. Plain black utility pants with two side pockets on each side along the thighs, and a plain black shirt tucked under her outer belt that holds a handgun, handcuffs, a radio, and a few various items. But the one item that pulls everything together and gives her an intimidating look is the thick bulletproof vest that ends right where the belt begins. To top it all off a thick blue and black utility jacket sits loosely on her shoulders. Lindsey looks at me with a steady gaze she gave me when we first met, then and now it still makes me feel sheltered.

Her general walk to my desk makes me stand, high and alert. But when she slowly runs a finger on my dusty thick oak wood desk I can't help but get closer. I can smell a fresh scent of mint and coconut spill from her skin and leak into her thick jacket. Moving around her to sit in the plush rolling chair my gaze lingers on the bulk of her gun that's attached to her waist.

Putting my feet up on the desk and leaning back I can't help but ask, "Why are you in my office? And most importantly where are your newbies?" When she tilts her head to the side, I get a clear view of her strong jaw. It's a reminder of what she's capable of, and all the hard work she has done over the long stressful days. I boost up and place a hand on the very brawny part of her neck. When she looks at me her vigorous eyes soften, "They are with Emma, she's more than ready to help lead them as well. And I'm doing my daily rounds, which I always like to finish on your floor." I hum as I thumb through some heavy stock paper, but a buzz pulls me out of focus. Lindsey digs into her thick pants pocket and answers the text.

A heavy smile creeps onto the strong features of her face. "Jonathan invited us over for dinner. And he also said that he already took Shadow on his run. So what do you say? Are you up for Johnny's cooking?"

I shudder. "Bloody hell, no. He burnt grilled cheese sandwiches last time. One of these days I need to offer him prepaid cooking courses or something." I earn a snicker from Lindsey as she begins to walk out of my office. Her ponytail standing out against the black of her uniform. The tiniest of a limp is all that remains of the day that feels like years ago. My heart aches to see her go. I glance at the clock quickly and decide that my day ends within ten minutes.

I grab my phone and pack my bag and call to her, "Lindsey! Wait!"

Taking quick strides to the door, I almost get knocked over by the figure standing in front of me. "Linds, Christ you scared me." Her body is stiff, and her hands are clasped behind her back. A menacing glow radiates from her when she's on guard and it scares me from time to time.

"I have to finish my rounds," Lindsey says boldly. I know that it's an act for the people watching but it still hurts to be called out by someone you love. Even more so when everyone here already knows that we are dating.

I look at her, and state my case, "I'm clocking out for the day, and I thought we could take this round together. You know then we could go have dinner." She loosens her shoulders, nods, and turns to continue her way down the hall. The slight thuds of her combat boots are the only noise to be heard.

Lindsey keeps her body straight and steady and she doesn't even glance twice at the people who are giving her strange looks. She keeps walking and monitoring those around her. I can see the soldier side of her now and I find myself respecting everything she has done, endured, and overcome.

From the sacrifices and all the challenges, she has overcome to be standing here today. From the people, she has loved and lost. And in a weak and low blow, I thank the Lord that all that stuff happened to her because now I have her.

I found family and understanding by sticking by her and weathering the storm. And now I'm walking beside the woman I love…and I found someone who taught me what it's like to be a soldier. But by weathering everything we've been through together we've both learned that at times some things are best to stay hidden. Speak it once and let it go.

As we walk through the last remaining halls I can't help but think about our future, and all the dark days that we will face together. I grasp her strong hand in mine and clear my head and focus on the now. I focus on Lindsey.

I focus on letting the dark days disappear.

I focus on finding myself and remembering what I've gained through all the storms I've had to face. I know the road ahead will not be easy, but as long as I have someone who loves me standing alongside me I know that I can overcome all that is bound to tear me apart.

Through the storms, I've learned who I am and what I am willing to do to keep those that I love safe and well cared for.

I've learned so much since I met Lindsey and the one thing that remains through it all is that the past can be painful and merciless but it is those who we encounter that can bring us peace when we need it the most.

Through pain and tragedy, we can all rise again and face the new day. Through weathering the storms we can grow into a person who can save ourselves.

And if we are all lucky, we can all have a warrior standing beside us, holding back the world until we are ready to embrace the true struggles of life.

For a while now, I have been ready.

Lindsey has let the braces in my life fold, and now, I am standing on my own two feet again. I am able to breathe and keep fighting.

I am a survivor who is ready to take on the challenges.

I am a survivor standing alongside a warrior.

Chapter 31

Hero is in the Name

Staring at the clock, watching the seconds tick by makes my heart beat rapidly. The steady pound in my rib cage seems to evolve with each advancing minute.

My hands begin to grow sweaty as I wait. The glow coming from the TV offers no distractions from my growing anxiety. Not even the comedic laughs that the sitcom offers can distract me from the sweat clinging to my palms.

I keep running my hand through my gelled hair, waiting for my first glimpse of Lindsey's outfit for tonight's party. I can't help but think that I am underdressed in my dark blue dress shirt and black blazer with black trousers. My metal watch adds class, but I can't help but feel miserable. I so badly want to see Lindsey in this dress that her brother personally picked out for her.

Those two are like a team, and if there is a secret, like what my girlfriend is wearing to a very important party, it tends to stay a secret until the very last minute. *To be fair,* I chatter in my head, *Jonathan has been keeping a secret for me too.*

Placing my hands in my pocket and pacing back and forth, I let my mind run wild. The intense feeling of dread inside of me has been eating away at my soul. I don't want to let anyone down, and lately, I've been wondering if it's worth all the pain to keep the business open. Deep down, in the deepest part of my gut, I have this feeling that at the end of all this, it may not be worth it. Every company already has been questioned for its reliability. And if not for Lindsey's unconditional support, I don't think I would have made it this far.

Becoming fidgety, I sink down onto the couch and watch the show unfold for a minute. As a sarcastic remark is released, I hear movement in the back room.

As I rub the back of my neck to release some of the tension, a steady set of footsteps comes in my direction. Jumping up and shutting off the television, I turn to the footsteps. A heavy weight lifts from my shoulders as Lindsey enters the living room. Her halo of blonde hair hangs elegantly between her shoulder blades, and the muscles contract in her back as she fixes the charm necklace that I bought her around her sturdy neck.

Her strong eyes radiate joy when she looks at me. Moving from my position, I come to stand beside her. The material of her classy black dress is soft as silk under my fingertips, and the battle within me is silent as I take her hand in mine. Slowly, I crave my touch into the hollow of her neck and kiss the side of her face.

Leaning into her touch, I ask, "Are you sure this party is a good idea? I don't want to make a fool out of United Forces or you, Linds." Lindsey turns so she's facing me. Her hand rests on my chest. With my head tilted down, I meet her knowing eyes.

"Thomas, there is one thing I've learned throughout my years; you only fail when you officially give up." Planting a kiss on my cheek Linsey mutters through hooded eyes, "Tom, you haven't given up. You have been fighting this whole time. You deserve to enjoy yourself." Rolling her eyes affectionately, she laughs. "Maybe in your mind, you've let go, but I haven't seen it. You've been fighting an uphill battle. But at this party, I'll be beside you, don't worry. Anyway, the opinions of a few competitors shouldn't bother you. You are doing great, trust me." She hums as she walks into the kitchen, leaving me barren and still anxious.

I follow suit in the kitchen as she continues to gather everything she needs for the evening. I got a text from Jonathan that he would meet us there, and he wants us on time no matter what.

I can't help but think as Lindsey walks lightly on her feet in her black flats that highlight her skin tone that we have overcome one battle just to face another. And while she's busy, I can't help but notice every elegant detail about her. From the strong jawline to the graying-cold, late-night eyes down to the shimmer of her hair. But the one thing that I respect the most about her is her strong character. Lindsey is willing to do anything to ensure that the people in her life either remain safe or get what they deserve. That good people get a good return, and bad people get slapped in the face by karma.

And right now, as we both hold an extreme amount of power, I see that hunter-like strength returning to her form.

"Thomas, are you ready to go? I think I've got everything. And Johnny is heading there already." Lindsey's strong face comes into view as she peers into the room. The steady thumping of my heart in my chest fills my ears as I look at her. Gasping, I swallow my thoughts as she stares at me.

Looking at her now, I see her natural beauty. "Yes,"

I called into the other room. With the thudding of my plain dress shoes, I pull my outer jacket close to me. As she leans into me, I pull her in tighter. "That dress," I murmur into her ear, "is amazing."

"You like it?" Lindsey presses her chest closer to mine. Stopped in my tracks, I feel my mind become foggy. With a heavy look, she captures my lips with hers, wasting no time. Opening my mouth, she equals me out. Empty of thoughts, my hands roam her silky back. As my hands work, her tongue attempts to go deeper. Feeling her jaw flex, a shot of pleasure rips through my muscles. Moaning as her tongue meets mine viciously, I shift my lips and pull back. "Stop," I pant out.

"No," Lindsey lays her hands on my chest, loosens a few buttons, and leaves a series of open-mouth kisses on me. Falling back against the door, she forces my coat off my shoulders. "We're gonna be late," I tell her as my lips clasp her neck. "Then don't make me wait," she mutters. Switching places, I push her into the door. "We're gonna be late," I tell her again, against her velvety lips.

Looking at one another, I so badly want to give in to her.

I want to give her what she wants.

But not now. With her brother waiting and the party still hovering over us, we have to go.

"Please," she moans, pushing closer and harder into me. Touching my slicked hair Lindsey hikes her leg up, and with the slit on the side of the dress, I touch her tight thigh muscle, stroking the bullet scar. Leaning in, I shut my eyes and lick at her neck. Feeling her tremble under my lips and licking at her pulse point, I feel my mouth widen as she moves up and rests her lips on mine.

Feeling the air become stuffy and feeling my heartbeat triumphantly, I groan out, "Later," through locked lips. "Lindsey," I try to plead with her. "The party, honey, we'll do this later."

As her bright eyes meet mine, with her chest rising and falling steadily against mine, I almost dread breaking the moment. But as she smiles and tugs on my tie, she just smirks. "I'm holding you to that."

Seeing her hair flood around her, I take her coat off the rack and retrieve mine from the floor. "I know it," I say as I help Lindsey slip into her coat. As we bound down the stairs, Lindsey remains silent, but the small, steady touches she offers make me mad at myself.

Once outside, I feel the blistering cold slip through my coat. "Bloody hell," I mutter as I watch Lindsey hail down a cab.

Watching her shoulders move and seeing her graceful movements, I come to stand beside her. As a car comes to a sliding halt beside us, I aid Lindsey into the cab. Just as my foot reaches inside, a biting breeze cuts through me. The cold night air seems restless tonight, almost syncing with my heart.

****

The soft glow coming from the house-style bar stuns me. I know these people. My father always told me that they were his most loyal clients. They got their money from him. He used to swear to me while sucking on his whiskey.

I'm pulled out of my wandering thoughts when a shadow appears in front of me. His glossed black hair and thick beard almost blend into the darkness around Lindsey and me.

But Lindsey isn't frightened even a little bit.

"Johnny! It's been a while. How are you?" Jonathan's face flares into a deep smile. And a rough chuckle melts into the air around the three of us. It seems like a party is brewing inside, yet I'm comfortably boisterous, staying outside with the people that mean the most to me.

Jonathan and Lindsey have become my family, and they are the two most important people in life, now and forever.

Jonathan ends up pulling Lindsey into a tight hug as my mind travels through the memories I have with the two of them. "I'm doing great. But getting in there and partying would really make me feel even better." Jonathan's hand clasps around my shoulder, and his face hovers above mine.

I can see the mischief in the core of his eyes.

He whispers to Lindsey, and she walks ahead of us, "I have to talk to Thomas for a second. I'm going to be stealing your gentleman for a bit."

Nodding, Lindsey heads off to stand by the entrance of the bar with her coat spilling around in the breeze. Grinning as I look at her, Jonathan chuckles at my expression.

"Did you ask her yet?" He aims at me in a hushed voice. My eyes grow wide when I understand what he means.

Shaking my head fiercely, I shoot down his remark. "No, no. There's been no time. I just…I don't want to ruin what's going so well between us." Jonathan constructs a pouting face but nods. His eyes are shockingly light when he looks at me.

Jonathan places a heavy hand on my shoulder once again. "Thomas, she cares so much about you. And I know that you feel the same way about her. Just don't wait too long to ask her. Trust me, that ring that we picked out together will look great on her." I nod, and together we both head in the direction of the party to find Lindsey. Not seeing her by the door, I already know where she is.

Scouting through the mass of bodies, I try to locate her. But it wasn't that hard to spot her by the bar, sitting on a metal stool with a bottle of water in her hand, giving the strangers around her the cold shoulder.

With Jonathan walking by my side into the bar, I feel secure. His cologne fills my nose, and I feel less nervous about my attire for the evening. He, too, is wearing a casual dress suit. We end up taking a seat on either side of Lindsey due to the packed dance floor. Lindsey places her water down and casts us both a knowing look that makes me shiver.

I can never get anything past her. She may not know the details of Jonathan's and my conversation, but she knows that something is up, and she never lets anything slide.

I know that she will find out eventually.

And it will probably be my fault. I can never keep a secret for long.

Lindsey places her left hand over mine and offers some knowing words, "You need to go and socialize. People are expecting the man that defied all odds." Seeing my eyes widen, Lindsey chuckles through a gentle embrace. "Don't worry. I'll be here, and I'll jump in if things get a little uneasy. But I know you, Tom, go out there and prove to some rich pricks that you are going to be the last man standing."

I end up looking at Jonathan, trying to convince him to come with me, but he gives me a smirk of defiance.

Knowing I have to go socialize, I take the liquor in front of me and take a long pull from the beer bottle. "Order me a burger?" I ask Lindsey, getting ready to walk away. I have a feeling that this event will turn into one of my many board meetings this week.

She nods, and pats my shoulder. Sighing and pointing back one more final look of annoyance, I give Lindsey a steady kiss, then stalk into the middle of the function, slightly sulking.

The mobs of familiar faces seem to blur together as I make my rounds around the room. Among the few people I have had the liberty to speak with, I've learned that London as a whole is in crisis. Roughly half the legendary businesses I've been hearing about for years have finally pushed the bankruptcy papers forward. I can almost feel the horror of the future clawing at my throat and stomach. But now I know that if I sink, so do many others who don't deserve it.

After speaking with one of my father's old company buddies, I feel drained having to tell him what happened to my dear old pop. He didn't take the news like I thought he would. All he did was nod, take my shoulder in his fragile boned hand and say he was sorry. "You are a good man for making the best out of that situation."

"Thank you, Mr. Geller," I say, shaking his hand. "Have you met my girlfriend, Lindsey?" I ask, wanting to steer my way back to her so I can be with company that I enjoy.

"No," Mr. Geller beams, "I haven't. But right now, I must mingle with a few colleagues of mine. It has been great seeing you again. I wish you all the best, Thomas. You still have my number?" Mr. Geller asks, pointing his boney finger closer to me.

"Yes," I say through thin lips, "I do, sir." Watching Mr. Geller's swaying walk as he approaches a woman, I blow out a sigh. Long, hard evening. Feeling ready to leave the social circle, I try to find Lindsey or Jonathan in the crowd. I'm ready to sit down with them, eat and drink, and then just head home.

Grinning as I think about my promise to Lindsey, my muscles contract.

With dizzy eyes, I find Lindsey, an older man with blond hair and dark eyes is, talking with her. Lindsey's shoulders are pulled back and tight along the material of her silky dress. For the first time in months, I can almost sense her tension and nervousness.

My heart is catapulting thoughts into my brain as I make my way to her. For once, my thoughts aren't about the threat of the company falling. It's the fear that everything we have already faced will come back and bite us far worse than before.

With the steadiness in my joints, I center my focus on Lindsey and the man at the bar. With a clear walk of dominance, I make my way through the people dressed in heavy suits and blinged-out dresses. My efforts don't go unnoticed. People move and give curious looks. Ignoring them all, I finally reach Lindsey's side. She is cold as stone, pale as a cloud on a sunny day, and her body is rigid like a brick wall.

Jonathan notices the onlookers and begins his assault on us. "Lindsey, what did that man want?" My eyes bore into hers. But at the moment, she looks like the woman I met at my house before hell broke loose. Determined and angry. I can see the defense shining in her blue eyes.

Lindsey takes my hand and glances at her brother.

The two seem to have a silent conversation. As she shoves off the stool, I pinch our coats and wrap them in my arm. Walking through people again and pushing through the thick glass doors of the entrance to the bar, we finally step outside. The night air hits me head-on, the chill seeps into my bones...or it's the fear, I'm not sure yet.

She doesn't even shudder from the cold. Her eyes are deadly daggers as she looks at the both of us. Jonathan looks more composed than I feel. "He said that he knew our father," Lindsey aims her focus at her brother, and the air around us almost felt like it dropped a few more degrees.

Just as a gust of arctic cold comes in, I watch as a few strands of hair slip from Lindsey's braid and blow around in the wind. Swallowing my own words, I try to focus on what that could mean, but my thoughts don't last long as a chill settles in again.

Seeing Lindsey shiver now, I peel her jacket from my arm and drape it around her. She smiles slightly before she speaks again. "He said that our father had something to share with us." Her jaw clenches as she thinks about what to say. I can tell that she is trying to stay on point, but the flare of anger dances in her eyes as she looks up at the sky.

Lindsey sighs and angles her face even with both her brother and me, "Dad knows about the people that are trying to destroy London. He wants us to do something because he has ties with them." Blowing a cloud of breath from her throat, Lindsey seethes, "He fooled us, and now the Ghost Crew is after us because they think we know something."

Seeming to plow through her thoughts, Lindsey

rants, "They think because Wolf is our dad, Johnny, that he told us vital information. Thomas," Her eyes dart to mine. "The company is no longer safe. I don't think it ever was. They were just biding their time. I think our downfall has come *moya lyubov'*."

"But," Jonathan interjects, "I thought everything was settled with Dad? That he's paying for his crimes?" Bewildered, Jonathan pushes a hand through his hair. "Military or not, he is serving his time for what he did overseas." Lindsey shrugs. "I don't know, Johnny...I don't know what to do. I wish I had listened to his warning when Thomas and I spoke to him in prison." I open my mouth to speak, but Lindsey holds up her hand to silence me.

"I should have known." Lindsey murmurs. "He never speaks in Russian. He warned me," Rolling her face away from me, I can see her bottom lip quiver with tears I know won't spill. "I toyed with him, for God's sake!" Lindsey shouts, and a mist of warm breath hits the cold atmosphere. I look at Jonathan for advice. I look at him wanting to know how to take some of Lindsey's pain away from her.

I try to step forward to take her in my arms, but she wraps her arms around herself and shrinks into her coat. "Now he's telling us that we are running out of time. That it really wasn't over. That in the end, this was the plan all along." Her lip quivers as a stray tear runs down her cheek. I was wrong. I shiver. A tear would fall.

I sigh through the ache in my abdomen, my stomach twisting together. I want to wipe the tear away and comfort her, but at the moment, it would have done nothing to calm her.

She looks at us both and continues, "Wolf Vasiliev

was hired by the *Privideniye* Crew. He played us all, and now he realizes that they betrayed him to the authorities. He's warning us that they are coming." She raises her arms in front of her and gestures all around us. "Not just for the business and money scattered around London, they want us. They want to defeat the ones that slipped through their best assassin's fingers." Lindsey shivers again, but this time in anger. She glares into the distance and bares her angry eyes to on-goers that are passing by.

I feel sorry for those who have to witness those eyes, but I don't go to her side yet. It's best to let it seep out of her, then offer support. It's the only way to help Lindsey.

As the jacket around her shoulders billows in the wind, she turns her murderous eyes to the stars above and whispers, "He said that it wasn't over…he was right." Pacing back and forth, Jonathan and I just watch as she keeps trying to figure everything out.

"He warned us then, and he's warning us now. They're coming, and they won't hold back." The anger inside her seems to slip away into the creeping night air. Now I take her shivering body into my arms, and Jonathan takes his phone from his pocket. The light from his phone shadows his face in places, and at that moment, he slightly looks like his father. The dialing tone is all that's heard, and the party inside continues on. Everyone inside is oblivious to the danger that's coming.

No one knows yet that the world they know is about to crumble and become like the rubble under our feet. It hasn't hit me yet, but it will. We lost this battle, and so will countless others.

The hollow feeling in my gut grows as I hold Lindsey. Panic, fear, anger, hate, and a slight sense of gratitude glide through my veins. The man that vowed to destroy us is now the one helping us.

Not perfectly, but at least he gave us a chance.

At this moment, I can't help but realize that his inside knowledge will either be our saving grace or the ember that will burn the world down.

I can't help but remember what he told me when I thought I lost Lindsey in that warehouse, that he may not be the one to kill me, but my time is coming. My heart hammers at my rib cage. He knew…he knew, and he knows that I'm willing to die for his daughter. Hell, I'm willing to die for Jonathan as well. They've become my family.

As I hold my defeated soldier in my arms, I make a promise, I may fall tomorrow or at any point soon, but these revengeful Ghosts will fall long before me.

I won't let them near the ones I care about. I keep promising and reminding myself of that as the cold air slips through my button-up shirt. Glancing up, I notice the stars feeding us their light in this ever-growing night of darkness.

I shall not die today, but maybe tomorrow. And these soul-seeking predators will not live to see the sunrise, for they shall die before I take my final breath.

As I close my eyes and draw Lindsey closer to my chest, I plant a kiss on her head and whisper, "We will win. The only time evil wins is when we fail to show up to the fight." Cooing onward, I keep my arms looped around her to block out the cold. "It's time to fight. It's time to let the anger boiling within our blood lead us into battle. It's time to make a choice. Them or us, and the darkness that is clinging to the night to be set free." Shuddering, I feel my blood boiling. "It's time to end this, Linds." I twist my arms around her even tighter and bring a lock of her hair between my fingers to hold onto.

I don't know what the future holds, but I know that the future is never set. And it's time to rewrite this story of betrayal. It's time to harness the darkness within us.

It's time to save the world and the ones I love in it. I whisper into the night sky that this battle can be won and that if a soul must be claimed on Lindsey's and my side of the battle that it's mine. She cannot go down for me, not again. "Me," I mutter, reminding the angels. *It has to be me...*

I'm willing to claim that grave. I'm willing to do anything to end this once and for all.

Jonathan's voice slips through my thoughts. "Let's do this. It's time to be the true children of Wolf and Stepanov Vasiliev. It's time to claim the name that people have feared for so long. Let's let these people know who they've decided to mess with."

And with that, the three of us look up to the stars, embracing the calm while we can because at this time, we know the force of the storm that's coming. And we embrace each other, knowing that this might be the last time.

We hold onto each other and the memories that we have created. As Lindsey puts her arms under my coat, she whispers, "I guess tonight will have to wait."

Placing my head on hers, I just smile through the cold. "Yeah, but we will have plenty of nights to make up for it."

Slowly, we all embrace our inner strengths as we cling to each other.

We all unleash the demons within, and we welcome them to the war that is about to begin. With fire in our eyes and hatred for the disruption in our hearts, we finally admit the truth: "Let's get ready for this war."

A word about the author…

Carrie Pierce is a young woman with a passion to inspire and adapt to the world of the unknown through her writing. While a cadet in high school with the local police department in Placerville, Carrie witnessed the acts of bravery and victory, as well as the loss and pain. Seeing the world through fresh eyes, and seeing the truth of the world's kindness and conflict, the need to write bloomed and took hold. As a native of El Dorado County, Carrie lives in a remote town with hard work and determination in their blood. At the end of the day, Carrie enjoys writing strong and independent characters that know how to take a hit. At the end of the day, Carrie enjoys watching films, reading novels, and lounging with her two dogs. She can always be found with a notebook in hand and ideas that scream to be written in her mind.